For Lack of a Title

by Nathan Wright

Grand Central Station was a bit busier this spring day than usual. More of everything it seemed flowed past as I sat in the gentleman's lounge waiting for my departure notice. There were more ladies in flowing dresses, each with a hint of spring color. There were more men in Bowler hats rushing off to either home or office. Wide eyed children walked hand in hand with a parent or caregiver, all the while watching the excitement taking place in one of the world's busiest train stations.

As I sat sipping my drink, I wondered how much different my final destination would be from my present surroundings. These thoughts flowed through my mind as easily as the travelers flowing by the window next to my table. It wasn't long before I was awakened from this peaceful noontime panorama by the black porter who had been instructed to notify me the moment my suite was available on the Pullman car which would be my home for the next two days.

The porter's name was Holmes, which to me bordered on the eccentric. It seemed his mother, who was literate, had taken a fancy to the name while reading stories about the clever English detective. She decided that if she were ever to be blessed with a son she would name him Holmes. Holmes seemed to honor the name as much as his mother; he never offered his last name when presenting himself, only Holmes.

"Excuse me, Mister Burton."

I turned from the window. There stood the tall porter holding some papers in his gloved hands. "Yes Holmes, I hope you have good news on our departure time."

"Yes Mister Burton, I do. The train will leave on schedule and your bags have already been placed in your suite on the sleeper car. I took the liberty of putting your things away. The locked bag though is on the table in your sitting room by the desk. If you're ready we can board now and I'll show you to your room. Dinner will be served in the dining car about an hour after your train departs the station. I hope all this will be acceptable to you?"

"Very good Holmes, and who will I be seated with this evening at dinner?" A good porter always knew who would be traveling on the train. And especially those passengers who might be of wealth or importance, and would tip heavily for the kind of treatment they were accustomed to.

"Mr. Wilcox, a Wall Street banker, Mr. Sweeney from the railroad and a Mr. Rooms, who hails from West Virginia. They have all boarded and been shown to their suites."

Burton stood for a moment, his eyes in a trance like state. He was in deep thought.

"Is everything alright Mr. Burton?" the porter asked.

Burton suddenly snapped out of his trance and said, "Yes Holmes. I was just trying to place the names you just mentioned. This Mr. Rooms, can you tell me anything about him?"

"Yes Sir Mr. Burton. He is an attorney from West Virginia."

Hash Burton was suddenly caught off guard and not the least bit astonished by this sudden turn of events. This was a misfortune he had not planned on or even anticipated.

Or was it misfortune at all? Perhaps lady luck had just smiled upon Hash Burton. The attorney Rooms was a partner in the law firm of Parsons, Wiggle and Rooms. This particular firm handled matters in Eastern Kentucky for a man by the name of William Haskell Conley. Mr. Conley, as it turned out, was the primary reason Hash Burton was on the train in the first place.

It seemed that Mr. Conley was one of the largest land holders in the entire state of Kentucky. This in itself would not have posed a problem except for where in the state his land was located. The bulk of the Conley holdings were in the mountainous eastern region. This land was rich in natural resources. Timber, natural gas, some trace amounts of oil and the most important of all, coal, lots and lots of coal. The mountains of Southeastern Kentucky were so rich in coal that mining had been going on there for the past one hundred years and could possibly continue for the next hundred.

The problem was that Conley wasn't a coal man, wasn't interested in coal, and didn't attempt to mine the coal that he owned. His interests lay in horses, cattle, and farming. Coal, Conley knew, was as important to the economy of the region as his cattle and horses were. He had no problem with the mining of coal or its transportation out of the region. It supplied the state with badly needed jobs, jobs that supported both his friends and neighbors.

The irritation that had just recently began to rub against old man Conley was a strange unseen undercurrent that was starting to take shape. Men from outside Kentucky had started to come into the area. Land was being acquired in large quantities by some sort of trust that operated under many different corporate names, and which was headed by a group of men known only as The Board. One man might sell his property today only to find the proceeds for the transaction

4

held up by another corporation tomorrow due to a problem with the original deed. More than one unfortunate farmer had his land taken from him because the title he held contained a flaw. A flaw could be as simple as a misplaced marker on the property or a misspelled word in the deed.

Once the trust had the landowner's signature on a bill of sale, any means possible were used against the previous owner to hold up the proceeds. Most families were forced off the land as soon as the deed was signed. Without a home or any income it didn't take long for a hardscrabble farmer to be forced to take much less than what was originally agreed upon in order to settle any disagreement and receive a portion of his money.

Many of the farms, using this bait and switch tactic, were eventually sold to the trust for less than half of the original agreed upon price. The only reason for any agreement in the first place was that the trust offered double and even triple again more than the farmers thought their properties were worth. But in the end the price received was much less than the property's value. The trust moved with such speed and vigor that many properties were involved before anyone knew of the potential for problems with the actual landholder's deeds. When the alarm was finally spread and the holdout landholders refused to sell without payment in full, more than forty percent of the land in some counties had already been acquired by the trust.

After the initial scheme with the deeds had played out as far as it could go, the trust moved into a new and much more odious second phase. Anyone who wouldn't sell now, or hadn't sold in the beginning, was handled by roving bands of armed toughs who would materialize at the most inopportune moment and threaten life and limb if the landowner wouldn't sell.

When the local county sheriff or one of his deputies would investigate, it seemed that the perpetrators had vanished into thin air. With so much land already under the control of the trust it was impossible for local authorities to get to the bottom of all the trouble. It was strongly suspected that the gangs moved in and out of properties controlled by the trust. After an attack they simply disbanded for a few days, holing up on the properties already under their control, knowing full well that local law enforcement couldn't get a judge's signature on a search warrant for every property owned by a trust that worked under so many different corporate names.

Hash Burton boarded the train just after four-thirty in the evening. His ticket, which was in actuality a rail pass possessed for the sole purpose of traveling anywhere in the country without purchasing an individual ticket, was checked by the conductor. These passes were very expensive and carried only by those with substantial means or strong political connections. The rail pass possessed by Hash had been obtained for him by The Board.

Once through with the conductor, Holmes escorted Mr. Burton to his room on the Pullman. Burton preferred that the Pullman be attached to a special, but due to the destination the train was a mix of Pullmans, along with regular passenger and freight cars.

Holmes wouldn't be traveling on with the train. His job was to see the most important passengers onto the train, along with all their belongings, and make sure all boarding went without a hitch. Holmes handed Burton his door key and introduced him to the room steward who was in charge while the train was in motion.

"Thank you Holmes, I find your services to be most efficient."

"Thank you Mr. Burton. I hope your trip is comfortable and successful."

Hash reached into his vest pocket and pulled out a ten dollar gold piece, which he then placed in the porter's hand.

"Thank you again Mr. Burton, good day." With that the porter turned and left the train. The smile on his face was a burden to hide.

Hash made sure the room steward saw the large tip as this would certainly guarantee superb service during his time on the train. Hash now turned his attention to the young steward, asking his name.

"My name is Quincy Talbot sir, and please don't hesitate to call on me if you need anything."

"Yes Quincy, I'll do that. Do you mind letting me know five minutes before dinner will be served? I'd like to close my eyes for a few minutes and then change into my dinner jacket."

"Yes Sir Mr. Burton. Dinner should be in about an hour."

With that the steward turned and left the room. Hash closed and locked the door and then made a survey of his surroundings. His suite consisted of a bed chamber and a small sitting room with a lavatory attached. Each room was done up in red oak panels, which were hand carved, hand rubbed and hand polished with lacquer. Other woods were also used throughout, inlaid by hand, with precision, into the oak itself. All the fittings were of polished brass that accentuated the oak very nicely. The furnishings along with the full length bed were upholstered of a deep green and burgundy design. The entire suite was lit by nine center lamps of brass which added a feel of warmth to the rich wood and fabric.

One advantage to traveling in such a way was the full length bed, although narrow it was still of adequate length. Any man of more than six feet will tell you the agony of a bed that allows his feet to hang over. The lavatory was of porcelain and mahogany. Hash thought this odd since the rest of the suite was of oak. He chuckled as he thought of the designer who worked out the car on paper and then, realizing he hadn't ordered enough oak, substituted mahogany instead hoping no one would notice.

The entire suite, and the remainder of the Pullman, was heated by hot air delivered by pipes that ran through the floor and walls out of view from the passengers and guests.

The exterior of the car was painted in a dark olive green polished to an extremely high gloss. The exterior trim and pin stripping was done in burgundy and gold. Anyone waiting by the rails as the train passed couldn't help but be impressed by such a highly polished and elegantly decorated Pullman on its way to parts unknown.

The surroundings thus far were highly acceptable to Hash. He was sure his surroundings in Kentucky would be quite a step down from the trappings of this lavish Pullman, which in a matter of minutes would be leaving his beloved city of New York and transporting him on the first leg of his journey southwest.

Hash heard the double whistle of the engine which meant the train was about to depart the terminal. With a slight jerk the car began to move. Hash lay on the sofa and closed his eyes.

Within a few minutes there was a knock at the door.

"Dinner in five minutes Mr. Burton."

Hash rose up with a start and realized his right hand had reached for an imaginary gun he wasn't even wearing. He had drifted into a deeper sleep than expected. After gathering his thoughts for a brief moment he replied, "Yes Quincy, thank you."

Hash rose from the sofa and went to the adjoining lavatory. He quickly shaved and put on his dinner jacket. This took ten minutes which would make him five minutes late for dinner, just as he had planned. A quick look in the mirror confirmed what he expected to see and now he was ready to go. When he had almost made it to the door he paused. He turned and went back to the locked bag on the table by the desk. He reached into his upper vest pocket and pulled out the key to the lock. Reaching over he unlocked the bag and removed a double shot derringer. In the bag were two more Colts, along with holsters, ammunition and a Stetson. These he left in the bag as he relocked it and returned the key to his vest pocket. He checked the loads and action of the small gun with the smooth experience of a man who had trained himself well. The workings of firearms was something almost second nature to this tall New Yorker.

Hash slipped the derringer into his lower vest pocket where it would be concealed from view by his dinner jacket. With that he locked the door to his stateroom and made his way to the dining car.

Hash had traveled the rail long enough to know that dinner this evening would consist of fine Angus beef in one form or another. Railroads like to patronize their freight customers. If at all possible the roads liked to purchase from these same customers what they needed for the operation of their trains. Anyone who knew anything about the railroad industry knew that big railroads hauled beef, and lots of it. With the advent of a nationwide rail network, beef from as far away as the Midwest could now be transported to the East Coast. Beef made up a large portion of the freight that was being brought into the cities of the east. With each passing year the consumption of beef would see record gains. So as beef became more and more a part of the nation's diet, it also became a staple in the Pullman dining cars.

The fare being served on the rail wasn't just any beef, it was Angus. The Angus of the Midwestern and Southern States had become the favorite of the well-to-do, and Pullmans were noted for their well-to-do. Chefs loved to work the Angus. It had a better quality and consistency than other varieties. It also went well with more sides and wines, which made it easier to provision the dining cars.

Hash Burton entered the dining car and stood just past the door for a brief moment letting the guests already seated take him in, all six foot four inches, before moving to his assigned table and being seated by the waiter. Three gentlemen were already seated ahead of him and this was just the way Hash had planned it. The waiter introduced the newcomer and greetings were exchanged. After shaking hands Hash took his seat and placed both forearms on the edge of the table. This was a maneuver Hash had learned many years ago. To sit at a table filled with strangers with your hands in your lap made the typical stranger a bit standoffish and harder to befriend, and the only reason to befriend anyone was to acquire information. This evening Hash not only wanted to enjoy a fine meal prepared by some of the best chefs in the business, but also to find out what Mr. Rooms had been doing in New York.

As it turned out Mr. Sweeney from the railroad wasn't just a minor functionary, but none other than Vice President of expansion and new rail services. Mr. Wilcox was the fund manager for several large railroads. Hash knew of Mr. Wilcox and knew of his dealings with the rail interests that were in direct competition with some of the big names that were involved in the trust.

Wilcox was the only one seated at the table who knew anything of Hash Burton. He thought Burton was only a minor functionary of several banking houses in the Northeast. He also knew that Burton was a Yale trained lawyer by profession and a Shootist by sport.

The fact that Hash was a well-trained attorney who had the ability to take care of himself was what led the members of The Board to recruit him in the first place.

After the waiter took the drink orders Wilcox started off the conversation with the news that the New York Central was in talks to acquire a small rail line, the Eastern Kentucky Railroad, with main offices in Ashland, Kentucky. The deal once complete, would give the New York Central its first business dealing with coal freight. The deal according to Wilcox only required his signature. Upon his arrival in Ashland two days from now signatures would be exchanged and the New York Central would be officially in the coal transportation business.

Rooms, as it worked out, was the attorney for the acquired railroad. He said he had been to New York to finalize the deal. Burton asked if he had traveled North on strictly railroad business. It was a very straight forward question and he expected little in return. Rooms looked as if he were pondering whether or not to answer such a question. Finally he took the bait, but then only responded with a clue.

"I travel to New York quite often, and always for business. My duties require too much of my time for any to be spared on sights or theater."

"Do you try to do two or three projects at a time while in New York, to save on the time wasted while traveling?"

"Oh yes, I've never made the trip with the sole purpose of working on only one project. The firm, of which I am a full partner, requires that I tie up several loose ends for different clients during each trip. Due to the attorney-client confidentiality agreement, I'm not at liberty to say any more than that.

Wilcox now spoke up, "Oh, I'm sure Mr. Burton here knows of the attorney-client clause Mr. Rooms."

Rooms looked at Burton now with more than just curiosity.

"And why is that Mr. Burton?" Rooms asked as he interlocked his fingers and placed them on the table in front of him.

Before Hash could answer Wilcox blurted out, "Why Mr. Burton is a Yale trained attorney himself."

Hash didn't speak, he only looked at Rooms with the slightest of smiles, and all the while cursing to himself the fool Wilcox for divulging who Hash was before more information could be extracted from Rooms.

Rooms leaned back in his plush chair and folded his arms across his chest. Hash knew this to mean Rooms was on guard and would divulge in no more idle chatter about where he had been and why he had been there.

At that moment the drinks arrived and each man took his in hand. As a jab at Rooms, Hash raised his glass and said, "To attorney-client privilege."

Hash now knew that the attorney Rooms would guard each and every word. Information was one of the most valuable commodities either man traded in, or kept secret from, an opposing business operation. Still all may not be lost if Burton could change tactics a bit. Years of acquiring knowledge from those who strived to keep it secret had honed Hash Burton's skills to a razor's edge. He looked directly into the eyes of the railroad executive and asked, "Mr. Sweeney, you say you're the Vice President of new rail services?"

"That's right. I implement any changes that may be required to bring new acquisitions into the New York Central family."

"I've always had an interest in the railroad business, what can you tell me about this Eastern Kentucky Railroad that you and these other two gentlemen are about to take over?"

Sweeney looked first at Rooms and then at Wilcox. "Well gentlemen I suppose there's no harm in a little conversation while we wait for our steaks to arrive, what do you say?"

Wilcox and Rooms only shook their heads, knowing full well that Sweeney enjoyed nothing more than talking shop.

With that the four men again took a drink. The conversation from that point forward consisted mainly of the Eastern Kentucky Railroad, with Rooms on guard just in case Sweeney divulged anything that should be kept confidential.

To Rooms pleasant surprise, Sweeney was not only a superb railroad man, he also had the rare ability to say quite a lot without saying much of anything. No secrets were revealed that could be used against the New York Central and Eastern Kentucky Railroad deal that would be consummated in forty-eight hours. Rooms was pleased that Sweeney and Burton carried the conversation while the banker Wilcox and himself were quite content to only sit back and observe. Rooms couldn't quite put his finger on it, but there was something about this Yale trained lawyer that made him uneasy. Rooms watched the newcomer with great interest, all the while sizing up the man as a potential rival.

Dinner was soon served and each man ate with an appetite that befits the meal, prime rib.

During dinner Sweeney told Burton about the small time railroad that would propel the New York Central into the heart of the coal fields of Eastern and Central Kentucky. Burton took all this in as the quiet observer, asking a well-placed question now and again to keep Sweeney talking.

Burton learned that the Eastern Kentucky Railroad was a small affair but what it lacked in rolling stock and rails it more than made up for with its location at the junction of the Mighty Ohio and Big Sandy Rivers. The Big Sandy ran all the way from the Virginia State line to Ashland, Kentucky.

The little railroad had only a hundred and fifty miles of track in service but that would soon be more than tripled. The engines and rolling stock were old but meticulously maintained. With the cash and resources of the New York Central the Eastern Kentucky Railroad would be propelled into one of the leading coal carriers in the United States. The line, which already reached to the town of Drift, in Floyd County, would be pushed all the way to the towns of Weeksbury and Wheelwright in the far southern end of the county.

At that time it would be connected to a tunnel system currently being constructed by the famed horseman William Haskell Conley.

Their meals now finished Rooms cleared his throat and said, "Gentlemen, enough talk of railroads tonight. What do you say we make our way to the smoking parlor?"

At this point Sweeney knew he had said a bit too much. Hash Burton also realized he had just heard a tidbit that was in itself quite astonishing. Conley, who was thought to have an affinity to coal, would now control a large portion of the industry. This wouldn't be by actually mining the dirty black rock, but by controlling the transportation of it. It was sheer brilliance on the part of the Horse Baron, as Conley was sometimes referred to. Conley could control the entire region by being a transporter rather than as a producer.

If knowledge meant power then this had been a very productive meal after all. Burton couldn't be more pleased and also more disturbed by what he had just heard. Conley had been a problem in that he wouldn't sell any of his farmland, which sat atop vast quantities of coal. Now he would also control more than two thirds of the coal flowing from the region on his new rail line. At the first stop Burton would telegraph his bosses in New York with this news and await new instructions.

With dinner complete, each man made his way to the smoking parlor, which was at the rear of the adjoining car. The room was filled with plush leatherback chairs, again in the dark green and burgundy material found in Hash's suite. On one of the heavy tables, flanked by two swivel armchairs, was a chessboard made of oak and mahogany squares inlaid with the same quality and precision found on the wall panels of each car. The board had been thought out nicely with the oak making up the lighter squares and the mahogany the darker ones. The chess pieces were of the same wood with each having a brass bottom, the weight necessary to keep the pieces in place due to the swaying of the train car.

Hash, still feeling a bit superior from his ambush of the lawyer Rooms and the railroad man Sweeney, and now wanting to make the fleecing complete, looked at Rooms and asked, "Do you play?" Hash had been an outstanding player at

Yale, and had even won the school title during his graduating year. Hopefully he could bait the backwoods lawyer in for a little sport.

Rooms, still smarting from having been led into the conversation earlier by a stranger who happened to be a Yale lawyer, felt the need to redeem himself. He had played throughout school and took up the game whenever he found a worthy opponent. His most worthy opponent of late was none other than William Haskell Conley, the number one client of the law firm of Parsons, Wiggle and Rooms. It seems Conley was a natural at the game and seldom lost. It had been good training for the attorney Rooms and it would come in very handy against this 'Champion from Yale'.

A broad smile spread across Rooms face. "Well yes, I have played a little in the past but my game is probably a bit rusty. I think I still know the basic fundamentals of the game though."

Burton smiled and said, "Please choose a color and let's pass off a little time with a friendly wager, if you're a gambling man."

"Well Mister Burton, I have been known to bet on a horse now and then and maybe even some five card stud from time to time. What would you feel comfortable with?"

Burton felt the wording and tone from Rooms was meant as a slight. Managing to keep his words, and temper, in check he threw out what he felt was a large enough number to put his opponent on the defensive and also to impress the others in the smoking parlor who had been listening.

"How does a hundred dollars sound Mr. Rooms?"

The room grew very quiet and all eyes were on Rooms. Rooms wasn't surprised by the steep amount of the wager. He had suspected that there was more to this Hash Burton than what on the surface appeared as only happenstance. He now felt the eyes of the other men on him. Not to be outdone a second time by this young upstart from Yale, Rooms smiled and said.

"Well as long as we are going to make a wager, why not make it interesting. How does five-hundred dollars sound to you Mr. Burton?"

The room was suddenly alive with chatter about the amount of money about to be bet on a single game of chess.

None of this was lost on Burton who now wondered how good Rooms understood the game about to be played.

"Done and done!" announced Burton.

"Please make a suggestion on how to determine who makes the first move, if you don't mind," replied Rooms.

With that Wilcox, who had been hanging on every word, stepped forward and said, "Gentlemen, if you both are intent on playing one game of chess for the steep sum of five-hundred dollars to the winner, would there be any objection if a few of the other gentlemen in the room made a side wager or two."

Burton looked up at Wilcox, and with a broad smile on his face said, "I think that is an excellent idea as long as the parlor will remain totally quiet during the game."

Wilcox looked around the room. "Is that acceptable to everyone here this evening?"

All the men in the room nodded in agreement and began to gather in the opposite corner to make their individual wagers.

"And as for who goes first Mr. Rooms, how about a toss of the coin to determine that." With that Hash Burton reached into his vest pocket and pulled out a ten-dollar gold piece.

Rooms asked, "Who shall toss, who shall be heads and who shall be tails?"

About that time the young porter, Quincy Talbot, entered the smoking parlor. Hash Burton, upon seeing the porter, was quick to seize the moment.

"Mister Talbot, the good Mr. Rooms and I have agreed upon a little game of chess which also entails a small wager. Would you be so kind as to flip this gold piece into the air for us? Upon it landing in your hand, just flip it over onto the back of your other hand so we can establish who will have the first move."

The young porter glanced around the room and realized that all eyes were upon him. About this time Mr. Rooms spoke up, "Yes Talbot, an excellent choice, will you do the honors?"

The young man stepped forward and as he took the gold piece from the hand of Hash Burton said, "I would be delighted."

Burton looked at Rooms and asked, "Which will it be Mr. Rooms, heads or tails?"

Rooms smiled at Burton and said, "Well Burton, most men in this situation would automatically choose heads, but I think tonight I would prefer tails."

Rooms noticed the briefest moment of discomfort in the eye of his adversary. And at that instant Rooms realized that the gold piece was probably weighted so as to always land on heads. When the gold piece was then flipped over on the back of the other hand it would show tails. If Burton always allowed his opponent to choose first, and if it was also true that most people choose heads, then a coin that always fell on heads and was then flipped over onto the coin tossers other hand would give Burton an advantage. Rooms was about to find out.

The room was as quiet as a funeral parlor. Talbot lowered his hand toward the floor and then with a smooth toss let the ten dollar gold piece fly toward the ceiling of the smoking car. As it neared the ceiling it slowed for the briefest of moments. And in that second the coin seemed to be suspended as by a string, the only movement was its rotation around its axis. No one in the room moved, possibly some didn't even breathe. Then as to not defy the laws of gravity the spinning orb began its descent and as quickly as its journey began it was stopped by the left hand of young Quincy Talbot. With a loud slap Talbot had done exactly as instructed and placed the coin on the back of his right hand, but didn't uncover it. Talbot slowly looked Rooms and Burton in the eye.

"Are you going to steal that gold piece or show us who won?" asked one of the spectators. Talbot seemed to enjoy this moment, knowing that he had the undivided attention of each and every man in the room. Finally young Quincy Talbot held both hands waist level and removed his left hand.

"Tails he shouted."

Rooms, who had been watching Hash Burtons eyes, saw in them what he had expected; Burton wasn't surprised in the least. To help prove, at least to himself, what he suspected had just happened, Rooms asked Burton, "If you don't mind Mr. Burton I would like to buy that gold piece from you. I wish to possess it for the memory of the moment."

Burton immediately reached into Talbot's right hand and retrieved the coin. With a testy tone Burton looked at Rooms and said, "Nonsense Rooms, there will be no sentimental value in this coin when you lose this match to me." With that Burton quickly sat at the table and began smoothing his wood and brass chess pieces into the exact center of their respected squares. Rooms couldn't be one-hundred percent sure but he felt confident that his suspicions were now confirmed about the weighted coin.

Rooms walked over and took his seat across from Burton and watched intently as the very anal Burton fussed with his chess pieces. Watching this display gave Rooms an idea that might just help throw his opponent off his game. He would purposely, with each move, place his own pieces as haphazardly as possible; not centered on their position and facing any way except forward, etc.

The porter was sent for again and drinks were ordered before the game was to start. Hash Burton ordered Jack Daniels, Stanley Rooms ordered coffee. Burton didn't seem to notice the disparity, which the ever observant Rooms made a mental note of. The other men in the room, having finished their side bets ordered drinks also and as the porter walked away the room fell silent. The only sound was that made by the train itself, steel wheels clicking on the joints in the rails.

"Rooms you have the first move," announced Hash Burton. With that statement Rooms noticed another mannerism of Burton's that might prove useful, Burton had no patience. He wanted everything to happen now and not a second later.

Rooms began play as he always did against William Conley with the goal of setting a defensive posture. Taking his time, even on this first move, would help agitate his opponent. When the pawn was in place, a little off center and turned to the side, he removed his hand and looked at Burton, who was looking back with nothing less than a sneer.

"Well that took long enough Rooms. I promise to defeat you in short order as to not be here all night."

Rooms only smiled in return. His evaluation of Burton seemed to be correct.

Hash quickly made his move. The second his hand left his pawn he said, "Your move."

Rooms slowly looked at Burton and said, "I know." He said this in a slow determined voice. Burton rolled his eyes in response.

After three or four moves each, Rooms realized that Burton was a time player. Move fast, attack fast and hard. Being a time player meant that Burton would give almost any of his pieces in order to get to an attack position. His strategy was to be one step ahead of his adversary and to keep him always on the defensive.

Rooms lived for this type of game. Nothing intrigued him more than maintaining a good defense and to exploit any weakness that might come up.

Burton, true to form, gave away pieces and in the process within an hour had a strategic advantage. He had given up more pieces by point than had Rooms but his strategy seemed to be working.

Within two hours it appeared Rooms would be defeated, but then Burton made a blunder. Rooms knew that within four moves the game would be over and Burton would be defeated. Only Rooms and Burton realized this. The other men in the room were too busy enjoying drinks and cigars. Even if they had been paying attention it is doubtful that any would have understood the situation that Burton had gotten himself into.

Hash Burton now understood he would be beaten. How could this be? Rooms wasn't acquainted with the aggressive style of play that Hash had used. Everything about Rooms said he would collapse against fast-paced aggressive play. But there it was right before his eyes. He looked up at Rooms. The West Virginia lawyer only sat there, smiling back.

Burton slid back his chair and stood up. "Two hours of play without a break requires me to go to the lavatory in my suite for a moment. What do you say to a ten-minute break?"

Rooms, wanting to conclude the game, could do nothing but agree. "Sure thing Mr. Burton, I could use a break myself."

With that Hash Burton stood and left the room. Stanley walked to the back of the smoking car and exited onto the outside covered platform. Soon another of the spectators joined him for a breath of cool night air.

"Well Rooms, how is the game going, any predictions on the winner?"

"Burton is a defeated man. Within three moves I will have check-mate and the game will be over."

"What good news Rooms. If that is true then I've just made two-hundred dollars, I bet against him you know."

Rooms looked at the man and asked, "You knew neither of us before the game?"

"That is correct."

"Then how did you come to the conclusion to bet your money on me rather than Mr. Burton?"

"Simple! I just don't like the man. He seems as a bully and someone who is used to getting his way. I predict that a candidate will someday win the presidency because of just such an abrasive nature."

Rooms smiled, "We better head back in, the ten minutes are about up."

As the men turned to the door they were suddenly flung against the rear bulkhead of the car. The train was screeching to a halt. Both Rooms and the other man were thrown to the floor of the platform. As each man scrambled to his feet Rooms asked, "What happened? Have we collided with another train?"

The stunned gentleman could only look back at Rooms. After a moment he said, "I don't think so. It felt like the emergency brakes have been applied."

The train had come to a dead stop allowing the two men to re-enter the smoking car. It was a shambles. Tables and chairs had been overturned and the carpet was scattered with glasses that had been thrown to the floor, their contents splattered everywhere.

Rooms noticed the chess board, upside down lying beside the overturned table. Some of the pieces were still rolling about on the floor. His immediate thought was that Burton had upset the train's emergency cord to end the game he was about to lose. But there he was, standing with a slight cut on his forehead.

Rooms walked over to where Burton was standing. They stood side by side looking at the chess pieces.

"What has happened to your forehead Mr. Burton? You have a slight cut."

"Oh, it's nothing Rooms. As the train was sliding to a stop someone's package fell from an overhead and clipped me. Do you have any idea what happened?"

No sooner had the words left Burton's lips than the door to the parlor flew open and the conductor hurried in.

"Is everyone alright in here, are there any injuries?"

Rooms spoke first, "Apparently only Burton here, but I think it is only slight. Do you know what's going on?"

"Yes, well apparently someone wanted to exit the train before our next scheduled stop. As soon as I regained my footing I pulled down a window and guess what I saw. A gentleman jumped from the second car ahead of this one and ran toward the trees. The crew and I shall do a quick check to see who this saboteur might have been."

"Well Burton, I guess that clears you," Rooms said.

"What are you talking about Rooms?"

"Well, a man about to lose five-hundred dollars on a simple chess game might be tempted to upset the train."

Hash took a step forward. Towering over the shorter attorney from West Virginia he said with a deep low growl, "I resent the implication Rooms. I think you owe me an apology." Burton couldn't press his anger any further though, not in a room full of witnesses.

The attorney from West Virginia dusted himself off and took a step toward Burton. "There will never be an apology from me Mr. Burton, and furthermore in the future don't try to intimidate me, it just won't work."

With that Stanley Theodore Rooms turned and went out the door followed by the conductor.

As soon as the two were in the leading car Rooms turned to the conductor and asked, "Did you notice anything at all about the man who ran off into the trees?"

"Well it was quite dark, but there was enough light from the passenger car for me to notice what he was wearing as he leapt to the ground. He had on a plaid top coat, Bowler hat, dark gray trousers and black cowboy boots."

Rooms looked at the conductor as if he didn't believe the accuracy of the description. The conductor, realizing the doubt in Room's eyes said, "It is part of a conductor's job to be observant."

This seemed to satisfy Rooms who said, "Very good. And may I ask if you have any clue as to who the man may be?"

"Not a name yet Mr. Rooms, but I do have a very good lead."

"And are you at liberty to say what that lead is?"

"Well, you being an attorney and all I feel I can confide in you. The man, dressed as I just described was talking in the passageway just outside the suite of the gentleman you just had words with in the smoking parlor."

Room's mouth gaped open. "You mean to tell me that just before the train was set to emergency stop, Hash Burton was talking to our jumper. But exactly how long before, that made all the difference, one minute or ten minutes?"

"Not more than two minutes time sir."

"Thank you very much. If you find out anything more would you please inform me."

"I'll do more than that, pulling the emergency cord for any reason other than an emergency is a federal offense. If I can find out who the bastard is, the railroad will prosecute to the fullest extent of the law."

Rooms smiled and said, "Good hunting." Both men shook hands and went their separate ways. Rooms went straight to his room, locking the door behind him. As he sat on the edge of his bed he made a mental list of what needed to be done about this Hash Burton. As soon as the train stopped at the next town the first thing to do was send a wire to the home office in Beckley, West Virginia. Wouldn't hurt to start a file and gather some information. Something told Rooms that Burton was trouble, and not just chess trouble, or train trouble.

Rooms had already checked earlier with the conductor and found that Burton's ultimate destination, as far as rail service was concerned, was Prestonsburg, Kentucky. This put him much too close to the operations of one of the law firms most valued clients, William Haskell Conley.

For the duration of Room's trip he made it a point not to be seated at the same table with Hash Burton.

Burton, who had been questioned by the conductor about the gentleman who jumped from the train, could only answer that he didn't know the man. They had only exchanged greetings as each squeezed by in the cramped passageway. The conductor, not exactly believing this explanation could only accept it for the truth.

Upon the trains arrival at the Ohio River town of Portsmouth all who were going over to the Kentucky side disembarked and made arrangements to ferry across to catch a train of the Eastern Kentucky Railroad.

When the Kentucky train made its first stop in Ashland, Sweeney, Rooms and Wilcox departed. Each wished Hash Burton a pleasant journey, but only out of professional courtesy.

Rooms had already wired his firm the previous day. As Hash stepped onto the southbound train he didn't realize that at that very moment an agency in New York was in the process of obtaining information about him.

The train jerked to a stop in front of a small rail depot. It had been several months since a town this small had been his destination. Hash Burton, who had finally managed to doze off while sitting straight up in his seat, was jarred awake by the rattle of the train brakes. He immediately looked to his right, through the side window of the passenger car, to get his bearings. All he could see were trees and a few dilapidated buildings used by the railroad to store material and equipment that it really didn't need or want anymore.

One of the worst of the shacks had smoke coming out of a flue that ran through its roof. Beside it was a clothesline with a pair of men's bibbed overalls and a plaid shirt gently swaying in the morning breeze. Surely someone wasn't living in that old shack Hash thought.

The rundown storage sheds were adjacent to the tracks, but there was no sign of a depot. Farther off were a few houses fenced in white picket, each with neatly kept yards. Finally realizing that he was seated on the opposite side from the depot he jumped to his feet and slid into an empty seat on the other side of the train.

There before him was a well-kept depot building with the words splashed down the side, 'Prestonsburg, Ky.' Hash Burton grabbed his leather bag from the top of the overhead and moved toward the rear of the car. His first few steps were stiff and painful.

Stepping out onto the rear platform Hash heard the noise of fast moving water. He soon noticed the runoff of a recent downpour filling small streams on either side of the tracks. The storm though must have been long gone. Looking up at the sky he noticed that the clouds had parted and were making way for clear skies. Within an hour or so the sun would be breaking over the tops of the hills.

Hash stretched as he stepped from the train's rear platform onto the wooden walkway in front of the depot. The air was cool but sticky from the high humidity that Eastern Kentucky was noted for. He stood there for a moment looking at his surroundings while trying to shake off the stiffness of riding in a passenger car for the past twelve hours. He had been unable to book his ride in a private berth, having instead to take a seat and endure many hours sitting straight up, rather than being able to relax.

He was not used to traveling as an ordinary passenger and his body could feel it. He had sorely missed the private suite on the Pullman from New York all the way to Portsmouth, Ohio. As he found out though, Pullmans didn't ride the rails between Ashland and Prestonsburg. Only one passenger car was allowed on each train between the two cities because one more passenger car meant one less coal car. The railroad couldn't be using up such valuable space for more than one passenger car on each coal train.

To help speed the coal to market most of the line was double tracked so trains could pass both day and night without needing to be sidetracked to let traffic through.

At the moment, as he looked back down the line, he remembered what the railroad man Sweeney had said about the improvements the New York Central would be making to its newly acquired Eastern Kentucky Railroad. The Eastern Kentucky extended to Prestonsburg and then on to the mining town of Drift. Burton knew the railroad did extend past Drift a few miles to work some of the new mines that were being driven into the side of the mountains there. But how much farther he wasn't sure. The railhead was only a dot on a map.

Now if what Sweeney had said proved true the railhead would be extended on up Left Beaver to the town of Weeksbury. And in the process it would connect at some point to the tunnel project now under construction by the renowned horseman William Haskell Conley.

Hash Burton thought of the reason he was in Prestonsburg, Kentucky and knowing what was at stake knew he must succeed. His plans were elaborate and very well planned. But all hinged on wresting the tunnel project from the hands of old man Conley. Without that everything else would come crashing down. This was such an unpleasant thought, Burton knew that he must immediately put it out of his head.

Hash Burton knew these thoughts were unwarranted. He wouldn't fail, he had never failed before and he wouldn't fail now. The stakes were just too high. If all the months of planning were to be seen through to fruition then Conley would have to be eliminated from the picture. Either by the legal sale of his property to 'The Board', or by means that would make other men squeamish. Burton would succeed and the tunnel project, when completed, would be his.

As he stood there on the platform and took in his surroundings, he noticed that the rain that had fallen the previous night had been hard enough to raise smaller streams to near their full capacity. The humidity he noticed earlier from the platform of the train seemed even heavier now as he looked at the fast moving water. Spring humidity in the Appalachian Mountains was nearly as bad as that which frequented the land that ran along the Gulf of Mexico, from Florida all the way to Louisiana.

The wooden decking of the depot floor was extremely slick from not only the moisture of the rain and humidity but also from any number of oily spills that stained the dock. One of the hazards of small town train depots was that passengers, along with freight, used the same loading platforms. In the smaller towns, cargo was cargo, human or otherwise.

Hash carefully edged his way across the dock to the front of the train station and then stopped just short of grabbing the knob to the door. Burton stood there taking it all in and wondering how a region as rich in mineral deposits as this could still be so far behind the times. This could be the train depot of any number of small backwoods towns in America, but it wasn't. It was in the heart of the coalfields.

The first thing he would need to do was establish an office and a place to stay while he implemented his plans. Plans that were nothing short of dominating the vast coal deposits of the region and also to market what had become known as black-gold. He had come down from New York with a plan that should make him and his backers very rich. Anyone who took the time to notice this tall man dressed in city clothes wouldn't suspect the powerful people he represented, or the amount of money those people were willing to spend in order for his plan to succeed.

All that stood in his way was a few back-woods country bumpkins who could easily be bought out for a few pennies on the dollar or pushed aside with a little of the heavy persuasion that Hash had become famous for up North. Anyone that wouldn't sell would soon be pushed aside by the progress that was taking place throughout the country since the end of the Civil War. The post-war economy needed coal, and lots of it, for the ever growing factories that turned out vast amounts of everything from farm machinery to any number of household goods. Not only did the factories use large amounts of this dirty black rock, but also the nation's ever expanding rail and shipping industry required their own unending supply. Everything it seemed needed coal and up until now it had been supplied by a small and fragmented army of uneducated miners who toiled in the mines for meager wages and hardship that rivaled the harsh conditions of the war itself.

What this industry needed was organization, and Hash Burton had decided that he was the man to not only form this organization but also to control it and in the process become rich beyond anyone's wildest dreams. Even the investors who backed him were not fully aware of his own elaborate plans for the total conquest of the industry. Hash Burton would one day become to the coal industry what John D. Rockefeller had become too oil, and Andrew Carnegie had become too steel. And in so doing, he along with his backers and stockholders would become wildly rich.

For Lack of a Title

He put together this group of investors from the northeast and pooled a vast amount of cash to start his march through the coalfields. His first target was an area in the southeastern part of Kentucky where mining had been carried on for years, though be it in a very limited fashion. The majority of the coal in this region was virtually untouched. Scattered mines for years had extracted coal, the easy coal that lay near the railroad lines.

Now with advancements in both mining technique and technology, coal could be mined in ever greater quantities and in more remote areas. Also with these improvements the mines could be driven deeper into the ground and much greater quantities of coal removed from each mine than ever before. Hazards such as roof falls and gas explosions could be managed better with the new technologies that were being developed, such as placing mammoth steam driven fans in adjoining shafts to move fresh air underground, removing any gas or dust buildup and preventing explosions that not only killed and maimed the underground miners but also damaged the precious mine itself. Burton had little regard for loss of life. Men to him were a commodity easily replaced. And even if a few miners died in the process, Burton told himself it was the price of progress.

The labor in Eastern Kentucky was experienced with the art of mining coal, with some families having three and four generations of men going underground. Burton had long heard the stories of miners so racked with Coal Dust Disease and other injuries that by the age of forty most could no longer work to support either themselves or their families.

This was of little concern to Burton or his backers; he was here to bring order to an industry that had up until now known only a fragmented sense of purpose. Now the emphasis would change from small town mine ownership to a large coal trust with Hash Burton as its head.

Prestonsburg and its surrounding coal fields had something else that was very important to this new trust, a well-established rail network, which could, with only slight improvement, be made capable of handling the increased tonnage necessary for any plan of such size to succeed. The double track line that ran for miles allowed trains to pass without the necessary precaution of siding entire trains for hours to wait for a train going in the opposite direction to pass. Of the seventy miles of track that lay between Ashland and Prestonsburg more than fifteen percent was double tracked. With the good fortune of the New York Central acquiring the Eastern Kentucky Railroad, Burton knew that the fifteen percent could be increased to forty or fifty percent. Train traffic would benefit greatly from the New York Central acquisition.

No one in this sleepy little town on the banks of the Big Sandy River could have guessed that this one man, standing at the railroad depot on a humid April morning, was about to bring so much change so fast. Change that could make Hash Burton and his backers in New York the dominate force in the coal industry, or if there was any resistance, start a war between big coal and the small town landowners that could result in the lives of many locals being lost. It made no difference to Burton, he had the money to hire an army if need be. Nothing was going to stand in the way of big business, or for that matter, Hash Burton.

Burton grabbed his bag and headed into the depot office. There he found a young man in spectacles perched on a three legged stool, reading a dime novel about the West and the men who roamed there with gun in hand. For a moment the railroad clerk was unaware that anyone was standing before him. Burton cleared his throat to get the young man's attention. With that the clerk took a startled glance at the tall stranger standing before him and nervously put down his book and said, "My apologies mister, may I help you?" Burton stood in silence for a moment, a trick he had learned long ago, allowing the much shorter and younger man to take in his entire six foot four inch height, it almost always made anyone Burton was addressing a little nervous.

"Young man, my name is Hash Burton and I would like to ask you a question."

With a nervous look the clerk spoke, "Yes, please do."

"As I was standing here I had the chance to notice only part of the name of that book you were reading. You seemed to be enjoying it so much I thought you might grant me the name and where I might find a copy."

With that the young clerk smiled and said, "The Winning of the West by Charles Willis." With a little nervousness the clerk then added, "It's not mine, I took it out of the mail bag a little while ago. Thought I would read a little and then put it back before the postmaster came in and caught me."

A frown came across Burton's face. "Do you mean to tell me that anyone in this town can read anyone else's mail?"

The young clerk looked as if he were going to run away and hide. "No sir, it gets kind of quiet here at night so at times I open the mailbag and find something to read." Burton thought of a way that this might come in handy. "Young man, do you realize that it is a federal crime to open a United States mailbag without the presence of a postmaster?"

"No sir, I mean yes sir, but I didn't mean any harm. You're not going to report this are you?"

After another long pause Burton said, "No son, I think that we can keep this little matter to ourselves, but remember I can still report it in the future if I so choose."

"Thank you sir, I don't want to lose my job, it would mean going back in the mines and I surely don't want that."

"Neither do I son, neither do I. Maybe in the future if there might be a particular piece of mail that I was looking for, I could count on you to retrieve it for me before the postmaster arrives, what would you say to that? Also there would be a twenty dollar gold piece in it for you, but I would need your word to keep quiet about this little arrangement. And remember, I can still report what I have witnessed this morning if you deviate from our arrangement in the least."

The young clerk only thought about this for a second before he stuck out his hand and said in a hushed voice, "Sure thing, twenty bucks is two weeks' pay for me and don't worry I won't say a word to anyone." With that Hash Burton shook the man's hand, turned to pick up his bag and headed for the door that lead out onto the street opposite the train tracks. Before he reached the door he turned and said to the clerk, "I don't believe I got your name young man."

"Name's Eisner sir, Jeremy Eisner."

"Well Jeremy Eisner, I have two bags on that train, could you keep them here under the name of Hash Burton until I have someone come down and retrieve them?"

"Yes Mr. Burton, I'd be glad to."

With that Burton tossed the boy a dollar coin and as he turned said, "Thanks Eisner, I'll be seeing you about our little deal very soon."

Burton stepped out on the other side of the train station and looked across the street at the well-kept frame houses which faced the depot. The street was nearly deserted as he stepped down onto the road that lead toward the large bridge that spanned the Big Sandy River. He knew from his reports of the area that the depot was located on the west side of the Big Sandy, the river which pretty much cut the town in half.

He also knew from his scouting reports that accommodations in this backwater settlement would be far simpler than what he had become accustomed to in New York or Washington. Surely in this town he could find accommodations that suited his refined tastes. He had grown quite accustomed to the finer things in life. His time spent in the coalfields required not the use of a hotel room or even an apartment, but a substantial house. He would spend his first few days in a hotel though, assuming his contact at the local bank hadn't acquired the house he needed. His last telegraph indicated that acceptable quarters had been found, and it implied they were just what he was looking for. The house would need to be spacious and have the ability to be segregated into living quarters and offices. Offices that could accommodate several staff members who would need to be recruited locally as to help gain the respect and trust of the local population.

First stop would be the local bank to set up two accounts. One account would be for his personal needs, the other to use for business. Purchases of large tracks of land for mining would be the first thing on his list. More than a quarter of the property needed had been already acquired. This was the easy stuff owned by men who were either too eager or too simple to know they were being swindled. Now the holdouts were next, and this included the famous horseman William Haskell Conley.

After the land issues were settled the next step would be the purchase of equipment that modern mining techniques required. Land for right of way, because once the coal had been mined it then had to be transported overland to the rail sidings. As soon as both accounts were set up then money would flow in from the northeast in amounts of which had never been seen before in Eastern Kentucky.

The distance from the train station to the bank was no more than half a mile. The trip took him over the Big Sandy River via the swinging bridge he had seen from the train depot. As he approached the bridge he noticed it to be a rather elaborate structure for such a small town. Both ends of the bridge were anchored to the opposing banks by large stone and masonry towers. The towers must have been at least seventy or eighty feet tall. Strung between the towers were two large diameter cables of at least two inches thick. More cables were attached that hung down and were then connected to the actual bridge deck itself. The bridge deck was wide enough for a wagon with room for pedestrians to pass by on either side. The deck had an arch that made the middle at least five feet higher than either of the ends. As Burton stepped onto the bridge and made his way across he could look down into the lazy flowing river below. The water was high and muddy. So muddy it almost looked thick.

The height of the water was almost alarming. Apparently the muddy runoff from the previous night was also adding to the water's color. He chuckled to himself as he thought of the future of this river. Fishing, he knew from his reports, had helped sustain the local population for years. It would no doubt be short lived when his mining operation got into full swing, oh but it would be in the name of progress.

When he stepped down on the opposite bank he noticed something attached to the mason work of the tower. The townsfolk must have been very proud of their bridge because at the pier on the city side of the river was a plaque giving the year the bridge had been built and the cost of construction, not only in dollars but also in lives lost. According to the plaque three men had died during construction. This gave Burton a bit of amusement as he thought to himself that apparently coalminers make very poor bridge builders.

The local bank was easy enough to find being the second tallest building in town, the county courthouse being the tallest by one additional floor. As he approached the building he took in as much of the town as possible, wanting to familiarize himself with his surroundings. His research had included a map of the town and with little effort he realized that the streets on the map were highly accurate. Burton stepped into the bank building, which had just opened, through a wood and glass double door. The lobby was a spacious affair with deep cushioned chairs covered with green cloth. The bank had only been open for a few minutes. No customers were as of yet in the building, Hash was the first customer of the day.

Hash was very impressed with the building that contained the bank. It looked to be no more than five years old. The exterior was of a reddish-brown brick that ran to the corners which were done in white limestone. The interior was also made of brick but of a lighter color, almost white or cream colored. The same dark brick that made up the bulk of the outside design was inlaid into the white interior brick to create intricate patterns. The woodwork and trim was of a dark stained oak that was made to match the darker of the two brick veneers.

It always seemed that banks in small towns liked their furniture covered in cloth that was of the same color as the money they so greedily dispensed to the local population at rates much higher than in any city back east. Burton knew that bankers in small towns were notorious thieves and he assumed that the men who ran the three different banks in Prestonsburg were of the same variety, if not worse.

Burton approached a teller's window and asked the lady standing on the other side if the bank had a president, and if so would he be available to conduct some business at such an early hour, or would it require an appointment. The teller stood speechless for a moment, not accustomed to having such a question asked of her. Most of the customers she encountered were dressed in bibs and spoke in a heavy Kentucky accent.

"Please wait here and I'll check for you." The teller stood, turned and walked back to an adjacent office. Soon she returned and before speaking sat back down at her window straightening out the wrinkles in her dress with the palms of her hands.

When she was sure her attire was as neat as it had been before her quick errand to the back she looked up at Hash and said, "I'm sorry but Mister Reed isn't available at the moment, if you could leave your name and where you are staying I'll let him know you were asking about him. Then perhaps you could schedule an appointment at a future time."

Now Hash Burton was a man who had dealt with politicians and corporate presidents on a much higher level than any small time Floyd County banker could imagine. Being shunned on a local level was something that Burton was unaccustomed to and it wouldn't be tolerated under any circumstances.

"Tell Mr. Reed that Hash Burton from New York is here to see him and I have two deposit slips in my pocket, one with five figures and the other with six, to discuss with him. Also you may tell him that my time is valuable and I will not waste it shuttling messages between a minor functionary such as yourself and Mr. Reed, is that understood?" The teller's mouth gaped open as if she was going to speak, but no words came out.

She was just about to deliver the harsh message, when the man who had been in the adjacent office, and overheard everything, came out and approached the teller window.

"Mrs. Simmons didn't tell me that it was you Mr. Burton, I must apologize. Mr. Reed has been expecting you. My name is Gregory Spurlock, Assistant Vice President here at the bank, but you can call me Greg.

The man offered a hand shake and soon regretted it. Hash made it a point to nearly break the man's hand with a powerful grip that nearly brought Spurlock to tears. "If you would follow me I will show you to Mr. Reed's office." Spurlock pulled back his right hand and rubbed it with his left. The two men walked toward a large staircase at the rear of the bank, leaving a rather angry looking teller at her window, still unable to speak and trying to figure out who this tall well-dressed so-and-so was.

As they proceeded up the stairs Burton noticed the total lack of security at the bank.

"I notice that you don't have a bank guard stationed in the lobby Spurlock, is that customary of banks in the area?"

"We do have the local Sheriff and he employs five county deputies and one detective. The bank has never felt the need to hire its own security."

"If this were New York, your bank would be relieved of its funds before lunch, with one or two of your employees and customers left to color the floor tile red."

Burton was amused when he noticed the worried look on the face of the 'Assistant Vice President' as they continued to climb the stairs to the top floor. That was one thing that Burton took pride in, making people worry. When they reached the second floor it opened up into a large waiting area with offices on all sides. At the farthest end from the stairs was a large glass door with two sidelights and a glass transom over the top. Before the young man could speak, Burton said' "Is that the office of Mr. Reed?"

"Yes sir, I'll let him know you're here."

"No need, I can handle it from here. Thanks for your help Mr. Spurlock."

"But Mr. Burton, I must insist......."

Before the man could finish his sentence Burton turned and held a hand in front of the bankers face. Burton was a powerfully built man who stood well over six feet tall in his stocking feet, with boots on at least six feet five. When he looked at most people they gave in to whatever he wanted and it was no different now. The banker stopped, remembering the pain that still radiated through his right hand, and took a step backward. For a moment Burton thought he was going to turn and run away.

"Yes Sir, have a nice day." The banker turned and with as much speed as he could manage without actually breaking into a run, went back to the head of the stairs and proceeded down, more than glad to leave this tall stranger with his boss, Mr. Reed.

Hash Burton put a powerful hand on the doorknob and gave it a turn without knocking. As he swung the door open, a man at a large desk looked up but said nothing. Burton went on in, closing the door behind him as he went. As he approached the oversized desk he noticed that the man sitting behind it was also just as oversized. Burton assumed this to be the man he was looking for. He adjusted a chair and sat down opposite the banker. The bank president was a neatly trimmed man in his late fifties by the look of it. The time he spent behind a desk was taking a toll on him though; he had to be at least fifty pounds overweight.

As Burton sat down the man put down his pen and closed the ledger he was working on. He leaned back in his chair and put both hands in his vest pockets. Burton could tell that the bank president wasn't used to being barged in on, especially by a total stranger. Both men sat there looking at each other for the longest time before the banker finally spoke. His voice was deep and raspy, probably from too many imported cigars. The large office had the faint hint of tobacco smoke and there was a mahogany humidor on top of the desk and to the side.

"Do you usually invade a private office in this manner without knocking, or is this a habit you've recently acquired in New York, Mr. Burton?"

Burton reached over and opened the cigar case and took out a Cuban. He used the imported cutter on the desk by the case to clip the end. Then he produced a Lucifer from his own vest pocket and lit it with his thumbnail. Burton slowly puffed the cigar as he held the match to the end. After crushing the flame between his thumb and forefinger he tossed it into the large pedestal ashtray beside the desk.

"Reed, you knew I was coming, don't act so damned surprised to see me."

It was true that Samuel J. Reed, or J.R. to those who knew him well, was expecting a new client from New York, but he wasn't expecting someone quite so overbearing.

Burton took a puff on the cigar, holding in the smoke for a moment before releasing it toward the ceiling. He held the cigar in his left hand, rolling it between thumb and fingers before looking at the banker with piercing gray eyes. "Not bad Reed, how is it that a man who lives in some of the finest tobacco country in the Union smokes Cubans?"

"I like what I like Burton. Now did you come all the way down here from New York to talk about cigars or is our deal good to go?"

"The deal's good Reed, all is in place on my end. Did you acquire all the information that's needed on your end?"

Reed stood up and walked to the window. "I have got all the information and most of the deeds that we will need for the first phase of the project in my possession. We've been forced to use more than ninety percent of the original deposit to acquire the first set of deeds. These were the easy ones. It would have cost twice as much if not for your Baldwin-Felts boys. I never saw so many unhappy transactions in my life. Most of the land owners who had dealings with the bank, before they had their land stolen for a pittance of what it was worth, have closed out their accounts and more than a few would like to see me hanged. I've had to post a guard at my home and if things get much worse I'll need to do the same thing at the office. I swear if the money weren't so good Burton, I'd tell you to go to hell.

Burton took another puff on his cigar, all the while looking at Reed.

"Most of the deeds are not all of the deeds Reed; we need everything in place before any mining can take place."

"I've ran into a little problem up on Left Beaver Creek. The biggest land owner in the county won't sell and I don't have a mortgage on any of his property. He won't listen to reason Burton and without his property we can't get at the coal on Mud Creek or the head of Right Beaver, not to mention the counties on the other side of his property."

"We can still mine the other coal without that track of land Reed, so what's the problem?"

"That's right Burton, we can mine the other coal, but the railroad goes up Left Beaver. Without William Conley's spread we can't get the coal to the railroad. The Conley farm is the key to this whole operation. Also you may not have heard but Conley has gone into the transportation business. He has two-hundred men building a damn tunnel system through the mountain at Wheelwright all the way to Knott and Letcher Counties. He'll control all the coal in those two counties as well. That's three times as much coal as Floyd County can produce on its best day. Story has it he wants to run a line through the Boone and connect to the railroad at Stearns. He has hired some of the best engineers in the business and he has more than enough money to accomplish just about anything he sets his mind to. Hell one of his engineers is rumored to be a genius, a man by the name of Winston Roy Martin. He can take a set of drawings and tell you in minutes how many man hours it will take and how much money it will cost."

Burton wasn't hearing anything new, except maybe the plan for Stearns and the engineer named Martin. After another puff on his cigar he looked at Reed and asked, "What kind of man is this William Conley to turn down what you've been offering him Reed?"

"William Conley doesn't need the money Burton. He made a fortune during the war selling horses to the north. The man has some of the finest stock in the nation and any northern officer above the rank of major wouldn't settle for anything less than a Conley horse during the war, or after for that matter. I hear tell that some of those horses were so good that some of the men stopped calling them horses all together and just started calling them Conley's."

Burton just sat back in his chair and rolled the Cuban around in his lips. "You just sit back Reed and watch how big business is handled up north. I'll have that land before you know it and the coal will make it to the railroad. It won't be a problem. And as for that tunnel system that's being built, if we can't acquire it then we'll destroy it along with William Haskell Conley."

Reed, continuing to look out the window, spoke again without looking around at his guest.

"Conley has powerful connections from his war days Burton, more than one politician and judge considers him a friend. If you go pushing too hard you may just get more than you bargained for. The last thing we need now is for some Federal Marshal to go looking around at the way we've been doing things around here lately. Some of what we've been doing ain't exactly legal."

"My friends back east have a few friends too Reed and some of them go all the way to Washington, DC. If push comes to shove then it's only a matter of whose friends can push the hardest."

"I hope you're right Burton; I damn well hope you're right."

"Now Reed, what arrangements have you made for my stay in your quaint little county, something a little nicer than that railroad depot I was dropped off at earlier today I hope. If at all possible I would like to get situated and rest up a bit after my train ride last night."

"I think you'll be impressed with the house I've acquired for you, Burton. It's a big Victorian that sits on a corner lot on the upper end of town. It's close to the Town Branch freight yard and around the corner from the nicest restaurant in town, the City Steak House. There's plenty of room for offices if you choose, and nice enough to entertain."

"The City Steak House you say. Sounds slow and stuffy Reed. Is there anything around here where a man can get rough grub and a drink after a hard day?"

"You bet. The Depot Saloon next to the freight yard serves good old fashion home cooking. They don't serve alcohol with the meal, but the bar room is attached. I eat there myself from time to time. Still though, the City Steak House is my favorite."

Burton thought to himself that a man of Reed's girth might want to stay away from grain and molasses for a while and just stick with straight hay.

"Have I said something funny Burton, you seem ready to bust out laughing."

Hash Burton, at that did laugh and laugh loudly, "Sorry Reed, just thinking about hay and the such. Pay it no mind."

Reed took all this as just Northern humor and let it pass.

After Burton calmed down he asked, "How did you come about this place where I'll be staying Reed, fair and square I hope?"

"Let's just say that I've held the mortgage on the place since a few years back. With a little adjusting of the books at the PVA's office, the taxes became a little more than the previous owner could afford. There was the usual court case which, thanks to a judge who would rather not have his own property re-evaluated, found in favor of the bank. It also took some help from the Sheriff, but the house did become vacant just in time for your arrival. The Sheriff wasn't happy about evicting one of his old friends, but the law is the law and he took an oath to uphold it.

"Also I took the liberty to have it cleaned and the furniture aired. It has the bare essentials in culinary necessities, such as coffee and tea, not knowing your preference. The house has a rather nice bar in the study. I had all the alcohol thrown out and then re-stocked with a variety of spirits." Reed looked at Burton with a smile and said, "I hope you don't mind."

Hash Burton stood up and adjusted his vest. He ground out his cigar in the well-used ashtray that stood on a pedestal beside the banker's desk.

"Reed, I am impressed. I should have known that you small town bankers could be just as ruthless as any of the Wall Street money men I've been acquainted with in the past. Now if you could make arrangements to have someone show me to my living quarters and also send someone to acquire my luggage from the railroad depot, I would be much obliged. Also I would like the luggage delivered at 4:00 this afternoon, I want to rest up from my journey on the midnight special." Reed knew there was no midnight special; it was just a jab at the local railroad.

"I can do better than that Mr. Burton; I shall accompany you to the residence myself and on the way we'll go over some other details you need to know about concerning this new endeavor of yours. In the mean time I shall send someone to fetch your belongings from the depot."

Both men made their way down the stairs and through the bank's lobby. It was starting to get busy now. Several customers had entered and were conducting their business at the teller windows. As Burton passed the teller he had insulted earlier he gave her a smile and a nod, it was not reciprocated. Reed, not knowing of the earlier run-in, made a mental note to talk to the teller about being friendlier in the future. Both men exited the large front doors of the bank and were instantly bathed in bright sunlight.

"Beautiful morning, the rain seems to have cleansed the air."

"Do you enjoy such humid mornings Reed?"

"Oh sure, humidity in the mountains is something you get used to. Don't think it'll go away soon either. Most farmers I've talked to say this will be a wet year. We've had too much rain already. The Big Sandy's been running about twenty feet above normal. Any more rain and there'll be a flood for sure."

As the two men made their way up the street from the bank, they drew more than a few stares. In a small town like Prestonsburg where everyone knew everybody else, any stranger was likely to draw attention, especially one wearing big city clothes and walking with the president of the county's largest bank.

The walk to the Hatfield house was only a short distance from the bank. Reed pointed out a few of the buildings and businesses that would probably interest Hash Burton, such as restaurants and the store which special ordered the Cuban cigars that Reed favored.

The house they came to was better than the banker had made it out to be. One thing that Samuel J. Reed had learned long ago was to under promise and over deliver, it usually got favorable results. And in this case it had worked out perfectly, Reed could see the approval written all over Hash Burton's face.

The Stanton Hatfield house was without a doubt the nicest house in Floyd County. It was a very large Victorian style, with a wide porch that went around three sides and was flanked by gardens. There were stables in the rear with enough room for six horses and also a carriage house.

Stanton Hatfield had made his money when the railroad first came to the area. He had owned most of the bottom land that ran beside the Big Sandy River in Floyd County. The railroad was following the river due to the need to not move the mountains that ran along the river banks. The path of least resistance, so to speak, was the bottom land which was owned by Stanton Hatfield.

It was quite a windfall for old man Hatfield. With all that money he built a magnificent house and stable right in downtown Prestonsburg, Kentucky. During the Civil War though Mr. Hatfield's sympathies were with the south and when the end of the war came most of his money, which he had converted to confederate currency, became worthless. As the years went by he had to take out a mortgage on his home, and Mr. Samuel J. Reed, was more than happy to give it to him. Reed knew that someday he would own the Hatfield house lock stock and barrel. This coal deal had forced him to move up his timetable a bit though. He was more than happy to allow Hash Burton to use the house for a while. When the coal deal was finished Burton would move back to New York and Samuel J. Reed would move into the house.

Reed went through the house showing Burton each room and then the two went out back to inspect the stables. With no one living at the house since old man Hatfield had been evicted there were no horses in the stalls.

"That does bring up a topic you may have touched on earlier Reed, where do I find some good horses to use while I'm staying in town?"

"How good of a horse do you want Burton, I didn't think city boys had much need for riding stock."

Burton resisted the urge to joust with the big banker, not liking the fact that this man, who he had only just met, had formed such an opinion of him.

"Let me just say Mr. Reed that I can ride and shoot as good as, if not better than, any man in this county, or any of the surrounding counties for that matter."

It was the first time that Burton had put a Mr. in front of Reed's name and by the tone and the language used Reed thought that an apology was in order.

"Please let me apologize Mr. Burton if I have offended you. I promise you sir that I didn't mean to belittle you in any way what so ever."

Burton looked at the pudgy banker for a while, knowing that his silence would help to intimidate the banker even more.

Finally he spoke, "Mr. Reed, in the future please don't judge my abilities in any way what so ever, I have spent my life doing many things that you would not even begin to understand. And also Mr. Reed please let it be known that I am a man who knows how to take care of himself, do we understand each other?"

Reed looked a bit shaken and nervous at having been lectured to by a man who without a doubt could and would not hesitate to pound him to a pulp right here in his own house in his own town.

"Yes sir, Mr. Burton, and again please accept my most sincere apologies."

With that the banker turned and walked out the front door, and then with a sudden stop he turned and walked back to where Burton was standing. "I almost forgot, here is the key to the front door." And with that the banker turned and hurriedly walked back down the street toward his bank and his upstairs office.

Burton walked over to the overstuffed couch in the front parlor and stretched out. Before long there was a knock at the front door which startled him. He must have fallen asleep. When he went to the door he was greeted by a gentleman who worked for the railroad. "Mr. Burton, I have your baggage from the depot."

"Please bring it in and place it on the floor by the couch if you don't mind."

When the luggage was inside Burton gave the man a dollar, which was a half a day's wages in this town.

"Thanks Mister, if you need anything else you can find me at the depot, names Josh Osborne."

"Yes Osborne, I met a young clerk there this morning by the name of Eisner, know anything about him?"

"Yes sir I do, he's the head of the Prestonsburg depot for the railroad, and he got me my job."

"Is he a man who can be trusted with his job?"

"Oh yes, he prides himself on his reputation."

"Thanks."

With that the baggage boy turned and almost skipped back toward the depot. It was amazing at the information that could be had in a small town with a dollar here and a dollar there. The difference a little money makes, Burton thought to himself as he stood there on the front porch of his new home. Burton stepped back inside and locked the door behind him. He walked over and opened the middle sized trunk with a key from his inside vest pocket. He reached in and pulled out a well-worn gun belt and holster. In the holster was a nickel plated .45 caliber revolver, manufactured by the Colt Arms Company. This was a special built weapon that Hash Burton was extremely proud of. It had an extremely sensitive trigger which took very little effort to fire. The front sight was a little taller and wider than on other versions and the overall length was slightly shorter than factory models, which improved the draw speed. The well-worn walnut handles had four notches on the right outside grip where they were visible to anyone who cared to notice.

Not many men notched their guns anymore but Burton was not just any man, he was his own man and he was proud of those notches. Two were from duels when he felt his honor had been tested, one was for a man who had tried to hold him up in a dark alley one night, and the fourth was a murder that eliminated a competitor in a business venture that was about to go sour. Hash Burton had spent many an hour practicing his draw and his aim. He had spent money on the best instructors in the care and use of a Colt. Burton almost felt he was the fastest gun alive and he was always ready to add another notch to those handles.

The double shot derringer was still in his vest pocket. It had been there ever since the chess game on the New York Central from New York to Portsmouth. Not that he ever felt threatened, but as things had worked out he thought a little extra caution was necessary.

He dug into another trunk and pulled out a flat brimmed Stetson hat and put it on. He went over and stood in front of the mirror and admired the look he saw. After adjusting the hat he strapped on the gun belt and loaded the six empty chambers in his Colt. He removed a carton of .45 cartridges and refilled the six empty loops on his gun belt.

Hash sat back down on the big overstuffed chair and before long his eyelids grew heavy. The little sleep he had gotten the night before on the train into town was growing pretty thin. He planned on an hour nap before he went in search of supper. That hour actually turned into five before he came to and looked at his pocket watch. It would be dark in a few hours. He went out the front door and locked it behind him before heading off to the saloon.

He walked right past the City Steak House, where he had been told the best food in the county was served. His preferred spot for dinner on this night, his first night in Prestonsburg, was none other than the Depot Saloon, a much smaller establishment near the freight depot beside the old Town Branch Bridge. He wanted to see what he could find out about this town and information would be easier to come by in a saloon. There was also another newcomer in town that had been there for the last few days. This newcomer worked for Hash, and he took his meals at the Depot Cafe.

Hash entered through the batwing doors and stood there for a second to look the place over. There was a long bar of oak that had been polished to a glossy shine. There were maybe a dozen tables where men played cards or just talked as they drank. In a side room were more tables where food was being served. Hash walked over and entered the dining area and looked around. Over in a corner was the man he came to see sitting at a table, alone with a plate full of food which meant he hadn't been there long.

As he walked over the man looked up and said, "Bout time you showed up boss, I was beginning to think that you backed out on me."

"I just got into town this morning on the seven o'clock train. I've spent most of the day with that fat banker getting myself situated. How's the food in this place?"

"Not bad boss."

"No boss anymore Riley, just call me Hash, I don't want anyone to know you work for me."

"Sure thing, Boss."

Riley looked over his plate and smiled at Hash. "Just kidding Hash, ain't had anybody around to talk to so I guess I just felt like a little humor."

Hash gave Riley a look that said no more humor, and then asked, "Have you been up on the Beaver Creek section yet?"

"Sure have. The train goes that way and back every day, it's the easiest way in and out. On horse it's about thirty miles one way, not a trip for every day travel if you're thinking of doing it by horse."

A waitress came over and Hash asked her about the special. "Roast beef, potatoes and cornbread," she said.

Hash looked at the woman with more than just casual interest, and then said, "Sounds good, bring me some coffee with that would you miss?" As the woman walked away Hash watched her and thought to himself that this town might have more possibilities than he had first thought.

Riley chuckled, "You sure ain't changed a bit over the years Hash, and I can tell you something else, that menu ain't changed either, that's the same special they been serving every day for the last week, roast beef, potatoes and cornbread."

"Don't look like you mind very much Riley, you keep coming back."

"Well I do like roast beef and anyway the view from over here of that waitress ain't that bad either. I done a little checking around town and it seems her husband ran off with some feisty bar maid a few months back and that little lady had to take a second job here just to make ends meet."

"A second job, where else does she work?"

"Don't know, but she must be dependable, she has been here every night this week. And if you think that gal has looks then you should see her two sisters, twins named Pam and Nancy."

Hash looked back at Riley. "You don't say. Would they be older or younger than our waitress over there?"

"I can't really tell but they are probably mid-twenties, at least that's what Burt over there tending bar said. But they both don't look a day over eighteen, I seen them a few weeks back talking to that waitress lady who is their sister. I tell you right now them two got the looks, either one could stop a train dead in its tracks."

"Dead in its tracks, that is quiet an analogy Riley."

"I would have to agree with you Hash, especially if I knew what analogy meant."

It wasn't long before the waitress brought back the food, and a steaming pot of coffee to go along with it. Hash tasted the food and then sampled the coffee.

"Not bad Riley, not bad at all."

"Told you the food ain't bad, a man can never get to much roast beef."

"Yes you told me, now can we focus on the job at hand?"

With that the two men ate their food and filled each other in on what had happened for the last couple of weeks.

The news wasn't what Hash had hoped for.

"Water's been getting big up that way Hash. Today's the first sunny day we had in the last two weeks. Them creeks up toward Drift and beyond look like rivers. It almost got over the rails couple of days back. Gone down a little, but it wouldn't take much to bring it back up. Ground's so full of water it squishes when you take a step. Farmers round here say the rain ain't nowhere near done. Say we're in for one of them big floods that their daddy's told em about when they were young"

"Now how bad can it be Riley? Seems to me the creek comes up and then it goes down, what's all the worry?"

"It ain't that way here in the mountains Hash. All that water gets corralled between these mountains. They say it comes bustin out fast enough to wash out a railroad bridge. Ground water fills the mines and takes weeks for it to drain out. Just makes all kinds of mess. And that's just the regular floods. These folks round here been talkin bout a really big flood coming due."

"Flood can't last forever Riley. We'll pump out the mines with the new equipment we got coming if it takes it."

The pretty young waitress stopped by each table from time to time to check on the last of her customers. Just as Hash and Riley were about to finish she informed them that the restaurant would be closing in a few minutes, but the bar in the next room would remain open as long as Burt, the saloon's bartender, had customers.

Hash and Riley quickly finished. "Riley, what would you think about a drink to finish off this fine meal?"

"Sounds good to me Hash, you buying?"

"Don't I always Riley?"

Riley laughed, "Yep' I reckon you always do."

Dinner over, the two got up and walked into the saloon. Before doing so Hash left two five dollar gold pieces to cover the two meals and the tip, knowing that the waitress probably hadn't seen a tip like that the entire time she worked there. Maybe she would remember him the next time he came in.

Just before Hash went through the batwing doors to the saloon he looked back at the table he and Riley had just left.

The waitress walked over to clean up and looked at the two gold pieces Hash had left lying there. She looked his way and a slight smile came upon her face.

Hash gave a slight nod as he touched the brim of his Stetson with the forefinger of his right hand.

As Hash and Riley walked up to the bar Riley said, "Maybe this ain't such a good idea Hash." Riley nodded over at a table in the corner where three men were playing cards, five card stud. Hash noticed that each of the three wore tied down guns.

"Them three's trouble Hash, they seem to pick fights just to help pass the time. Stranger had a run in couple weeks back with them three. He was found back shot the next day. Sheriff couldn't prove who done it, just another unsolved murder.

"They work for a small time coal operator over in the county and they don't like strangers. Seems that some of the folks around here are a little suspicious about all the land that's getting bought up and the man who pays them boy's wages ain't about to sell. They're hired guns from down state, here to make sure that nothing happens to their boss's coal operation."

Hash looked over at the card players and said, "Pay them no mind; we just came in for a drink."

"Too late for that Hash, looks like we've just been noticed."

Hash didn't respond to Riley. He looked at the bartender and said, "Whiskey for the two of us. And by the way make it your best Kentucky whiskey; I want to try it out while I'm in your fine little town."

The three men threw their cards on the table, stood up and walked over to the bar. "Howdy mister. You new here in town, or maybe just passin through?"

Hash just kept facing the bar. He could see all three in the mirror behind the bar. The view was only partially blocked by all the whiskey bottles sitting up on shelves in front of the mirror which also obscured the fact that Hash was looking at them.

"Maybe you didn't hear me mister, I'm talking to you. When I talk to a man I spect him to answer."

The bartender set two glasses on the bar and filled each with whiskey. Hash picked up the glass with his left hand and took a sip. While that had everyone's attention he loosed the leather strap on his gun with his right.

Hash put down his drink and turned to face the man, and in doing so he straightened up to his full height. The three seemed a little surprised at the size of the man they had just spoken to, each took a step backward.

Hash looked at the three and sized them up in a matter of seconds. He could tell which one was the most dangerous, which one was the fastest and which one was the craziest. In that amount of time he had formulated a plan and before anyone else could speak he hit the tallest, and meanest, looking of the three and before either of the other two could speak his Colt was out and in there face.

"I'm sorry fellas, but were you talking to me?" Hash asked.

The one that Hash hit was on his back lying on the floor out cold. The other two were caught off guard so bad that they couldn't even think of an answer for Hash.

About that time from behind the bar the bartender pulled back the hammer of a Greener shotgun. "Logan, I told you and your two gun-hounds to never start trouble in here again, now I'm gonna hafta ask you three to leave."

"Wait a minute Burt, we didn't start nothing, we just wanted to talk to this new feller here and before we knew it he done knocked Russell out."

"I heard what you were asking, and I saw how you were asking it, so until you learn some manners get out and don't come back."

"Alright Burt, you win but don't think this is over by a long shot."

"I try never to think Logan, it takes too much of my time, I'd rather just react; now shoo before my thumb gets tired of holding back the hammer on this here Greener."

The two still standing helped the third one to his feet and headed for the door. The one with the busted head said, "What happened Logan, did I get into a fight or something?"

"Weren't any fight to it Russell, now just shut up."

After the three left Burt put the shotgun back under the counter and said, "Mister, I don't know who you are but I been waiting a long time to see them three loudmouth bullies put in their place. They been running off my customers for the last couple of months and I was about to get tired of it. Name's Burt if you didn't already hear. Burt held out his hand and Hash took it, "Hash is my name, Hash Burton."

"Pleasure Mr. Burton, what brings you to the big city of Prestonsburg?"

"A little business Burt, just a little business."

"Well you be careful of them three you just had the ruckus with, they're mean and I suspect not above waylaying anyone that shows em up, especially the way you just did."

"Good advice Burt, I'll try to watch my back. I was kind of hoping this was a friendly little town."

"It used to be up until a couple of months ago. I've seen lots of new faces in here lately, all heading up the Beavers, either to work in the mines or to protect the mine owners."

Hash thought about what the bartender had said before he finally spoke. "What's going on up in the Beavers, Burt?"

"Lots of coal mining been going on since the war ended. Most men up that way just work for wages, bringing that black stuff out from under the mountain. Some of them fellers are getting rich though, you know the ones who own the mines and all."

Hash knew more than he was letting on, but enjoyed the conversation. He wanted to keep the talk going to see if he could learn anything useful though so he asked Burt if he knew where he could get a few good horses. Burt didn't have to think long before he said, "Try William Conley's, he's got the best stock in all of the state. I warn you though, Conley's stock ain't cheap. Some say he can get as much as four hundred dollars apiece for his best horses."

"Four hundred dollars sounds a bit steep to pay for a horse Burt. I don't know how my twelve dollar saddle would look on such an expensive animal as that. What do you think Riley, me and my worn out saddle atop a four-hundred dollar horse?"

"Hash, if you got the four-hundred for the horse I think you could spring for a new saddle. Any man on a horse that expensive better be sitting a good saddle. Don't want anyone thinking you stole the horse now do ya?"

"Leave it to you Riley to spell out the obvious. First thing in the morning I think I'll take the train up Beaver Creek and talk to this William Conley fellow about a few things, including a horse."

"Conley won't be there," replied the bartender. "Seems he was on a little business trip through West Virginia and on up into Ohio a few weeks back and he ain't been heard from since. Some folks think he might have run into a bit of trouble."

Hash rubbed his chin and knew that this was the type of conversation that could produce some valuable information.

"Now what kind of business would a backwoods horse trader be conducting in West Virginia and Ohio Burt?"

"Hash, William Conley ain't no small timer. He made it rich back during the war and he's got business dealings from here all the way to Washington and even to that Wall Street place up in New York City."

"You don't say, well what kind of business does he conduct in Floyd County besides horse trading?"

"Mister Conley is big in tobacco, corn, and beef. He ships off some of the best cattle this side of the Mississippi River. And I do know for a fact that he has his own mining operation with enough coal they say to last for a thousand years."

Now this was something that Hash hadn't expected. Every rumor up until now had it that William Haskell Conley wasn't in the mining business. And for that matter even his tunnel plans were something less than a year old and just now getting started.

"Burt, did you say that Conley mines coal?"

"Well actually the mine is run by a brother of his named Cecil, or Big C as everyone likes to call him. He's Haskell's youngest brother and the mine is in his name. Everybody knows though that Haskell Conley is the real backer of the Big C Mine.

Hash had heard of the Big C Mine in the reports his scouts had been sending. But no one had associated this particular operation to the William Haskell Conley family. The Big C was an impressive operation. Eighty men employed underground in two shifts. Thirty five on the outside, not counting office personnel.

Hash thought to himself how these thousand years of coal would be mined in ten years or less if all went as planned. This little conversation with the bartender had turned out better than Hash had hoped. Burt was a man who, in his position, heard everything this small town had to say. If handled properly he could be a future source of information that could prove well worth a small financial investment.

"Well Riley, what do you say we walk over to my place? Need to talk to you about a few things."

Burt looked at the tall stranger, "Your place, you live here in town do ya?"

"Sure do, living in the Stanton Hatfield place."

Burt chuckled, "Stanton Hatfield's ain't no place, in my mind it's a mansion."

Burton knew a mansion when he seen one. The Hatfield house might be a mansion in Floyd County, Kentucky but it was a shack compared to some of the places in New York.

"Sorry Burt, the Hatfield Mansion."

"I heard that fat banker Reed stole it from Hatfield."

"I don't know about any of that Burt, but I'll be staying there anyway. Let's just say that I'm renting it from the bank for a while." Hash reached into his pocket and pulled out another five dollar gold piece and laid it on the bar. "Will this cover our drinks?"

Burt looked at the coin and as a big smile consumed his face said, "You bet Mr. Burton, ain't often anybody plants that much coin on this here counter. Much obliged."

Hash smiled at the bar-keep as he turned and headed for the door, Riley right behind him. Just as Hash and Riley were ready to exit, Hash stopped dead in his tracks.

"Riley you got a throw down?"

Riley gave Hash a puzzled look, "You know I got one hiding under my coat. It's in that new-fangled shoulder holster you sent me."

Hash turned back to Burt, "There a back door to this place Burt?"

"Sure thing Mr. Burton. Just through the back stock room and on the right, here let me show you."

With that Burt turned and went through a door at the side of the bar. The room was small and poorly lit. Hash knew that anyone exiting through this door probably would be hard to see from the outside. The light outside was almost gone and no light would shine through the back door as it opened.

"This will work just fine Burt. After what happened earlier I feel better using this door instead of going out the front. Using that front door would be no different than paintin a big target my chest."

"Know what you mean Mr. Burton. You humiliated them three pretty bad, they might be thinking about getting even. And just between you and me, I don't think it'd be the first time."

"So long Burt. Hopefully I'm just being a little too cautious, but a man can't be too careful these days now can he?"

Burt rubbed his beardy chin and said, "I reckon so Burton, I reckon so."

Hash and Riley eased out the back door and let it close very slowly back against the jamb. Hash could hear Burt sliding the bolt that locked the door from the inside. It was almost completely dark now, especially on the back street. As the two men made their way around the side Hash decided to go two more doors down before entering the main street in front of the saloon. Upon reaching the front of the alley that ran to the concrete walkway the two men first looked left, back in the direction of the saloon and then right. The street was deserted.

Riley stepped up on the sidewalk first but before his second boot touched the concrete a shot rang out. Riley went down but didn't make a sound. Before he hit the ground Hash grabbed him and pulled him back into the alley.

"How bad you hit Riley?"

Riley didn't answer at first, he just slowly put his hand on his shoulder. "Not bad boss, just in the left shoulder I think."

Riley had forgotten and called Hash boss again, but under the circumstances Hash was just glad he wasn't hurt worse than he was. Riley was holding his shoulder with his right hand to stop the bleeding. A quick look and Hash knew the shoulder had only been grazed by the bullet. There was neither an entrance nor an exit wound, only a graze but a deep one at that.

"Riley, did you see where that shot came from?"

Riley looked up at Hash and with clenched teeth said, "Sure did boss. Over there by that rail shed, see it?"

Burton eased his head out ever so slightly and looked at the shed. I see it Riley, now what?"

"You see on the porch in the shadows there are two benches. The shot came from the bench on the right."

Burton was looking hard but the porch was only darkness and shadows. "Riley, how in blazes did you see any benches? That porch is completely dark."

"I know that the benches are there boss, I seen em in the daylight before. When the shot went off I could see his outline, just sitting there like he'd been waiting on us. He knew we couldn't see him in the darkness like that."

Hash looked at Riley and said, "You stay down. And if you have to shoot make damn sure what you're shooting at, it might just be me. I'll be back in a minute."

"Sure thing Boss, you be careful, whoever is shooting out there is shooting to kill."

Hash turned and went back down the alley and then ran back up to the back door of the saloon. Hash knocked as quietly as he could on the bolted door and said, "Burt open up, it's Burton."

The bolt slid back and the door flew open. Hash was looking at a Greener shotgun not more than six inches from his face.

"That you Burton, what the hell's going on out there anyway? I heard a gunshot."

"Yea Burt it's me. You got a lantern in there?"

"Got one right here, hanging on this nail right by the door."

"Let me have it. And stay inside away from the windows."

"You got that right," replied Burt.

Hash grabbed the lantern and headed back down to the alley where Riley was waiting. As soon as he turned he heard the door behind him close and the same sound as before of the big interior slid-bolt being rammed home. Hash eased back to where Riley lay in the alley.

"Riley, it's me Hash, don't shoot."

"Don't worry boss, I knew it was you. I could tell by the way your boots click on the boardwalk," Riley whispered. "You got a plan boss?"

"Sure do. You think whoever tried to bushwhack us is still over there?"

"Yea, those dry-gulchers are still there, waitin to finish the job. They don't think we know where they are or else they would've already headed out. I saw em easin out to try to get a better look at what mischief they had already caused. I counted three of em."

"Three. You reckon it's those same three from the saloon?"

"That would be my guess boss."

"How's the shoulder doing?"

"Bleedin's stopped. It ain't no more than a scratch."

"Is your other shoulder good enough to throw this lantern over on that porch?"

"You bet, what's the plan?"

"Give me thirty seconds to get around to the next alley. Stay behind the cover of this building and after you light that lantern let her sail right on that porch." With that Hash disappeared around the back of the next building.

Riley pulled a match from the brim of his hat and when he thought the time was right he struck it on the side of the building. As soon as he touched the match to the lantern's mantel the fire took. Riley held the lantern with his good arm and let her fly. Before he could get back behind cover two shots rang out in quick succession from the other side of the street. Something hit Riley, spun him around and he hit the ground.

In the next alley Hash was ready. As the lit lantern sailed across the street Hash heard the two shots go off and hoped Riley had made it back to cover. When the lantern hit the street in front of the porch it burst into a brilliant flame lighting the entire porch where the three men were hiding.

Hash stepped into the street, gun in hand. One of the three stood up and leveled his gun at Hash, it was too late. The gun in Hash's hand roared and the man went down. Another one stood up, but before he could fire, Hash, in a booming voice shouted, "Drop it, both of you."

The one that stood up was already taking aim at Hash. At that same instant another shot rang out, but this one was not from Hash's gun. The man that had stood up was jerked back by the slug. He went against the wall of the porch, both hands holding his chest. He slowly slid down the wall; a dark stain smearing the stucco as he went.

"Don't shoot. Don't shoot," the third man shouted.

Hash shouted, "Throw your gun out onto the street."

Only a second later a six shooter came sailing out from behind the horses watering trough.

"Now stand up. And don't try anything."

"Mister, I'll do exactly as you say, but you make sure that other feller with the scatter-gun doesn't shoot me."

"Riley, you fire that other shot?"

No response from Riley. A second later Hash heard the unmistakable voice of Burt.

"Burton, are you and Riley alright?"

"I'm alright Burt, don't know about Riley."

"I got that second feller with my Greener. You check em out and I'll keep you covered."

The Greener explained why the second man went to the wall. A twelve gauge shotgun with two-ought buck can make a real mess out of a man. If the wall hadn't caught him he would have been blown into the next street.

"You there on the porch, come out with your hands up and remember you got a Greener trained on you."

The man slowly got up and walked out on the street.

"Put your hands over your head where I can see em."

The man did exactly as he was told.

Hash hollered, "Just the three of you or is there anyone else?"

"There's no one else, just the three of us."

Hash yelled at Burt, "Keep em covered while I check on Riley."

Hash cautiously headed over to where Riley had been. As he approached he heard other voices as people began to investigate what all the shooting was about.

Hash found his friend lying face-down in the alley. He removed the gun from Riley's hand. Hash checked for a pulse. Riley was still alive but not by much.

Hash stepped from the alley and asked one of the men coming down the street how long it would take to get a doctor.

"Not more than a few minutes, he lives a couple of blocks over."

"Can someone get him and tell him it's urgent."

No more had the words left Hash's mouth than the man said, "Don't have to, here comes Doc now."

Hash saw an older gentleman coming up the street at a fast trot carrying a small black bag. One of the men said, "Over there Doc, lying in the alley."

The doctor came up to Hash and asked, "Is this one still alive?"

"Yea Doc, but I think he's been hit pretty bad."

A quick check and the doctor hollered for a couple of men to get some stretchers.

"Just need one Doc, the other two over there don't need a doctor, they need an undertaker."

The doctor frowned and said, "Damn-it Sam then just get one stretcher before the undertaker has three customers. And Sam, you run for it as if your feet just grew wings." The man named Sam took off at a full gallop.

The doctor, who was trying to stop the bleeding with what little he had available to him from his bag, looked at the faces in the crowd that had gathered. "Someone get the sheriff and tell Doctor Sables to meet me at the clinic." With that two more men took off at a dead run.

"You men, pull that buckboard over here." It was apparent when the doctor spoke, men listened. Four men grabbed the rails of the buckboard and pulled it over to the side of the street where the doctor was working on Riley. Burt had come from the saloon with two more lanterns and men were holding them up on either side of the doctor as he worked.

Running footsteps could be heard as Sam came back with a stretcher. It was placed on the ground beside Riley. The doctor stood up, blood on both hands and the front of his pants and shirt. "This man has lost a lot of blood. I've got it stopped for the most part." The doctor reported this to no one in particular.

"I need four men, two on each side, to gently lift him onto the stretcher." With that four men jumped forward and did as the doctor ordered.

"Easy now boys, don't want to start him leaking all over again."

In a matter of seconds Riley was on the stretcher. He was out cold and never made a sound.

"Now pick him up on the stretcher and ease him into the back of the buggy."

"But doc, there ain't a horse. It'll take ten or fifteen minutes to hitch up that rig," Sam said.

This threw the doctor into a tirade that would make a strong man tremble.

"Damn you Sam. I didn't ask you about a horse. You just do as I say and put that stretcher in the back of that buggy."

Sam didn't say another word. All four men gently picked up the stretcher and slid it into the back of the buggy.

"Now, I need every man here to push this buggy to the clinic. Sam you run on ahead. Here, take my keys, unlock the clinic and stoke the fire. We're going to need a real hot fire for water."

With that Sam took the doctor's keys and took off at a dead run. When he was almost out of sight the doctor shouted, "Put on some strong coffee too Sam, it's going be a long night."

The men eased the buggy down the unlit street for a few blocks. The doctor was in the back with his patient. Two men walked along side holding the lanterns high enough to shine in the back where the doctor continued to work on Riley.

Burt had now gone back into the saloon. When Hash walked in Burt looked up. He was in the process of pouring a straight shot of whiskey.

"I need something to calm my senses Burton. You want I should pour you one too?"

"Yea Burt, sounds like the best idea I've heard all day."

Burt poured another glass and slid it to Hash.

Hash had barely grabbed the glass when Burt said, "Bottoms up." The bartender raised the glass to his lips and killed the entire glass in one gulp. He wiped his mouth on his sleeve and began pouring himself another.

Hash looked at Burt and noticed that the bartender's hands were shaking.

"You better slow down on that stuff Burt. When the sheriff gets here he's gonna want to ask you a few questions."

"I know, just need this one last drink." With that Burt turned up the glass and, same as before, killed it in one big gulp again wiping his mouth on his sleeve."

"What do you think the sheriff is gonna want to talk about?"

Burton gave the man a harsh look.

"Well, most likely he'll talk about the weather and then maybe how the bartender business has been lately. Oh, and he might have a question or two about them two dead men out there in the street."

Burt looked up at Hash. A big grin came over his face as he said, "Do I look a bit nervous to you Burton?"

"Yea, just a mite Burt."

"I ain't ever killed a man before, at least not in this town Burton."

Hash took another sip of his whiskey.

"By the sound of that, you telling me you killed a man before, someplace else Burt."

"Keep your voice down, Burton. There's some things about me I'd just as soon people round here didn't know about. And it weren't just one man either."

Hash put down his drink and looked at Burt.

"If it wasn't just one man Burt, then how many was it?"

"Is this just tween me and you Burton?"

"Yea Burt, you got my curiosity all riled up now. How many was it?"

"In my whole life?"

"You gonna tell me or should I start guessing?"

Burt poured himself another drink. He held the glass up to his lips but didn't drink. He just held it there thinking.

"This one just put me into double-digits."

Burt put the glass to his mouth and again gulped down the whole thing. This time when he finished, he slammed the empty glass down on the bar.

Burton took a step back from the bar looking at the bartender all the while. This didn't add up. How could a run-down old bartender have killed ten men and not been apprehended by the law for at least one of them? It must be a lie. That must be it, the old barkeep was lying.

Burt looked at Hash and said, "You don't believe me do you Burton?"

Hash still didn't speak. He just stood there looking at the bartender.

They could hear voices outside. Hash went to the batwing doors and stepped out onto the sidewalk. The sheriff had arrived and was talking to some of the men on the street. Hash walked over and introduced himself to the sheriff.

The sheriff was a stout looking man of average height. He had a handlebar mustache, seemed that all lawmen wanted to look like Bat Masterson. He had a full head of black hair which was lined with streaks of gray. The gray must have been premature because he didn't look forty years old, more likely in his mid-thirties.

The sheriff looked at Hash and asked, "You see what happened here tonight mister?"

"Sure did sheriff, names Hash Burton."

The sheriff looked at the tall stranger and said, "Okay Hash, what do you know about what happened here tonight?"

"Sheriff, me and the man the doc just hauled away to his clinic were set upon by those three. They were hiding and tried to bushwhack both me and Riley as we came out of the saloon."

"Say you and this man Riley was coming out of the saloon huh. Well then tell me why your partner was shot up so bad in that dark alley two doors down Hash? The saloon is at least fifty of sixty feet from there."

Hash looked at the sheriff and realized he was about to be set up.

"Sheriff, Riley suspected something was going to go down, so we went out the back way and came down to this alley to avoid trouble."

Hash noticed the sheriff slide the leather strap off the top of his gun. The sheriff took a step back and said, "Slide that gun out of your holster real slow mister, butt first, and let her drop to the ground real easy like."

The sheriff had his hand over the handle of his gun ready to draw if he felt the need.

Now Hash had a decision to make, be arrested by a local sheriff in a town where Hash had just killed a man. Be brought before a local judge and then hung on a local tree.

Hash took a step back and eased his hand real slow over his gun just like the sheriff had told him. But instead of easing the gun out of the holster butt first as the sheriff had directed, Hash drew. Not a man saw the draw, not even the sheriff. But there it was, a Colt forty-five pointed straight at the sheriff's nose. No one moved, not a man spoke.

Hash looked at the sheriff and said, "Don't try it sheriff, there's already been too much killing done here tonight."

Hash heard one of the men say, "Here comes two of the town's deputies. Now what are you gonna do stranger?"

Hash took his left hand and pulled back on the hammer with the edge of his palm. "That all depends on the sheriff here. All that stands between him and the gates of hell is the strength in my left hand. I ain't done anything wrong here tonight. All me and Riley done was defend ourselves. And for that I find myself about to be arrested. Well I don't fancy to being arrested tonight, or any other night for that matter."

The two deputies saw Sheriff Barnes standing in the street. They also saw the tall stranger holding a gun on him. Both drew their guns and shouted, "Drop it mister or you'll be dead before you take your next breath."

Hash stood straight and still, not taking his eyes off the sheriff.

"Naw fellers, I don't think so," replied Hash. "You see this Colt I'm holding will blow a third nostril in your sheriff before I hit the ground. My hand slips off the hammer here and your boss is a goner. The sheriff didn't take his eyes off of Hash's gun. He just stood there and said to his deputies, "Put em away boys, I believe what he says. You try anything and I'm a dead man."

With that the two deputies holstered their guns. The sheriff looked at Hash and said, "Now what do you plan on doing Hash, you're the one with the gun?"

"Send someone to the saloon and get Burt, if he ain't drunk already."

One of the men ran to the saloon and in just another minute he and Burt came down the street. Burt didn't look too steady on his feet and Hash wondered if the local law enforcement would believe a drunk man.

"Here he is Sheriff." Burt stood on the sidewalk and weaved in the cool night breeze.

One of the deputies looked at Sheriff Barnes and said, "Burt's drunk as a skunk Sheriff, how can he know anything about this?"

Apparently Burt was as drunk as he looked. Upon hearing his name he looked at Hash and said, "You got the wrong man there Burton. That's the sheriff you're holding a gun on." Everyone in the crowd began to laugh.

One of the deputies said, "There's your bartender stranger. Now what is it you wanted with him?"

Hash didn't take his eyes off the sheriff. "Burt, tell the Sheriff here what happened tonight."

Burt stepped closer and said, "I done killed the man who shot Riley Sheriff. I have been trying to tell you for the last few weeks that them three weren't nothing but trouble."

The folks in the crowd got deathly quiet. No one spoke, no one moved.

"Sheriff, did you hear what I said; I'm the one who shot that no good skunk. Burton would you put down that gun so the Sheriff can arrest me?"

One of the deputies noticed a bead of sweat running down the sheriff's face. He knew Barnes wasn't going to make a move with that gun in his face.

"Burt, that explains just one of the bodies over there, what about the other one?"

Burt steadied himself on a hitch-in post by the street. "They shot Riley and were going to kill Burton there too, until Burton got one and I got the other."

The sheriff, who had been quiet as a mouse up until then; finally spoke, "Sorry stranger, I reckon that just about explains it. Now if it wouldn't be too much to ask would you please get that damn gun out of my face?"

Burton smiled and looked at the two deputies. "You heard your boss boys. Are you two going to behave yourselves if I put my gun away, or do you have anything else in mind?"

The two deputies took their hands off the handles of their holstered guns and as they did one of them said, "I reckon you're innocent, at least until we can sober old Burt here up and see if that story of his will hold up as well with strong black coffee as it did with whiskey."

Hash slowly put away the big Colt. The sheriff eased his hand off the top of his gun and wiped his forehead with his shirtsleeve.

"No hard feelings Sheriff?"

"None Hash, next time though I may not be so forgiving."

Hash stepped over and put a hand on the sheriff's shoulder and said, "Deal Sheriff, what happens now?"

The sheriff looked at the two deputies, "Jake, you and Scrappy get the undertaker. While you're at it, roust Oscar out of bed. Have him wait at the jail. After I talk to that man over there holding his hands up I'm going to put him up for the night at the expense of the taxpayers in that new jailhouse of ours."

"Sure thing Sheriff but the jailhouse ain't ours until day after tomorrow. Mayor ain't even had his dedication yet."

"Well what better way to dedicate a jail than to have a guest. Who on earth would want to dedicate an empty jailhouse anyway?"

"Well Sheriff, you been itching to move into that new building long enough. I reckon one day early won't make any difference."

"Stranger, did you say your name was Burton?"

"That's right Sheriff, Hash Burton. But you can just call me Hash."

"Yea I remember that now. If you don't mind Hash, how about coming by my new office in the morning, say around nine-o'clock. It should be easy to find, it's brand new. Entire building smells a lot like new paint and wet plaster."

The sheriff began to walk across the street and almost as an afterthought he asked one more question over his shoulder.

"And one more thing Hash, where you staying while you're in town?"

"I'll be at the Stanton Hatfield house Sheriff."

The sheriff stopped dead in his tracks and turned around.

"Did I hear you right Hash, you staying at the Stanton Hatfield house?"

"You heard right Sheriff."

"But I thought that was now the property of that fat banker Samuel J. Reed."

"That's right Sheriff. Reed and I have a little business to attend to over the next few months. I'll be staying at the Hatfield house during my time here."

The sheriff was no fool. He knew the way Reed had acquired the house. The banker even had a court order, signed by a judge that forced the sheriff to evict the old man.

The sheriff and his deputies didn't just throw Hatfield's belongings, what few the court had allowed him to keep, out in the street though. Barnes borrowed a wagon and horse from a friend and hauled what was left of the proud old Hatfield Estate to a run down one room shed across from the town's train depot. It did have a potbellied stove in the center so the old man wouldn't freeze to death. Barnes stopped in to check on Hatfield almost every day, on occasion bringing something his wife had cooked for the old man.

Old man Hatfield had been instrumental in getting the sheriff elected three years earlier. The next election was less than a year away and rumor had it that Reed and some powerful men, both in and out of the county, wanted nothing more than to have a new sheriff elected.

The sheriff said, "See you in the morning Hash." He then turned and headed across the street to gather what information he could about what had happened, and to oversee the removal of the bodies.

Hash watched as one of the deputies helped Burt down the street. Most likely they were heading to the new jail. Burt, probably spending the night there, would be sobered up in the morning with strong black coffee and ice water.

It had been a very long and quite eventful day. Before it was over Hash would find his way to this clinic the doctor had been talking about and check on Riley. The thought of his old friend being shot to pieces would have brought a lesser man to tears. If Riley died, Hash would be hurt deeply. But tears never changed anything. Hash could never remember a moment in his life when he had ever shed them for any reason. The kind of pain Hash felt could always be expressed better with anger.

Hash started down the street. As he made his way toward the center of town he noticed that the streets were lit here and there by kerosene street lights. He knew the clinic was near the courthouse and not far from the bank that Reed ran. It shouldn't be too hard to find for a man who was used to living in a city like New York.

Sure enough, as Hash rounded a corner, there was the horseless buggy that had served as an ambulance to transport the wounded Riley. Hash walked to the front door which was open and went in. The entire building was well lit by kerosene lights. There was a small chandelier in the center of the ceiling. Along two of the opposing walls hung sconces, each about a foot and a half below the ceiling and they both flickered hard trying to chase away the darkness.

Hash could see down a long hallway that ran from the lobby to another large room at the back. Along each side of the hall was any number of doors. Again, as with the lobby, the hall and the room at the end was extremely well lit. The doctors, being up in years, probably needed a lot of light to do their jobs.

Just as he was entering the hall that led to the back room he met the four stretcher bearers coming out. The last man out closed the door behind him as he went.

"How's he doing boys?" Hash asked.

The one named Sam said, "He's still out, both doctors are in there with him now."

Another one of the men said, "Mister, you mind if I ask you a question? "

"Not at all."

"I saw you draw on the sheriff out there a little while ago. Sheriff Barnes prides himself on his gun handling. Some say he practices an hour or two every day. Well Mister, I seen you and the sheriff toe to toe out there and you got the drop on him like it weren't nobody's business. I seen you out draw him, or should I say I thought I seen it. It was really more like a blur. Where in tar nation did you learn to draw like that?"

Hash stood in the lobby as the four men waited for an answer. "Oh I guess it just comes natural to some of us is all I know." Hash hoped this explanation would satisfy the four stretcher bearers. Apparently it did, the four men continued toward the door. Just before exiting the building the one named Sam turned back to Hash.

"Doc said if I see you out here to let you know that coffee is in the kitchen, that's the first door on the left. Hope your friend makes it." With that the four men were out the door and gone.

Hash found his way to the kitchen which turned out to be an elaborate affair. A wood burning Western Windsor Stove, equipped with several different cooking surfaces, was against the back wall, and on top of the warming shelf was a pot of coffee. On the counter beside the stove was a bag of Arbuckle Coffee. This wasn't his favorite brand but it would do just fine. A stack of cups sat beside the sink. If any of the buildings in town had running water it only made sense that one of them would be the clinic.

Hash took a cup from the stack and set it beside the stove. He poured what looked like some very strong coffee from the steaming pot. There on the table was some sugar in a covered bowl. Without using a spoon Hash tipped the bowl over his cup and let a generous serving slide into the black liquid. Not bothering to stir he eased the cup to his lips and very slowly took a taste. Not bad he thought, not bad at all.

Hash stepped from the kitchen of the clinic into the long hallway. He stood there looking at the closed door at the other end and wondered how his friend was doing, still not knowing if Riley had been hit two times or three. Hash stood quietly and tried to hear what might be going on behind the closed door, not a sound could be heard. He knew about the wound to the shoulder, which in itself did not appear to be life threatening. But there had been two more shots. If both had found their mark and depending on where the slugs had hit, Riley could be near death, that is if he wasn't dead already.

Hash turned and went back to the waiting room. He picked out the most comfortable of the chairs and sat down, but not before adjusting it to face the front door. On a table in the corner were some newspapers and a few magazines, the new glossy ones that no one had the heart to throw out. He sat his coffee down on a side table and retrieved the entire stack, knowing it was going to be a long night.

As he rummaged through the print, looking for something interesting, he heard the door at the end of the hall open, and then after a few seconds the door closed again. Footsteps could be heard coming toward the waiting room. A man entered the waiting room and looked at Hash who was sitting in one of the chairs with a magazine in his hand. Hash presumed this to be Dr. Sables. Hash set the magazine he was reading down on the side table and turned toward the hallway. The man standing in the doorway had on a white full length apron. On the front was the red stain of blood.

"Hello, my name is Dr. Sables," the man said. "May I help you?"

Hash stood up and said, "My name is Hash Burton. I'm here on behalf of the man you got down the hall there, Joshua Riley. How's he doing Doc?"

"Well, for a man who's been shot three times, I'd say pretty well."

Hash now knew that Riley had been hit by the two bullets fired when the lantern was thrown. This made him feel even more responsible for the wounds that Riley had received.

The doctor turned and went into the kitchen. Hash got up and followed.

"Were you able to get the bullets out Doc?"

The doctor grabbed two coffee cups and sat both on the table. As he took the pot from the stove and began to fill both cups he looked at Hash and said, "One of the bullets is out, the one that was below his right thigh. Didn't break the femur, but it only missed it by the smallest of margins. If the bullet had hit the femoral artery your friend wouldn't be here right now, he'd be at the undertaker's office with those other two unfortunates. That was the easy one. It made it to the back of the leg without actually exiting the other side. All we had to do was clean the wound, sew up the entry point and then we made a small incision and pulled the bullet out the back. The graze on his shoulder only needed a few stitches and some bandage."

"You say that was the easy one Doc. What's the rest of the story?"

The doctor finished filling the two coffee cups and then got a spoon out of a drawer. He put one big scoop of sugar in each cup. He then opened the icebox and took out a small pitcher of milk which he then used to finish filling each of the cups almost to the top. As he stirred each with the spoon he looked at Hash.

"Your friend has a second bullet lodged just behind his ribs and very close to his heart. Dr. Barnes and I will attempt to remove it next. The wound itself isn't necessarily the problem. That bullet can't stay there so we have got to try and get it out. One wrong move and your friend could die. Neither Dr. Barnes nor myself have worked on a patient before with a bullet that close to his heart."

The doctor picked up both cups and headed back down the hallway. Just before pushing the door open with his foot he looked at Hash and said, "You're more than welcome to spend the night in the lobby, just push a couple of chairs together if you get sleepy. And if you don't mind, keep plenty of coffee on the stove. Barnes and me been known to drink two, even three pots, on a night like this."

"Sure will Doc."

After the door closed behind the doctor, Hash refilled his cup from the pot and added a little of the milk that was still sitting on the table. As he put the milk back in the icebox he couldn't help but notice the doors were of hand carved ash. The inside had a porcelain finish and the tag attached to the door said it held forty pounds of ice. This was good news. The town had an ice making plant. He hadn't noticed an icebox in the Hatfield place earlier but was now sure one was there. A luxury he had assumed was not available here was the ability to keep cold beer at his new residence.

Hash rinsed the coffee pot in the sink and then put another pot of coffee on the stove. He noticed that the fire was growing cold so he added a log from a stack that sat next to the side door. He used a poker to position the log just right and then closed the door to the firebox.

Carrying his coffee cup back to the front lobby Hash resumed his place in the same chair. By the time he finished reading what was of interest from the stack of newspapers and magazines it was a quarter past four in the morning. He stood up and stretched. As he stood he removed his Colt from the holster and removed the one empty cartridge from the cylinder, then replaced it with a fresh one from his belt. He was sure to leave the hammer on an empty, just for safety's sake. He put the gun back in its holster and picked up the coffee cup. Just as he was about to go back into the kitchen he heard footsteps on the boardwalk out front.

Instinctively Hash switched the cup from his right hand to his left. He then rested his right hand on top of the revolver and removed the leather strap.

The door knob turned and then the door swung open. It was the sheriff.

"Howdy Burton, how's the patient?"

Hash took his hand off of the Colt.

"So far so good Sheriff, Doc was in earlier, said the second bullet will be a mite tricky. They've been working on it for a few hours now."

The sheriff rubbed the five-o'clock stubble on his chin and then looked at Hash. "Hash, I been over to the undertakers office trying to get some information that might help me understand what happened tonight. We went through both men's pockets. On the first fellow we found the usual stuff. Pocket knife, chewing tobacco, comb, and twelve dollars cash, nothing really unusual about that. The second fellow though was anything but. He had two fifty-dollar gold pieces and another hundred and fifty in cash in his pockets."

The sheriff saw the cup in Hash's hand and said, "There any more of that coffee left? I could sure use a pick-me-up. My body can't figure out if it's late or early."

"Sure thing Sheriff, that's my new job around here; keep the coffee pot hot and full, done been put in charge by none other than Doctor Sables himself."

Both men went into the kitchen and the sheriff grabbed a cup and filled it to the brim. He blew the steam off the top and took a sip.

He looked back at Burton. "That's a lot of money for a farm hand to be carrying around these parts Hash, don't you think?"

Hash thought for a second before saying, "Could be at that Sheriff."

"There's something else I found. This was in his boot."

The sheriff took out a folded piece of paper and handed it to Hash.

Hash looked at the note and before he unfolded it said to the sheriff, "This note couldn't have been in his boot long, it looks brand new."

"That's what I thought too, go ahead, read it."

Hash unfolded the paper and began to read.

'Two-hundred fifty now, same again when the job is done. Tall man, more than six feet. Dark hair, clean shaven, dark mustache and slight sideburns. Gray eyes that pierce.'

Hash refolded the note and handed it back to the sheriff. "I see why you came looking for me this late Sheriff, much obliged."

Both men went back into the lobby and took a seat. The sheriff looked at Hash and asked, "Now who do you know that would want you dead Burton?"

Hash looked up from his cup and said, "Up North, could be any number of old acquaintances, and each of those men would pay a lot more than five hundred dollars for it. Here in Prestonsburg, shouldn't be anybody. I ain't been here long enough to get to know anyone."

"Well somebody knows you're here. That was a damn good description of you on that piece of paper you just read. And your first night here they knew right where to find you, in the saloon with that Riley feller, you know the one. He's in the back room full of holes that were meant for you." The sheriff thought about what he had just said and realized it probably sounded a bit harsh.

"Sorry Burton. I got two dead men at the undertaker's and another back there that may or may not pull through. Senseless killing tends to make a man say some things, you know."

"Yea Sheriff I know what you mean. I just hope that I'm not next."

Sheriff Barnes got up and took his coffee cup to the kitchen. As he came back in he put on his hat and said, "Still need to talk to you in the morning, nine-o'clock."

"I'll be there Sheriff."

With that the sheriff turned and went out the door. His last words were, "You watch your back Burton." And then he was gone.

Burton sat on the chair thinking about what he had just heard and also what he had just read. He pulled the Colt again from its holster and opened the cylinder. Reaching behind his back, he pulled another cartridge from a loop on his belt and inserted it into the one empty chamber. He then closed the cylinder and gave it a spin, listening to the smooth sound it made until it finally came to a stop. He sat the gun in his lap and pulled his Stetson down low over his eyes. Just as he was about to drift off to sleep the door at the end of the hall opened again.

Burton heard both doctors talking as they came up the hallway. Both went into the kitchen and poured coffee. As they stood and gulped the strong brew Burton entered and looked at the two tired men. Both looked at Burton and each man wore a big smile.

"How's he doing in there, is he going to be all right?"

Doctor Barnes spoke first, his voice tired but full of hope, "Mr. Riley as of twenty minutes ago is bullet free. But you know Mr. Burton how lead seems to be attracted to him. I'm not sure how long he can remain lead free."

Doctor Sables gave his colleague a sour look and then looked at Hash.

"I'm sorry for Doctor Barnes' sense of humor Burton. After a day like today he is a little off his edge when it comes to conversation. Your friend is doing fine for the moment. Both bullets have been successfully removed and he is resting comfortably."

"When will he be able to talk Doctor?"

"Tomorrow, when he comes to you should be able to talk to him but only briefly. We gave him some ether to keep him sedated while we were working on his chest. We didn't want him coming to while we were in there working so near to the heart."

Doctor Barnes put down his cup and rubbed his chin. "You know Mr. Burton, that man lying in there is probably the luckiest son of a bitch on the planet right now. If either of those bullets had gone a quarter of an inch in either direction he would have bled to death in a matter of minutes. As it is though, he's still lost a lot of blood. The good news is that the human body can replace the lost volume in a day or two so long as no other complications arise."

Dr. Sable chimed in at this point. "Another thing Burton, he was shot by two different men last night."

"Two different men, how can you know this?"

"The two bullets we removed were each of a different caliber. Now take into account that neither Dr. Barnes nor I are ballistics experts, but we do know that two different size bullets had to come from two different guns. We saved the bullets to turn over to Sheriff Barnes in the morning. Now the best thing for you to do is to head on out of here and get some rest. You look like you ain't slept in a couple days."

"If it's alright with you two I think I'll just get a little sleep right here in this chair until daybreak."

The two doctors looked at each other and then Dr. Barnes looked at Hash and asked, "You mind telling us why you need to do that, we done told you your friend's gonna be alright."

"Well Doctor Barnes, the sheriff was in here about a half hour ago. Seems our little run-in down at the saloon wasn't just an accident. Somebody paid them boys, at least one of them, to shoot me. I can't be sure where Riley fits in to all this but if it's okay with you two I'd just as soon stay here and guard that front door. Especially with him being all laid up the way he is.

Also I really don't fancy walking down dark streets in the dead of the night going to a house I ain't ever slept in before."

The two doctors just looked at Burton. Finally Dr. Sable spoke up.

"Well what do you think about that Barnes? Two killings, one attempted murder and an assassination attempt right here in downtown Prestonsburg, and all that in the span of one night. You stay right here Mr. Burton if you like. The day nurse comes in at seven in the morning. I'll be staying until then. Me and old Barnes here drew high card on who stays and who goes home tonight. Barnes here drew an ace. I knew better than to play that game, especially with him wearing long sleeves."

Barnes took the abuse rather well. He just took his coat off the rack and walked out the door. Dr. Sable looked at Hash and said, "Why don't you put us on another pot of coffee while I go check on our boy back there."

Burton did as he was told and went to the kitchen. The coffee was boiling by the time the doctor came back.

"How's he doing Doc.?"

"He's so out of it; he doesn't know whose little boy he is. He has to be a tough critter to have been shot three times in one night though and still be on this side of the here-after. If you're worried about somebody coming in here and doing some more mischief though, I got a gun in my desk drawer."

"Thanks Doc. I appreciate what you and Dr. Barnes done here tonight. I'll see that you both get paid well for saving my friend's life."

"Well now that's just music to my ears. Old Doctor Barnes and me only collect about twenty-five percent of what we bill. Most of our patients are coal miners and farmers. We usually get paid with produce, a live hog or some block coal for our fireplaces. We eat pretty well and stay warm, but it would be nice to have a little extra jingle in our pockets from time to time."

The clock on the wall showed five-thirty in the morning. Doctor Sables went to the kitchen and refilled his coffee cup. Hash followed and refilled his own.

"You know Burton, I've been around a lot of trouble in my time, but never was part of it. Closest I ever come to trouble is patching people up after all the damage has already been done. You might say that I get the last word in every argument."

"I never thought of it that way Doc. In my life I've seen my fair share. Don't get me wrong though, I'm not a troublemaker, not by a long shot. But it just seems that any man who stands for change kind of draws attention to himself. Some of that attention usually is accompanied with trouble and gunplay."

"Makes sense, most people don't like change, good or bad."

The Doctor rinsed out his cup and sat it on top of the ice box.

"Well Burton, I'll be in there keeping an eye on Riley. I got some reading to do between now and when Rebecca gets in at seven. You still set on staying till morning?"

"That's right. You won't even know I'm here unless I start snoring."

The doctor turned and headed down the hall. After Hash heard the door to the back room shut, he topped off his cup and went back to the waiting room. He picked up one of the magazines that he had overlooked earlier and tried to read. Before long he could feel his eyes starting to cross and gave up. He went to the door and turned the knob on the kerosene lamp. The room was bathed in darkness. After a few minutes he noticed that enough light came in from the street to throw shadows on the walls. He looked out the window and noticed that the town had a few gas lamps along the street. The town of Prestonsburg was slowly clawing its way into modern times.

Hash resumed his spot in the chair and soon fell asleep. At about six-thirty in the morning he was awakened by a noise in the kitchen. It was Doctor Sable, again in the process of refilling his coffee cup.

"Good morning Burton. I trust you slept well."

"Not bad Doc, not bad at all." He lied. What sleep he did get was fitful at best. Hash had experienced gun battles in his dreams all night.

"How's Riley doing?" he asked.

"You wouldn't believe it. He came to bout an hour ago and asked for water. After that he wanted to know where he was and what had happened during the gun battle last night. I filled him in with a brief outline of what few facts I had. Before I could finish, he was back asleep. Most men in his shape wouldn't be talking for at least twenty-four hours."

"Think I'll be able to talk to him later today?"

"Shouldn't be a problem. I suppose the next time he comes around he'll want a little something to eat."

A key could be heard in the front lock and immediately the door could be heard to open. Dr. Sable and Hash left the kitchen and entered the waiting room. It was Dr. Barnes. He hung his coat on the coat tree in the corner and turned toward the men with a smile.

"Don't suppose the patient has roused since surgery last night?"

"Actually he came to about an hour ago, talked a bit and then went back to sleep."

"Good, Good. Don't suppose you two left any coffee for me in there did ya?"

"Sure did, but I think that's the last of it. When Rebecca gets here you should send her to the general store. Out of coffee and with a full time guest recuperating in the back we're gonna need some other provisions other than the usual stuff that you and I use. I'll stop by the café and let them know to send meals for the patient. Later today we'll need to do an inventory and mail off a letter to the apothecary in Ashland. Mr. Riley ran us low on a few things last night."

"Sounds good Sable, you go on home and catch a few hours. What about Burton here, he staying with us all day too?" Both doctors looked at Hash and waited for an answer.

"No I got an appointment with Sheriff Barnes at nine-o'clock sharp. I'll stop in later today to check on Riley and leave some cash toward the bill. Say how is it that one of the town doctors and the Sheriff have the same last name?"

Dr. Barnes looked at Dr. Sable and then back at Hash and said, "Me and the sheriff are first cousins, both our fathers were brothers. Now what the hell is he talking about paying cash Sables. We ain't ever had anybody pay up front before. I ain't used to hearing such talk, but I think I like it."

"You heard the man right Barnes. He told me the same thing last night. Now let's go check on our patient before he changes his mind."

Both doctors went down the hall and closed the door behind them. As Hash was putting on his coat the front door opened again and a young woman stepped inside. It was the same woman from the Depot Café that had been waiting tables the night before.

She looked a bit surprised to see Hash. He said good morning and informed her that the doctors were down the hall attending to a patient. They should be back in a minute.

The woman smiled and said' "Thank you. You were the one in the diner last night with that man who got shot."

"That's right. Riley and I were there."

"Are you here to check on your friend this morning?"

"Been here all night! Didn't know if I could find my way home in the dark, I've only been in town for a day."

She folded her arms. "By the looks of it, it was quite an eventful day."

The door at the end of the hall opened and closed again. Dr. Sable looked at the young woman and said, "Ah Rebecca, good to see you this morning. Your father is in the back room with Mr. Riley, our new patient. I don't suppose you've met Mr. Burton. Mr. Burton this is Rebecca Barnes, her father is Doctor Barnes."

Rebecca looked at Dr. Sables and said, "Yes, I met both of them last night at dinner. I waited on them at the Depot Café."

Hash Burton was quite surprised. Rebecca, the morning nurse was also the daughter of Dr. Barnes. But how did it fit in that she also worked at the Depot Café. He made up his mind then and there to pay the Café another visit that very night.

She smiled, turned and went down the hall. The last thing Hash heard her say before the door to the back room closed was, "Good Morning Dad."

Hash put on his hat and went out into the street. The sky was painted with low overhanging clouds, most a very dark puffy shade of blue but some, here and there, were a very distinctive black. According to his pocket watch it was now half past seven. He had just enough time to head over to the Hatfield house and clean up before his meeting with the sheriff. On the way he passed by the front of Tucker's General Store located on Main Street.

Hash looked inside through one of the big front windows and saw that they were open for business. He stepped inside and walked up to the front counter. Behind and about half way up the wall he could see what he had stopped in for. A very neat display of tobacco went from floor to ceiling. There was anything from cigarette makings to chewing tobacco and snuff, but no cigars.

A middle aged man in a store apron stepped up on the other side of the counter and asked, "Anything I can help you with this morning Mister?"

Hash looked at the man and asked, "I was just wondering if you keep any imported cigars in your establishment? I was informed by a reliable source that you might stock a few Cubans here."

"Sure do Mister, but you won't find em on that wall. I keep them in the back in a big humidor. The Cubans sell slow and if we don't keep the air right they won't last. I also roll them a quarter turn each day, seems to do better that way."

The storekeeper's face was that of a man who thoroughly enjoyed his job. His appearance, both neat and trim was just like the contents of the store. "I'd like to see what you've got then if you don't mind."

"Sure thing. Sally would you watch the front while I show this gentleman some cigars in the back?"

A tall woman with shoulder length red hair came from a side room, probably the office and told the man in the apron, "Sure Joe, take your time."

With that the man named Joe led Hash to a stock room in the back. There against one wall stood a rather large humidor. It looked as if it were built by a local carpenter. The wood was rough and the sides not exactly true. But when Joe opened it up you could tell that all the attention had been dedicated to the inside. There were eight shelves, each about ten inches apart. The shelves weren't solid but made of slats about two inches wide and spaced about a quarter inch apart. The walls were lined with a dark felt material. On each shelf were several stacks of rolled cigars, each stack spaced a few inches from the next.

"See anything that interests you Mister?"

"Do you happen to know what brand Mr. Reed buys? I had a sample of the ones he keeps in his office while I was there yesterday and found it rather to my liking."

"Mr. Reed likes these." He pointed to the biggest stack in the cabinet. "He buys three boxes a month, twenty to a box."

"That's quite a few cigars for one man to smoke."

"Naw, he doesn't smoke all of them. Gives most away I suspect."

"Joe, I think I'll take a box. What is your best Kentucky rolled cigars?"

"That would be these over here. They're called Burnt Bark brand. Old man by the name of Eliza Reynolds down around Mt. Sterling has a tobacco farm there. Got him five Mexicans hired. They roll cigars all day, six days a week. He cures the paper in Kentucky Bourbon before his Mexicans can do the rollin. These are some of the smoothest you'll find and about half the price of the Cubans.

"Well Joe, looks like you talked me into a box of them too. I wouldn't want to leave Kentucky without sampling the local leaf."

The store keeper's eyes lit up. It was obvious that he rarely made any good sales when he first opened up in the morning.

Hash and Joe went back out to the front counter. Joe put the two boxes on top of the counter and asked, "Anything else Mister?"

"Who delivers the ice in town Joe? I'm gonna be around for a while and would like to set up an occasional delivery."

"I do! Soon as the other help arrives I make the rounds, usually between ten-o'clock and noon. You need a delivery today?"

"I think I do Joe. I'm staying at the Hatfield place, know where it is?"

"Sure do." The store keep looked up at Hash, a look of suspicion on his face.

"Well if that house has an icebox I'd like you to keep it filled."

"It has an icebox sitting out back in the carriage house. I can keep her nice and cold without you even needing to be there."

"Now why did old man Hatfield put the icebox way out there Joe?" Hash asked.

"I asked him the same thing. Said his blood was old and thick and flowed slowly and he was cold all the time. He just couldn't stand the thought of ice in the house."

"Well that makes about as good a sense as any. How much do I owe you?"

"Fourteen dollars and twelve cents and that will include ice for today."

Hash reached into his pocket and pulled out a twenty. "Here you go Joe. Keep the change toward future ice. I'll be in from time to time."

Joe put the twenty in the register. "I didn't get your name Mister."

"Burton, Hash Burton." With that Hash picked up his two boxes of leaf, turned and went out the door.

Joe looked over at Sally. "If he's living in the Stanton Hatfield house then he probably knows something about how your grandfather lost the place. Don't mean he had anything to do with it though."

Sally looked at Joe. "We can't be worrying about that now. What's gone is gone. It does break my heart to think of granddaddy living in that shack down by the depot though. He still won't come and live with us, I asked him again just yesterday. It's his stubborn pride." With that Sally began to cry. Joe came over and put his arm around his wife.

Hash headed up Court Street and over to Riverside. As he approached the Hatfield House he fished the key from his vest pocket that Reed had given him the previous day. Hash unlocked the door and pushed it open to find a large sad eyed Beagle dog sitting on the front rug looking him in the face. The Beagle made no attempt to be unfriendly. He stood and walked over to where Hash stood.

"Howdy boy, how in the world did you get in here?"

Hash rubbed the dog's head as he pushed the door closed with his boot. The Beagle was lean but not poorly. The coat had a good shine and there were no marks to indicate mistreatment or abuse.

He looked at the Beagle with a bit of amusement and then said, "I'd like to stay here and rub your head a little longer boy but if I'm not at the sheriff's office by nine this morning then he might just come looking for me."

Hash sat the two boxes of cigars down on the sofa table in the living room. He grabbed his two bags which still sat where the railroad boy from the depot had dropped them the day before. Heading up the stairs and over to the right he entered the master bedroom. Attached was a dressing room and a lavatory. Hash quickly shaved and bathed. As he was dressing he knew he would need to hire the services of a washer woman, or better yet, maybe the town had a cleaner where his clothes could be cleaned and pressed.

As he descended the rather elaborate stairs, there at the base sat the Beagle as before.

Hash opened the front door and turned to face the dog. "Come on boy, out you go." The dog did exactly as told and went out the front door. Not stopping the beagle went to the sidewalk and headed down the street toward the northern portion of town.

As Hash made his way to the sheriff's office he wondered how the dog had gotten into the house. As he replayed the showing of the house the previous day by Mr. Reed there had been no dog in sight. The dog must have entered while they were upstairs looking over the rooms. That must be the answer. No problem now though, both the dog and Hash had gone their separate ways.

Hash entered the new jail at a quarter to nine. The building was a rather nicely built affair, roomy and well lit. Offices occupied the front portion and at the rear through a heavy iron plated door, which was open, were the cells. There were eight of them in all, with four on either side of a hallway. The hallway itself was at least fifteen feet wide. At the rear of the hall was another heavy iron door, same as the one in front, which must have led out the back of the building.

In the first cell Hash could see the third shooter from the previous night. There was no sign of Burt.

"What do you think of our new jail Hash?"

Hash turned around to see Sheriff Barnes leaning against the door frame of an office at the very end of another hallway that ran the full length of the front of the building. On either side were rooms that could serve as offices or interrogation rooms.

"Very nice Sheriff, very nice." The new paint smell was enough to turn a Billy-goat's stomach but Hash thought best not to say anything. "What happened to Burt?"

"He went to his place as soon as it got daylight. Looks like you made it through the night without any more trouble. How's that Riley feller doing?"

"Doc says he'll be alright in a few weeks."

"That's good. If he pulls through I won't have to file murder charge against that man in cell number one. Come on in and let's fill out a report about what happened last night."

Hash headed down the long hall to where the sheriff's office was. One of the offices had a deputy at a desk filling out some paperwork. He looked up at Hash and frowned. Hash recognized him as one of the deputies who had gotten in on all the excitement the previous night.

"Come on in," the sheriff said as Hash entered the room. "You like a cup of coffee? I promise that it's better that what you got last night at the doctor's office. Them two pinch pennies on everything except their doctoring. Can't say as I blame em though. Most people round these parts don't pay with cash. The coffee here is paid for by the taxpayers, and taxpayers don't like it when their deputies fall asleep on the job, so I buy good coffee."

"You talked me into it Sheriff."

The sheriff said, "Come on into the kitchen, we can talk while the coffee brews. Hash followed him out a side door of the office and into a large room that must have been meant for meetings. To one side was a stove almost like the big Windsor that was in the doctor's office. On top were two pots of coffee instead of one. The sheriff reached Hash a cup as they waited. The smell of coffee filled the room and almost hid the smell of new paint, but not quite. After a couple of minutes Sheriff Barnes picked up the first pot and filled both cups.

"Try it and tell me what you think."

Hash took a sip and was quite impressed. The flavor was as good as anything he had experienced in New York.

Hash looked at the sheriff and said, "Very good, where in town can a man find this brand?"

"Only place I know is at the City Steak House. They have the coffee beans imported from somewhere in South America and then grind it themselves. Rumor has it they grind two or three kinds of beans together to come up with the flavor. If you eat there you can order it with your meal or for those with the money, they sell it in two pound sacks so you can brew it at home."

Hash pondered this for a second before asking, "Well Sheriff, what did you need to know about last night?"

"Not much now. Once we got old Burt sobered up he told us everything that happened. Said how those three picked a fight and that was why you and Riley felt the need to use the back alley instead of the front entrance. One thing is for sure though, if you two had gone out that front door, instead of the back, then those three would have made another two-hundred and fifty dollars. You got any idea who would have paid them boys to murder you?"

"Not really. I do have a hunch though. Whoever paid them boys must have done it yesterday. If we can find out where they went and what they were doing while they were in town that might narrow things down a bit. We also know that our man is literate and we have a sample of his handwriting on the note you found in the dead man's boot."

"Burton I am impressed. You could be a detective."

"When a man's got a price on his head he tries to cover all the angles."

"Well Burton, the county does employ a detective. He's been out of town for the last few days, be back on the seven-o'clock in the morning most likely. With all the flooding going on he may or may not make it tomorrow. Soon as he shows up, I'll put him on the case."

"It's your town Sheriff. I plan on catching the first train heading up Left Beaver in the morning. If your detective needs to see me I'll be back tomorrow night."

"Okay Burton, thanks for letting me know. One more thing though."

"What's that Sheriff?"

"Whatever you do, don't let anyone know what your plans are. Don't tell anyone when or where you're going. Try not to make it too easy for someone to set up another ambush. And one more thing Burton, I think that whoever wrote that note and paid them three killers got a good look at you yesterday. That would explain the note unless you think someone from New York City is involved."

Hash thought about what the sheriff had just said. "You know Sheriff, you might have a point."

The sheriff continued. "I would like for you to think of everyone you spoke to from the time you got off the train until the time you and Riley were confronted in the saloon last night. Maybe we can narrow down the list of suspects a mite. And let's just keep the list to men; I don't think a woman would be involved in a murder for hire unless you think otherwise."

"That is going to be a very short list Sheriff. There were only four men I met after leaving the train yesterday. Jeremy Eisner, the clerk at the depot. Gregory Spurlock, the Assistant Vice President at the bank. Samuel J. Reed, the President of the bank and Josh Osborne, another employee of the railroad, that's it."

The sheriff was impressed with Burton's ability to remember the names of men he had only met the day before and for the first time at that. "Of the four names you just mentioned you can mark off Eisner and Osborne, the railroad employees. They are too young to be mixed up in something like this and anyway, I have known both their entire lives," the sheriff said.

"What about the two men who work at the bank Sheriff? You think one of them could be a possibility?"

The sheriff thought over the question that Hash had just asked. "How well do you know Reed? You said you have some business dealings in the works with him didn't you?"

"That's right though I'm pretty sure we can rule him out for the moment."

This raised the eyebrows of the sheriff. "What do you mean rule him out for the moment?"

Hash laughed, "Well, as our business together starts to prosper I would not let my guard down around him. When it comes to money never turn your back on a banker." Both men laughed now.

Hash looked Barnes, "That only leaves Gregory Spurlock Sheriff. How well do you know him?"

Barnes went over and topped off his coffee cup. When he was finished he pulled out a chair and sat down. Finally after the longest time he looked up at Hash and said, "Spurlock came here several months ago, maybe even a year. He hails from Chicago. Apparently Reed has some business connections up that way and one of those connections sent Spurlock down here to help grow the bank. From what I gathered at the time Reed accepted the arrangement without a word. Apparently the firm in Chicago that sent Spurlock has some serious money invested in Reed's bank."

Now it was Hash's time for reflection. Chicago had some extremely large business entities that even rivaled the ones in New York that Hash represented. Could it be that The Board had competition in the coal fields that up until now had remained in the shadows?

"Do you know anything else about Spurlock that might shed some light on this situation?"

"I don't have any actual facts Burton, but I have had my suspicions since right after Spurlock arrived in town. I found it strange that he goes back up there to Chicago about every six weeks. It almost seems like he is taking information to his bosses up there and don't trust the telegraph. I know this because every other week or so me and Reed have drinks at the City Steak House. He likes to keep me posted on anything that might concern his bank and this county. Lots of taxes are deposited at the bank and he runs his ledgers like a general. If anything looks out of place then he fills me in, just good business. Anyway, a month or so ago he was complaining about Spurlock being out of town again."

"Sheriff, if you get any more information about this Spurlock that you feel might be of help would you let me know?" Hash asked.

"Yea Burton, the more I think about it the more it doesn't add up. I'm going to do some more checking around and in the mean time you be careful."

"I'll try to remember that Sheriff, if that's all for now then I would like to go check on Riley."

"That's all I got at the moment. Check back in from time to time. If I hear anything I'll leave a message at the doctor's office."

Hash turned and left the jailhouse. It had begun to rain, light stuff that wouldn't require anything more than a hat. He hurried down the street to the doctor's office. He entered and hung his wet jacket and hat on the coat tree in the waiting room. Rebecca was in the kitchen cleaning up from the night before.

"Good morning," Hash said as he entered the kitchen.

Rebecca turned from the sink. "Good morning Mr. Burton. I thought I heard someone come in."

"Came back to check on Riley, how's he doing?"

"He woke up a little while ago. I gave him a little broth and he went right back to sleep."

"When do you think I can talk to him?"

"Let him rest a few more hours. Stop back in this evening around dark."

"I'll do that, thanks for your help."

Rebecca gave Hash a smile and said, "You're welcome."

Hash retrieved his jacket and hat from the tree. Stepping out onto the covered part of the walkway in front of the doctor's office he noticed that the rain had gotten heavier. The trip to the train depot would get him drenched. The General Store was only two doors down. With any luck maybe they had umbrellas for sale. Hash pulled the collar of his coat up high and his hat down low. A few quick steps later and he sprinted through the front door of the store.

"Hello Joe."

"Hello Mr. Burton. I won't be able to deliver your ice today; the rain is just too hard."

"No problem Joe. I just stepped in to see if you sold umbrellas?"

"Over there, standing in that barrel."

Hash walked over and chose the sturdiest one he could find, a black one.

"Here you go Joe, how much I owe you?"

"Let's see Mr. Burton, looks like three-dollars."

As Hash counted out the three-dollars he noticed the woman named Sally standing at the end of the counter. She seemed to be scowling at him.

"See you later Joe." Hash stepped outside and opened his new umbrella. The rain was steady and hard. By the look of the sky it wouldn't end soon.

The trip to the train depot took Hash back across the suspension bridge he had used the previous day. The river was still big and fast. If anything it was a few feet higher than the day before.

Hash hurried up the steps and into the depot. Young Jeremy Eisner was at his small ticket counter reading another dime novel. He looked up and saw a tall man standing in the doorway struggling to close a large black umbrella. When Hash turned around Eisner jumped to his feet and said, "Some storm we got out there Mr. Burton!"

"Yes Eisner, much more rain and that river of yours will be too big for its banks."

"I got a telegraph from the Depot at Pikeville about an hour ago. Said rains been coming down in buckets for hours now. We do a wire check every hour in weather like this; make sure everything is still working between here and there."

At that moment the key started to chatter.

"Excuse me Mr. Burton, need to write down that message."

Eisner went to the pad beside the key and began to write. After only a minute the key stopped. Eisner sent back the received code and then sat down and looked at what he had just written.

"That was from the big rail yard at Martin. Water's high and looks like it might flood. They still got wires to Drift, the depot about ten miles on up Left Beaver. If the rain stops soon then the flood might just be a bad one not the catastrophic one that everyone in town says is past due.

"Eisner, I need a schedule of the trains on Beaver. I might need to take a trip up that way soon."

"Sure thing, Mr. Burton. I've got one right here."

Eisner reached under the counter and then handed Hash a neatly folded sheet of paper. Hash glanced at the schedule and said, "First train out leaves at seven-thirty each morning. Is that a passenger or coal train?"

"Both. Always have at least one passenger car attached to the coal trains. It's how people up on the Beaver Creeks get their mail. You need a ticket for tomorrow morning Mr. Burton?"

Remembering what the sheriff had said about not revealing his plans Hash looked up at Eisner and said, "Not sure. Can a ticket be purchased on the spur of the moment, say right before the train leaves?"

"That shouldn't be a problem Mr. Burton. Trains going that way first thing in the morning carry mostly empty coal gondolas and mail, not many people. You just try to be here fifteen minutes before the time on that schedule there and you'll get a ticket."

"Thanks Eisner. By the way, was there a trunk delivered on the incoming freight this morning?"

"Freight ain't all been sorted yet. My help didn't show up today, so I've had to do everything myself."

"I'll check tomorrow. Can you tell me who lives in that old rail shack over there, the one with the smoke coming out of the flue?"

Young Eisner walked over to the window on the rail side of the depot. "Old man Stanton Hatfield. He used to own that big house you moved into yesterday."

Hash Burton felt a deep sadness start to take hold as never before. He had run over wealthy men in the past but never actually seen the end result with his own eyes. Most of his adversaries in the northeast had only been taken down a notch or two. What he witnessed before him now was the total destruction of a proud old man.

"How is it that he now lives on railroad property?" Hash asked.

"That ain't railroad property. Hatfield owns it. He used to lease that shed to the railroad. Lease ran out about six months ago and the railroad didn't renew. Some say it's the only thing the old man has left."

Hash stood and looked at the shack through the depot window. The longer he looked the more responsible he felt for the misfortune of the old man. He reached into his pocket and pulled out a twenty dollar bill.

"Eisner can you do something for me."

"Sure thing, Mr. Burton."

"Have some firewood delivered to that shack. Make sure it's good stuff. Also send him a bag of the coffee from the City Steak House. The kind they grind for their customers. And then have the Depot Café deliver him supper every evening and to send the bill to Mr. Samuel J. Reed at the bank. If old man Hatfield asks who it is from, tell him it's from the railroad as a small courtesy for all the years they had done business together."

Eisner looked at Hash like he had just told a joke and was waiting for someone to start laughing.

"Yes Sir Mr. Burton. But can I ask you why?"

"No Eisner you can't. Just do as I ask and don't forget about our earlier agreement."

"Yes sir. I'll see that it is done today."

Hash looked at the young clerk and said, "Please see that it is done every day."

Hash grabbed his umbrella and went out the door on the rail side. He looked close at the old shack. He thought he seen movement in the crawlspace underneath. The longer he looked the more he knew he did see something under that shed. Hash turned and went back inside.

"Eisner can you tell me what that is under the old man's shack?"

Eisner walked over and looked across the rails at Hatfield's shack again.

"Looks like old man Hatfield's Beagle under there trying to stay dry."

This might answer something that Hash had thought of on and off all day. "Did Hatfield have that beagle when he still lived in his house in town?"

"Sure did! Hatfield and that old Beagle been around forever, seems like. That was one of the best hunting dogs in the county just a few years back. Poor old hound looks a mite thinner now than he did when he was living in that mansion. When hard times fell upon old man Hatfield I guess they fell on the dog too. Hatfield's youngest daughter is married to Joe, the storekeeper in town. They been trying to get Hatfield to move in with them, but he won't hear of it. Don't want to be a burden on anyone."

"And Eisner, one more thing, other than Reed don't speak a word of who paid for the wood or the food. If the old man knew he would just refuse. And another thing, have the café send a bone or two each day for the beagle, include it on Reed's bill."

Eisner looked at Hash and wondered if he was the same man he had met yesterday. Yesterday he was tough as nails and today he was worried about an old man and his dog. "It will all be taken care of Mr. Burton and not a soul will find out about who is paying. Hatfield would probably starve before he would accept charity."

"Well Eisner, this ain't charity, that old man was done wrong and before I leave town I'll see that things are set straight again." Just before he went back out the door Hash stopped and added, "Thanks for your help Eisner."

With that Hash picked up his umbrella and headed out the front door of the depot. As he walked across the high part of the suspension bridge, still deep in thought, he looked down and saw the fast moving river below. If the rain continued there was going to be a flood for sure.

Again he stopped at the bank and had a long talk with Reed. He wanted to spend a little time with the banker and try to find out who else might have known he was in town. After a while he felt he could rule Reed out as the man who wanted him dead, after all they did have business together. He told the banker about the arrangements he wanted made for old man Hatfield and to his surprise Reed readily agreed, and seemed happy to do so. So the banker wasn't all about profit after all.

Hash descended the stairs of the bank and noticed Spurlock busy behind a teller window. When he noticed Hash in the lobby he nodded but it was more out of necessity than courtesy. Hash nodded back and headed toward the big front door. Fifteen minutes later he was back at the clinic.

Before entering Hash took off his coat and hat and shook them out on the covered walkway. He stepped inside leaving them, along with the umbrella, lying on a bench on the porch. The waiting room was warm and had the strong smell of bad coffee. After being introduced to the City Steakhouse brand the thought of clinic coffee was not appealing to him in the least. Still though, the pot was only a few steps away, and hot.

Hash entered the kitchen, which was empty, and poured a cup of the very strong black liquid. After taking a sip he put in two big spoons of sugar and just stood at the counter stirring. The whole time he stirred he thought of the old man and the Beagle. When he left New York a week earlier he was his same old self. Now after nearly being killed by an assassin's bullet he was starting to look at things differently. Life meant a little more now, people meant a little more.

Hash was startled by the voice of Dr. Sables. "Your friend has slept all day. If he wakes up tonight I'll try to get a little warm food down him."

"You still think he's going to make it Doc?"

"I think so. Rest is a good thing for him in his condition. Now the only thing is getting him to eat. I don't think he should be bothered right now though. Can you stop in tomorrow?"

Hash thought about his early morning departure on the first train up Left Beaver in the morning.

"I've got some business tomorrow, but I'll stop in late tomorrow night."

"That will be just fine Mr. Burton. He should be awake and alert by then."

Hash turned but before he left he asked the Doctor, "Is the lady named Rebecca still here?"

"No, she got off at three-o'clock. She has a second job at the Depot Café in the evenings."

"Thank you Dr. Sables. I'll see you tomorrow."

Hash stepped out the front door and onto the porch. The rain hadn't let up. He put on his coat and hat and grabbed the umbrella. It was nearly dark when he arrived at the Hatfield house. He unlocked the door and stepped inside. There sitting on the rug was the Beagle. Neither man nor dog moved. Hash for the life of him, couldn't explain how this had happened twice.

The dog was soaking wet. Water was dripping off his coat onto the rug. Hash was in a hurry so he stepped around the soggy dog and ran up the stairs to his bedroom. Less than ten minutes later he came down wearing a different shirt. The beagle still sat in the same spot. Hash opened the front door and stepped onto the big wraparound porch. He turned and snapped his fingers at the Beagle. The dog, as if on cue, stood and walked to the front porch. Hash locked the door and went down the street, umbrella in hand. The beagle sat on the porch and watched him go.

The Depot Café was busy tonight. Customers filled more than half the tables. Hash walked to an empty table at the far corner and took a seat in his favorite position, facing the entrance. Before long Rebecca came from the back carrying a tray full of plates and food. Hash watched her as she sat the plates on a table where four people were seated. As she turned to go back into the kitchen her eyes met those of Hash. For a moment she froze and then a slight smile came to her face. As she walked past his table she said, "Hello Mr. Burton."

"Good evening Ms. Barnes. You look very busy tonight."

"Rainy evenings seem to bring in a crowd. I'll be right back."

She turned and headed for the back. Hash couldn't figure out this arrangement of the doctor's daughter working two jobs to make ends meet. Also, he wondered what kind of a man she was married to who would abandon her to leave town with a bar girl.

As Hash sat and thought about the events of the past twenty-four hours the sheriff walked into the restaurant and scanned the room. Sheriff Barnes saw the man he was looking for and headed in that direction.

"Evening Burton, I see you took my advice and sat where you could observe anyone entering the room."

"You got that right Sheriff. I picked this spot real careful like you told me to do. I was just getting ready to order some supper, why don't you join me, it'll be my treat. Might make the both of us feel better after the bad introduction we got on the street last night."

It didn't take the sheriff long to make up his mind. "Don't mind if I do Burton. Did you say you're buying?"

"Sure did Sheriff, it would be my pleasure."

"Then I'll take you up on it. I don't eat out much thanks to my meager paycheck as sheriff." Both men laughed.

What brings you out this way on such a rainy night Sheriff?"

"Well Burton, it's the rain that's got me out looking for you. I was over at the train depot about an hour ago. I had some telegrams to send, and while I was there Eisner got a bunch of wires from Martin. Seems something is going on up both Beavers. Messages from the Drift Depot said the water was rising fast, even said something about an engine and tender trying to outrun a tidal wave of flood water coming out of Left Beaver. Just as I was leaving Eisner got another message from the Martin yard. The lines to the Drift depot had gone dead and they don't know anything else about that missing train, it never made it to Martin with two men onboard, the engineer and his fireman. Brave son-of-a-bitches if you ask me. I just came to let you know that the railroad has decided to suspend all rail service up both Beavers until more information can be gathered about the flood."

As the sheriff was saying this Rebecca Barnes came back to the table. She was carrying a coffee pot and two white porcelain cups. "Howdy Sheriff, I seen you come in and thought you might like some coffee. I was just going to take Mr. Burton's order, would you like to have some dinner too?"

"Thanks Rebecca. Burton here has offered to buy my supper tonight. Now how can a man refuse an offer like that?"

"Well that sounds like a great offer. What will the two of you have?"

Hash looked at Rebecca and smiled. From what Riley had told him the special was always the same, he was about to find out, "What's the special tonight?"

"Tonight is the same as last night Mr. Burton, roast beef, potatoes and cornbread. If you would like something other than the special I can have the cook prepare it for you, that is unless you're hooked on the special."

"The special will be just fine," Hash told her.

"And Sheriff, what will you have?" Rebecca asked.

"Just make it two specials, and if you don't mind throw on an extra slice of that cornbread."

"Sure thing." She filled both coffee cups and returned to the kitchen.

The sheriff looked at Hash and said, "Like I was saying Burton, the water up both Beavers is pretty big and from what those messages from the Martin yard said it's getting bigger by the hour."

Hash thought about what Barnes had said. "Can I borrow, or for that matter rent a horse, I really need to get up that way tomorrow to look over a few things Sheriff?"

"You could, but let me tell you you'll never make it. The roads in Floyd County follow the creeks and ninety-percent of them are under water by now. Even if you tried to follow the timber it would take days and a horse might lose its footing on sodden earth. Best I can tell you is to put off your travels until this rain stops and this flood recedes. Even then I doubt the going will be easy. Tracks will need to be repaired and the roads will be washed away."

Hash thought this over and tried to find a silver lining. There was always some advantage to be found if you looked hard enough. "Tell you what Sheriff; I think I'll take your advice. I'm expecting a few packages on the seven-o'clock train in the morning and I might as well be there to receive delivery myself. I never did like muddy water and from the looks of the river by the depot that is one thing that Floyd County has got plenty of right now."

Just then Rebecca came from the kitchen with two large plates and a basket of cornbread. After she sat them down and left, Hash looked at the sheriff and asked, "What do you figure happened to that stranded engine and tender somewhere above Martin?"

Rain continued to beat hard against the windows of the tiny rail depot which sat in the sleepy little mining town of Drift, located far down in the southeastern corner of Kentucky, the Bluegrass State. This particular rain however was not just a simple spring shower which usually would last only an hour or two. This was turning into something much worse.

There was something about this rain that was a little bit strange and a whole lot different than previous rains...... it came down, straight down, as if the drops were too large and too heavy to blow sideways or do anything other than just race from cloud to earth taking the shortest possible route. It came in quantities the man sitting at a small table had never seen before in all his travels. It brought to mind the overused analogies of, coming down in buckets or, raining cats and dogs.

It had been doing this now for the better part of three days and the creek in front of the depot was well out of its banks. Another foot and the railroad itself would be covered with muddy fast moving water. The railroad clerk who worked the office in this long forgotten part of the world said he had never seen the water over the tracks before, never. As a matter of fact in his fifteen years of living in this muddy little town, he had never seen it even as high as it was now. The fact that it might touch the rails before everything was said and done was unheard of.

Suddenly off in the distance there was the faint sound of a locomotive's whistle. It wasn't the toot, toot, toot of a normal steam engines whistle, it was constant. It was as if the engineer had tied down the handle so the whistle would let out one continuous scream; no breaks, no pauses, no let up, just one long unending scream.

Oscar, the railway clerk, who up until now had been busy reading and preparing messages to send down wire to Martin got up and headed toward the front of the depot. He looked at the man sitting at the table and said, "Sounds like trouble up the line Pack."

Pack looked at Oscar as he went by. He raised one of the double-hung windows that faced the siding in front of the depot. When the window was at its most open position he leaned out and looked up the track to see if he could determine what was going on. The whistle continued to grow louder. Oscar turned toward the three other men in the room and said that in all his years this was only the second time he had ever heard the panic whistle of a locomotive.

Pack looked at Oscar and asked, "What do you mean, panic whistle Oscar?"

"Panic whistle means that something is very wrong, and what that something might be we won't know until that locomotive gets here. Engineers are only allowed to set a panic whistle in one of two situations; to avoid a collision, or any other event that could end in a fatality."

"Well I don't think we'll be waiting very long to find out Oscar, because here she comes now," Pack said.

Around the curve coming out of Beaver was a tender and locomotive doing thirty, maybe even forty miles an hour........ In reverse. About a half mile from the depot the engineer applied the brakes hard and the big Baldwin 4-8-2 began to slide on the steel rails. She came by the depot with the big drive wheels still sliding. As the engine slid past the down creek switch the engineer released the brakes. Still going backwards, he put the engine into its forward gear and released steam to the drive wheels. With the engine and tender still going backward the eight powerful drive wheels started trying to pull forward in a hail of sparks and noise. Slowly she came to a stop two hundred feet below the depot and started pulling back. The down-creek switch, which was always in an open position, allowed the engine and tender to pull onto the siding directly in front of the depot. The engineer pulled up to the water tower and his coaler, a tall muscular man, jumped up on the catwalk and raced toward the pull down pipe that put water into the engine's tank.

The engineer hollered with a big booming voice that was in a near panic, "Johnson, hurry your ass up before the water boils off the plate and we all get blown to hell."

The coaler moved with the skill and speed of a man possessed. Within less than a minute the big hinged drain pipe was down and water flowed into the thirsty engine. Oscar hollered up at the engineer and asked what was going on. The engineer, who had been busy resetting his brakes and making sure his gauges read safe, finished up and climbed down to the depot platform and came inside out of the downpour.

"Oscar, we got big trouble up the line. Flood is covering the tracks almost faster than we could outrun it. We passed up water for the engine twice to stay ahead of it. We couldn't make it any farther without blowing up. Had to stop, water was almost gone. I figure we got twenty, maybe thirty minutes before that water covers the track here. Have you still got wires to Martin Oscar?"

Oscar was still taking in what he had just heard, when the engineer suddenly grabbed him by the shoulders with two big gloved hands and shook him hard.

"Oscar, this is not the time to be daydreaming. If you got wires I need to contact the depot at Martin."

Oscar snapped out of his trance and looked at the engineer.

"Talked to Martin about an hour ago Caudill. We'll give them boys down line a shout again, if all this excitement ain't made my key fingers go slack."

With that Oscar sat down at his telegraph key and began to send a message to his counterpart at Martin. After a minute or so he stopped and looked up at the engineer.

"Well Caudill, we'll know in a minute or two if the line is still up. Hope they could understand what I was trying to say, excitement makes my messages a little murky."

Everyone in the room looked at the key and waited. As each minute passed it began to look more and more like the telegraph had become disabled by the torrential rain, or possibly even the flood itself had done some sort of mischief to the poles. At any rate, you could have heard a pin drop as each of the men studied the telegraph key waiting for any sign of life. All that could be heard was the heavy rain on the tin roof and the big engine outside letting off steam.

Just when it seemed the wire was dead, the key began to tap out the magical alphabet that only operators seemed to understand. Everyone in the room almost jumped out of their skin, that is everyone except Oscar.

"Lines good Caudill, what did you want to say?"

"Tell them I'm only minutes ahead of the worst damn flood since Noah's time. Ask if I can be cleared through to Allen, it's the only way to save the engine and tender."

With that Oscar began to transmit the urgent message while the others watched in amazement as the water outside began to rise even faster.

After Oscar sent the message he looked up at the engineer and asked, "How come the water's coming so fast and hard all the sudden Caudill?"

"All I can figure Oscar is that all the water from each of the hollers on Beaver kind of meets at the same time up past McDowell. After that it sort of made a wall of water about three feet high on top of the flood that's already going by. Johnson and I saw it as we were backing out of Frazier's Creek. We made it to the main line switch only minutes before it got there. Didn't have time to switch her around, just kept running hard in reverse. We managed to pull away from the big water on the straights. Oscar, last time I was that scared was when, when.........well come to think of it, don't reckon I ever been that scared before."

Oscar looked at the big engine and then at Caudill. "Looks like you were running her pretty hot Caudill."

"Yea Oscar, we kept heavy steam all day, trying to finish our switches and get back to Martin before things got worse up here. When Johnson and me seen that wall of water up past McDowell, we didn't hold nothing back. Johnson kept the boiler hot and we ran all the way with the gauges almost touching the red. That's why our engine is so thirsty, takes a lot of water for a hot engine that's running full go." Even now the train was throwing off excess steam in large white hissing clouds.

The telegraph key began to chatter again and Oscar started writing down the message as it came in. After the key fell silent Oscar handed the note to Caudill. As the engineer read his expression went from anticipation to anger. After he read it twice he wadded it up and threw it on the floor. Oscar, who already knew what the message said, looked at Caudill and asked, "You leaving her on the siding or moving down to the curve where the line is slightly higher?"

"I ain't going to do neither Oscar. I been working that old engine for the better part of six years now and I ain't about to let the flood get her."

Just about then the coaler, Johnson, came in and said, "All watered up and waiting on you boss."

Oscar looked at Caudill and said, "Don't Johnson have a say in this too?"

Caudill quickly picked up the crumpled note from the floor and shoved it in Johnson's grimy hand.

"Read what them pencil-pushers down at the Martin yard want us to do with the engine and tender."

Johnson quickly read the note and looked back at the engineer.

"You got to be kidding me boss, if the flood takes the engine and tender you and me are out of work. You know any crew that loses their ride loses their job."

"Yea Johnson I know. It's not only that, a flood ain't any way for a lady like that to die."

"What do you want to do boss? You know I'll do whatever you think is right."

"Well, if you're up to it, I'd say we make a run for it and see what happens. We outran it this far, maybe our luck will hold just a little longer. What do you say we climb on board and let that old engine feel some wind before that water shows up and drowns her?"

About that time Oscar, who had been looking out the front window said, "You two better come over here and get a look at this."

Every man in the building ran out on the depot dock in spite of the pouring rain to look up the creek. Coming hard around the curve was what looked like an ocean wave? The engineer was right about the height of the water; it looked at least three feet tall and stretched from one side of the valley to the other. And the noise as it rounded the curve was something straight out of a nightmare. What began as a low rumble soon turned into a roar. As the four men stood spellbound by the sight in front of them, the engineer and his coaler scrambled up the side of the massive locomotive.

Oscar hollered at the top of his lungs, "Caudill, don't be a damn fool, you and Johnson can't outrun a monster like that."

"No choice Oscar, if we leave a fired up locomotive sitting here as hot as she is she'll blow sky high when that cold flood water hits her boiler. Everything within a hundred yards will be scalded."

With that Caudill yanked the lever that put steam to the big eighty-inch drive wheels. All eight at once began to spin in reverse in a hail of sparks and noise. As the big engine started out of the depot you could see Johnson shoveling hard to increase the fire in the already hot firebox.

The four men still on the dock stood in the rain and watched as the engine and tender gathered speed and moved onto the main line. As soon as the last wheel cleared the switch Caudill pushed the valve that regulated the steam for the drive wheels to full open. That big Baldwin grabbed the rails and shot down the line as if she had a life all her own. Black smoke shot a hundred feet in the air from the stack. None of the men had ever seen the power that could be generated by a big Baldwin engine that was turned loose and running for her life. Just then the whistle blew again and never let up. Caudill had tied down the rope to warn anyone down the line that an engine was coming, and coming hard.

As the engine rounded the curve and went out of sight the wave began to pass the depot. First the ties went under water, and then the rails as the full height of the wave passed the depot. It was now only about two feet below the top of the platform on which everyone stood.

Oscar turned and went back in out of the rain. The rest of the men followed. There was nothing now for James Arthur Pack to do but just sit and wait.... and wait and sit. And anyway, where could he go? The road and wooden bridge that led from the depot to the other side of the narrow valley was underwater and in all likelihood, washed away. Pack had never seen the bridge. It had been submerged from the moment he had gotten off the train two days earlier. There had been no one in or out of the depot since the deluge started, except for Caudill and Johnson. Besides Pack and Oscar Simms, who was the rail clerk, there were only two other unfortunates trapped by the rain. These two didn't talk much and kept mostly to themselves, playing a game of cards at a small table in the far corner of a building that seemed to shrink a little with each passing hour.

Pack, who had kept a close eye on these two, was a pretty good judge of character. In sizing those two up he knew they were two men not to be messed with, they just had the look of trouble. You see, it was James Arthur Pack's job to size people up, especially strangers who didn't know they were being sized up in the first place. He was a detective for the Baldwin-Felts Detective Agency whose headquarters were established in Charleston, West Virginia.

Baldwin-Felts Detective Agency wasn't the best organization that Pack had ever worked for. As a matter of fact Pack loathed not only the organization he worked for, but also the assignment he was currently on. Pack had been sent down to gather information about certain individuals and mining operations in and around Floyd County, Kentucky. He had been in the area for the last two months and this was his third trip up Left Beaver Creek. On his first two trips he had encountered snow almost a foot deep and now with April almost over he was in the middle of a hundred year flood the likes of which, according to the depot clerk, no one had ever seen before. This could even be a five-hundred year flood.

"Well, it's over the tracks a good three feet deep, never seen the like," The clerk commented as he looked out the depot window.

Oscar went over to the telegraph and sent the message to the train master in the main yard down at Martin, which was about ten miles downstream.

'Drift Depot, Water on Tracks, Seven O'clock'

'Caudill and Johnson running hard toward Martin, hope they make it.'

Being a bit curious about how the local railroad authorities handled things in a crisis, Pack looked at the rail clerk and asked, "Oscar, what do you think is going on down track now that they know this is the biggest flood to be heading their way in the known history of Floyd County?"

"Well Pack, the railroad has a plan for almost everything, and some of those plans are pretty damn good. I reckon for the last twelve hours they've been moving out anything that can be loaded on a train and taken down river. Probably be trying to keep the rail bridges from washing out too, them higher ups don't like it when one of their expensive bridges gets damaged."

"How in the world do you keep a railway bridge from washing out in something like this Oscar? I ain't ever seen that much swirling muddy water in my life, it looks like the Mississippi River out there, only faster."

"Well Pack, they'll be backing some loaded coal cars up both beavers and leave two sitting on every trestle that crosses the creek. Each of them cars weighs about fifteen tons empty,

121

and if they're loaded that's another thirty tons. Altogether that's about ninety tons holding down each bridge. If the water don't wash out the footings or get overtop too much then they should hold."

"Think ninety tons is enough?"

Oscar rubbed the stubbly point of his chin as he looked out the window facing the fast moving creek.

"You may have a point there Pack; Mother Nature can be a contrary bitch when she wants to be. Might lose a trestle or two, but that's better than losing the whole damn line from here to Allen. Those sledgehammer boys can repair a bridge in less than a week. One thing about this railroad young feller, they know that the coal has got to get through. Factories as far away as Pittsburg waiting on the stuff and believe me, they don't like to wait long."

"How will Caudill and Johnson get through if the bridges are blocked by loaded coal cars?"

"Martin knows they're on the way, they'll clear that engine through before they start parking cars on the Left Beaver bridges."

Oscar wasn't telling Pack anything he didn't already know. Pack had been studying rail operating procedure for the better part of two years. He had a better grasp of the situation than most railroad veterans. The whole reason he was in the area in the first place was to gather more information that would increase the mining and rail operations in the area by a factor of four. Big interests up north had set their sights on Eastern Kentucky, and they were going to make the coal pour out of the area.

The coal industry in this part of the country, up until now, had been small time. Now a few men from New York were going to push out all the small time operators and run the coal business under a trust. This trust, as yet to be named, would gobble up everything and everyone in sight. When they were done in fifteen or twenty years they would leave a barren wasteland behind, with polluted streams, eroded soil, and every miner that was left would be a broken down wreck, unable to breathe from all the dust piled up in his lungs. This was why Pack, along with eight other Baldwin-Felts men, were here and in the surrounding areas.

As soon as all the information was gathered and in place, legions of armed detectives would be working the area to protect the mining operations of the trust. At first most people would welcome the trust with open arms, thinking that the local economy would explode from all the money being pumped in. But within a year or two they would start to realize that the vast profits of the coal industry were being siphoned off and taken out of the area. It would be just like the days of the California or Alaskan gold rush. Many would seek fortune, but only a slim few would actually attain it.

All these thoughts ran through James Arthur Pack's mind as he sat at his small table and watched the rain fall and the Beaver Creek rise. The water was now touching the floor joists of the platform and continuing to rise. It was only about one more foot from actually entering the depot itself. Oscar still sent and received messages on the telegraph and the two who never seemed to have anything to say just sat at another table and played their cards.

After two days the four men were about to run out of food and the only options left to them was to stay and hope the water stopped rising, or move to another rail shack about two hundred feet away and on slightly higher ground. But one and all didn't want to abandon the telegraph; it was their only link to civilization, and to cut and run now, before the last possible minute, was out of the question.

According to Oscar the shack on the hill behind the depot was used as a bunkhouse for the track crews that worked the area one week out of each month. Usually there were cases of canned goods and maybe some coffee kept there after the track crew left out, which in this case had been about two weeks earlier.

All of the men were reluctant to leave if for no other reason than the telegraph. It was comforting to know they could send and receive information. It made each of them feel like they were not so alone in the world. At the moment the telegraph to them meant they were not forgotten.

"How long Oscar, before the operators at the Martin telegraph office jump ship and head for higher ground?"

"Not long, I think. Water at Martin comes from both Beavers, outside you're looking at only half the water that's about to hit that town. Won't matter anyway, won't be long until we lose the line between here and there; water will take down one of the poles that run along the side of the track. When that happens, and the telegraph goes down, we'll head on over to that rail shack for safety and also see what kind of provisions them track boys might have left behind."

Caudill and Johnson had been gone about twenty minutes and the men could still hear the panic whistle, although very faintly.

"How far you think they are now?" Pack asked Oscar.

"I was just thinking about that same thing Pack. At the speed they left out of here they should be almost to Martin by now. By the sound of their whistle I think they ain't even made it more than two miles, not even to Hunter Straight. The depot there is called Jump.

"What's going on Oscar, you think they ran into trouble?"

"You want my best guest Pack?"

"Yea Oscar, I think I do."

"There's a three trestle bridge this side of Jump. I think them dunderheads at Martin already had some loaded cars parked on it and that's why they wanted Caudill to abandon his engine here. Somebody down there made a mistake and left an engine on the wrong side of the bridges. That same somebody didn't telegraph that piece of vital information up the line. I believe Caudill and Johnson are trapped between a blocked bridge and a screaming bitch of a flood."

"Do you think Caudill saw it and was able to stop in time?"

"Caudill is good, probably about the best engineer on the line. Yea he could have stopped her in time."

"And if he did stop in time what are they doing now? They must still be with their engine because we can still hear the whistle."

Oscar thought for a second before finally saying, "Knowing them two for as long as I have, I'd say they hooked up to the loaded cars and are trying to push on ahead of the flood. Problem is, it takes time to hook up and then release the brakes of the parked cars before they can proceed on down the line. That engine of theirs is powerful, as you seen when they took out of here, but they would have to push them loaded rail cars from a dead stop and that takes time even for a big Baldwin. This is pretty scary stuff Pack, pretty scary stuff."

No sooner had the words left Oscar's mouth than there was a bright flash that lit the entire sky. It revealed the low hanging clouds overhead, black and ominous, that seemed to descend into the valley itself. In no more than a second a tremendous explosion could be heard. The depot building itself shook as if caught in an earthquake. The thunder from the explosion lingered for several seconds until it was upstaged by the sound of steam and steel as the big engine tore itself apart from the inside out.

Each of the men in the Drift Depot saw and heard what could only be described as Hell itself. For an eternity that could have been no more than a few seconds no one said a word. Everyone knew that Caudill and Johnson had met their end when their beloved engine was overtaken by the fast moving flood. They would not have felt any pain, only a tenth of a second of bright light as the steam scalded their bodies. The men just stood in silence. It looked as if Oscar said a silent prayer as they moved back inside out of the pouring rain.

Pack stayed near the front windows, which faced the raging torrent that had just claimed the lives of two men. He just couldn't take his eyes off the water. It was fast and black with mud. After finally snapping to his senses he spoke, "Oscar, I don't want to raise any alarms but that water is all the way around our building now and it's starting to move even faster than before."

No sooner had the words come out of his mouth than there was a loud crash and the depot shook with a terrible force. Next thing they knew the entire building moved an inch or two downstream. The men all ran out onto the loading platform to see what had happened.

Outside in the driving rain they were astonished to find that the water tower, which was used to add water to the locomotives, had been knocked from one of its footings and had leaned over against the upper end of the depot. The fast moving water must have eaten out one of the footings which held the supports. Without the help of even one support the heavy tower had eased over and was pushing against the depot. The flood waters were gathering behind that water tank's legs and threatening to push the entire tank and depot into the raging creek. The men each moved back inside the depot.

"Oscar, I think that unless we abandon this shack, and I mean right now, the four of us are gonna drown."

Pack looked at Oscar and could only think that he had never seen fear take hold of a person as it had taken hold of the railroad man.

"Oscar, did you hear what I just said? We're going to drown right here in this depot unless we get out of here, and I mean right now."

The old man just looked out the big window facing the raging flood as if caught in a daze or a spell of some kind. He cast his eyes on Pack and with a voice that was less of conviction and more of fear said,

"No, no, you fellers go on, I got to stay with the telegraph." He looked each one of the men in the eye before adding, "It's my job."

"Oscar, that's crazy talk, the telegraph line was knocked down when the water tower fell; you can see the wires hanging from the side of the depot now."

"Pack, I can't swim, I'm gonna stay right here in the depot, I'll be all right."

Now Pack had been in worse places than this, although at the moment none came to mind. He had made up his mind that he wasn't going to let that old man drown if there was anything he could do about it. Whatever they were going to do would have to be done fast because the depot had begun to shake more violently and at any minute the whole structure might be swept away, along with the four occupants.

"You two, I don't know your names but you're going to help me get Oscar to that shack over there on the hill."

The two card players looked first at Oscar and then at Pack.

"The hell with you mister, we ain't helping nobody. We're heading out of here and there ain't anything you're gonna do about it."

With that the two headed toward the back door of the depot to make an attempt for the higher ground, leaving the old man to drown. Oscar looked at Pack. He already had the look of a man who was about to die. Come Hell or high water, and they already had the high water, Pack wasn't about to let that happen. He pulled his Colt .45 from a shoulder holster under his jacket and lifted it toward the ceiling and pulled the trigger. The shot went through the roof, spraying pieces of plaster and splinters throughout the room. Then he lowered it toward the two selfish bastards who had almost made it to the back door. Both stopped dead in their tracks at the sound of the shot and turned to see the heavy revolver pointed straight at them. Neither one spoke.

"As I said gentlemen, you're gonna help Mr. Simms here, who can't swim, over to that rail shed, do you understand me or do I have to explain it again?"

The smaller of the two looked at Pack and said, "We ain't helping nobody and I don't think you're going to shoot us down in cold blood."

Pack pulled back the hammer of that big Colt and raised it to the face of the man who was doing more talking now than he had in the last two days.

"If they find your body after the water goes down, it'll have a bullet hole right between the eyes unless you decide to help me get this man to safety, and I mean you better decide in the next two seconds."

The two men looked at each other and then looked at the .45. They knew by the look on Pack's face that he might pull the trigger at any second. Before either man could answer, the building shook hard and moved a few more inches.

"All right mister, we'll do what you ask, let's just do it quick before this whole damn place falls into the water."

Pack didn't know if it was the Colt or the flood that made the two change their minds and at the moment he really didn't care. All three men just looked at him as if they were waiting on a plan, and then he realized he still had the Colt in his hand. He holstered the weapon and then turned to Oscar, "Is there any rope in here?"

"Sure thing Pack, almost a full spool is stored in the back room."

Suddenly a new sound, much louder than the raging water, got their attention. It was a loud scratching sound as if the claws of some giant beast was scraping on the outside of the depot and at any moment it might make its way inside and devour the four. They each heard the sound and for a moment the fear of the water was replaced by the fear of the unknown. At least the flood was a known fear and as bad as the fear of drowning is with any man this new sound seemed even more ominous. What was it that was trying to claw its way inside, what could be out in that flood and still survive.

The answer came soon enough. A large tree, with a trunk at least three feet thick, swept by. Branches from the tree clawed and scraped at the sides of the depot as if trying to hold on and not be swept away. As fast as it was there it was gone, but not before a branch broke out the big front windows and even came inside the building a few feet before being swept away. Nothing was said by anyone as they each tried to gather their thoughts and allow the fear of the moment to pass.

Finally Pack snapped out of his trance and grabbed Oscar by the arm. "Oscar is there any rope about."

"Sure thing Pack got a big spool in the back room. I already told you that once." Oscar's voice was shaky and broke a few times but he said what they needed to hear. Apparently the first time he had answered that same question Pack was too preoccupied to hear his reply.

"Alright, cut about eighty or ninety feet from the spool, and do it fast."

All three men went after the rope as Pack looked back out the window. The water was only inches from the top of the platform where the water tower had wedged itself against the building. The men only had a matter of minutes if not seconds before the flood claimed this building and everything in it.

When the three came out of the side room they were carrying a good size piece of brand new rope. Pack asked the two lowlifes if either one of them could swim? They both said that they could. Pack had the one with the big mouth to tie the end around his waist and then measured about twenty-five feet and tied that around Oscar. The third man tied himself with about another twenty-five foot space. That left about twenty or thirty feet from the last man to Pack.

"Alright now head to the door and let's get onto that back loading dock."

All three men were more than glad to obey because that building was shaking up a storm and water had begun to seep in the front door and up through the floor boards. The first man to the door was Oscar. He grabbed the old lever over the door lock and twisted it with all his might, but the door wouldn't open. The biggest of the two card players pushed the old man out of the way and grabbed the handle with both hands. With a mighty heave he broke both the handle and the lock completely off the door but the damn thing was still shut tight. The rest of the men looked at the handle in the big man's hands. He had used so much force in breaking the lock that blood was oozing from some of his big meaty fingers.

"I'm real sorry fellers; I didn't mean to break off the knob like that. Now it looks like the door to this depot is the lid to our coffin."

Pack grabbed a straight-back chair and swung at the door with all he had, but the chair just shattered. Apparently when the building shifted on its foundation the door became wedged tight in its own frame.

Just beside the front door of the depot was an old oak bench that was about eight feet long. It was made of heavy timber and looked like their last chance to break through the jammed door.

They all thought what Pack was thinking and without saying a word the four grabbed that bench and headed for the door. They placed the end against the spot just above where the lock had been and on the count of three they all took a couple of steps back and with all their combined strength they hit that door as hard as they could. The door gave way and the four escaped to an even more hellish scene on the outside.

Out on the back dock, which was about a step higher than the floor of the depot, all their fears were confirmed. Flood water was racing by almost as fast as it had been at the front of the depot, which was on the creek side. Pack scanned the area and saw that the back dock ran down the full length of the building. From there it was about twenty feet to another shed and from there another twenty feet to higher ground.

Pack noticed that the water ran by and then back under the depot about halfway down. Past that the current was not nearly as fast. If a man could make it to the protection of the other shed it would slow the current even more. They all ran to the end of the dock.

Pack looked at the other three and said, "Alright here's what we've got to do. You three stay at the end of the dock here. I'm going to make a try for that building over there, if I don't make it to that shed just haul me back in and then we'll try something else, got it?"

The three nodded in agreement, glad that Pack was going to be the one to try first, instead of making one of them go. He picked up the loose end of the rope and tied it around his belt. Then after making sure the knot was good and tight he took off and with as long a jump as he could make he landed about half way between the depot's back dock and the shack. The water was cold and powerful but he managed to stay on his feet. Luckily the ground must have been a little higher there, that would explain why most of the water was going back under the depot and not on down this side to the end of the structure.

With extreme difficulty he made it to the shack and none too soon, there wasn't any more slack on the rope between himself and the next man who was tied twenty-five feet back. He turned and told the next man to do as he had just done. Without hesitation the second man jumped and was in the water. He must have hit something or something in the water had hit him, because as soon as he went in he was taken out of sight under the black swirling deluge. Pack pulled hard on the rope and almost as fast as he went down he came up coughing and spitting muddy water. Pack continued to pull and in a matter of seconds the man was safely behind the shed, although breathing very heavy.

It was now Oscar's turn and just as he was about to jump there was a grinding sound that could mean nothing but trouble. The entire building swiveled on its axis and began to nose down into the black churning waters. If it took Oscar and the other man down, then it would also pull the two men at the shed down with them and all four would drown.

The two men screamed as the water came up around their legs. At that moment Pack and the man tied beside him began to pull with everything they had. They completely yanked those two off the dock just as the whole thing started to disappear into the flood. As they pulled on the rope they noticed that the depot was going down like a sinking ship. The last part of the building to go under was the upper gable which held the sign, 'Drift Depot'. It seemed to stay stationary for a brief moment and then it just slowly sank out of sight. It was all gone; the only thing left in its place was the black angry water.

The two continued to pull on the rope but the other two men were nowhere to be seen. They had gone under as soon as they were yanked off the dock. There was still tension on the rope and the two continued to pull hard. For a moment the two men thought they were going to join them. Finally the rope began to edge out of the water and then Oscar's head popped up. He soon got to his feet and was clawing hard toward the shed. A second later and the fourth man came out of the water and they pulled them both in.

All four men huddled behind the relative safety of the rail shack for a moment to catch their breath. They were standing on the foundation with water up nearly to their knees. Before long the water began to swirl around them again. Apparently without the protection of the depot the current was released now fully on the new position. The four eased to the back side of the shack and looked at about twenty more feet of fast water.

"Oscar, how does the ground lay between here and the hill?"

"Don't know Pack, I think it's about level," he said with exhausted gasps. The exertion thus far had been hard on the old man, but he was still alive.

"The water is still raising and getting faster, if we don't go now we probably won't live to tell about it."

The other three looked at Pack with exhausted frightened faces, but all three nodded in agreement.

"All right, we're going to do it the same way as before, me first, and so on. If I get in trouble though, don't bother pulling me back. You just cut me loose and then the next man can try, the water is rising too fast to try to pull me back, got it?"

The three looked horrified at the suggestion, but no one argued. With a quick nod Pack turned and left the three men, along with the relative safety of the calmer water behind the shack, and dove for the far bank. The water was above his knees and pushing hard. It was a struggle to lean into the current and try to hold the rope up out of the water; he didn't need it dragging him under along with the current.

About ten feet out, the ground started to rise up a bit and as he proceeded a little further his knees and then lower legs were out of the water, he had made it. Then he heard screaming from behind and as he turned around he saw a sight that stopped the breath in his throat. The water tower now had broken totally free from its footings and had wheeled around toward the shack where the other three men were standing. It was only feet from crushing those men and then dragging Pack to his death.

"Come on, it's now or never," Pack yelled.

With that all three were pushing through the water hard with that water tank right on top of them. Pack was pulling to beat the band and those three were looking like the grim-reaper was riding on their shoulders as they fought for their lives. Within seconds the four were on the bank just as that water tower went by and sucked the shack right along with it. The four collapsed on the bank right at the water's edge, totally exhausted.

After a few minutes the water made it up to their new resting area as they just lay there in the pouring rain. Pack got up and pulled out his knife and began to cut the rope off himself. He didn't want to be attached to any more trouble at the moment than he had to. The others soon were up doing the same, all were grateful to be alive.

They made their way up the slope to the repair shack, thankful to be alive. It's funny how a man's mind works, after almost getting killed only minutes before they were now all hoping the previous track crew had left some grub and coffee behind. Maybe thinking about food took their minds off the close call each had just experienced.

When they made it to the side of the shack they found it had one of those big railroad locks on the door. Pack looked at Oscar and asked.

"Oscar, where would the key to this lock be, you got any idea?"

Oscar looked at the man and frowned before saying, "Bout half way to Martin by now, it was in my desk drawer under the telegraph set."

One of the other two said, "How we gonna get in, we ain't got nothing to break a lock like that."

Pack un-holstered his Colt and said," You three better take cover behind the building just in case this slug ricochets."

He didn't have to say that twice, those three tripped all over themselves getting behind the shed. As soon as they were in the clear he stepped back and let a .45 cartridge do the job faster than any key. With that the three men came back around the shed and forced the door open and went inside. It was nearly dark now and inside the shack it was almost pitch black. If any of the three had matches they would be useless after their little swim.

"Oscar, you know if there is a coal oil lamp and dry matches kept in this building?"

Almost before the words came out of his mouth a match sparked and old Oscar was lighting a lantern. He just looked at Pack and grinned. With the light from the lantern and a quick look around, the men could tell that the railroad took pretty good care of its track crew. The room had eight or ten bunks with a big table and several ladder-back chairs in the middle. In the center of the room to one side was an old pot-belled stove, the kind with a flat top for cooking. Beside the stove was a stack of dry firewood and kindling. Before long old Oscar had a nice hot fire going and with the help of that lantern the place almost looked like the inside of one of those big hunting cabins men stayed in out in the Rockies.

Next on the list was food. The four were starved after their little adventure. It amazed Pack at how hungry almost losing his life always made him. Even before their clothes began to dry they were tearing that place apart trying to find any food that the previous track crew might have left behind. Up on a top shelf they found a sack of soup beans and some coffee. Not a good situation, soup beans have to cook for quite some time before they become edible. They kept digging around and finally came across a case of canned peaches. With some difficulty they finally found a can opener and started eagerly opening the cans. It didn't take long before the four were cooking beans, eating peaches, and sipping strong hot coffee made from rain water that ran off the roof. The two card players ate with particular gusto. It was as if they either liked canned peaches a lot or were just plain famished.

After all the four had been through Pack hoped the little incident between the card player and himself had been forgotten, but it wasn't to be. The man whom he had leveled his gun at just keep looking at him until he finally asked, "Is there a problem there Hoss?"

"Damn right there's a problem; you pointed a gun at me when I was unarmed."

Everyone had stopped eating, and all three were looking at Pack for a reply. He put down his food and gave them one.

"It ain't in my nature to let a man drown if there's anything that can be done to prevent it."

"Well when you feel man enough to put that big Colt aside, I'm gonna teach you a thing or two about not being so overbearing," the card player said.

Pack stood up and took off his jacket and undid the shoulder holster, reaching it along with the gun to Oscar.

"Oscar you mind holding this for me while this big mouth son-of-a-bitch teaches me that lesson he was just talking about."

Oscar took the gun and before Pack could turn around that card player had pulled out a knife and was coming at him with the look of a man who wanted to kill somebody. As he came at

Pack he waited and at the last minute stepped aside. As he was going by Pack grabbed the back of his neck with his left hand and the wrist that was holding the knife with his right and as he slid by he rammed a knee into his chest. There was a loud gasp from the man as the air left his lungs. He landed against one of the bunks and collapsed to the floor. He had no sooner than hit the floor until his partner came at Pack with a skillet that had been hanging on the wall. Oscar thought that if this man fought as poorly as his friend then it should be over pretty quickly. As he came, he swung the skillet in a big arching overhead swing that was easy enough to step away from. As the skillet came down into nothing but thin air Pack caught the man with a powerful right to the side of his jaw. He stood there for a second and then his knees got a little wobbly. Before you knew it his eyes rolled back in his head and he fell right on top of his friend.

Pack sat back down and picked up his can of peaches and fork and began to eat. Oscar was looking at him in astonishment.

"I ain't ever seen the like of that in my life. Where on God's green earth did you learn to fight like that?"

"Oscar, that wasn't a fight that was just two tired old boys who had bit off more than they could chew."

After Oscar and Pack had finished their peaches they helped those two up and onto a bunk. The fight had gone out of both of them, they just wanted to sit and finish their grub without any more excitement. Oscar tended the big pot of beans for a couple of hours. On a shelf next to the pot-belly stove was a bottle of beef-stew spice, whatever that was. Oscar kept adding a spoonful at a time about every fifteen or twenty minutes. He said the railroad men always used the stuff in their beans to add flavor. He guaranteed the three men when it was finished it would be the best beans they had ever eaten. None of three really cared. They were to the point that they could almost eat them raw.

During the evening Pack kept a close watch on the rising water. The track crew's bunk house sat about twelve or fifteen feet higher on the hill than the actual depot. He used the lantern to gauge how fast the water was raising, with the help of a yardstick that he had stood in the ground at the edge of the flood water. Each time the water raised six inches he would note the time and then move the yardstick back to the edge of the water again. He still couldn't believe that his pocket watch worked after being under water, but it did.

In the course of four hours the water had come up another two feet. At that rate the shed the men were in would be in the water shortly after daylight. The thing about rising water though is that as it rises it spreads out. So as it gets wider it takes a lot more of it to get deeper. The rain had also slowed considerably and that should begin to help. Oscar said the water could still rise for another six to eight hours even if it stopped raining now altogether. They were still a good fifteen or twenty miles from the head of Beaver and it would take that long for the rest of the high water to make it there.

"Well Oscar, all we can do now is just sit tight and wait it out. I don't believe any of us is going anywhere for some time."

"That sounds good to me Pack. After our close call tonight this bunk house feels like the place to be. You boys all fetch you one of them tin plates over there on that shelf and come and try these beans I been telling you about."

The two troublemakers had been sitting in the corner on their bunks with not much to say to anyone. Each had just sat and rubbed their chins and looked at nothing in particular.

With Oscar's invitation to try the beans they both jumped up and pushed Pack out of the way as they grabbed a metal plate and headed for the stove. They didn't even wipe the dust off, just held them out for Oscar to fill with the big ladle he had found hanging on the wall. They both started eating with their fingers. Oscar looked at Pack and just shook his head. "Them beans are hot fellers, would either of you two like a spoon?" Both of the card players looked at Oscar who was holding a big spoon in each hand. Both grabbed a spoon and headed over to sit down. The four all sat and ate and Pack would be the first to admit, Oscar did know how to make good beans.

"Told you them was good beans didn't I Pack?" Oscar asked.

He looked at the old man and asked, "No cornbread?"

Oscar laughed and told Pack to go to hell.

Finally about midnight one of the two, the one who Pack had held the gun on said, "Mister, who did you say you was?"

Pack just looked at the man for a long second and finally said, "Name's Pack, James Arthur Pack."

The two went back to talking in a low mumbling tone which was too low for Oscar or Pack either one to make out. They could mumble the rest of the night for all anyone cared as long as they didn't start any more trouble.

Then the man with the sore ribs spoke, "You wouldn't be the same James Pack from out Arizona way would you?"

"Yea, I reckon that would be me."

"You mean the one who's a gunfighter?" The other one asked.

"You're right again boys."

With that both men went back to mumbling and that's when Pack noticed Oscar looking at him.

"You know Pack; I thought I had heard of you before. It's been a long time since the town of Drift has had a celebrity to roll through."

"Well Oscar, I don't reckon that I'm a celebrity but I do seem to get more attention after people know who I am."

"Pack in case you hadn't noticed it yet, you got quite a bit of attention from them two and they didn't know who you were."

About that time the two trouble-makers got up and started to walk toward Pack. He stood up, not knowing what to expect. These two hadn't been very friendly as of late and he wanted to make sure he was on his feet if they wanted to resume their conversation from earlier.

"Mr. Pack, I'm Jess Reynolds and this here is my cousin Arlee. I just wanted to apologize for all the trouble we been causing and wonder if you could just forget about everything that has happened between us?" With that he held out his hand to shake. Now Pack was still a little leery of these two, and didn't want to give up his gun hand for the sake of a handshake, and on top of that the man had been eating soup beans with that hand before he grabbed a spoon, nasty!!!

"I reckon we can shake after we get out of trouble with this flood, if you don't mind?"

With that Jess put down his hand and then went back to rubbing his jaw. After a few seconds he looked back at Pack and said, "You don't trust us, and I don't say as I rightly blame ya."

"Well let's just say that I didn't live this long by taking any chances."

Jess looked at Arlee and then back at Pack and then started to grin. "So anyway Mr. Pack, no hard feelings."

"None here Jess, as long as we're being neighborly though, how about you two telling me and old Oscar here how it is that you two ended up in the town of Drift during this kind of weather?"

"We were sent for by a man name of William Conley, see me and old Arlee here are two of the best farriers in the whole state of Kentucky. We were promised six dollars a head to put some new iron under a few of Conley's prize horses. That would be about four times what we been getting out Bowling Green way. He said he would furnish everything we needed along with room and board, we just couldn't pass up a job like that."

All this time while Jess was talking his cousin just stood there with nothing to say, just shook his head in agreement every now and then. Finally he decided to chip in a little to the conversation.

"We both left Western Kentucky with the hope of making the trip in four or five days. We used our last twenty dollar bill to buy train tickets to get us here. We only had less than two dollars left between us and thought we could scrounge some food along the way. After four days and very little luck with the scrounging for food part we made it to this depot about forty-eight hours before it got washed out from under us."

Then Jess added, "We were both pretty hungry and a mite testy when all this happened. When you started telling us what to do, well Mr. Pack, it was just the last straw. Hope you don't hold no grudges cause we sure don't."

Well that was about the best explanation Pack had ever heard from anyone and it pretty much explained everything that had happened so far. He couldn't help but feel sorry for the two, there had been times in his life when he hadn't eaten for a day of two and it makes a man do some crazy things. Pack reached into a pocket and pulled out a ten dollar gold piece and tossed it to Jess. He caught it and looked at Pack for the longest time and then finally spoke.

"What's this for."

"Just call it an advance on your first couple of shoeing jobs."

"But we're going to work for William Conley as soon as this flood lets us go on upstream to his farm."

"That's right and you can pay me back after we get there, after you shoe your first horses."

Jess and Arlee both looked at Pack and at nearly the same time both of them said, "We?"

"That's right; I'm on my way to the Conley farm myself. Mister Conley and I have got a few business deals to work out. Once this water goes down, you two can travel on with me if you'd like."

"Well Mr. Pack, I think we'd like that a lot."

"Then it's settled, once this flood is gone I'll rent a few horses, that is if they ain't all been drowned, and we'll make our way together to the Conley farm. Don't look like a train will be back in this part of the country for a while, and anyway, the train only goes part of the way past here."

This was a plan that had come to Pack at the spur of the moment. He would go to the Conley Farm with these two farriers. It might be the only way to see the old man without getting shot.

The Baldwin-Felts higher-ups had at times planted people inside of certain organizations to gather information. Maybe these two horse shoe boys could check out the crew and fill Pack in on the goings on at the ranch.

He only hoped that his reputation as a gun for hire wouldn't interfere with his first meeting with old man Conley. But then again maybe that could be a commodity that Conley needed, time would tell. There were still a lot of unanswered questions. He still didn't know who had planted that bad information he was given while in Prestonsburg but if all went well he might be able to find out. Something told him that there was other competition in play for the coal business of Eastern Kentucky.

By now the rain had stopped and before long both farriers and Oscar had each selected a bunk and were sound asleep. Pack stayed awake for another hour or so taking a look now and again at his yardstick water gauge. By the time he assured himself that their new home wouldn't be claimed by the flood waters it was a few minutes past two in the morning. He chose a top bunk on the opposite side of the shack and hoisted himself in. He convinced himself that the floodwaters sounded not that much different than the sounds of the ocean waves crashing on a quiet beach. Before long, sleep had claimed him too.

When Pack awoke a little sunshine could be seen through the cracks in the gables of the old bunkhouse. In the hills of Eastern Kentucky if you wanted to see the sun you usually had to look straight up so he knew it must be at least thirty minutes past sunrise. He stepped outside the track shed and looked at the destruction. Water continued to flow by at an alarming speed. The flood was so far out of its banks that there wasn't anything to slow it down. Anything and everything was floating by. Wasn't long before the body of a cow went by, apparently it was unable to make it to high ground before the waters of Beaver Creek claimed it as a victim. Pack could hear noise from inside the shed and before long the other three came out and took in what looked like a large lake........going by at about ten miles an hour.

The four pulled some chairs out onto the covered platform that was attached to the front of the shed and sat to watch the show. Pack still had his yardstick in the water to measure the size of their little fast moving lake. By about three that afternoon the water had stopped rising. Within three or four hours the level of the water had receded by an inch or two. Without any more rain the water should be back down below the railroad track by morning, according to Oscar.

Being only about fifteen or twenty miles from the headwaters, according to Oscar, meant that without any more rain the flood would be gone in about a day and a half. By Thursday morning, with any luck, the three could continue the journey to the farm of William Haskell Conley, most likely on foot.

Oscar took one last look at the flood and then said, "You boys hungry? I sat that big pot of beans back on the stove before I came out here. Should be warm in a few minutes." All three indicated they were and followed him back into the bunkhouse. As they sat eating they thought they heard talking outside the shed. Oscar looked at Pack and asked, "Am I hearing thangs or do any or you boys hear somebody talking?"

"I thought I heard something too Oscar," Pack told him. "We better go and have us a look."

Pack knew they were isolated and didn't know how anyone could be outside unless they were in a boat. When all four went outside they looked around but couldn't see anyone about. Just as they were about to go back to their breakfast there was a shout from the tree line.

"Hello the cabin. You boys got any food for a couple of hungry groundhogs?"

The four looked up the hill behind the shed and low and behold there was Caudill and Johnson coming down the mountain. Oscar looked at Pack and said, "Well Pack, I guess that proves it. We all did drown last night cause here we are reunited with them two dead crazy bastards that thought they could take an engine and tender through the worst damn flood in history."

Not another word was said as the two railroad men made their way to the shed. Caudill spoke first. "Bet you didn't expect to see me and old Johnson here again now did ya?"

"No Caudill, we shore didn't, last we heard of you was when that big engine of yours blew you both straight to hell," Oscar said.

Johnson looked at the four and asked, "What happened to the depot?"

Again Oscar spoke, "Well Johnson, we didn't like that old depot very much so the four of us decided to move up here, better view and all don't you think?"

Johnson looked around, "I have to agree with you Oscar. The view up here is a lot better, what do you say about that Caudill?"

Caudill looked at the rest, "You got any grub in that shed fellers? Me and old Johnson here been trudging around that mountain all night trying to get back here and we are plum starved."

Oscar slapped Caudill on the shoulder and said, "We got beans and peaches and you will be glad to know the two are in different pots, come on in and you can tell us what happened last night after you left us."

"Yea and you can tell us what happened to the depot. The railroad ain't in the habit of misplacing property unless there is a pretty damn good reason for it." Everyone laughed as they headed back inside.

Oscar got down two more of the tin plates from the shelf and filled both with steaming hot soup beans. When he sat both of them in front of the men Caudill looked up and asked, "Where's the cornbread Oscar?"

Pack couldn't help but laugh, and then old Oscar set them up real good when he said, "Oh we had plenty of cornbread but these three ya-who's ate it all up when they seen you two coming out of the hills, now tell us what happened after you headed out of here last night with that devil of a flood hot on your heels."

Caudill wiped his mouth on the back of his wet shirt sleeve and asked if there was any coffee. Pack got up and poured each of the two men a cup. After Caudill took a sip he looked at the four and started the story.

"Well, you seen the way that water was coming after us and how we lit out of here trying to get away last night. We made it almost to Jump and things were looking like we might be able to save the engine and tender after all. As we rounded the curve that lines us up with the straight stretch that has them three trestles in it our worst fears were sitting right there in front of us. Six loaded coal cars sat on top of the trestles. But that ain't the worst part. Whoever sat the cars didn't keep the six buckled together. They had sat two to a trestle. Only thing I can figure is they must have thought that if one trestle failed then all six cars coupled together might pull down the other two. Anyway, I locked the brakes hard as soon as I seen the loaded coal cars. The tracks were wet and that old engine slid long and hard into the first set of cars, we hit pretty hard and it damn near threw me and Johnson off the train. I first thought we might have broken the coupler on the tender or the one on the car but when Johnson got off and inspected they was both okay.

"Johnson ran back to release the brakes as I eased the engine in to set the couplers. It takes time to turn the crank on a coal car to release the brakes and Johnson had to climb up and do it on two. Well anyway, I got the couple done and Johnson had both sets of brakes loose in just a few minutes. He stepped aside and I pushed them two cars into the next set of cars for another couple. Johnson was already releasing the next two cars and as he did I got ready to push back again to hook up with that last set of cars when we saw that water bearing down on us again. We weren't going to make it. By the time we could have gotten all the cars coupled and the last set of brakes released the water would have been up to the cab on the locomotive.

"I hollered at Johnson and told him to come to the engine. He seen the water and knew the gig was up. I told him to hit the hill and I would be right behind him and believe me I didn't have to tell him twice. He took off like a scalded dog, and if the flood hit that hot boiler and we were anywhere near it then that is exactly what we would have been, scalded dogs.

"When Johnson started up the hill I dropped that old engine in forward gear and put every bit of steam she had left in her to the drive wheels. With only four cars and a tender holding her back she took off like a rabbit, a big mean rabbit. When she started pulling forward I jumped clear and took off after Johnson. I knew the two of us only had a minute before that engine with her superheated boiler hit the cold water and then there would be hell to pay.

"I saw Johnson jump down into a little gully about a couple hundred feet from the track and part way up the hill and I only hoped I was lucky enough, or should I say fast enough, to make it there too. Well I did and both of us turned to watch what happened next."

Caudill took a big bite of soup beans and just sat there chewing until Oscar said, "Caudill damn your hide, don't start eating now you steam jockey, finish the story."

Again Caudill wiped his mouth on the back of his soggy sleeve and then continued his story. "Well let me tell you something, that big old engine looked mighty proud going forward instead of running away like she had been doing while me and old Johnson here were trying to get her back to Martin. She had good steam and not much holding her back. She charged that wall of water and I swear to you it looked like she had a mind to push it all the way back to Wheelwright. And as she was plowing forward she was also protecting me and Johnson." Again Caudill took another big bite of soup beans and sat there chewing like it was nobody's business.

This was more than Oscar could stand. He, just like the rest of the men, was hanging on every word. He reached over and took Caudill's plate and said, "You finish the damn story if you want another bite and I mean it this time."

Caudill looked at Oscar and said, "Alright Oscar, but while I'm talking how about you filling my plate again?"

"You start talking first and then I'll fill your damn plate, now what do you mean she was protecting you, she couldn't push back a flood."

Caudill continued the story. "Well she was protecting us you grouchy old bastard and I'll tell you how. If she was anywhere near me and Johnson when she blew-up then the both of us would have been scalded to death by boiling hot water, terrible way for a man to die, just terrible. Every foot that she made it away from where we were hiding in that gully helped to increase our odds. As she went forward she was also picking up speed but I still didn't think either of us had a chance in hell. When she did hit we were still too close, but then something amazing happened." Caudill stopped and took a sip of his coffee. "Say what kind of coffee does the track crew get anyway, it shore is better than the crap we get down at the Martin Depot," Caudill asked.

Oscar said, "Pack, pull your Colt and point it at his nose until he finishes his story."

Again Caudill lit into the story that each of the men couldn't wait for him to finish. "Well, when she hit that water I thought we were goners. Funny thing happened though, when the flood and the engine hit the flood came up over the big cattle catcher in front and completely covered the engine. And you know what, she just kept going forward. It only took a few seconds for that cold water to find the boiler though. When she blew she was completely covered in water and that must have helped contain the steam. Also she was pointed away from me and Johnson and had a tender and four loaded coal cars behind her which also helped to contain the blast heading our way. Me and Johnson seen the whole thing and ducked down just in time as the blast went over top of our position. We still got some hot water but it was raining so hard we barely felt it. We still could have been hit by pieces of falling steel but the Lord must have been watching over us. Hot iron fell all around us but neither of us was hit and here we are, now give me back my plate Oscar."

Oscar slid the full plate back to Caudill and then the four just watched the two eat; trying to absorb the story that each had just heard but were still trying to comprehend.

Caudill looked up at Oscar and asked, "Now tell us the story of the Depot that used to be here and how the four of you ended up in this here track crew bunkhouse."

Oscar stood, then stretched and said, "Not much of a story Caudill, after you and Johnson left last night I took charge and got everyone here to safety." Oscar winked at Pack and then busted out laughing.

After breakfast was over the six took a few more of the old ladder back chairs that were in the bunk house out onto the front porch of that old shed and sat and watched the muddy water roll by. Pack looked at Oscar and asked, "How long do you think our food will hold out?"

Oscar scratched his stubbly chin and said. "I'd say probably two maybe three days Pack."

Pack looked at the others and then added, "We got six men now Oscar and that sack of beans is near the bottom. You really think we got enough food for three days."

Oscar looked at Caudill and Johnson and said. "Well we were in pretty good shape before these two showed up. You done seen how they eat, if the water don't go down soon we'll be getting pretty hungry around here. It shore was bad luck for the four of us that them two didn't get killed when that engine exploded, just plain bad luck pure and simple." All six had a good laugh. For the next few days all they could do was sit on that porch and watch the flood.

After dinner with the Sheriff, Hash paid the tab and again left a substantial tip for Rebecca. He had rethought his opinion of her. She was a hard working gal with brains. She held down two jobs and was smart enough to help the two doctors in the clinic. But it was more than just that. True she was a beautiful woman, but more than anything else it was the way she carried herself. Her mannerisms were truly magnificent. Hash found himself attracted to her style more so than her beauty and for Hash Burton this was truly uncharted territory. As he left the dining room and headed into the saloon he noticed that she glanced his way and there was that smile again, a smile that would stop any man dead in his tracks. He touched his hat to her as he left.

He scanned the saloon and saw maybe ten men at different tables and two more at the bar. Burt was there and as soon as he saw Hash he took down a tall glass with a handle and filled it with beer. Hash walked over and sat at the bar as far away from the two men who were already there as he could get. He sat sideways on his stool as to keep a better view on the other patrons in the room.

Burt walked over and sat the tall glass of brew in front of Hash. "Say, how's it going there Burton? Seen you and the sheriff having dinner in the restaurant, you ain't in no trouble over that shooting the last night now are you?"

Hash picked up the glass and took a long pull. The beer was cold and tasted just right after a big meal. After he sat the glass down he smiled and said, "No Burt, I'd say that everything worked out pretty well unless you was one of the two unfortunates that got killed, and don't forget about poor Riley over at the clinic."

Burt thought about that and asked. "How's he doing anyway? I never did find out how many times he got shot."

"He got shot three times. One was in the chest and it was real bad, the other two bullets didn't do as much damage as that one. The doctors think he is going to pull through unless something else happens."

"All in all Burton I still say that we handled that situation pretty good don't you?"

Hash thought over the question and then had to agree with the barkeep. It for sure could have been a whole lot worse. "I think you bout got it figured out Burt, and by the way thanks for your help. If you hadn't shot that second varmint when you did then I am pretty certain that I would have been sharing a room right now with either Riley or the two corpses. Both thoughts are unpleasant."

"Don't mention it Burton. I done told you, that ain't my first gunfight. It shore brought back memories of younger days." Burt had a far off look on his face as if he was thinking about events long past.

"Say Burt, I was wondering, do you know anything about that dog that belongs to Stanton Hatfield?"

"What do you want to know Burton?"

"Well I have yet to spend a night in that old house thanks to all the attention I've been getting around here but every time I open the front door there sits that hound on the rug in the front parlor. I put him out when I leave and then just like a magician there he sits the next time I open the door. I'm starting to believe that beagle has his own key. Any way you can explain that?" Hash asked.

The old barkeep, who had been wiping down the bar top as Hash talked looked up and said. "I might be able to shine a little light on that mystery. As Mr. Hatfield got up in years he didn't want to get up and let that dog out and then ten minutes later get back up and let him back in so he hired them two Reynolds brothers to put a small door off to one side of the kitchen. Well those two Reynolds boys are about the best carpenters in the county. They can take a piece of wood and make anything you want out of it. Anyway, they figured out a way, with old man Hatfield's help mind you, to make a door that hinged both out and in and then put the hinge part on top, that way the door always hangs down in a closed position. If the dog wants to go out then he takes his nose and pushes that little door and jumps out. If he wants to come back in then he just does everything in reverse. Hatfield made sure that the door worked smooth, he didn't want his best friend to get caught in it and hurt himself."

Hash finished off the last of his beer and asked, "That explains that. You wouldn't happen to know the dog's name would you Burt?"

"Shore do, he calls him Gray Bob."

Hash looked up at Burt. "What kind of a name is Gray Bob?"

"Well I think you are going to like this little story Burton. Old man Hatfield was a staunch supporter of the South during the Civil War. His favorite General was Robert E. Lee, he took the name Bob which is short of Robert and then combined it with the color of a Confederate soldier's uniform which is gray and put the two together, Gray Bob." As Burt finished the story he slapped the top of the bar and busted out laughing.

Hash slid his empty glass to Burt and said, "Well what do you know? That was pretty clever of old man Hatfield, how about another beer?"

As Burt refilled the glass Hash asked another question. "You think there would be some kind of leftover food around here that I can take home with me. I would really hate to not take Gray Bob his supper because I would bet just about anything that when I open that big front door tonight he will be sitting there on that rug looking up at me."

Burt looked at Hash with a grin and said, "Burton, me and you is a lot alike."

This statement caught Hash off guard; he couldn't see any similarity between himself and the wooly barkeep. "How do you figure that Burt?"

Burt slid the refilled glass of brew back to Burton and said, "Well, the both of us done killed a man apiece last night, and you and me both got a soft spot for dogs, yea I would say that puts you and me about as close as brothers." Again Burt slapped the bar with his hand and started laughing, Hash laughed a little too.

"You know that old man Hatfield got himself a patent on that doggie door he invented. Said it was his idea and he wants people to know it. Let me run over to the kitchen and see if there are any leftovers you can take home to Gray Bob." And with that Burt turned and headed to the restaurant side of the building.

With all the conversation between himself and Burt going on Hash had let his guard down and failed to monitor the saloon. He felt that with Burt in the room and that big Greener twelve-gauge shotgun of his under the counter that he had an edge, still though it wasn't a good idea for a man to turn his back on strangers in a town where there was a contract out on his head. Hash quickly scanned the faces of every man in the room after Burt left. Didn't seem to be any sign of trouble but then sometimes trouble came without a sign.

Burt came back in with a paper sack and sat it down in front of Hash. "I done hit the jackpot Burton. They had a big ham bone back there and it still had lots of ham on it. I told the cook what it was for and he said give it to Gray Bob along with a pat on the head. I think everyone in town feels a little sorry for old man Hatfield and his dog."

Hash picked up the bag and then sat it back down. "Pretty heavy Burt, I'm sure Gray Bob will appreciate it."

With that said Hash finished off his beer and reached Burt five dollars. Burt looked at Hash and said, "You going to use the back door again tonight Burton?"

Hash looked at the old barkeep and asked, "Well Burt, I'm going to let you decide that for me, you know this town way better than me."

"Use the back door, and this time go the other way and come out two doors up. If I was you I wouldn't make my movements to predictable."

Hash thought this was really good advice. He was starting to wonder how it was that Burt had ended up in Floyd County, Kentucky. It was obvious the old man had seen his fair share of trouble going by what he had said the previous night. "Sounds like good advice."

Hash picked up the sack that contained the ham bone for Gray Bob and headed for the storage room where the back door was. Just before Burt closed the back door the old barkeep said, "Try to keep your head down brother." As the door closed Hash could hear Burt laughing on the other side. He was really starting to like the old man.

The street was dark and not a soul could be seen as Hash stepped onto the boardwalk. He remembered that the previous night neither he nor Riley had seen the men who were hidden and intent on killing him. He stayed in the shadows for a moment to let his eyes adjust to the darkness. The sky had cleared late in the day and now the moon was casting a light that made everything look pale gray. When Hash felt certain that no one was waiting under the awnings that covered the walkways of the businesses on this end of town he began to move down the street. As a precaution he had taken the leather strap off his Colt. He was carrying the paper sack in his left hand and had his right hand on his belt just above the big revolver. It is never a pleasant feeling to be on constant guard against dangers either real or imagined but this was what the situation required. His boots on the boardwalk were a little louder than he liked. He wondered why the other side of the street had a concrete sidewalk and this one was wood. The concrete would have been much quieter.

While in New York Hash had a few similar experiences but at least there he had the expanse of the city to help conceal his movements. Here in the small river town of Prestonsburg, Kentucky he felt exposed and vulnerable. It was as if the danger here was more focused and he had fewer options available to him. Hash was torn between the need to hurry his pace or proceed with caution. He did a little of both, dark corners meant caution, out in the moonlight meant a quicker step. Before long he was at the Hatfield house.

Instead of going right up on the front porch and using his key he stood in the shadows available to him on the street. Using caution Hash pulled his Colt from its holster and proceeded to circle the house looking for any sign of trouble. There was none.

He hurried up the front steps and eased the key into the lock as quietly as possible. On the other side of the door he heard the low throaty sound of a dog growling. This believe it or not was a good sign. Hash felt that if Gray Bob was inside then there was little chance of anyone else being there. He sat the hambone on the porch and put his left hand on the knob and slowly turned. The growl was suddenly replaced by a vicious bark. Hash felt the need to speak so as not to be mauled by the very dog he was bringing the hambone to.

"Gray Bob, easy boy."

He slowly eased the door open and there on the rug sat the hound. The bark was replaced by the sound of a friendly yelp. Both Gray Bob and Hash were relieved.

As soon as the door was fully open the dog must have been able to smell the ham that was sitting just outside the door. He got up and proceeded to where the brown paper sack sat by the front door and sniffed. He then picked up the entire sack with his mouth and just before he headed off the porch he turned and looked at Hash. He stood there for a moment and wagged his tail. Hash walked over and patted him on the head. "Almost forgot boy, this goes with the meal." With that Gray Bob headed down the front steps and off toward the other end of town, no doubt to be with old man Hatfield.

Hash now had two friends in town that he was almost certain didn't want to kill him. Burt and Gray Bob. He went in and closed the door, locking it from the inside with the key. There was also a big slide bolt above the key lock and he also locked it. Not having the time to properly inspect the house the previous day he went from room to room checking the windows. He counted three exterior doors and he made sure each was secure before going upstairs. In the kitchen he found the doggie door that Burt had talked about earlier. It was just as he had explained it. Hash took the toe of his boot and gave it a nudge. The door swung out and then immediately came back. It teeter-tottered back and forth for a few seconds until gravity stationed it back to a closed position. It was just the right size for a dog to get in and out, maybe even just a little too big. Hash hoped there were no possums or raccoons that knew how to use the device; that could be an unpleasant experience.

Confident that his new residence was secure he went upstairs and finished unpacking his bags. The clothes he had with him were in need of a good cleaning. It had now been seven days since he left New York and he was down to his last clean shirt and pants. In the morning he would put the worn clothes in a bag and deposit them out back on top of the ice box. On his way to the depot he would stop by the general store and see if the friendly store keep could pick them up when he delivered the ice and deposit them at a local cleaner. Hash would pay the man for his trouble. With that problem solved he took out his Colt and cleaned it, making sure the action was working smooth and easy.

By the time he was ready to lay down it was going on eleven o'clock and he was exhausted. He really hadn't gotten a good night's sleep since he had left New York a week earlier. Once his head hit the pillow he was out and didn't wake a single time during the night.

During the early morning hours he had a very pleasant dream. He was out on the town with the most beautiful woman he had ever seen. They had dinner together and then attended the theater, something he loved. When he dropped her off at her house later that evening he leaned over to give her a kiss. She also leaned toward him and both closed their eyes. Instead of the kiss he anticipated she licked him across the mouth with her tongue. Startled at what had just happened in the dream Hash woke up and opened his eyes. There stood Gray Bob with both feet on the edge of the bed and his face not more than an inch away. Hash's mouth was wet with dog slobbers. "Damn you Gray Bob!" Hash shouted as he spit and gagged. Gray Bob didn't seem too upset at being cursed at this early in the morning because before Hash could move he licked him in the face again. The breath smelled of hambone.

Hash jumped to his feet and went to the lavatory that was next to the master bedroom. He used a towel and lots of soap and water but just couldn't seem to get clean. If anyone called him dog breath today he told himself he would shoot them for sure.

After he cleaned up and shaved he put on his last set of clean clothes. When he came out of the lavatory he found that Gray Bob had climbed up and fallen asleep on the bed. Hash made up his mind that tonight the bedroom door would be locked from the inside. He just hoped old man Hatfield hadn't installed one of his patented doggie doors somewhere in the bedroom. He didn't bother waking the mutt up before he left the house, hell that dog had the run of the place as it was.

Hash deposited his clothing bundle on top of the icebox that stood in the carriage house and then headed down the street. It had just gotten daylight and he could see that the sky was mostly clear, just a lingering white fluffy cloud here and there. This would make nearly two days in a row without rain if indeed it didn't rain today. From what he gathered though the big river that ran through town wouldn't reach its full height for eight or ten more days. As he walked down the street he could hear the fast moving water and the river was at least five hundred feet from where he was. He would judge its height when he made it to that big swinging bridge that crossed to the depot.

His first stop was the General Store. When he got there it was a little past six thirty. The store was open and he could see the storekeeper inside sweeping the floor. Hash entered and said 'Good Morning.' The man with the broom looked up from his work and greeted Hash.

"What can I do for you this morning Mr. Burton?"

"Just stopped in to see if the ice would be delivered today?"

"Sure thing. As soon as my morning help arrives I can make the rounds, will you need anything else brought along with the ice delivery?"

Hash thought a second and then said. "Actually I would like that ice box stocked with some beer, where do I find that in this town other than the saloon?"

"I can take care of that for you. We stock a brand at the store that is a notch better than what they sell at the saloon. If you want me to keep a case in there it won't be any problem."

Hash was pleased that almost everything he needed in this little town was so readily available. He pulled out a ten dollar bill and said, "A case will do just fine. I only drink one or two a day, if that much."

The store keep took the money and said. "Sure thing Mr. Burton, I'll keep an eye on it and as soon as that case gets low I'll stock you a fresh one. Anything else?"

Hash had almost forgotten his laundry bundle. "I left a large paper sack of my clothes on top of the icebox. Would it be possible for you to drop them off at a cleaner in town?"

The store clerk smiled and said, "I will be glad to. There is a cleaner near here that I use from time to time. They are reasonable and do a very nice job."

Hash again pulled out his money and began to reach it to the man when the store keep said. "Tell you what Mr. Burton, how about I start you an account. You can stop in and settle up once a week if that is alright with you?"

Hash reached the man a twenty dollar bill and said, "That sounds just fine with me. Go ahead and put this against the

161

account. I'll stop in every few days and settle up." With that he turned and left the store.

As he headed toward the clinic he picked up his pace. He was in a hurry to check on Riley and then to make it to the Train Depot in order to meet the seven o'clock train. Hash entered the door to the clinic and saw that the front room was empty. He looked down the hall and saw that the door to the back was closed as well. He could smell coffee and went into the kitchen, there stood Dr. Sables.

"Good Morning Doctor. I just stopped in to check on Riley."

"Morning Burton. Your friend had a pretty rough night."

"What happened, I had hoped he was on the mend by now."

"He was, as a matter of fact he was doing better than me and Barnes could have expected. Last night just before nine he had a bad spasm. That wound to his back must have brought it on; anyway he tensed up real bad and started his chest wound to leaking again. Me and Barnes worked on him for a couple of hours and got everything patched back up. He lost more blood and the man didn't have that much left to begin with. We both agreed to keep him sedated with laudanum for a couple of days. By then hopefully he won't tear anything loose again."

Hash didn't respond, he just stood there and thought about what the doctor had said. He pulled a check from his pocket and reached it to Dr. Sables. Sables took it and looked at the amount Hash had written in. "Five hundred dollars, his bill ain't even half that much Burton."

"That's okay Doc. You and Doctor Barnes use what's left until Riley is well enough to get out of here. I will settle up any remaining balance then. I didn't know who to write the check to so I left that part blank. Reed over at the bank knows me and will cash it when you present it to him." Hash was talking low and slow like he was in deep thought. When finished he turned and slowly left the clinic. As he went out the front door Dr. Sables couldn't help but feel sorry for the man.

Hash walked to the Depot and on the way he saw the sheriff coming out of the new jail. He walked over and filled him in on what the doctor had just told him about Riley.

"I'm real sorry to hear that Burton. I don't know the man but if he is a friend of yours then that's good enough for me."

Hash looked at the Barnes and said, "I appreciate that Sheriff."

"Where you headed to now Burton?"

"Over to the depot. I got a couple of packages arriving on the seven o'clock train this morning."

"Train might be a little late this morning. The Big Sandy is running way past full and it just keeps on rising."

Hash wondered how that would affect the train schedule. "I fail to see how that would change the train schedule unless the water is over the tracks somewhere Sheriff."

"Water ain't over the tracks Burton. The problem is that when the river is this big the railroad higher ups are afraid a fast moving train might vibrate the road bed enough to cause the ground underneath to break away and then the whole thing could slide into the river. Now tell me that ain't a scary thought. We have been dealing with that for years. Every time that river gets up the railroad higher ups are afraid of a disaster. It actually happened about twenty years ago. An engine, along with the tender and fourteen freight cars, had a real close call. The ground under that rail bed broke loose and set down about ten feet. Didn't go into the river but it was a pretty frightful event. Most engineers don't want to run fast when the water is big just for that reason.

"How many men did you know in Prestonsburg when you arrived the other morning Hash?" the sheriff asked.

"Just Riley, can't say that I knew anyone else in the entire county except for that banker Reed and I only knew of him, hadn't even met the man in person until I got off the train that morning. Why do you ask Sheriff?"

Sheriff Barnes looked up the street at nothing in particular and didn't answer the question for the longest time. Hash could tell that he was deep in thought and troubled about something. Finally he did reply, "There have been a lot of new faces in town lately. Been quite a few street fights and the such, none of them compare to the tussle you and Riley had with those three men the other night but still we're getting our fair share of trouble and I am starting to get a mite worried. My small force of deputies can only do so much and at some point they got to find time to eat and sleep."

Hash wondered what the sheriff was getting at. None of the strangers in town had anything to do with the deal he and Reed had going. Or did they? Suddenly Hash had a thought. "Sheriff, have you had any luck with that note you found in that man's boot the other night?"

"Nothing yet, but it's still on the top of my list. That third gunman from the other night, you know the one that didn't get killed by you and Burt?"

"Yea Sheriff, I know the one. Have you been able to get any information out of him yet?"

"Not much, he is convinced that he's a dead man. Says if he talks then the man that hired him will kill him for sure. And if he doesn't talk he says he will be killed all the same to keep him from talking in the future. He is one pretty scared puncher if you ask me."

"That's interesting Sheriff. How much do you believe him?"

"I don't know the man, never seen him around here until a couple of days before you got here. I tend to believe him though. He never looks out that small window in his cell just like he's afraid that someone might have a high powered rifle trained on him or something. Even locked in his cell he is jumpy as all get-out. Every time there is a loud noise he about jumps out of his skin."

Hash and the sheriff were walking as they talked and had just about made it to the bank. They both crossed the street and went over to one of the benches that were in the town square. Both men took a seat.

"Can anyone get to him in your shiny new jail Sheriff?"

"No way, we always have at least one deputy in there all the time. If a stranger comes into the front lobby with mischief on his mind then he still can't get to the jail cells unless he has a key to the big door that separates the offices from the cells. I mean it ain't fool proof by any means but it ain't a walk in the park either. I think he is as safe as he can be right where he is."

"What happens next?"

The County Attorney has the paperwork now; I dropped it off to him yesterday. The prisoner will be brought before the judge first thing tomorrow morning on two counts of attempted murder. And if Riley doesn't make it then the charges will be amended to one count of murder and one count of attempted murder. The judge is getting a little anxious about everything that's been happening around here lately. He will speed that trial along and have our man in front of a jury in less than a week. How's that for frontier justice Burton?"

Hash Smiled. "Sounds good to me Sheriff, will that County Attorney try to make a deal with him."

"He told me that as the charges stand right now he is looking at twenty years. If Riley dies then we will hang him right here in this courtyard. Yea I think he will talk and talk fast in order to avoid some of the twenty years and if worse comes to worse, avoid the hanging. He'll talk; you can damn well count on it."

It was now nearly eight o'clock and Hash saw Samuel Reed walking up the street toward them. "Sheriff I guess you were right about the train delay, I haven't heard a whistle. In a situation like this how late do you think it will be?"

"Usually four hours, should be here by eleven o'clock."

"In that case I need to meet with the man you see coming down the street there."

Sheriff Barnes looked up the sidewalk and saw Reed approaching. "You got business with Reed and I need to check on my prisoner and relieve the night shift deputy, see you around Burton."

"Sheriff if you can spare a few minutes then I would like for you to join me and Reed there in his office. I can promise you a big fat Cuban cigar if you agree."

The sheriff had never had a foreign made cigar before; his paycheck just wouldn't allow it. He looked at Hash and said, "You got yourself a deal Burton."

When Reed got to the bench where the two men were sitting he said, "Good morning gentlemen, the two of you are out early this morning. Hope it doesn't have anything to do with that monster of a flood that is about to cruise through town."

Hash stood and said, "No Reed it doesn't, although that flood is starting to worry me a little too. I need to speak with you about a couple of things this morning and I just asked the Sheriff here to sit in if that is alright with you?"

Reed smiled at Barnes and said, "My door is always open to the both of you. Come along and let's get started. I wasn't going to the office for another hour but we can go there now anyway."

For a man of Reed's age and girth he walked with a spring in his step. Fleecing people must give the fat banker extra energy Hash thought.

The three men walked up the front steps and into the front lobby of the bank, which had been opened for a few minutes. As the three headed for the staircase Hash looked over at the teller windows wondering if the lady he had spoken to when he first arrived in town was at one of them. She was not but he did notice Greg Spurlock giving the three a funny look. It was as if he was worried. His was one of the four names Hash had given to the sheriff when the note with the murder instructions was found. Of the four men mentioned to the sheriff Spurlock's was the only one that could not be completely ruled out as having a part in the murder plot. Also he was the man from Chicago. Hash would use more caution around this man if they ever met on the street.

After climbing the stairs Reed took out a key and unlocked the door to his office. All three men entered and Reed told each to please take a seat. He then opened the wooden box that contained the Cuban cigars and offered one each to the two men. Each gladly accepted.

"What is it I can do for you this fine morning Mr. Burton?" Reed asked.

Hash cut the end of his cigar and lit it with one of the matches that stood in a small brass box on the desk. Barnes did the same and each man sat back farther in the two plush chairs and looked at Reed.

Hash again rolled the big cigar around between his thumb and fingers as he had on the first morning of his arrival. He held the Cuban in his left hand leaving his gun hand free and this did not escape the notice of either of the other two men in the room. It reinforced Reed's opinion of Burton as a bully and Shootist and made him nervous. It reinforced the sheriff's opinion of Burton as a smart man who might come in handy if there was ever trouble.

"I was on my way earlier to meet the morning train when I ran into the Sheriff here. He informed me that the train would most likely be delayed due to the river and as it turns out he was right. What I need to talk to you about Reed is the banks security."

Reed looked first at the sheriff and then at Burton, "I can assure you Mr. Burton that this bank has one of the finest safes in the state. It is only a little over four years old and would take a wagon load of dynamite to destroy. You can rest assured that anything you put in our bank will be safe."

At this Hash didn't respond at first. He just sat there and toyed with his cigar. He leaned over and put the stogie in the large pedestal ashtray that stood between his chair and that of the sheriff's. After almost a minute he returned his attention to Reed and said. "Oh, I am very impressed with your safe Reed. I have a complete set of the blueprints from the manufacturer for it in my office in New York. I also have a set of prints for this bank from the builder. Your bank building is an impressive structure."

Reed looked astonished. How could this man whom he had only met a few days prior have so much information on his beloved bank? He had been assured by the builder ten years ago and the safe manufacturer four years ago that all plans of this nature were extremely sensitive and would under no circumstance be shared with anyone. He was now being told by a man he barely knew that nothing about his bank was secret.

"Please explain to me how anyone from New York could possible obtain confidential information of the type you just described Burton?" Reed's voice was a notch or two above normal and there were beads of sweat now appearing on his forehead.

Burton looked at Reed and said in a very calm and casual tone. "The men I represent are each cautious business men. They are also very powerful. Information and the art of acquiring it is something they mastered years ago."

This didn't soothe Reed in the least. "Well let me tell you something Burton, if your backers up North acquired the information we are talking about by way of theft then I can assure you that I will bring suit." Reed's voice had returned to normal when he said this. Now his tone was low and authoritative. The banker knew how to conduct an argument, probably from years of practice.

Hash retrieved his cigar from the ashtray and looked at Reed. "Calm down Reed. Your precious bank, with its expensive safe, is not in jeopardy due to the fact that my associates in New York possess the blueprints. If anything you should be grateful that you now possess the knowledge that nothing is truly secret, especially the blueprints of banks."

"How did you come to acquire my blueprints Burton if you don't mind me asking?" Reed asked this hoping to see if a law had been broken.

"That is simple Mr. Reed. My associates bought the company that built your bank along with the company that manufactured your safe. As an officer in the corporation that owns those companies I have the authorization to see any prints that I choose as long as it pertains to a project that I am working on. But it is not the prints that I came here to talk to you about this morning. It is the lack of security that worries me."

The banker seemed satisfied that no laws had been broken when the blueprints of his property were obtained by Burton. "What do you mean security; I am positive that this bank along with anything in it is safe. You have my word."

Hash put his cigar back in the ashtray and stood. He looked at Reed and then with lightning speed he drew the big Colt and said, "Accompany me downstairs Mr. Reed and instruct your employees to empty the safe. There are six men just outside the door who will assist me in removing every nickel this bank possesses. Then I plan to lock each and every one of you up in that expensive safe while me and my men ride out of town."

The sheriff didn't make a move; he just kept puffing his cigar as he said, "You know Burton you were right, these Cuban cigars are about the best I have ever had, although the ones that Eliza Reynolds produces in that Bourbon soaked paper are pretty damn good too. I think he calls them Burnt Bark Brand, or Triple B."

Hash put his gun back in his holster and sat back down. He retrieved his cigar from the ashtray and took another puff. "I bought a box of them day before yesterday but haven't had a chance to try one yet. If they are as good as you and the store keep say they are then I am in for a treat. I didn't know they were called Triple B though."

Both men sat there puffing their cigars while Reed sat stone faced. He hadn't said a word or for that matter moved a muscle. Finally Reed said, "What the hell just happened? Sheriff you heard what he said."

"Yes I did Mr. Reed. Burton here told me outside that he wanted to demonstrate how easy it would be for someone to rob your bank. He told me to just sit tight and observe and he would prove it. Well I have got to agree with him. This town as of late has seen some pretty rough looking men blow through. The shooting at the saloon the other night proves it. Now Reed, I believe you will agree with Burton here that this bank is an easy target."

The banker pulled a starched white handkerchief from his pocket and wiped his face. He got up and walked over to a large cabinet which sat on an opposite wall. When he opened it there were several bottles of whiskey inside. He took out a glass and then selected the bottle he wanted. He didn't fill it while at the cabinet. He picked up the bottle and the glass and returned to his desk. After sitting down he opened the bottle and poured a liberal amount of the amber colored liquid in. He tipped that glass and swallowed the entire contents in one gulp. He sat the glass back down and then poured himself another.

Reed looked up from his glass and said in a low growl, "I hate you Burton." With that he drank the second glass.

When he finished he slammed it down on his desk and said. "Would either of you gentlemen care to join me?"

Hash got up and retrieved two more glasses from the cabinet. "I can't speak for the Sheriff here but I might just take a small taste. If your liquor is as good as your cigars then we are again in for a treat."

Reed poured all three glasses and then picked up his. "Cheers," he said to the other two men.

Hash picked up his glass and looked at Sheriff Barnes who said, "No boys I can't, I'm on duty and anyway I never take a drink before five o'clock in the evening." As the Sheriff was saying this he reached over and picked up the third glass." The three men chinked their glasses together and then all three drank. As the Sheriff sat his glass down both Reed and Burton noticed the sheep-killing-dog look he had on his face.

Reed, now with three drinks under his belt said, "I surrender. You two put together a plan on how to better protect my bank and I will implement it."

Hash was starting to like Reed. He could take a joke and hold his liquor too. The banker had taken three shots and never flinched. The drink Hash took had damn near stopped his heart.

The sheriff looked at Reed and asked, "Would it be possible for you to hire a couple of guards to be stationed in the lobby during business hours?"

Reed answered the sheriff without hesitation. "I will be glad to, especially after that little demonstration Burton here just put on."

Hash had noticed that during their conversations the banker had stopped using Mister in front of Hash's name. This didn't bother Hash in the least. He had always felt he could trust people who used his last name only, another mark in favor of Reed. Hash had always used Mr. to intimidate people. The lack of it was a sign of familiarity.

Reed thought a minute and said. "I will need you to make a list of the men you feel comfortable recommending Sheriff. I would try myself but am not good at picking men with backbone. How soon should I have the guards posted?"

The sheriff thought a second and said. "I have an idea. One or two of my deputies could use the extra work. They mostly work evenings and nights. Each could fill in a few hours a day.

For Lack of a Title

Anyone else I can think of I will run it by you first in case you might know of a reason not to trust them. Also, anyone you hire, other than my deputies of course, should be deputized. That badge goes a long way in stopping trouble."

Hash thought that was an excellent idea. Reed thought a minute and said, "Done and done. How soon can they start Sheriff?"

"Monday, I will talk to a couple of the men who are off duty and send them on over to talk to you. Make out some sort of schedule so I can coordinate with the duties that need to be maintained with my department. I won't allow my station as Sheriff to be weakened. Anyone who works at the bank will still need to maintain the schedule they already have with me."

Reed smiled and said. "Today is Friday. If your men agree to the arrangement then we will start them first thing Monday morning."

The Sheriff thought about this and then looked at Hash. "Burton, you are the one with the big banking experience from New York. Do you think Monday will be sufficient?"

"Maybe Sheriff, I would have liked for the security to have started immediately but if Monday is the soonest you and Reed can put together a detail then Monday it will have to be."

Reed looked at the sheriff and asked, "Would it be possible for one of your deputies to swing by a few times during the day until we get the full time guards stationed?"

"Sure will and I will do better than that. During the day and evening I will also make the rounds. Good idea for everyone to see a badge in here from time to time. May I ask why all the sudden this bank needs all the extra protection?" Barnes asked.

Reed chimed in, "Well Sheriff my guess is that it has something to do with the packages that Burton is expecting on the seven o'clock train. You know the one that arrives now at ten thirty or eleven." With that Reed burst out laughing. The three stiff drinks were beginning to kick in.

Barnes looked over at Burton. "That so Burton, would you be at liberty to say what might be in those packages?"

Hash finished his cigar and crushed it out in the ashtray. "Sure thing Sheriff, I figure the three of us can keep a secret. The packages on that train contain well over a million dollars in gold and government certificates cashable anywhere."

When Hash said this Reed's eyes lit up. He already knew to expect a substantial infusion of money from Hash Burton's backers in New York but hadn't been filled in on how much it would be. "That's a very substantial amount of money Burton. Why is some of it in gold and the rest in government certificates if I may ask?"

"That is only part of the money on the train Reed. Along with the gold and certificates is four hundred thousand dollars in brand new bills, mostly hundreds but also other denominations in order to make the kind of transactions that will be required. In our purchase of land it might be easier if you can pay with the kind of money that people prefer. I have found that some people just like gold."

The Sheriff had sat listening, taking it all in. "What in the world is that kind of money doing coming in on the seven o'clock. Hell if word got out then every two bit criminal from New York to here would be riding after that train trying to get the gold and cash," he said.

This was a good question and now both Barnes and Reed were looking at Hash waiting for an answer.

"The money is not coming alone gentlemen. It is being escorted by three Baldwin-Felts operatives, I chose the three men myself. They are not men to be trifled with. Furthermore no one knows about the shipment except the three of us, isn't that so Reed?"

Reed now had the look of a child who had just got caught with his hand in the cookie jar. Both Hash and the sheriff noticed and Reed knew it, he felt compelled to explain. He picked up the bottle and started to pour himself another stiff drink until the sheriff stood and took it away from him. "I think you have had enough Mr. Reed."

The three men sat in silence as Reed worked up the nerve to explain. Finally he cleared his throat and said. "The other morning Burton when we first met you informed me that a substantial sum was going to be deposited in the bank and would arrive by the end of the week."

Hash looked at the sheriff and said, "That is correct, I told Reed about the delivery." Hash then looked at the banker. "But I also told you to keep that piece of information between just you and me, no one else, did I not?"

"That is what you told me Burton but I felt the information would be safe if only a few of the people at the bank knew about it."

"A few of the people at the bank, if I wanted your people to know then I would have told you that Reed. Just how many is a few and I mean everyone you talked to about this?"

Reed looked at the bottle but this time made no effort to reach for it. "Well we had to make room in the vault. I told Greg Spurlock to have the valuables already in there condensed and to make room for a bunch of cash. He asked if he was to do this alone or would it be possible to have a few of the other employees help. I told him to use whoever he needed."

"Sheriff, would you be so kind as to retrieve Mr. Spurlock so we can determine just how many people know about this?" Hash asked.

"Be glad to Burton. If that kind of money is arriving in town this morning then I want to know just how many people know about it myself."

Barnes rose from his seat and crushed out the remainder of his cigar and then went downstairs to find Spurlock. Hash and Reed sat in silence until the sheriff returned with the Assistant Vice President in tow. When the two men entered the room the sheriff closed the big oak door and locked it. Barnes walked over and sat back down in the same chair in front of the big desk. Spurlock just stood and wondered why the High Sheriff of Floyd County had just escorted him up the stairs to his boss's office. He looked at Burton and knew it must have something to do with the money his boss had told him about a few days prior. He also noticed that his boss's eyes looked a little bloodshot almost as if he had been drinking.

Reed looked up at Spurlock and said. "Remember the other day when I told you to make room in the vault for a large sum of money?"

"Well yes Mr. Reed. You told me to clear out some space and that is what I did."

"How many of the bank's employees did you speak to about the money shipment?"

Now Spurlock knew what this was all about. "Well let me think. I told five I believe." He thought a minute and then said. "Five Mr. Reed, I told five."

Hash was astounded. He had told the president of the bank how important it was for his business dealings to remain a secret and now he finds out that five other employees of the bank were notified that very same day. When Hash was in college in the Northeast he had taken a class once which dealt with human behavior. A portion of that class was on the domino effect of human nature and the assimilation of knowledge. He had always felt that it was one of the most productive classes he had ever taken. Knowledge he learned, especially that of the confidential kind, was nearly impossible to contain as the number of people in the confidential control group grew.

In the classes' own experiment there were three people from outside the class selected. They each were given some information about the college itself and told that the information was extremely important and to share it with no one. Four days later the members of the class, Hash included, were sent out by their professor with instructions to interview as many students at the college as possible in a one hour period and to report back to class in exactly sixty minutes. The question they were to ask the other students dealt with the confidential information that was given with the instructions not to be shared under any circumstance.

When all the students returned to class a pie chart was constructed using the information gathered. In that chart could be found these statistics. A total of one hundred and thirty two students were interviewed. Of this number ninety one had knowledge of the secret. And of the remaining forty one it was determined that thirty seven knew that there was a dark secret about the college being circulated but had no more information than that.

The same test was then conducted with the only difference being that the next information given was not to be contained or guarded by the three new test subjects. The results of that test were nearly the polar opposite of the previous test. Almost no one knew of the non-secret information, it hadn't spread at all.

Summation; information spreads at a much faster rate if it is considered confidential. The more people in the initial control group also increased the speed at which the information spread.

As Hash sat and tried to contain his anger he looked at Spurlock and asked. Of these five people, how many have keys to the bank and combination to the safe?"

Spurlock shrugged and said, "Why all of them do."

Hash had seen and heard enough of Spurlock. "You are dismissed Spurlock. That is all we need from you at this time." As Spurlock opened the door to leave Hash added, "Try not to tell anyone else on your way back downstairs."

Spurlock wasn't about to let this go unchallenged. "I have done nothing wrong Mr. Burton. In the future I expect a little more respect from you. I do not answer to you or for that matter the likes of you." Apparently Spurlock had gotten over the intimidation of his first meeting with Hash, the one where he nearly got his hand crushed.

At any other time, in any other place, Hash would have gotten out of his chair and pummeled the smartass but there was something else going on here and he wanted to wait and find out what it was. When Spurlock left and closed the door behind him the sheriff looked at Hash and smiled. "Well Burton, I think you just got you ass handed to you."

Hash looked at the sheriff and said, "You know what Barnes, I think you're right."

He then turned to Reed and said, "I am going to need a list of all the people who have keys to the bank Reed. Then on a second list I need a list of all the people who have the combination to your safe. And finally I want you to make a third list with the names of everyone who has both the keys and also the combination. When that is completed you can give it to the Sheriff. Oh and Reed, please include any employees that have since retired and no longer work here."

Reed, who looked like he needed a strong cup of coffee said, "Shall I put your name on that combination list Burton? You said yourself that you have the blueprints to both the building and the combination to the vault."

No Reed the Sheriff is aware of everything that has already been discussed. But what you can add is the names of everyone who has left the bank that might still have a key or the combination."

Reed looked at the sheriff and said, "Now why would you need that?"

Barnes now chimed in. "Reed, just make the lists and give them to me as soon as you can, say lunchtime today?"

Reed got up and carried the bottle of Tennessee whiskey back to the wall cabinet. He closed the door and turned toward the two men in his office. Now grasping the full weight of what had been going on he took charge.

"I will have your lists made within the hour and you can stop back by and pick it up personally. I don't want anyone to know what names the lists contain or for that matter that they even exist. Also I think it would be a good idea if we started the extra security now instead of waiting until Monday. Please send the two off duty deputies over this morning and I will station them where I feel it will do the most good. The bank will reimburse the Sheriff's Department in full for the amount of payroll the guards generate. Just give me an itemized list at the end of each week and I will have a check prepared. Also Sheriff, I would feel better if you and an additional deputy will meet that delayed train along with Burton here."

Both the sheriff and Hash were impressed with the way Reed had finally realized the seriousness of the situation and then taken control. When it came to money, especially such a large sum of money, they knew Reed didn't want to take any chances now that all the dangers were presented to him.

Hash and Sheriff Barnes both got up from their chairs. As they headed for the door Reed added. "And gentlemen, when you head this way with the delivery from the train please send Jeremy Eisner over ahead of you. I intend to empty the bank of customers and close down for an hour and thirty minutes in order for a quick inventory to be made of the contents of the packages and then to lock it up safe and sound in the vault. Burton, do you have anything to add?"

Hash indicated that he didn't.

"How about you Sheriff, have I got all the bases covered or do you think maybe I have forgotten something?"

"No Reed, I think you pretty well got it covered."

After Hash and the sheriff left Reed got up and closed the door to his office. Before he went back to his desk he turned the lock on the door. Satisfied that he had now thought of everything he sat down. Almost as soon as he touched the seat he thought of one more small detail. He went over to the wall safe in his office and spun the dial. After he entered the combination he swung the door open and got out a Smith and Wesson thirty-eight special with a short barrel. He reached back in the safe and retrieved a box of cartridges and a leather shoulder holster. He relocked the safe and then returned to his desk. He removed his jacket and put on the holster. After pulling his jacket back on he opened the box of shells and fully loaded the revolver. He was never a man to rest the hammer on an empty cylinder. If he carried his Smith he meant

For Lack of a Title

business. He put the gun inside the holster and then eased his jacket over the shoulder rig. He walked over to the lavatory which was adjacent to his office and looked in the mirror. The gun was completely hidden.

Reed was a good twenty five years past his prime but he didn't let that deter him from the fact that this was his bank and he would damn well help defend it if the time came. In his younger days when his father ran the bank he was branded as a rich man's wild child. He drank heavily and loved to target shoot with some of the other ruffians he ran around with. Reed didn't look the part but at one time he was feared by more than a few of the other men in and around Prestonsburg. All this came to a chilling end when he was challenged to a duel by the meanest man in the entire county, Bradford Billings or Bastard Billings as he was called behind his back.

None of Reed's friends could talk him out of it. It seemed to them that he actually looked forward to the duel. The whole thing had started when Bradford had started taking a liking to the girl Reed was seeing. Reed had every intention of marrying the girl and he wasn't about to let the likes of Bastard Billings get in his way.

On the morning of the duel both men met below the town down by the river bank on a sand bar. Reed thought it poetic to be re-enacting the most famous duel in history which also took place near water, that duel was the one between Aaron Burr and Alexander Hamilton. Reed only hoped he fared better than Hamilton.

Both men brought seconds and the rules were established. There were no matching pistols so each man was allowed any revolver he felt comfortable with. Bastard Billings brought a Colt 45 revolver and Reed possessed none other than the gun he now carried in his shoulder holster.

Both men stood back to back and the seconds stepped back to a safe distance. When the signal was given both men advanced fifteen paces each. The reason the distance was not the historically significant count of twenty paces per man was that the sand bar they stood on just wasn't long enough.

When the men stopped and turned they each pointed their guns and fired. Billings was slightly faster than Reed and his bullet hit the young man in the lower left side. The round hit only soft tissue and exited without any serious damage. Reed fired after he was hit and his aim was a little off due the injury he had just received. His intent was to injure and not kill Billings. Reed was an extremely good shot due to years of practice and he always hit what he aimed at. This time he also hit what he aimed at but either due to the injury or the fact that Billings was aiming his Colt to finish off Reed he had rushed his shot a little, the shot hit Billings squarely in the chest. The shot was instantly fatal.

When Reed and the two seconds were arrested and charged with murder it looked like twenty years for the banker's son. Reed's father Augustus Quinton Reed vowed not to interfere with the legal process. He could call in any number of favors but knew this would look bad to the people of Floyd County. He sat on his hands and allowed his son to receive whatever fate God had in store. When all the facts were presented to the county attorney and the judge it was decided that Reed acted in self-defense. Bastard Billings had fired first and fully intended to finish the job until Reed's bullet found its mark. If Billings had been more of a likable fellow then it is possible that the judge and the county attorney might have found reason to pursue the matter but so goes it when a villain meets his end.

The girl that was at the base of all this drama was eventually won by none other than Samuel J. Reed. They were both married and lived happily together for thirty-eight years. She had passed away only two years prior and this had shaken the soft hearted Reed to the core. In the two years he had spent as a widower he had begun to drink again. The moderation had given way to heavier bouts of 'Glass and Bottle' in order to relieve the pain of being alone.

As Reed sat at his desk he reminisced about days gone by and the happiness that was now gone forever. He made himself a vow, he would now stand up to anyone who got in his way or threatened the bank that his father had left to him. No more would he consider himself the timid banker who was more concerned with what people thought of him that the way they treated him. He also decided then and there to shy away from the bottle and to push back from the table. He didn't like the man he had become. Things were going to change.

He picked up a pencil and then a stack of paper and placed them in front of him on the desk. He started on the three lists that the sheriff and Hash wanted and was determined to finish quickly in order to look the names over himself.

As Hash and the sheriff left the building Hash asked him if he intended to escort the money from the train station to the bank as Reed had requested. Barnes indicated that he did and that also he considered Reed to be the best suited to dictate what happened as far as the money went. "If the president of the bank asks the sheriff to do something then I will gladly do it. He may not look the part but I have a great deal of respect for him. In all the years we have known each other the only problem we ever had was over a couple of evictions I was forced to participate in. But even they were signed by the judge and who am I to disagree?"

Hash looked toward the big swinging bridge and then asked. "Sheriff, what do you think of that Gregory Spurlock, do you trust him?"

"Not a damn bit Burton. There is something about the man that spooks me. He just doesn't fit in with this town or this county."

"I'll bet his name will be on two of the lists that Reed is probably preparing right now. Hell, he might even be on the one with the retired employees too," Hash said.

Barnes thought about this for a second and then said, "I would just about bet you a dollar bill on that one Burton. I'm going over to the jail to check on my prisoner and to see if I can find a deputy to lend a hand escorting that money of yours from the train to the bank. Damn sure would be an embarrassment on my part if one of your gold coins got misplaced."

Hash slapped the sheriff on the shoulder. "You sure got a way with words Sheriff. See you in a bit."

With that both men headed off in different directions, Hash toward the Depot and the sheriff toward his jail. Sheriff Barnes had made it about half way to the jail when he spotted one of his deputies heading his way in a hurry. By the time he got there the deputy was completely out of breath.

"Jake, what in the world is going on, you look plum tuckered out."

The deputy, who was bent over with both hands on his knees and completely out of breath finally managed to say, "It's the prisoner Sheriff, something has happened to him."

Barnes first though this meant he had somehow escaped. "What do you mean Jake; I can't imagine he has escaped from a brand new jail."

"No Sheriff, he is lying in the floor and throwing up something awful." By now Jake had somewhat caught his breath and was standing up looking at the sheriff.

"Did you leave him there all alone?"

"Naw Sheriff, Scrappy is there with him, I came straight here to find you to see what you wanted me to do."

"Go straight to the clinic and see if one of the doctors is there and tell him to come right over to the jail and bring his medical bag. I'll meet the both of you at the jail.

With that both men headed off in different directions, the sheriff running and Jake trotting along as fast as his burning lungs would allow. When Barnes got to the jail the front door was standing wide open. He went in to find the big iron door that separated the offices with the jail cells to also be open. The sheriff drew his gun and entered the common area of the cell block. There, standing in front of the occupied cell was Scrappy. On the floor of the cell was the prisoner and his face was as white as snow. It was apparent that he had thrown up everything in him and there was also a small amount of blood oozing from his mouth.

"What's going on here Scrappy, did you see anything before this happened?"

Scrappy looked at the sheriff and said, "It was terrible Sheriff, truly terrible. Me and Jake were in the next room when we heard coughing, a little at first so we didn't think much of it. But it didn't stop, just kept getting louder and louder. We both came in here and seen him holding both hands to his neck like he was struggling to get his breath. Jake told me to go back out and get the keys so we could open the cell. When he came back with the keys the prisoner came off his bunk and landed on his knees still holding his throat. I told Jake to not open that door just yet. I didn't want to go in there and possibly catch whatever it was he had. I think Jake had the same thought as me. Neither one of us had the guts to go in there. Then it dawned on me that maybe he was trying to pull a stunt to overpower one of us and take away a gun. You know, a way to escape. All of a sudden he started throwing up something awful. After a few minutes he just fell over and then I told Jake to run and fetch you."

Sheriff Barnes asked where the keys were and Scrappy reached them to him. "Here you go Sheriff, you intend on going in there?"

"Yes I do. By the looks of things he ain't in any shape to try and escape, hell it looks like he's dead anyway."

The sheriff took the biggest key on the ring and unlocked the door. He pulled his gun out of the holster and then cautiously entered the cell. Scrappy had pulled his gun and covered the sheriff for no other reason than to feel like he was doing something.

"Did he ever tell you his name Scrappy?"

"Naw Sheriff, he shore didn't. Me and old Jake just been calling him 'Bushwacker' you know for the way he and them other two shot that Riley feller and tried to do the same to Burton."

Just then Dr. Sables came running in with Jake hot on his heels. When he saw the way the prisoner was sprawled out on the floor with blood oozing from his mouth and nose he said, "Sheriff, you better come on outta there and let me have a look."

For Lack of a Title

Sheriff Barnes was more than happy to exit the cell and turn it over to the Doc. "Alright Sables, you can go in but we will be right outside the cell in case you need a hand with him."

Sables went in with his small case. He noticed the tray of food on the edge of the bed; it had what looked like only a few bites missing. He guessed that when the prisoner started feeling sick he sat the food down on the bed. Sables eased around the man careful not to step in any of the vomit or blood on the floor. He gently pressed two fingers into the side of the man's neck and waited.

"Is he dead Doc?" Scrappy asked.

Sables didn't answer at first, he just shot the deputy an annoyed look and then said, "You want to shut the hell up Scrappy or should I come out of here and let you take over?" The doctor had always hated it when something like this happened while a man was penned up like a wild animal. He also suspected that the deputies might have had a hand in whatever had happened to the prisoner. It wouldn't be the first time he had been sent for because a prisoner alone in a locked cell had the crap beat out of him. Until he figured out what happened he didn't want either of the two deputies to speak.

After a few more seconds he looked at the sheriff and said, "He's still alive but I suspect not for very long. His heart is beating eight or ten beats a minute but his breathing has completely stopped. I can't do anything for him because there is no apparent injuries to treat."

"If his heart is still beating then he might pull through, right Doc?" Jake asked.

"I don't think so. His heart is still beating but without oxygen it can't do it for long." Sables bent beside the man again and checked for a pulse, there wasn't one. The man was now officially dead.

When the doctor rose from the floor the sheriff asked, "Dead?"

Sables shook his head yes.

"Scrappy, you go and get the undertaker." With that the deputy left the cell room and was glad to be doing it. He had seen more than he cared to and wondered if he would ever be able to take another bite of food in his life. As he was heading out the front door he met a man carrying a tray of food covered with a white cloth.

"Howdy Scrappy, I brought breakfast for that prisoner you got in the jail, sorry I'm late. I been trying to get here for hours but every time I was about to leave we got busy, probably cause of the flood. You want me to wait for you to get back?"

Scrappy stopped dead in his tracks. He looked at the man holding the tray. "You say that's the tray of food for the prisoner's breakfast?" The man nodded that it was.

"Bring it on in and let me get the sheriff, just stay out here by the stove and I'll go fetch him, he's back in the cell area."

Scrappy rubbed his stubbly chin as he went into the back to get Sheriff Barnes. "Sheriff, I got a man out here that says he has the breakfast for the prisoner."

Dr. Sables and the sheriff both looked at Scrappy and then at the tray of food on the bed. "Doc, I think you better not touch anything else in here until we figure this thing out."

The doctor looked at Barnes and said, "I think we just figured it out Sheriff."

Barnes went out to the front room of the jail where he saw a man standing holding a covered tray of food.

"Howdy Bennie, what you got there?" The sheriff asked.

"Fern sent over breakfast for the prisoner Sheriff. This makes three days in a row I brought breakfast. Why is everyone acting so squirrely this morning? I know it's nearly noon but I been running late, I told Scrappy."

The sheriff looked at Scrappy. "Where did that tray in there come from?"

About this time Jake came out of the cell area and seen the second tray of food. "Howdy Bennie, how come Fern sent two trays this morning, we only got one prisoner, or at least we had one prisoner."

The sheriff gave Jake a look that could only mean one thing, 'Shut the hell up.' Jake knew he had said too much and returned to the cell room with the doctor.

"What's he talking about Sheriff? This is the only tray that's been sent over. You told us to send breakfast, lunch, and dinner each day and this here is the breakfast."

"Thanks Bennie, just set it over there on that chair beside my desk. I might be over in a little while to talk to you and Fern. For now though we got a little situation here and need to clear out the building."

Bennie scratched his head and then headed back to the Depot Café. When he left Barnes looked at Scrappy, "Where did that other tray of food come from and what time did it get here deputy?"

Scrappy hollered at Jake. "Hey Jake, what time did you find that tray of food this morning?"

Jake came from the back and looked at his pocket watch. "It must have been about nine o'clock this morning."

The sheriff looked at his pocket watch, it was past eleven o'clock. "What do you mean you found the tray Scrappy, didn't someone deliver it?"

Scrappy looked at Jake and then said, "Well Sheriff, it was delivered to the jail about nine this morning I suppose. I went outside to stretch and see what the day was looking like and there was the tray sitting on that bench out front. There was a note on it that read, *'Knocked but nobody came to door. Here is food for prisoner.'* Me and Jake figured we must have not heard him."

"What happened then?" The sheriff asked.

"Well, I brought the tray in and set it on the table by the stove over there. It must have been there ten minutes or so until Jake took it back to the cell for Bushwacker. He raised the cloth that had it covered and said for me to get a look at what a load of food. I walked over and let me tell you it was one of the best looking breakfasts I had ever seen. There were scrambled eggs with gravy and biscuit and a big piece of ham. We both wondered why a prisoner in our jail ate better than either of us ever did."

"After you took the tray back how long was it before the prisoner started coughing?" The sheriff asked.

"Oh, I don't know Sheriff, couldn't have been more than a few minutes. You say that would be about right Scrappy?" Jake asked.

"That's right Sheriff. No more had he gotten his food than he started coughing," Scrappy added.

The sheriff looked at both men and then at Dr. Sables who had now entered the room. "Did he say anything at all when he got his food or when he first started coughing?"

Both deputies thought about this for a minute. "You know Sheriff, he did say something about the pepper on his gravy. Something about he never seen so much pepper on gravy before, right Jake, ain't that what he said?"

Jake looked at the sheriff and added, "That's right, he did say that his gravy had an awful lot of pepper on it, and then he dug right in. Next thing you know he started coughing. What do you think happened to him Sheriff?"

Doctor Sables went in and retrieved the tray from the bunk and brought it out and sat it down on the big oak desk. All four men gathered around to have a look. The only thing that looked like it had been eaten was the gravy and a biscuit that had been crumbled up and stirred in. There were dark spots in the gravy, and a lot of them at that. Sables bent down and smelled the tray.

"It does have a peculiar odor, I can't quite make it out."

Barnes did the same and said, "You know Doc, I have to agree. That is it weirdest smelling gravy, here Scrappy, you and Jake see if you can identify that odor."

Both men bent and sniffed the contents of the tray. Neither knew what it was but Jake said, "I do smell the pepper. It is strong, like too much of it was put on. There is something else mixed in with the pepper smell but I don't know what it is."

The sheriff looked at Sables and asked, "Doc, by the look on your face I think you got an idea."

Doctor Sables looked at the sheriff and said, "Yea I do. Someone put a lot of pepper on the food to try and hide the scent of the poison they used to kill your prisoner. Pepper can do that you know."

Scrappy said *poison* as he and Jake backed away from the tray.

"That's right poison, and my guess is they used arsenic."

Barnes asked the next question without taking his eyes off the tray, "Why do you think it's arsenic Doc?"

"Arsenic is a white crystalline compound. It can be ground into a very fine powder as long as you don't breathe any of it in. My guess is that whoever done this put the powder in the gravy and then smothered it with pepper to hide the smell.

From the looks of things it worked out pretty well. I doubt though that they needed to disguise the poison at all. It doesn't have any taste and the white color would have just looked like part of the gravy."

Scrappy chimed in, "Yea, unless you're old Bushwacker in there. That ended up being his last meal."

Both Jake and Scrappy laughed until Barnes decided to put the two to doing something useful.

"Scrappy don't you have a little errand that I asked you to do earlier?"

"That's right, the undertaker. Sorry Sheriff, I'll go and fetch him right now."

"Jake, I need you to find Hansen and get him to go with you to the Depot to wait on that seven o'clock train," the sheriff said. "You know, the one that's three or four hours late."

Jake protested, "Hansen's been up all night guarding the prisoner, he probably ain't been home long enough to even fall asleep yet."

"I know that, but get him anyway. When you get to the depot you tell Hash Burton that I will be along as soon as I can, we got a little problem here at the jail. And Jake, grab two shotguns out of the gun cabinet there and twenty rounds of double-aught buckshot. You and Hansen might need to look a little more fearsome this morning."

This got the deputy's attention, "You expecting trouble over at the depot Sheriff?"

"The way this day is going Jake you just never know."

"I heard that Sheriff. I'll grab them two new Greener shotguns if you don't mind. I always like the way a Greener feels." Jake grabbed the two shotguns along with a box of shells and hurried down the street to the place where Hansen lived, which was a room he rented over the General Store.

That left Sheriff Barnes and Doctor Sables, along with one dead prisoner. "Doc, you got any ideas on how something could kill a man after just a few minutes? It looks like it must have taken hold of him pretty fast. He hadn't eaten more than a bite or two."

The doctor walked back to the big door that led to the cell rooms and said, "It is a very potent substance Sheriff. It's used to kill bugs and rodents, and even then it isn't full strength, it's thinned substantially. After he took the first bite he was done for but didn't know it. After another bite or two his throat started to hemorrhage." Sables noticed the inquisitive look on the sheriff's face. "His neck started to bleed. He then became very nauseated and started throwing up everything he had in him. That also contributes to the damage the poison is doing. As he gagged on his own blood he forced the poison back up so forcefully that it even came out his nose. You can tell by the blood coming from both his nostrils."

Sables looked from the cell where the dead man lay toward the sheriff. He noticed that Barnes looked a little pale and was about to get sick himself. "Sheriff, you look like you might have had a little biscuit and gravy yourself. Are you feeling alright?"

"Not really Doc. Just stop giving me all the nasty details and I think I'll be fine."

Doctor Sables laughed and wondered how it came to be that things of this nature didn't bother him anymore. He knew he had become desensitized after all his years of work. Just as he was about to say something else Scrappy came running in and said, "Doc, you better get back to the clinic, Doctor Barnes said he needs you real bad."

"Sheriff, I will be back later. Have the undertaker take that body in there to his preparation room but warn him to not touch any fluids that are on the floor or on the body. That stuff can still make you sick if you get it on your skin. Also take that tray of food and destroy it in a hot fire, tray and all. Do it now and don't let any of it get on you either. Later today I want to do a more thorough examination at the undertaker's office." With that Sable was out the door and heading down the boardwalk at a trot.

"Scrappy, were you able to get word to the undertaker?"

"Naw Sheriff, Doctor Barnes nabbed me as I was walking by the clinic, you want me to go back?"

"Yes deputy I do. And this makes the third time you've tried, if you don't bring back the undertaker this time I'm going to hold back a day's pay on you."

Scrappy laughed as he turned to leave the jail, "Don't you worry about me Sheriff; I will bring him back this time or else."

Sheriff Barnes walked over and looked back into the cell room. It must have been a terrible way for a man to die, choking to death while some evil poison ate your insides out. In all the confusion and excitement he hadn't even asked if either Jake or Scrappy had seen who had left the tray out front. Thank goodness a child hadn't walked by and smelled the food under the cloth. Right then and there Sheriff Barnes decided he would go out of his way to find out who done it and instead of a trial he might slip in a little old fashioned hanging if he could do it without too many people finding out.

He closed the big iron door that separated the cell rooms from the front lobby. As he walked over to his desk he looked again at the food on the tray. It looked no different than any other breakfast he had seen brought to the jail over the years other than it was so neat and abundant. Most jail meals were just average but this one was exceptional in appearance. He supposed that whoever put the tray together wanted the prisoner to dig right in. Thank goodness one of the previous deputies wasn't still on the payroll. That particular deputy had a bad habit of sampling the food before he took it to the prisoners. Said he was checking for poison. He would have found it this time.

Suddenly Barnes heard fast footsteps on the front boardwalk. In ran Scrappy completely out of breath.

"Sheriff, you better get over to the clinic fast, something has happened over there."

Barnes grabbed his hat and asked, "What do you mean?"

"As I was on my way to fetch the undertaker Dr. Sables came out of the clinic and said to find you quick and for you to come straight there."

"Damn. What else can happen this morning? You stay here and for heaven's sake don't touch that tray on my desk. Keep everyone out of here until I get back." With that the sheriff took off at a fast trot.

The clinic was no more than a ten minute walk from the jail but the Sheriff made it in half that time. The front door was open and a few people were standing out front talking. It was apparent that these people must have been in the clinic's waiting area and were ushered outside. Barnes heard a woman say, *here comes the sheriff, it must be bad.* He didn't stop to ask questions. The front room was empty so he walked over and looked down the long hallway. He could hear one of the doctors in the back talking but couldn't tell which one it was.

The sheriff walked down and knocked on the door at the end. He heard Sables say, *maybe that's the sheriff.* The door swung open and the sheriff was hit with a strong odor similar to soured milk. The two doctors were wearing cloth masks that tied around the back of their heads. Sables said, "Here Sheriff, you better hold this over your mouth" as he reached one of the cloth masks to him. "Come on in so I can close the door."

Inside, lying on the examination table was a man in rough range type clothes. He seemed to be unconscious but breathing. The floor at the end of the table was covered in vomit and a small amount of blood.

"What happened here Doc?" the sheriff asked.

Dr. Barnes had a bucket and was trying to scoop up the mess with a small broom and dustpan. Dr. Sables said, "Looks like we found the man who delivered that poison tray to the jail, or should I say he found us. He got here while I was up at the jail and Dr. Barnes was here looking after Riley. Said he complained with shortness of breath and upset stomach. Said he just couldn't breathe. By the time Barnes got him in here he started throwing up. Barnes went to the front door to find someone to come get me and that's when he saw Scrappy going by. You know the rest of that story.

"When I got here the coughing fit had gotten worse and then it looks like he passed out. I first thought he was dead but he wasn't. His heart rate is low and his breathing is labored but at least being unconscious has suppressed his cough reflex."

Sheriff Barnes paced around the room and thought about the events of the morning. "So you think this man had something to do with the killing at the jail?"

Dr. Barnes looked up from his cleaning and said, "What killing at the jail?" It was apparent that in all the commotion since Dr. Sables had returned from the jail there hadn't been time to share that piece of information between the two.

"Got the same thing at the jail, the prisoner they got down there ate some food I suspect was laced with arsenic. This man has all the same symptoms as the other one with one exception, he's still alive. I suspect he ingested some of the dust as they were grinding the crystals into a powder form. That is a very dangerous poison," Sables said and then added. "If anyone else was in the room when they were fixing that tray then they will be sick too, all depends on the amount of exposure."

"I need this man alive if at all possible Doc. If he can give me some information on who else is involved then it might shed some light on a few other things that have been going on around town. You think you can save him?" the sheriff asked.

Both doctors looked at each other. "Depends on the amount he breathed in. From the looks of things though I would say he won't last long. He's bleeding on the inside Sheriff. If he got enough to cause that then it's still working on him right now," Sables said.

The sheriff looked at his pocket watch and saw that it was now just past noon. At the moment he needed to be at three places at once. He put his watch away and turned to leave. Just before going out the door he turned back to the two doctors. "Do all you can for him that is if anything can be done? I was supposed to be over at the depot about an hour and a half ago. If anything else happens send for me. I'll be somewhere between the depot and the bank." With that he turned and left. The two doctors knew there was nothing more they could do.

As Sheriff Barnes went by the jail he stepped in to check on Scrappy. The deputy was sitting in the sheriff's chair holding a gun on the tray that sat on top of the desk. "What the hell are you doing Scrappy?"

The deputy quickly put his gun away. "Sorry Sheriff, I was just having a little fun. I figured that tray of food was probably the most dangerous thing I ever run up against since you gave me my badge. I was just making sure it didn't try anything." Scrappy laughed a little as he said this.

"Well, I'm having me a pretty damn bad day Scrappy and I don't want any more of your bullshit, you hear me?"

The deputy nodded that he understood.

"I'm on my way to the depot. I want you to go and fetch the undertaker and this time unless another Civil War breaks out you better bring him back. Make sure you tell him to not touch any of the liquids in there. Lock the front door as you leave so no one else gets in here, and set both those trays in the floor and scoot both under my desk." With that the sheriff was gone.

When he got to the bank on the way to the depot he eased his pace a little. He fully expected to meet Burton and Jake before he got there. Then he realized that he hadn't heard the train whistle indicating that it had arrived. He looked at his pocket watch again and saw that it was ten minutes past noon. As he walked on he remembered that he had heard the Presbyterian Church bell ring a few minutes ago, past noon and still no train. As he approached the big suspension bridge he could hear the flood waters. Once at the first concrete and stone pier he could see the fast moving water. He had lived in and around Prestonsburg all his life and had never seen the river this high.

When he was younger he had heard his grandfather talk of a flood in the early eighteen twenties that had covered the entire town. Back then there were only a handful of log homes and a few wooden structures used for commerce so the damage wasn't as bad as a flood of that size might cause now. About halfway across the bridge Barnes could see both up and down river for a great distance. The river was truly enormous and was still a week from reaching its crest. Another ten feet and it would start to flood some of the lower portions of town. These were parts where people gardened and had some livestock penned up. It would need to get another ten feet taller again to actually start giving the townsfolk problems. It just might make it.

Once across the bridge he could look down the tracks and see that there wasn't a train in sight. He did see Burton and Jake sitting on the dock in some chairs they had drug out from inside the building. Hash saw the sheriff coming and got up in order to meet him before he actually got to the depot, "I heard you had some trouble at the jail Sheriff."

"That's right Burton. Been a lot going on today, I guess Jake told you about the prisoner."

"Yes Sheriff he did. Did you ever get any information out of him, or for that matter even his name?"

"Not a damn thing. The deputies have been calling him 'Bushwacker.'"

"Under the circumstances I would say that name fit him pretty good," Hash said.

"You ain't heard the half of it Burton. The two doctors got another one at the clinic and he might just die like the first one. What's been going on here, did I miss anything?" the sheriff asked.

"Yeah Sheriff, that's why I came over here to talk to you, didn't want everyone at the depot to hear what I got to share with you. It appears that the train was late this morning because someone tried to waylay it somewhere between some towns called Paints Bill and Louisa. The telegram that Jeremy Eisner received about two hours ago was from a depot down in Johnson County. Said the train got shot up pretty good but they should be able to make it here within the," Hash looked at his pocket watch, "the next thirty or forty minutes.

"One more thing Sheriff, the telegram said to expect causalities and to have a doctor here along with a wagon to transport some of the injured to the clinic," Hash told him.

The sheriff hollered over to the men sitting on the loading platform, "Jake, come over here for a second."

He looked at Hash and said, "I know the town Burton and it's called Paintsville. I have never heard of an attempted train robbery around here before though. You think they were after that shipment you told Reed about?"

"Eisner said the train was all coal cars along with a single passenger car. He said the freight on that train was mostly mining stuff, nothing to rob a train for. So yes Sheriff, my guess is that they were after the cash and gold. What I can't figure is how anybody except a few here in town even knew the money would be on that train," Hash said.

"You figure anyone up your way might have tipped off the robbers about that delivery Burton?"

"No way Sheriff, we were very cautious about when and on which train the money would arrive. The three Baldwin-Felts men accompanying it are professionals. Their organization knows how to carry out deliveries like this; they do it all the time in the Northeast."

The sheriff thought a minute and then added, "Then it has to be someone from here. Let me talk to Jake a minute."

Just then Jake walked up and said, "You need me boss?"

"Yes Jake, I need you to go to the clinic and tell one of the doctors that we got some injured people coming in on the train and I need him to head this way with his medical stuff. And find an empty wagon with a team already attached and bring it over here as soon as you can. We need it to transport the wounded to the clinic. Tell the doc that I don't know how bad it is but to come prepared. Go by the jail and tell Scrappy to find the other off duty deputies and get them on the streets."

"Sure thing Sheriff, you want I should hurry?"

The sheriff said in a voice that indicated his mind was somewhere else, "I think so Jake, I think a little hurry is just what we need right now."

As Jake walked toward the big suspension bridge the sheriff continued to run things through his mind. "Burton, if you say that no one knew about the delivery today except me, you and the bank then something is really starting to stink at that bank, what do you say?"

Hash was way ahead of the Barnes. "The one thing I can't figure Sheriff is how they got word out of here and down river that far to set up the robbery."

"Had to be a telegram Burton, what do you say me and you go have us a little talk with Eisner?"

The two turned and headed toward the depot, both running ideas through their minds and trying to find a solution. When they entered the only sound inside the room was the click, click, and click of the telegraph keys. Eisner was at his writing table putting to paper what the sounds meant. When the noise stopped he put down his pencil and reread what he had written. Only when he finished did he look up at the sheriff and Burton. This at first startled the young man, he wondered if he was in trouble.

The sheriff spoke first. Before he did he made sure the door to the loading platform was shut. "Eisner, do you keep a log of all the telegraph traffic you send and receive during the day?"

Eisner didn't speak he just held up a black bound notebook, it was a thick one.

Hash reached for the book but before he could get it Eisner pulled it back. "This is the log book, but it's against company policy for anyone other than me or another telegraph operator to see it."

Hash frowned at Eisner and also raised his eyebrows. Eisner knew that Hash had caught him reading stuff in the mail bag but he wasn't going to break the most sacred rule of all, revealing what was sent and received on his telegraph unless it was addressed to the one asking.

Hash looked at the sheriff and asked, "Now what Sheriff. I don't know if we can get a judge to sign an order in time to help us or not?"

The sheriff reached across the counter and said, "Give me that damn book Eisner." He snatched it out of the startled man's hands and turned it around so both he and Hash could see inside. Both looked at the page for yesterday and scanned for names that might shed some light on the problem. Both stopped when they read the name *'Greg Spurlock, three-ten.'*

Hash looked at Eisner and said, "Does the three-ten designate the time Eisner?" He knew if it did then it was P.M. since the telegraph in this town was closed at night.

"Yes sir it does. I ain't going to lose my job over this am I?"

Sheriff Barnes looked at the nervous youth and said, "No Eisner. You are helping with an official Sheriff's Department investigation. If anything you might be commended." The Sheriff was just bullshitting him, but it did put the young man at ease.

Hash now asked what both he and the Sheriff wanted to know, "Do you still have the note that you sent the telegraph from Eisner?"

"No sir. He made sure he took it with him when he left. As he was walking back across the bridge I saw him throw it in the river."

"Well do you remember what the message said and who it was addressed to?" the sheriff asked.

"You know Sheriff, in the three years I been doing this I have never seen such strange messages. Every time he sends something it is just a bunch of gibberish. I can't make heads or tails of it. And as far as who he sends them to that is usually someone different each time. This one was for someone in Ashland by the name of Collins I believe." Eisner thought for a minute and then added. "That's right Sheriff, it was Collins, A. L. Collins." Eisner now smiled, happy that he had remembered the name.

"What do you make of that Burton?" Barnes asked.

"It's a code Sheriff. He has been using coded messages and unless we can find someone who knows that code then we will never know what the message said."

Barnes looked at Eisner and then at Hash. "I don't know what the coded message said Burton but I got a pretty good idea of what it meant."

"Sheriff, we need to take a further look at that telegraph log book and see if there were any more messages that might correspond with any of the other mischief that has been going on in town since I arrived."

"That's a good idea Burton, but right now we got bigger things to attend to, here comes the train."

The sheriff walked out onto the platform followed by Hash and sure enough in the distance downriver the engine came into view. She was going slow and not making a lot of noise. As she got closer steam could be seen escaping the right hand side of the engine. "That doesn't look right Sheriff," Eisner said.

It was a good thing the steam was escaping the opposite side of the engine or the loading platform would have been a pretty dangerous place to be at the moment. As the train slowed it passed the platform and then stopped so the passenger car was adjacent to the depot, before it completely stopped, a man wearing a tied down gun and also carrying a Winchester rifle stepped to the platform. He looked around until he saw the badge that Barnes was wearing and asked, "You the Sheriff?"

"I am, names Barnes. How bad is it?"

"Pretty bad Sheriff, we got two men killed and a few more injured. Do you have a doctor?"

"We do and he is on his way now. Were there any women or children on the train?"

"Not a one Sheriff. I think the big water has a lot of people scared, and that is the only good piece of good news out of all this. There was me and my two associates, both dead now, and five other men, three of them have injuries. The worst I'm afraid might not make it."

Hash stepped closer. "Did I hear you correctly; the two men with you were killed?"

The man looked at Burton. "That's right, both shot by whoever it was that tried to hold up the train."

Just then Dr. Sables arrived along with a wagon being pulled by a team of mules. "How bad is it Sheriff?" the doctor asked as he climbed down from the wagon.

"Pretty bad Doc, got three wounded men on the train and I reckon one is pretty seriously hurt," Barnes said.

The doctor didn't say another word; he just walked over and climbed onto the passenger car.

When Doctor Sables boarded the car he was astonished at the scene inside, it was pure carnage. The windows were nearly all shot out and the wooden trim and seats were splintered with multiple bullet holes. On the floor there were empty bullet casings and lots and lots of blood. He saw one man slumped in a seat and looked to be unconscious. Two more were trying to assist another man who was stretched out in the center isle of the passenger car. This one appeared to be in the worst shape.

"How many of you are injured?" He asked.

One of the two men, a tall angular fellow with a mustache turned and asked, "Are you a doctor?"

"That's right, I'm Dr. Sables."

"We got three men that have been shot. This one we got stretched out here is the worst. The other two are not so bad." The man stepped aside so Dr. Sables could move closer.

Sables looked at the man and determined quickly that he had been shot twice. Once low in the shoulder and again in the upper thigh. The two men had managed to stop the bleeding from the leg wound by placing a white pillow casing over the wound and then tying it in place with another pillow casing. The shoulder was a different story altogether. The two men had used whatever else they could find for bandages and Sable could tell that blood still oozed from the wound. He eased the man onto his side to look at his back and found the exit wound, which was also bleeding slightly but not nearly as bad as the entry point.

"We couldn't stop the bleeding Doc; all we could do was slow it down. The exit wound in his back wasn't so bad so we tried more to work on the front," the man with the mustache said.

Sables reached into his bag and pulled out a hunk of bandage and began to unroll it. He tore off a small portion and with his index finger he pressed it into the bullet hole. The bleeding stopped. "What's your name?" he asked the man with the mustache.

"Name's Lester Clay, you think he's gonna make it? I tried to do everything I knew how but I don't think I done so good."

Doctor Sables stood up and said, "With any luck he just might make it, he's lost a lot of blood though. He would have lost more if you hadn't stepped in and tried to stop it. If he does live it will be more because of what you did than me. Go to the front of the car and get some help in here, we need to get these men loaded onto that wagon out there and moved to the clinic as fast as possible." The doctor could tell that Clay was disturbed either by the shootout earlier or his feeling of helplessness as he watched a man possibly bleed to death. Sables was used to death from all his years of battling the Grim Reaper and mostly losing. As Clay headed for the stairs of the car Dr. Sables said, "You done good Clay, real good." He hoped this made the young man feel better.

Lester Clay went out the end of the passenger car and down the steps. He saw a man wearing a badge and told him what the doctor said. Soon there were three or four men in the rail car gently moving the injured outside. Sables stayed inside and oversaw what and how the men were moved. As soon as they were loaded up he climbed in the back of the wagon with his patients. He instructed the driver to move slowly but hurry.

"Now how the hell do you spect me to do that Doc? I can do one or the other but not both," the driver said.

Sheriff Barnes now chimed in, "Get that wagon moving Prescott, and do it just like the doctor said, 'Slow but Hurry.'"

The man named Prescott released the wooden handle that kept the wagon from moving and then tapped one of the mules with a long stick. As the wagon pulled out everyone could hear him talking to his two mules, "You heard the man boys, slow but fast, so Cob why don't you go fast and Short Shank you go slow and let's just see what we get."

As the wagon moved off the sheriff went inside to have a look at the passenger car with Hash right behind him. "This thing is shot all to hell Burton. I saw a lot of bullet holes on the outside of the car but this looks worse. Most of the shots must have come through the windows."

The other Baldwin-Felts man came in last. Down about halfway of the car was a body laying sprawled in the center aisle. At the far end by the back entrance was another one, both wearing the same black uniform that designated they were Detectives with the agency. The two men on the train that had survived the ambush were gathering what they could find of their belongings. One of the men must have had his suitcase in an overhead compartment and the latch was shot off. As he struggled to retrieve it the lid flipped open and everything inside spilled onto the bloody floor.

"I'm afraid you can't take anything from the train at the moment gentlemen," the sheriff said.

"Why not Sheriff?" the man with the mustache asked?

"This is a crime scene. Everything that happened here will need to be documented and the contents of the car cataloged to determine what belongs to who."

"But Sheriff we've been through a lot and I don't want to spend any more time on this train. All I want to do is get my suitcase and get on into town," the man said.

Hash knew why the sheriff wanted everything to remain on the train, to make sure the money and gold hadn't been tampered with. "Sheriff if I may, why don't we let these two men gather what they say is theirs and then take them into the train depot. You or a deputy can inspect what they say is theirs and document it. They can leave their names and where they will be staying with you and if they are needed further then we know where they can be found. That might help to speed them on their way," Hash said.

The sheriff thought about this for a minute and said, "Sure Burton. These men have been through a lot. Alright you two, grab your belongings and head into the depot building. I'll have one of my deputies get the information we need and a list of what you are taking off the train."

The two men smiled and quickly grabbed their suitcases. The sheriff saw Jake standing on the platform. Barnes leaned out a window, careful not to cut himself on the broken glass and told him what to do with the two men who were getting off the train. Jake herded the two men inside the depot and then Barnes turned back to Hash.

"This must have been a hell of a gun battle Burton. Of the eight men on board only three escaped without injury." No one spoke for a while as they took in the damage to the car.

Again the sheriff spoke, "With all the bullet holes it's a wonder that everyone in the car wasn't killed."

Burton looked up at the sheriff and said, "Too bad we missed it Sheriff. A couple more guns might have made all the difference."

"It might have at that Burton. What do you want to do about your delivery? I need to get it transported to the bank and then get these two dead detectives off the train before it gets too late."

Hash turned to the last surviving member and asked, "What is your name if I may ask? "Hash had chosen the three men from their reputations but hadn't actually met them.

The detective, who had been looking at his two dead associates, turned back toward the sheriff and Hash and said, "Mack Ramsey, I am the senior Detective on this trip. We were never warned of a possible ambush of the train or we could have had more men assigned. These were real good men. They died doing what they loved and that was being detectives. I guess no man can ask for more than that."

Hash and Barnes shook their heads in agreement.

After enough time had passed the sheriff asked, "Is the cargo you brought with you still secure Ramsey?"

Ramsey reached under a few of the seats and pulled out six suitcases, they were large and square, more like crates. All were dark brown leather and each had two heavy straps that went completely around and buckled at the top. Each case had a brass padlock attached to a heavy hasp. As each one was slid out Ramsey stood it in an upright position. Other than a couple of bullet holes in various places, mostly the top and bottom, they looked secure. When finished Ramsey pulled a paper from his vest pocket and reached it to Hash.

"This is what they gave us in Philadelphia three days ago when we picked up the six cases. I was present when the contents were packed. The count is correct and matches what is on the packing receipt you have there in your hand." He had been looking at the sheriff as he said this and Hash noticed.

"You can feel free to say anything in front of the Sheriff here. He and I have been through a lot in the last several days and I would trust him with my life," Hash said.

The sheriff was surprised at such a compliment. He stuck out his hand to Ramsey and said, 'My name is Barnes, Sheriff Barnes." As they shook Barnes said, "I will need you to fill us in on the events of the ambush Mr. Ramsey. We don't have time now but maybe you could come by my office and we can discuss it later today or even tomorrow. I would like to know everything that happened from the first shot until the last." Just as he was saying this he remembered the body in the jail and the poison fluids all over the floor."

Ramsey said, "Please call me Mack. Is there a hotel or a boarding house in town that you could recommend? I want to get cleaned up. I feel like blood and gunpowder right now."

"Got two or three around that might be sufficient but remember we are not New York."

Hash looked at the sheriff and said. "We'll need to get the undertaker over here. And then there is the matter of transporting the six bags to the bank." He looked at his bill of lading. The total weight of the six cases was two hundred and seventeen pounds. He knew it would be cumbersome to carry six cases, each weighing approximately thirty five pounds, from the depot to the bank. A wagon was needed. "And we probably need a wagon Sheriff. I don't think it would be safe to carry this much money any other way."

"Right Burton, tell you what, how about I go to the clinic and have that wagon sent back over after they wash the blood out of it, or I can get the undertaker myself and as he transports Ramsey's two men to the morgue he can drop off the six bags, with our supervision of course." Barnes said.

Hash looked at the Baldwin-Felts Detective and said, "Maybe we should use different wagons for the transportation.

These two men gave their lives and I think the extra effort is the least we can do Sheriff."

The Sheriff was a little embarrassed. "You're right Burton; sometimes I get a little complacent and try to figure the quickest way to get something done. As much death as I have seen this week it's a wonder I can think straight at all." He looked at Ramsey. "I can assure you that I meant no disrespect. I was just trying to get too many things done as soon as possible."

"Think nothing of it Sheriff. I can see that things around here are a little edgy right now."

The sheriff turned and headed for the undertaker's office. The engineer and his fireman were at the side of the engine trying to see what kind of damage had been done when a stray bullet from the gun battle had hit the right hand side and breached a steam tube. The amount of steam that had been escaping when the train entered the depot was slowly decreasing as the firebox cooled. As Barnes walked to that side of the engine he asked, "Did either of you get hurt during all the shooting?"

The engineer looked up from his work and saw the sheriff. "Naw Sheriff, me and old McCloud here just ducked for cover and hoped for the best."

"When the shooting started did you try to gain speed in order to outrun the men on horseback who were shooting at you?"

"Couldn't Sheriff, first shot punched a hole in this here high pressure steam pipe, I actually had to reduce speed to keep from splitting this tube wide open. Whoever tried to rob us knew exactly where to hit us. And I'll tell you something else Sheriff, whoever did this must have brought a big bore Winchester with them; say a .45-.75 big game gun. It would take a gun like that to breach this steam pipe. Regular Winchester wouldn't do it. The steel is just too thick."

"You think they came prepared to disable the engine?" Barnes asked.

"That's exactly what I'm saying Sheriff. We would have been sitting ducks. Me and McCloud kept nursing her along while that gun battle raged and let me tell you it was some kind of battle. I knew that if we stopped then them men in the passenger car were goners and if that happened, then me and McCloud were goners too. They would have killed us for sure to eliminate any witnesses, ain't that right McCloud?"

"Right!" was all the big fireman said.

Barnes turned and headed for the suspension bridge. As he crossed he was again amazed at the height of the river, and the noise it made was truly as scary as a nightmare. Fast moving water and all the runoff from the surrounding streams made for quite a show. When he made it to the jail he went inside to see what had happened while he was gone. The undertaker had come by and retrieved the body from the cell; Scrappy was scrubbing the floor with a mop and some strong bleach he had gotten from the General Store.

"What did you do with the tray of food Scrappy?" Barnes asked.

Scrappy looked up from his work and said. "I took it to the incinerator out by the river; you know the one where the city burns their garbage?"

"What about the tray, it wouldn't burn and everyone knows not to put metal in there."

"Well Sheriff, I thought about that long and hard. I knew it couldn't be put in the incinerator and for that matter it might come in pretty handy if we see another one like it, might give us a lead. Anyway I held my nose and banged it against the side so all the food would fall in the fire. Then I brought it back here and got it soaking in a bucket of strong bleach out back. It ought to be in good enough shape to handle but I don't think it ever ought to be used for food again. I thought after I dry it off I might get some paint and draw a skull and crossbones on it. Like I said, it might come in real handy as a piece of evidence."

Sheriff Barnes was truly impressed. "That was pretty good thinking Scrap. You might make a fine detective, especially if you would learn to read and write. Let that scrubbing go for a while. Me and you got some work to do."

Scrappy put down his mop and headed out the front door with the sheriff. He followed Barnes up the street to the clinic. Sitting out front was the wagon with the two mule team. The driver was cleaning out the back when the two walked up. He told the man to head back over to the depot and pick up six heavy bags and then to wait there until he and Scrappy arrived to help escort the cargo back to the bank.

The old hostler's eyes lit up, "We going to transport that train load of gold to the bank Sheriff?"

"Something like that, how long before you can move out?"

"Right now Sheriff, this has been an exciting day and it ain't over yet wouldn't you say?"

The old man climbed into the seat and released the brake. "Giddy up Cob, get some move on Short Shank, we gonna haul us some gold. You two are shore getting up in society. Bet none of your poor old mule friends ever hauled a wagon load of gold before."

Barnes and Scrappy watched as the wagon turned and went around the corner. Even out of sight they could still hear the old Hostler talking to Cob and Short Shank.

213

"We better get the move on Scrap. I want to get the undertaker and then head back over to the depot as soon as possible."

Scrappy looked at the sheriff. "Undertaker, don't tell me we got more trouble at the depot."

"We do, got two more bodies over there on the train."

"Hells got buttons Sheriff. I should have been an undertaker. That business has really picked up since your friend Hash Burton came to town."

"What makes you think he's my friend Scrap?"

"I don't know Sheriff, he ain't such a bad guy from what I can tell but he sure does have a way of piling up dead men. As much grief as seems to follow him around he needs a sheriff with him everywhere he goes. That's all I'm saying."

"I know what you mean Scrap. This is the most bloodshed I can remember in the history of this town, maybe even this county. Were any of the other deputies in today while I was gone?"

"Yea, they was. I told them to patrol the town and see if they came across any strangers that were coughing their heads off, and if they found any to come and tell me or to go and find you."

The sheriff looked over at Scrappy. He was truly impressed. "That was really good thinking Scrap. How the hell did you get to be so smart all the sudden?"

"Oh it wasn't nothing Sheriff. I knew you were busy today so I thought I would do some of the thinking for ya."

"Well that was some fine thinking at that Scrap. You just keep on doing that and some day they might just elect you as the new Sheriff. That is if you ever learn to read and write, we talked about it remember."

For Lack of a Title

"Well Sheriff, you know how to read and write and I done out thunk you all over the place today," Scrappy said and then started laughing."

Sheriff Barnes looked at his laughing, and slobbering, old deputy and said, "Out thunk, did I really hear you say something like that. If I ever use the word 'thunk' instead of 'think' then you won't have to run for Sheriff, I'll just give you the damn badge."

At this Scrappy lost his breath laughing and then said, "I thunk you done got yourself a deal Sheriff." Barnes could only shake his head.

It only took a few minutes to make it to the undertaker's office. It was right in front of the largest cemetery in town, which the undertaker also owned. Barnes noticed two men up on the hill digging a grave. In the last week there were more than a few new graves on that hill. Scrap was right, business was good. They both went in the front room but there wasn't anyone there. Voices could be heard coming from the back. Barnes and Scrappy went through the back door into the preparation room.

Dr. Sables looked up from his work and said, "Hello Sheriff, hello Scrap, anything I can help you two with?"

It appeared that the doctor was doing an autopsy on the prisoner who had died in his cell that very morning. As Barnes stepped closer he noticed that the doctor and the undertaker had cut the man's chest open and were looking inside. Barnes quickly stopped and stepped back to the door. Sables noticed this.

"It's alright Sheriff. I researched some manuals in my office this morning. Arsenic becomes less potent after it becomes wet, and also can't become airborne anymore. Me and the undertaker here are using these new rubber gloves Dr. Barnes

215

ordered a few months ago, until now we haven't had an opportunity to put them to use. I read that this poison can still be absorbed through the skin so we are being real careful."

"What are you looking for Doc?" the sheriff asked.

"Well Sheriff, that other man who came to the clinic coughing this morning is still alive but in pretty bad shape. I couldn't find anything about arsenic poisoning and how to treat it. Apparently everyone who takes it dies. For the moment we have that patient who breathed in the powder and is still alive. This created a very intriguing situation. If I can determine what damage is caused by the poison then I might possibly be able to help that poor man in the clinic." After Doctor Sables finished talking he turned his attention back to his ghoulish work.

"That poor man as you refer to him helped murder a prisoner of mine this morning. If he does survive then I expect him to give me the names of anyone else that might have taken part in their mischief."

Dr. Sables knew that his duties and the sheriff's differed in a lot of ways, but he wasn't going to be talked down to. "Don't lecture me on the morals, or should I say the lack of them, of society Sheriff Barnes. My job is to help all and in the process if I can discover something new then that is exactly what I intend to do."

The Sheriff and Dr. Sables had a long standing friction between them. Each would thrust and the other would parry. "Well Doctor, you do what you feel is right but right now I need the undertaker over at the depot to remove the two Baldwin-Felts men. Before he left the room he looked back at Sables. "Shouldn't you be looking after the three wounded men you just brought from the train?"

Sables looked up from his work. "Dr. Barnes is over there now. The two men that were only slightly injured have been bandaged and are resting. As for the other fellow, it was a clean wound. It was a quick job to stitch him up and apply bandages. He too is resting but the loss of blood is troubling, he should pull through alright though with any luck. Is there any other advice you require Sheriff or are we finished?"

"Finished," the Sheriff said as he turned and exited the room. Sables watched him go.

The undertaker, Herb Shufflebarger took off the rubber gloves the doctor had brought for him and laid them in the wash basin. "Them gloves are a trick Sables. You mind if I keep em, might come in handy on some of my duties."

"Sure Herb, I thought you might like them. When Barnes placed the order he said that you could use a pair so they belong to you now."

"Thanks Doc, well I better get the wagon and head over there. I already got it hitched up and ready to go."

"Why did you hitch it up Herb, you didn't know there would be any bodies to pick up today?" The dead man they were working on had been carried over on a stretcher.

"Just a feeling I get sometimes. When that feeling hits me then I latch old Josephine up to the wagon and then an hour or two later I get a body," Shufflebarger said.

Doctor Sables looked up from the body he was working on and said, "Are you for real Herb?"

"Believe me or don't believe me, but it's true," the undertaker said.

"Well if you ever get that feeling around me then please leave, I don't want to give you my own personal business, at least not for thirty or forty more years anyway," the doctor said.

Herb went out the door laughing. Sables quickly finished up with the autopsy and headed for the clinic. He wanted to write down his findings and also to check on the five patients that now occupied different rooms.

Sheriff Barnes went to the clinic after he left the undertaker's office. He wasn't mad about the little exchange he and Dr. Sables had just had. It was something the two had been doing for years. Barnes felt it helped to keep him on his toes. He actually liked the doctor.

When he entered the front room of the clinic he saw no one. Stepping around the corner he noticed Rebecca and her father in the kitchen, both were holding coffee cups.

"Howdy Sheriff," Doctor Barnes said to his cousin. "Didn't expect to see you today with all the trouble the town seems to be having. You got time for a cup of coffee?"

Sheriff Barnes grabbed a cup from the counter and filled it with coffee. "I just stopped by to check up on things. Dr. Sables says that the other poisoning victim is still alive. Can I talk to him?"

"Sure thing Sheriff, you can talk to him all you want but he won't be able to answer you."

"Is he asleep?" The sheriff asked.

"No he ain't asleep, he's dead."

Rebecca knew her father was tired and when he was really tired he didn't care what he said.

"You will have to excuse my father Sheriff; he loses any bedside manners he ever had when he's overworked. The man you spoke of died about thirty minutes ago. I was going to go over and get Herb but dad wanted me to wait until Dr. Sables got back. With four patients here that are not in need of the undertaker he felt that he might need me."

"Well, the undertaker isn't there now anyway. He's on his way to the depot, got two more bodies over there," the sheriff said.

"How did they die Sheriff, or do I already know?" Dr. Barnes asked.

"Gunshot, both were killed this morning when some men tried to hold up the train somewhere between here and Ashland. It has been so busy around here all day that I haven't had time to gather any more details. I plan on spending the entire evening trying to do some interviews and then to fill out my reports. Ain't even had time to grab a bite to eat. This coffee is the first thing I've had the entire day."

"Could be worse Sheriff," Doctor Barnes said.

The Sheriff sat down his empty coffee cup and asked, "How do you figure that Doc."

"Could be raining."

The sheriff looked out the window of the kitchen at the bright sunshine. "Glad it ain't, that river is still going to give us some bad trouble in a few days when the big water finally makes it here."

The sheriff left the clinic and headed for the depot. He wished he had saddled his horse this morning, the way he figured it he must have walked five miles already and the day wasn't half over. There were now two wagons on their way to the depot, one for the bodies and one for the gold. As he walked he thought of the fact that anytime gold was involved then men were going to die. It just seemed to be the way things were.

As he crossed the big suspension bridge for the thousandth time today he was so deep in thought that he didn't even notice the river. When he got to the other end he noticed the two wagons. Both had been turned and backed up to where their beds were against the loading dock. The most solemn sight was the loading of the two bodies, men shot down in their prime, men that had just been doing their job. After Herb had them in place in his wagon he covered both bodies with a large tarpaulin.

He was climbing into the seat as the sheriff walked up the ramp to the platform. "Hold up there a minute Herb while I check on something."

The sheriff walked over and boarded the passenger car. Both Burton and Ramsey were still onboard talking.

"Are there any special instruction for the undertaker Mack, they were your men and I don't know how the company you work for handles things like this?" the Sheriff asked.

Mack walked toward the sheriff and said, "Well Sheriff, the bodies will be transported back to New York on the next train. I have sent a wire but it will probably be late today before they send a response. Please have the undertaker take the necessary steps to insure a three to four day journey."

Sheriff Barnes walked back out and gave Herb the instructions. "That won't be a problem Sheriff. I can have them ready by tonight. Any idea when that feller needs to have the coffins brought back to the depot to be put on the train?"

"Right now Herb I don't know what the train schedule is. We got that damn flood slowing everything down and this engine may or may not be able to run. She's got a bullet hole in some sort of steam pipe. The engineer and his fireman are working on it now. As soon as I find out then I'll send someone over to your place, would that be alright?"

Herb thought a minute and said, "When you do send for me can I have whoever you send to help me get them loaded up and ride along with me, especially if it's after dark Sheriff?" Herb asked.

For Lack of a Title

Sheriff Barnes had known about the strange sixth sense the undertaker was noted for. People around town had talked about it for years. "Why do you need him to ride along Herb, you ain't getting spooked in your older days now are you?"

Herb rubbed his chin and said, "No Sheriff, it ain't nothing like that I don't believe. I just need help loading the two pine boxes up and once I get them here I might need some help unloading them, that's all.

The undertaker said this and his nervousness didn't escape the sheriff's notice. "No problem Herb, I'll have whoever I send to ride along with you and then he can follow you back to your place if you like."

"I would like that a lot Sheriff." With that Herb released his brake and tapped the back of Josephine with a long cane pole. "Giddy up Josey." The two eased out at a slow pace and Herb let the old horse have her way, she knew the trip back without being prodded. As Herb went across the big swinging bridge he slowed Josey down a bit, didn't want to shake anything on the bridge loose and fall into the river. The two dead men in the back probably didn't care.

Barnes went back into the passenger car. "Herb is gone Burton. We better get this luggage loaded up and headed toward the bank. The sooner it's locked up nice and safe in that big vault the better I will feel."

The three men each picked up a bag and headed to the door. The first three were easy, they contained the cash. Jake was positioned at the loading platform and he was holding one of the new Greener shotguns that had been brought from the sheriff's office that morning. The three men went back inside for the other three bags. Ramsey picked one up and then sat it back down.

"It might be better if someone got a two-wheeled dolly to use on these." He knew the bags of gold were extremely heavy, enough to possibly pull the handles right off the top if they weren't careful. Eisner found a dolly and in no time flat the three bags of gold coins were loaded beside the cash.

"Where is that other Greener you took from the gun case this morning Jake?" Barnes asked.

"Gave it to one of the other deputies this morning, got two men patrolling the town looking for anyone else who might have come down with a cough. It would do me good to find someone and to make that someone talk," the deputy said.

"When we pull out I want you to sit up top with Prescott. The three of us will follow about a hundred feet behind to keep a close eye on things." Barnes raised the little wooden gate at the back of the wagon and fastened it shut. "Get moving Prescott and don't shake that suspension bridge too much, you wouldn't want to go for a swim now would you?"

"Naw I wouldn't Sheriff but you are more than welcome to ride up here with me if you like." Prescott tapped Cob and said, "Giddy up boys, we got sacks of gold to deliver. I reckon right now you are two of the richest mules in the State of Kentucky." Just about then Short Shank snorted and bucked a little as if to say, "Hear that Cob, me and you done hit the jackpot."

The wagon moved off with Jake riding shotgun and the other three men following along at a considerable distance. None of the three set foot on the bridge until the wagon had cleared the other side.

Ramsey looked at no one in particular when he said, "You don't think anyone would make a play on the money in broad daylight do you Sheriff?"

"The way this town has come apart in the last week nothing would really surprise me Mack. The undertaker and the clinic have seen a years' worth of business in just the last few days. Hell even old Burton there has got a contract out on his head."

Ramsey looked at Hash and said, "For real Burton? This place is more dangerous than New York City at night."

Within ten minutes the wagon pulled in front of the bank building. Jake jumped down and walked up to the top of the steps and then turned to face the surrounding area, his Greener at the ready. The sheriff, along with Hash and Mack were still about a hundred feet back, maybe even farther. The town was a little busier than usual, probably due to the constant rains of the previous weeks and now everyone was out trying to take care of a little business before the big flood came. Everyone expected it to be a bad one.

Sheriff Barnes was a little nervous with all the foot traffic about, especially around the bank building. He noticed five or six men that he didn't recognize standing on the street corner across from the bank. Each was armed with revolvers in leather holsters and a couple even carried rifles. "Hey Burton, does anything look unusual to you about that group of men across from the bank?" Barnes asked.

Hash had already seen them and was about to ask the sheriff the same question. "Yea Sheriff I see them. I think they are a little heavily armed for a Friday evening don't you?"

Jake had seen them too and had gotten down on one knee just in case. He was now positioned behind one of the large stone columns that supported the big gabled roof over the front door of the bank. He checked the loads in the Greener and had it ready if and when the time came to use it, what he really needed though was a Winchester. He hollered at Prescott and told him to latch the brake and get down on this side of the wagon, just in case.

The sheriff and the other two men had stopped and were looking the situation over. They were a good hundred and twenty five feet from the bank. All three were watching to see what the strangers were going to do next. The men were definitely observing the bank and the wagon that had just pulled up in front.

"Burton, why don't you and Mack cross to the other side of the street and keep me covered while I go on up to the bank building. If shooting starts now as busy as the sidewalks are then there are going to be a lot of people hurt."

Hash and Mack did as the sheriff asked and moved to the other side. Both men had undone the leather straps that kept their guns secure and were ready to draw and fire at the first sign of trouble. Before Sheriff Barnes had made it half way the group of men stepped off the sidewalk and started across the street toward the bank. It was apparent that none of the men in the group had noticed the sheriff, or for that matter Hash and Mack.

Jake had seen what was happening and told Prescott to get away from the wagon and step into the alley to his left away from the men coming across the street.

"What about my mules Jake?" Prescott asked.

"Don't worry about them now Prescott, just get your ass out of sight."

"My ass is out of sight Jake; if you hadn't noticed; I'm wearing bibs, now what about my mules?"

"Those damn mules are alright, hell anybody that gets around either of them other than you is apt to get kicked, now hide around the corner before any shooting starts." With that Prescott moved out of sight.

Without Prescott to worry about Jake leveled the twelve gauge Greener and got ready. The men were now in the middle of the street and as far as Jake could tell hadn't noticed either the sheriff or Hash and Mack.

As the group of men made it to the other sidewalk the one who was in front asked, "You there with the shotgun, step out so we can talk to you."

Jake raised the Greener to his shoulder and asked, "I can hear you well enough from right here. What do you want?"

The man looked to the one on his right and said something. Three of the men then moved toward the wagon while the man who had spoken along with two more came toward Jake. "I just want to see if you know of any jobs in town. Me and my friends here just came in last night and could sure use some work. Being out on the trail can leave a man pretty hungry."

Jake had seen the men moving toward the hitched wagon and wondered if they were going to try to steal the rig knowing the money was inside. "Now with all the people out and about today why would you ask a man who is holding a shotgun on you about work?"

"You just look like a man who might know where we can get a job." He said, all the while getting closer to the building and the wagon. Cob and Short Shank were getting nervous without Prescott, the men getting closer and shouting wasn't helping. Cob pulled on the rig and actually drug it a few inches.

Jake was getting a little nervous himself, the three men that had broken off were now nearly at the wagon and his position wasn't as good as he would have liked. The column he was behind felt like it was getting smaller by the minute. Just then Reed, who had witnessed the goings on, came out of the building. He stood beside Jake and then reached inside his hidden shoulder holster and pulled out his revolver.

"What are you doing Reed? If you haven't noticed there are six of them and every one of them has a gun. Get behind that other column there before you get shot," Jake whispered.

Reed didn't take his eyes off the men as they advanced. He was feeling something he hadn't felt since his youth, the rush and excitement of doing something dangerous. He calmly raised his revolver and in a deep smooth voice he demanded, "Stop right there, any man who takes one more step toward that wagon will be shot." He cocked the hammer back and the sound carried to everyone approaching the building. The men all stopped.

The man who seemed to be the leader of the group held up his left hand and made a fist. This must have been the signal for the others to stop. Sheriff Barnes noticed this and realized these men must have been, at one time or another, part of the military. While this had been going on Hash and Mack had continued to move forward and were in an excellent position to catch the six men in a crossfire. Hash noticed that people were taking cover inside some of the businesses. They must have heard and seen what was going on. The street was becoming less crowded by the minute.

The man who had raised his hand asked, "Who are you friend?"

To Reed's own surprise he wasn't nervous in the least. His hand held the revolver steady and he wasn't sweating. He heard what the man had asked and decided then and there that he was the man he would shoot first if things got out of hand. "I am Samuel Reed, president of this bank. State your intentions mister."

The man lowered his hand and started laughing. "Well Mister Samuel Reed what do you mean coming out here and holding a gun on me and my friends. That might just be a good way to get yourself shot." Some of his men laughed at this.

Reed didn't lower his gun; in fact he took better aim on the man who had just spoken. "You are a very perceptive man."

The laughing stopped. "What do you mean by that, what is perceptive?"

Now Reed laughed. "Perceptive means you have a small inclination of the events that are about to take place."

The man reached his hand up to his hat and rubbed his head. "What does inclination mean?"

Reed realized he was talking to a bumpkin who probably knew the basics of the English language and little more. "I wish I had time to teach you and your ignorant friends a few things about manners, but it would appear that none of you are smart enough to understand anything I say." Reed was hoping to get the opportunity to use his gun. He didn't know what had taken hold of him but he was certainly enjoying it.

The man might not have known what perceptive or inclination meant but he had certainly heard the word ignorant more than once in his life and he definitely knew what it meant and he didn't like it one bit. "Well Reed you have gone too far now."

Before he could finish there was a gunshot somewhere behind him. He and the other five men with him were ready to draw and start shooting.

"You there, stand still and don't move a muscle," Sheriff Barnes said. Jake stepped up and leveled his Greener at the leader, at this range it would blow him in two. The six men didn't move. Barnes had gotten close enough to hear what was being said and knew that gunplay was going to erupt at any moment. Hash and Mack also heard and had drawn their Colts. The six men looked around as they put their hands over their heads. They counted five men, each with a gun pointed in their direction.

Mack and Hash walked up and removed the guns that each man carried. Now that the six strangers had their teeth pulled they were looking as meek as mice. Jake came off the porch and had the men line up on the sidewalk facing the sun. The sheriff walked up to Reed and whispered, "What in Hell's Blazes were you trying to do, get yourself killed?"

"Not at all Sheriff, I was merely keeping their attention until you and Hash got in position behind them. And by the way, it worked perfectly."

Barnes looked at the revolver in Reed's hand. "You know how to use one of those?"

Reed didn't answer; he simply raised the gun and shot the hat off the man who had been doing all the talking. When the hat flew off the man fell to the ground as if he had been shot. Reed shouted, "Approach this bank in the manner you just did, or talk to my friends here without being polite, and the next time when your hat flies off there will be a portion of your head still in it." With that Reed holstered his gun and went back inside the bank.

Hash and Mack walked up to the sheriff. All three men just stood there and looked at the six strangers. "What do you plan to do with them Sheriff?" Mack asked just low enough for the sheriff to hear. Hash was looking at the sheriff and also wanted to know what he was going to do.

"Well, I can't arrest them, as far as I can tell they haven't done anything wrong."

"They were approaching the bank in a menacing fashion. If we hadn't been where we were then things might have gotten ugly fast," Mack said.

"You got that right. They had something in mind and the three of us know pretty much what it was. The only thing is, we didn't allow that to happen. I can't very well arrest someone for thinking about committing a crime," the Sheriff said.

Just then Scrappy came down the street. When he saw Jake holding a Greener shotgun on six men he pulled his own gun and walked up beside the deputy. "What's going on here Jake? Looks like I might have missed all the fun."

"I don't really know Scrap but you definitely missed the show. Reed the banker came out here and single handedly apprehended these varmints. Why you should have seen them. Reed damn near took that one fellers head off," Jake said

Scrap knew the banker and the man Jake just described wasn't that feller. "I didn't know the town had another Reed that was a banker."

"Naw Scrap, it was Reed that runs that bank right behind us. I'm telling you the man was fierce and these six done folded their tents and gave up," Jake said. The conversation was carried on loud enough for the six strangers to hear, and it was meant to be.

The man who was hatless asked, "What do you think you're doing Sheriff? Me and my friends here haven't done anything wrong. Why are you letting these two deputies hold guns on us? And I would also like to press charges against that man you called Reed."

Sheriff Barnes looked over and asked, "Charges for what?"

"For attempted murder, he tried to shoot me in the head and missed. I got me five witnesses here that will testify at trial." The five other strangers began shaking their heads in unison.

"Attempted murder? Did I hear you right mister?" Barnes asked.

"That's right Sheriff. Now go in there and arrest that fat banker."

Barnes put his gun in his holster and walked up to the man who had just accused Reed of attempted murder. He walked right up to him and with his right fist hit the man so hard that it looked like he was lifted off the ground. He went backwards and landed in a pile. He didn't move. As Barnes rubbed his knuckles he looked at the others. "Anyone else here see Reed try to commit a murder?" All five who had been shaking their heads yes now were shaking their heads no.

"Jake, I want you to lead these men to the jail. Have the five that are still standing to drag that son-of-a-bitch on the ground with them as they go. When you get them there lock them up, all six in one cell. Scrappy, I want you to go along and make sure none of these men says a word between here and there. I have heard all I want from them for the moment," Barnes said.

"Why are we being arrested Sheriff? We ain't done nothing wrong," one of the men said.

"You're not being arrested, just taken in for questioning. As soon as the six of you answer for yourselves then I will let you loose. And if I hear anymore bullshit from any of you then I will find a good reason to arrest you, got it?" All five shook their heads as they picked up the one laying on the ground.

When they were gone Hash looked at the sheriff and said, "Nice left hook Barnes, that man won't come to for a while."

"Yea, well I knew I couldn't arrest them and I was just so damn mad at the time. You and me know what they had in mind Burton. We just got here and spoiled their little plan. That is six more men that knew what you had coming in on that train this morning. Hell it seems that the whole world knows."

"I think the man that sent that coded message in the telegram this morning is to blame Sheriff. Everything points to him," Hash said.

"It seems so Burton. Let me get Reed back out here and see how he wants to handle the delivery." The sheriff went up the stairs and before long he came back out with the banker.

"Well Reed, you seem mighty handy with an iron. I might have underestimated you," Hash said.

"Burton, in my younger and thinner days, I might have been a bit rowdy. Let me tell you sometime about the man I killed in a duel once. Matter of fact, I think tonight would be such a time, after we get things straightened up out here of course. How would the three of you like to have dinner with me at the Depo Café, my treat?"

Hash looked at the sheriff for confirmation. "You heard him right Burton. He really did fight a duel once and he actually let the other man shoot first. Not a smart way to fight a duel if you ask me?" The Sheriff grinned at Reed as he said this. "And by the way Reed, as to your offer of dinner I would be delighted. I haven't ate since yesterday thanks to all the trouble in town." Hash and Mack also agreed to have dinner with the banker and the sheriff.

Reed again took charge of the situation. He motioned for two of his male tellers to come outside. When they did he told them to conclude all business with the customers that were already in the bank and to hustle them out as quickly and politely as possible. The two men turned and went back inside.

Reed looked at Hash and said, "We have three more customers in the lobby to finish up with then once they have left I intend to close the bank until an accounting is made of your delivery. Would it be possible to turn that wagon around and back it up to the steps here?"

Jake went over to the alley and motioned for Prescott to come out. The old driver looked a bit shaken but when he saw that Cob and Short Shank were alright he smiled. Once told the plan to move the wagon it didn't take him more than a few minutes to have the rig moved with the back gate against the steps.

The last of the customers were just then leaving the bank. Reed had one of the female tellers to stand on the sidewalk and inform anyone trying to enter that the bank was closed for the next ninety minutes. Spurlock came out rolling a two wheeled dolly and within minutes the six heavy suitcases were inside.

"Burton, go back out and tell Prescott that we appreciated his help today if you don't mind. Tell him that Reed here will settle up with him later," Barnes said. "Oh, you can also tell him that we appreciate Cob and Short Shank too. I wouldn't want either of them two mules to feel slighted."

"I can do that Sheriff. Make sure none of the packages are opened until I get back inside though." With that Hash went out and spoke to the mule driver.

Reed had a big wooden table carried out and then he closed all the blinds on the front windows and doors. Once Hash was back inside the heavy front doors were closed and double locked. Reed instructed his tellers on how he wanted the delivery handled. As each case was emptied and counted then the money was to be put back in the case it came out of and relocked, then put in the vault for storage. He also stressed that at no time was anyone to be left alone with either the gold or the cash while the case it was in was unlocked.

Once his instructions were complete he looked at Spurlock and said, "Is everything understood Mr. Spurlock?"

Spurlock indicated that it was.

Reed turned to the sheriff and Hash and said, "I would like for you two to join me in my office if you have the time."

Hash was satisfied with the instructions Reed had given to his employees and he also had Mack Ramsey there to oversee the job. The Baldwin-Felts man was responsible for the shipment until it was safely inside the vault and then he would sign off and be finished with his part of the delivery. He also had the only keys to the six cases.

"I would like you to join us upstairs Mack as soon as you can," Hash told him. Ramsey nodded and then pulled the six keys from his pocket.

With that the three men climbed the stairs to the big corner office. Once inside Reed closed the door and went back to the liquor cabinet. He took out three fresh glasses and the same bottle of whiskey from that morning. He poured and then handed a glass to each man. "Sheriff, I know you are on duty and never touch a drop while sherriffing or whatever the proper verb for that might be."

Barnes took the glass and then said, "You know me too well."

Reed picked up the third glass and motioned for the men to have a seat in front of his desk. When seated himself he said, "I hoped the two of you would have a few minutes to spare so we could talk over something that is really starting to trouble me."

Both men indicted that they did. Reed smiled and then offered the sheriff and Burton a Cuban cigar. Both men accepted and then Reed began.

"Both of you are as up to date on the happenings concerning the shipment of money as I am. What I wanted to talk to you about is that there have been two attempts made so far today to relieve us of it. Men have died trying to get it here safely and the worst thing of all is that no one is supposed to know about the money except the three of us. I did make the mistake of assuming that my employee Spurlock was trustworthy. As of now he is my prime suspect. What are your thoughts on this matter Sheriff?"

The sheriff clipped the end of his cigar with a pocket knife and then lit it. After a few puffs he looked at Reed and said, "I believe he is part of it. I also believe he is just a minor functionary and someone else is calling the shots. Did you say earlier that he has taken a trip or two up north, I believe it was Chicago?"

"That's right. His most recent trip was about three weeks ago. I can look back through my calendar and be more specific if you want."

"That might be useful. You can give me the exact dates and times later; right now we need to worry about the money that is going to be stored in your vault. You saw what nearly happened out there. Six men could walk in here and take just about anything they could carry. My deputies can't guard this place and carry out their other duties; I just don't have enough men."

Hash took a sip of his drink and then spoke, "How about Mack Ramsey. I might convince him to hang around town for a few weeks to oversee the bank's security if that would be acceptable to each of you. He works for a company that makes a lot of money from my associates in New York. If he were allowed to implement the security the bank needs for the next three to four weeks then the problem will solve itself. The money by that time will hopefully have been used and will no longer pose a problem."

Reed smiled and said, "You think you can pull the right strings to get this done?"

"It will not be a problem. My biggest concern is security during regular business hours. If anyone tried to blow up the vault at night half the town would hear and come running. It is a daylight job for Ramsey at most. I have seen the plans of the vault and am confident it cannot be blown apart with dynamite."

It had been nearly forty-five minutes since the three men had come upstairs. There was a knock at the door and Reed got up and opened it to find Ramsey. He invited him in and offered him a drink. Mack looked at the sheriff and Burton and saw that each held a glass.

"Yes Sir Mr. Reed that would be nice. I came up to inform you that the money has been counted by your staff and I have signed off on it. It is now the full responsibility of the bank and I have no further involvement with it other than the tally sheet which I have here." He took the glass that Reed had just poured and took a sip.

"This is the tally sheet Mr. Burton. If you find it to be correct then I have accomplished my mission," Mack said.

Hash got up and pulled a chair from the corner over to where he and the sheriff sat. "Have a seat Mack; there is something I would like to talk to you about." Hash motioned to the chair and Ramsey came over and sat down. As Ramsey was sitting down Hash opened the tally sheet and then signed the bottom. He then reached it to Reed.

Reed looked at the numbers and nearly got choked. He looked up at Hash and said, "I don't understand. First I was led to believe it was four-hundred thousand, and then this morning you hinted it was a million and a half."

Hash took a sip and then said, "I have known for a while that a large sum of money in transit from up north to your bank would generate a lot of unwanted attention. It was a secret as you indicated but I doubted that it would remain one for very long. As the events of today have unfolded it is apparent to everyone in this room that secrets can't be kept. And gentlemen, the larger the sum of money the faster the secret travels. Just imagine what would have happened if everyone knew it was actually two and a half million?"

Sheriff Barnes stood and went to the widow. "You mean to tell me that you and your associates up in New York sent two million five-hundred thousand dollars by train with only three guards? That sounds pretty dangerous Burton wouldn't you say?"

"My associates came up with the plan; I protested but was dismissed as being overly dramatic. The result is two men are dead and two attempts have been made on the money, and that's just today. But in hindsight I would say that if the amount had been revealed and a hundred men sent to guard it then who knows, the money might have arrived alright but most likely with more deaths attributed to it," Hash said. "And remember, it didn't matter what the amount, someone here in this city is responsible for leaking the information and I intend to find out who it is."

Reed knew he was partly to blame for the leaked information but still wasn't one-hundred percent convinced that the blame lay with his bank's employees. "I almost agree with that but still am not convinced that your associates in New York are completely blameless Mr. Burton. What if one of the men on the board of your organization has decided to go into business for himself, can you say, with any degree of certainty, that you trust every man on that board?"

Hash studied his shoes for a minute. He had never thought about this angle until now. He thought he knew every one of the men who were subsidizing this project but now he wasn't so sure. "You have touched upon an interesting subject Reed. As to your question I must answer no. There is one or two that I would have had slight reservations about. I will give this some serious thought." Again Hash was impressed with the banker.

Reed didn't want to appear ungrateful for the work that Ramsey had done so he reached him one of the Cubans. Mack took it and looked it over. "Cuban made Mr. Reed. Not what I expected to find in Floyd County, Kentucky. What is it that you wish to speak to me about?"

Hash sat his cigar in the big pedestal ashtray and asked, "Mack, what were your instructions once you delivered the six packages to the bank?"

"I was to take the next available train back to New York along with my two associates. They will be traveling with me I suppose now anyway but more in the form of freight instead of as passengers."

"Yes well I am sorry. The ambush was something that none of us in the room could have anticipated. I believe there are forces at work here that have a great many resources and men. We here do not know when they might strike again but we feel confident that they will try. That is why I would like you to stay on here for a few weeks to oversee security here at the bank. I can contact your superiors up north and have you reassigned here but only if you agree."

Ramsey knew that Burton was only being courteous. If he wanted him to stay here in Prestonsburg then Ramsey could only say yes. The agency would grant any request Burton wanted. "I would be glad to stay and assist you in any way I can. There is the matter of the two caskets. It is normal for an agency man to accompany any fallen associates back to their home. I feel certain that they would have accompanied my casket if it were the case."

"I understand your concern Mr. Ramsey, you wish to accompany your associates home and that is very commendable of you. I think it is also an honor to them to see that the money that they died protecting remains safe until what time as it can be used for the purpose in which it was sent here in the first place. What if a telegram was sent, then someone could meet the train at; say Ashland, Kentucky or even a town closer if an operative could be dispatched from your firm in time?" Reed asked.

Ramsey thought this over. He knew he wanted to do what was right concerning the bodies. But he also understood the need to finish the work that had ultimately gotten the two men killed in the first place. "You make a very good point; I think we will try your plan Mr. Reed. If the train can be met and an operative of Baldwin-Felts can accompany the body's home then I will stay and organize the security your bank is in need of."

Sheriff Barnes had been thinking about what measures his meager force could provide. "Might I make a suggestion, it is now nearly three-thirty, what time does your bank close Reed?"

Reed looked at his pocket watch and realized that the day had flown by. "My goodness Sheriff it is three-thirty, we close at five on weekdays, why do you ask?"

"It is my suggestion that you do not reopen this afternoon. Allow your staff to finish up and then permit them to go home early. That will allow us to get a handle on what needs to be done. You can reopen tomorrow morning with a security plan in force. How does that sound?"

Hash thought it was a good plan. "Reed what are your hours on Saturday?"

"Nine until noon. After that three ladies work until four in the afternoon cleaning and getting the bank ready for Monday when we reopen at nine o'clock."

"I suggest that we follow the sheriff's suggestion and don't reopen this afternoon. Also I would cancel the cleaning tomorrow. You can have your staff tidy up in the time they have left today. Don't send them home early just let them finish out their day by doing what the cleaning staff would normally do on Saturday. Sending them home now might raise suspicions," Hash said.

Reed looked at everyone in the room. "Then it is agreed. We don't reopen today and the staff remains here until their usual quitting time. Tomorrow morning I would request that the four of us meet here at a quarter of nine. Once the bank is open then Mr. Ramsey can take over as our head of security."

After the meeting broke up in Reed's office Hash and the sheriff walked back through town toward the jail. Mack remained at the bank to familiarize himself with the layout of the building and also look over the employees. He wanted to take in as much as possible in what little time he had before the building was locked up for the night and everyone went home.

Reed came down from his office at a quarter to five and walked up to Mack. "What do you think of your new duties Mr. Ramsey?"

Mack looked at Reed and said, "Please call me Mack. I like the layout. With two men inside I think we can make your building reasonably safe. I do plan to have a man at the top of the stairs with a Winchester rifle. From that vantage point he can cover the front doors and the entire lobby. I would request that that large shrub you have in the corner of the lobby be carried to the top of the stairs and put to the left of the landing up there. It will help give our man with the rifle some cover. Most of your customers will not even know he's there. I want another guard to be posted at the end of the teller line where he can observe the entire lobby and every customer as they enter and also as they leave the building."

Reed looked at the two positions that Mack had mentioned, he was pleased; the Baldwin-Felts man knew his business. "Should the two men have their guns hidden and act as employees Mr. Ramsey, I mean Mack?"

"No, I want this to be an active response to anyone looking over the building that might have mischief in mind. To have them blend in would be a little too passive. I want everyone to know up front that the building has security."

Reed looked again to the top of the stairs where the guard with the rifle would be. "You said that the man on the landing should have a Winchester, I just wonder if a Greener twelve-gauge shotgun might get the message across in a more forceful manner."

Mack looked over the building once more. Reed had made a good suggestion. "From that distance a twelve-gauge might do more harm than good. The shot pattern from there would probably hit some of your customers. I say we leave the man up there with a Winchester and have the one down here carry the Greener. Do you think any of your customers will be alarmed by the sight of a man holding a shotgun as they enter the lobby?"

Reed rubbed his chin. "Actually after thinking about all the trouble this town has seen in the last week I believe that they might be relieved to see some added security. Do you think the sheriff could deputize the men you use? The badges might also have a good visual effect for the customers and also anyone else who might be looking the place over for other reasons. The sight of a badge means these aren't just security guards, they are deputies."

"It might be a good idea at that Mr. Reed; a badge sends the right message. Wouldn't want anyone to think the guards in here are actually robbers now would we?" Mack said.

Sheriff Barnes and Hash had nearly made it to the street that ran to the jail when both heard what sounded like a man coughing, and coughing badly. Sitting or more like lying on a bench in front of the courthouse was a man holding a handkerchief to his mouth and nose. Sheriff Barnes looked at Hash and said, "I need to go and ask that man a few questions Burton. Could I get you to go to the clinic and see if one of the doctors is there and if so come back here with you? I might have just found a badly needed witness."

Hash was unaware of the poisoned prisoner in the jail that morning or the other man who had died at the clinic later in the day. "Is that man over there a friend of yours Sheriff?"

"No, I've never seen him before in my life but I do know his symptoms. Try to hurry if you can, this man might be in pretty bad shape."

Hash hurried up the street toward the clinic wondering what that was all about. The sheriff approached the man all the while looking around to see if there might be anyone else about. If this man's cough was caused by breathing in the same thing that had killed the man at the clinic then he knew he was part of a gang and he didn't want to be caught off guard if any of the others might be around.

When he got close enough he said, "Howdy stranger."

The man weakly looked up at the sheriff and then went back to coughing.

"You seem to be sick friend; can you tell me what might be causing you to feel ill?"

This also never got a response. Again the man looked at the sheriff and then he eased from his side to his back and only looked up at the sky. The coughing came back and Barnes decided to wait for Hash to return, hopefully with one of the doctors. As he waited he looked around some of the houses and alleys hoping to find someone who might know the man. Just when he was about to give up he noticed someone peeking around a building a few doors down. He took the strap off his revolver and eased down the sidewalk. When the man saw him he darted down the alley. Barnes sprinted to the alley and ordered the man to stop. He had his hand on the butt of his revolver and was ready to draw if need be.

The man slowly held his hands out to his sides and about shoulder height. "Keep your hands up and slowly turn around." The man lowered his head and then turned toward the sheriff.

"Now slowly walk toward me and out onto the street where you and I can talk."

Again the stranger did as he was told. When he was out of the alley and in the sunlight Barnes got a good look at him. The man was about average height and slim, almost malnourished. He wore tattered clothes and had an old Navy revolver stuffed in his waist band. Barnes drew his gun and held it on the man while he walked over and took the gun from him. The old pistol was worn and looked in need of a good cleaning; it had only two shells in the cylinder.

Barnes stepped back to put some distance between himself and the stranger. "You got a name stranger?"

"Spokes," was all the man said.

The sheriff looked once more up and down the street. No one was paying attention to what was going on, that was good. He knew if the man had friends then they would be watching and at the moment he felt uncomfortable and very exposed out in the middle of the street. "Did I hear you right stranger, did you say Spokes?"

"Yes sir, you heard me right."

"Well what kind of a name is that?"

The stranger was paying attention to the toes of his boots, not wanting to talk. Barnes noticed that the end of his left boot was worn off and he could see a sock with a hole in it. The shoes were dirty and tattered and the big toe of his left foot could be seen.

The man looked up at the sheriff and said, "It's just a nickname I got because I'm so skinny, you know kind of like the spoke of a wagon wheel."

Barnes didn't know whether to arrest the man for being a vagrant or to toss him a dollar so he could go eat. His next question had nothing to do with anything but concern. "Well Spokes, when was the last time you had anything to eat?"

He looked up from his shoes and said, "This morning Deputy. I found a tray of food on the porch of that building over there and it had everything in the world on it, especially gravy and eggs. I saw that there were two biscuits so I took one. I know it was wrong and I promise I won't do it again Deputy, I was just so hungry. That's why I was peeking around this here building. I thought maybe that well-dressed feller who brought the breakfast tray might have brought back dinner too."

The sheriff could barely believe his ears. This skeleton of a man had taken a biscuit from the tray of food that had poisoned his prisoner. He had also seen whoever it was that left the food on the porch to begin with. "Did you get a good look at the man, the man who left the food?"

"I sure did Deputy. I was laying on that bench over there where that feller is now; you know the one who's coughing so much. Well, when I saw the man carrying that tray with the cloth on top I just acted like I was asleep and he walked right by me. I could smell everything on it. Well he never paid no attention to me, he just walked right up to that building there and then he started acting real funny. It was like he was trying to surprise somebody. After he looked around real good he sat the tray down and then went down that alley right beside where he sat the food. I waited a few minutes and then I eased over there and raised up that cloth that was covering everything up. It all looked and smelled so good. I started to take the whole thing but decided that it would be stealing. I did take a biscuit though and I'm real sorry Deputy. My momma, God rest her soul, didn't raise me that way. She told me that a man that steals should be struck down on the spot."

Barnes thought about that last remark. If he had taken the whole tray then he would have been struck down, not by God but by the poison. "After you ate that biscuit this morning have you felt alright? I mean have you felt sick in any way or had a coughing spell."

For Lack of a Title

Spokes looked over at the man who was doing all the coughing and asked, "Is it something catching Deputy. Was there something wrong with that biscuit I took this morning?"

Sheriff Barnes looked back up the street and saw Burton and Dr. Sables coming their way. "Spokes, I'm not sure if there was something wrong with that biscuit but that man there coming down the street with the small black leather bag is a doctor. Why don't you come along with me and we'll let him have a look at you."

When Sables and Hash got closer Hash asked, "Who you got there Sheriff?"

Spokes looked at Barnes again and said, "I'm real sorry Sheriff, I thought you was a deputy."

Barnes looked at the young man and said, "That's all right. Burton I found this young feller over there in that alley. I don't know much of the story yet but it is apparent that he ate some of the food off that tray this morning."

Hash had been filled in by the doctor on their way over. "Then why ain't he dead like the other two?" As soon as Hash said it he wished he could take it back.

Spokes turned a lighter shade of white than he already was. "Then there was something wrong with the food Sheriff. My momma was right all along, you steal and something bad is gonna happen."

Dr. Sables looked at the young man and asked, "What is your name son?"

"Spokes, my name is Spokes. Am I gonna die Doc?"

Sables looked in the man's mouth and asked him to try to cough. Spokes coughed for the doctor and then looked at the sheriff.

"How much of that food did you eat off the tray Spokes?" Sables asked.

"Just a biscuit, that's all Doc I swear."

"Have you felt alright since then?"

"I suppose, I mean I feel the way I always feel."

"And how do you always feel?" the doctor asked.

"Hungry mostly."

Hash knew the man was starving just by looking at him. His clothes were not much more than rags and barely hung on his thin frame. He also noticed the worn out shoes with the toes sticking out. "Sheriff, what do you intend to do with him?"

"He seen the man who left the tray on the porch this morning," Barnes said.

Sables looked over at the sheriff, "For real, you got yourself an eyewitness?"

"Apparently so Doc. He said it was a well-dressed man and he was acting real spooked and all when he sat that tray on the porch of the jail. That should narrow down my list of suspects."

Hash asked the sheriff, "How many people you got in mind as possibles?"

"Well Burton, I would say right off hand that maybe twenty on the short end and twenty-five on the long. Most of the men I can think of who fit that bill work at the banks in town or in the courthouse. Most of those would be at the largest bank which is Reed's. Burton, how about me and you step over here away from everyone so the doc can do his work? Doc the reason I sent for you is so you can look at that man over there on the bench. Me and Burton found him there about thirty minutes ago and he was coughing his head off." The Sheriff noticed that the man had stopped coughing. He wasn't making any noise at all.

As Dr. Sables headed toward the bench, Barnes and Hash stepped away from Spokes so they could talk in private. Hash knew what the sheriff was doing.

"Burton, that skeleton of a man over there is our only eyewitness and from what he said about the man who left that tray I for one would hazard to guess that it's Spurlock over at Reed's bank. Now if we don't get him put away someplace nice and safe then he won't live long enough to identify the man you and I both suspect."

Hash thought over what the sheriff had in mind. It was either put Spokes in jail or hide him somewhere in town. The jail wasn't an option, look what just happened to the third member of the gang that bushwhacked him and Riley. "Well Sheriff, what do you have in mind?"

"I'm going over to talk to the judge and see what he wants to do. He may want to have Spokes put in protective custody which isn't a very good option."

"Protective custody in your jail Sheriff is almost the same as a death sentence. Would your judge really be any help in a situation like this?"

"I don't know Burton. Maybe he can help me figure out what to do. This man hasn't broken any laws other than stealing a biscuit. I can't arrest him and put him in jail for that. But if he is left to roam the streets then he is most likely going to disappear once the culprit behind all the killings finds out we got a witness who can identify him."

"Will the judge be at the courthouse this late in the evening?" Hash asked.

"I'm going to try the courthouse first and if he ain't there I'm heading to his house."

"And in the meantime you just going to let Spokes stand here in the middle of the street Sheriff?"

Barnes thought about this for a minute. "Tell you what, Sables is probably going to want to walk him and that other feller over there on the bench over to the clinic so he can check them out. I hate to ask but how about you tag along with the Doc, just in case? I'd feel better knowing a fast gun was going along to the clinic with them Burton."

Sables, who had gone over to check on the man lying on the bench, came back over to the sheriff and Hash. "I guess that makes three men dead now from the arsenic. His breathing just stopped. I could tell by the blood on his face when I first seen him that he probably wouldn't make it," the doctor said.

Hash and the sheriff looked over at the bench. "Doc, how about you tend to Spokes here at your clinic, make sure he's alright. I'm headed to the courthouse to fill in the judge on the events of the day and see if he has any suggestions. Before I do that I guess I'll try to find Shufflebarger. I feel like the undertaker has buried half the town in the past week." The sheriff left and headed toward the undertaker's office.

Hash went along with Sables and Spokes. The three men were at the clinic in less than ten minutes. Hash went straight for the coffee pot. Doctor Barnes was in the back looking after one of the victims who had been shot on the train that morning and Rebecca was in one of the side rooms applying fresh bandages to Riley's wounds.

"How's he doing?" Hash asked.

Before she could answer Riley opened his eyes and said. "Howdy Hash, where the hell you been for so long? I bout got my ass shot off the other night trying to keep you from getting killed and it took you a month to come and see me?"

Before Hash could respond Rebecca said, "Now Riley, I won't allow language like that while you're laid up in this clinic.

Furthermore, Mr. Burton has been here every few hours to check on you. Why he even slept in a chair out front the night they brought you in. I would say he is a pretty good friend to do that wouldn't you?"

The look on Riley's face softened a bit after being scolded by Rebecca. "I know he was here, I was just having a little fun. I might have been unable to talk but I could still hear a lot of what was being said. I even heard them two sawbones say I might not make if they couldn't get that bullet away from my heart."

Rebecca was surprised at this. It seems Riley could hear the two doctors while they were operating on him. She would need to mention this to her father.

After the visit to the undertaker's office Sheriff Barnes walked back to the big courthouse in the center of Prestonsburg. He looked at his pocket watch and doubted if he would find the judge in, it was nearly five o'clock. He walked through the big front door and noticed a few people still in the foyer. He climbed the big staircase and went into the main courtroom. It was empty. The quickest way to the judge's office was through the back of the courtroom. The judge didn't like it when anyone used that door unless it was his bailiffs or court staff. The sheriff didn't care; after all he was the sheriff.

The door led into a long hallway that went the entire length of the back of the building. There were rooms along the way that were used by some of the court staff and at the very end was the door to the judge's office.

Sheriff Barnes knocked but didn't expect to find the judge there. To his surprise the door opened slightly and Judge Isiah Helton peeked around the corner. "Oh it's you Sheriff, please come on in."

When the sheriff walked in he noticed the judge was holding a Smith & Wesson 38 revolver in his right hand. He knew the judge kept a gun in his chambers but this was the first time he had ever seen him with it out in the open. The judge went to his desk and sat down. He put the gun in his top right hand desk drawer and then looked up at Sheriff Barnes.

"Sorry about that Sheriff, I didn't expect it to be you. With all the trouble that's been going on around here the last few days a man can't be too careful, especially a man who has put as many lawbreakers in jail as I have. You never know when someone might come up here and try to even the score."

Sheriff Barnes pulled a chair back from the judge's desk and sat down. In all the years he had been coming to this office the judge had never asked him to sit down. Didn't matter, as High Sheriff of Floyd County he felt he could sit pretty much anywhere he wanted, with or without the judge's approval.

Judge Helton turned around and got a bottle of bourbon and two glasses from the book case behind his desk. He sat the two glasses on his desk and looked up at Barnes. "I know neither you nor I drink during daylight hours and never while on duty but I need a drink and I want you to join me. As of right now let's just say that the two of us are on official break and this doesn't count, deal?"

The sheriff liked the judge for many reasons, one of which was for the bourbon he drank. He could see on the bottle the initials O.F.C which stood for Old Fire Copper, at least that's what the judge said it was. Others claimed it stood for Old Fashioned Copper but that didn't matter to either the judge or the sheriff, they simply liked the smooth yet extremely strong taste. It was a brand of Kentucky Bourbon that was purported to be produced in all copper equipment which supposedly made it more pure. Anything as strong as O.F.C. had to be pure, how could it not be?

Judge Helton poured two generous glasses and slid one to the sheriff. Both sipped slowly as the bourbon burned a path down each man's throat. "Now Sheriff, what is it you come to see me about?"

Barnes explained everything that had gone on for the last few days, most of which the judge was aware of. When he got to the part about Spokes the judge took special interest. Both men realized that the thin stranger probably wouldn't live very long once word got out that he had witnessed a crime, the crime of murder. The sheriff told of his suspicions about who it might be that Spokes had seen deliver the poisoned food to the jail. Judge Helton thought about this for only a minute before speaking.

"I tend to see it the way you have described Sheriff. I met that man a month or so ago and didn't like him. He seems a bit aloof if you ask me, never met a man from that far north that I liked anyway Barnes. Can you tell me why he is even here and how he got the job of Assistant President at the bank in the first place?"

The sheriff never really knew how Greg Spurlock landed on both feet in Prestonsburg. Reed wouldn't be specific but hinted that he was forced to put him in as Vice President or Assistant Vice President or whatever in hell he was. Apparently some concerns from Chicago had invested a substantial sum of money in Reed's bank and taking Spurlock as Vice President was part of the deal. It really smelled rotten.

"I really don't know the answer to that Judge. What do you think I should do about Spokes?"

Helton took another sip of his bourbon and closed his eyes as it burned another path down his throat. "Well, he hasn't broken any laws except for stealing a biscuit. Damn good thing he didn't take any gravy or we wouldn't be having this conversation right now. You can't really lock him up now can you, he hasn't done anything wrong. How about we send him out of town, say Pikeville or Paintsville? We'll put him up someplace cheap and cover the cost out of county funds. You keep him alive for two weeks, all the while building a case against Spurlock, then we will have us a jim-dandy trial. Produce Spokes as your surprise witness, Spurlock won't know what hit him."

"That won't work judge. We got a broken down train at the depot and I just heard the railroad ain't using any of the rails along the Big Sandy for a week or so, too much water."

"Well then just use a horse and buggy. You don't think anyone will try to take him out with a rifle on the road do you Sheriff?"

Barnes took another sip of his drink and tried not to cough. "That won't work either judge. All the roads along the river are starting to flood. As a matter of fact, I had one of my deputy's ride out this morning with instructions to report back to me on the condition of all the roads both in and out of town. As of right now we have only one road that isn't blocked and by tomorrow morning, it's my guess that it too will be under water. This time tomorrow Prestonsburg will be completely isolated. The telegraph still works but Jeremy Eisner says that could go at any minute. All it takes is for one pole to get taken out anywhere up or down the line and that's it."

Judge Helton thought about this for a minute before asking a question he had no answer to. "So what do we do with your man Spokes? We can't just let him walk about town, he wouldn't last ten minutes."

For Lack of a Title

Barnes had a plan in mind but he wasn't sure the judge would sign off on it. He had cooked it up as he walked to the courthouse earlier. All he could do was run it by the judge and see what came of it.

"Well Your Honor, I do have an idea but it requires you to initiate it and also to see it through. What I would like to do is have Spokes stay here at the courthouse. He can sleep in the basement and food can be brought here from the General Store and prepared in the small kitchen you use for the jurors when there is a trial going on, that way we can hopefully prevent another man from being poisoned." Barnes addressed the judge as Your Honor because he knew he liked to be addressed that way.

Helton poured himself another drink and then slid the bottle to the sheriff who declined. "Not a bad plan Sheriff, can you furnish security in the form of a deputy or two?"

Barnes knew this was coming and knew it could also be a sticking point. "I am a little shorthanded right now Judge. I only have five deputies and now on top of normal town and county duties I am going to need to provide a little extra security at the bank. Reed just had a substantial amount of cash and gold delivered and there have already been two attempts to take it before it even made it inside the vault.

"How would you feel about giving a couple of your bailiffs some extra pay in order to provide protection? No one ever uses the basement and it is a pretty big space. I'm sure Spokes could hide out down there for a few weeks as long as he is fed. You should see him, a walking skeleton, just a pelt and bones."

Judge Helton grabbed the bottle of O.F.C. and put it back in the cabinet behind his desk. By his manner the sheriff thought the deal wasn't going to take. When Helton turned back to Barnes he said, "I think you might be right Sheriff about that

253

boy being in a bad way. The way I understand it he is starving and about to be killed before he can testify. I think your plan has merit. The only problem is with my bailiffs. You've seen what I have to work with. These men are not what you would say in the prime of their lives. If it came to trouble I don't really know how they would react."

Sheriff Barnes knew what the judge meant. His bailiffs were a pretty sorry looking bunch. Most worked as bailiffs because it was the only work they could get. "If they lock themselves in and don't allow anyone around the basement then I think it will probably work. But try to keep them quiet about what it is they're doing and who it is that they are hiding."

Judge Helton thrust a hand across his desk and said, "You got yourself a place to hide one witness Sheriff. And remember that during the day I will also be roaming the halls with my little friend here." The Judge pulled out his Smith & Wesson and laid it on top of his desk.

The sheriff smiled and said, "Yes we met when you opened the door. Has it got any bullets in it?" With that both the sheriff and the judge laughed.

Spokes was sitting in the clinic's waiting area while Hash was in the back talking to Riley. As he sat there he took in the room and the furnishings. He noticed the magazines and went over to the stack. He picked out one of the glossy new ones and sat down. When Hash finished aggravating Riley he stepped back to the front to check on his skinny new friend. He found him sitting straight as a ramrod in one of the chairs looking at a magazine. He doubted the man could read and supposed he was just looking at the pictures.

"Find anything interesting in that magazine Spokes?"

"Sure thing Mr. Burton, I never get to read any of these glossy new magazines much. People don't seem to leave them lying around like they do newspapers."

Hash noticed an accent that didn't really belong in Prestonsburg, Kentucky. It would fit in better a little farther north. "Where are you from Spokes, doesn't sound like you're from around here?" Hash asked.

"You're right; I'm not from around here. I came to the area a few months ago looking for work. Seems though that a lot of other people had that same idea, any jobs that were here have mostly been filled. I still have hope that something will turn up. My home town was near Cleveland, Ohio. I used to work for some of the refineries around there but over production has got that whole industry in a slump. The economy took a turn for the worse and I found myself out of a job.

"When it seemed the oil industry might never come back I started asking around at the railroad depot up there. I asked the telegraph people and some of the passengers coming off the trains if they knew or had heard where any jobs could be found. Most said they had no idea but some of the train people said that Eastern Kentucky was a vibrant place at the moment and I might find work there in the coal fields. Trains use lots of coal and it just made sense that they knew what they were talking about. But apparently lots of other people closer than Cleveland got here first. Between the locals and some of the people who came here from the surrounding areas it soon became clear that I was too late."

Hash listened patiently to the young man's story. He wasn't sure what kind of work he did at a refinery, probably an unskilled laborer. "What kind of work did you do at the refineries Spokes?"

"I wasn't in production or shipping, I was a chemist. I worked at the Standard Oil Works. It was my job to find ways to get more kerosene out of a barrel of crude oil. You see in a barrel of crude you can only get so many gallons of good quality kerosene. Each month I worked there I was able to enhance the process to increase the kerosene obtained from a forty-two gallon barrel of crude oil by a pint and some months even a quart. Now that may not sound like a lot but when you take into account the thousands of barrels processed each month then you can appreciate the numbers.

"I was also working out solutions for the vast amount of by-products that could be created from the waste oil. But I was only one of the dozens of chemists working there. When the firings came they used the last hired/first fired approach. Some men who had very little experience but were hired before me were able to maintain their jobs. And here I am."

The more Hash listened the more he realized that he was listening to an educated man, and more importantly than that, he was probably someone who wasn't mixed up in the trouble brewing now in the coal region. He could possibly use a man like Spokes in the coal fields but at the moment he had no idea as to what that use might be. "You say you have been here a couple of months. How long have you been in the town of Prestonsburg?"

"Only a couple of days, most of my time in Kentucky has been out in the surrounding counties beating the bushes trying to find work. I ran out of money a few weeks ago. Since then my time has been spent scrounging for food. Not much luck there either I'm afraid. A farmer gave me a bag of dried apples about a week ago for helping him kill and carve up two hogs. I really wanted some of the meat but didn't want to seem ungrateful, so I took the apples. I thanked him and left. The apples lasted until day before yesterday. Then this morning I took that biscuit." Spokes was silent for a few minutes as if he was thinking of something else he wanted to say. "You know mister, that biscuit is the first thing I ever stole in my life and no amount of hunger will ever make me do it again."

Hash knew the man was starving and needed to eat something but he couldn't just give him some money and let him wander the streets. He would have to accompany him or go and get the food and bring it back to the clinic. That probably wasn't a good idea, the clinic was a very busy place full of sick and wounded men and Spokes was a starving filthy mess.

"How about you have a seat there and let me talk to the doctor?" Hash asked. Spokes agreed and sat down, after all where else was there for him to go.

Hash went back and found Rebecca. "May I speak to your father or Dr. Sables? It concerns the young man sitting in your lobby?"

Rebecca glanced into the front room of the clinic and saw the man Hash must have been referring to. She put down a box she was carrying that looked like it was full of cloth bandages. "They are pretty busy right now but maybe I can help?"

Hash lowered his voice so Spokes couldn't hear. "That man out there ate some food off the tray at the jail that was poisoned. I was wondering if either of the doctors had an opinion as to why he isn't sick or even dead already?"

Rebecca had heard the story and was wondering that herself but felt she should get one of the doctors to answer Hash's question. "Let me ask if one of them can spare a minute to speak to you." She went down the hallway to the door at the end and entered. Hash had finally figured that that must be some sort of surgery room. No one other than the doctors or Rebecca were allowed in there, except for the sick or wounded of course.

After only a minute Dr. Sables came out and went to the kitchen to talk to Hash. As he poured himself some coffee he said, "I left Rebecca back there to help Dr. Barnes while I came out here to talk to you. It was good timing on your part Burton because I was really in need of some coffee. What was it you needed to talk to me about?"

"I know you are busy Doctor, I'll try to be brief. It's about Spokes out there. He ate some bad food off that tray as you know. What do you think is going to happen?"

Dr. Sables smiled and said, "You know Burton, I have been thinking about that ever since we found him a little while ago. We have three dead men, maybe more, who came in contact with either that food or the poison itself. That young man said he only took a biscuit and I tend to believe him. I mentioned it to Dr. Barnes back there while we were changing the bandages on one of the wounded men from the train and he agrees with me. The poison was in the gravy. The dead prisoner had crumbled up a biscuit and was eating it with the gravy and that must have been how he died. The other biscuit, the one that Spokes took was not contaminated. Whoever done this put all the poison in the gravy and then smothered it with pepper in order to disguise the arsenic. Our young friend out there is one very lucky man."

"But doctor, the other two men that are dead, they didn't eat the gravy; you said they must have breathed in the powder when they pounded it from a crystal form into a powder form. Wouldn't that have also been on the two biscuits?" Hash asked.

For Lack of a Title

"You would think so but it must not be the case. They must have mixed the arsenic in the gravy and then brought it over to the tray and finished their mischief. The tray must have been several feet from the poison and didn't get contaminated. Spokes shows no signs of sickness and I believe he will stay that way. The only thing that looks like he is going to die from anytime in the near future is starvation." With that Dr. Sables picked up his coffee cup and went back to the surgery room.

Hash went back out to the front room where Spokes sat reading another of the glossy magazines. "I just spoke to the doctor; he says you are free to go. Apparently that biscuit you took this morning wasn't your last meal after all."

Spokes put down the magazine and looked up at Hash. "That is good news, but what I am more concerned about right now is my next meal. That biscuit and them dried apples I had are running pretty low." With that he got up and headed for the door.

Hash wondered what the man had in mind. "Where are you going Spokes?"

"I thought you said I was free to go Mr. Burton. I know where there's a turnip patch at the edge of town, thought I might try to find something that got left in the ground from last year."

Now Hash felt really bad for the young man. Without help it was a good possibility he would starve to death. "Well Spokes, if I have anything to do with it you will have a job pretty soon. In the meantime why don't you let me buy you some supper, I know a place where the food is good and you can have all you want. How does that sound?"

"Well that sounds pretty good to me but I can't accept it unless I can work it back out."

This was truly a rare human being Hash thought. He wouldn't let anyone help him unless he could do something in return. "Well Spokes, you are kind of on the payroll right now. The sheriff thinks you can identify the man who put that poison tray on the front porch of the jail this morning. Until that happens you are a ward of the city. And I would also add that the food that was poisoned was meant for a man who shot my friend who is back there in one of these clinic recovery rooms. You help us figure out who is at the source of all the evil around here and you will more than earn your keep. And like I said, I intend to check out your story about who you worked for up in Cleveland. If everything is the way you say it is then I can guarantee you a job, how does that sound?"

Spokes smiled and stuck out a dirty hand. Hash was reluctant to shake it but didn't want to hurt the boy's feelings. "You can check out my story and then you'll know that you can trust me. The Standard Oil Company has offices on the Cushing Block in Cleveland. If you send a telegraph then I am certain they will verify my former employment," Spokes said and then released Hash's hand.

"Alright then, how about you and me head to the Depot Café and I will set you up with some supper?" Before they left, Hash left word with Rebecca of where they were going in case the sheriff came back from the courthouse looking for Spokes. The walk to the café took a little over ten minutes. Hash kept the young man talking the entire way. As he listened he kept a constant vigil in case there might be an attempt on the witness. He doubted that word had gotten out about Spokes yet but he still didn't want to take any chances.

Once at the café Hash and Spokes entered through the Saloon and then headed toward the restaurant. Hash nodded at

Burt as they went by the bar. It wasn't very busy in the dining room but the few who were there immediately noticed Spokes. Hash pointed to a table way over in the corner and had him to sit down. A lady Hash had never seen before came over and almost gasped when she saw the threadbare skeleton sitting in the chair. She regained her composure when she noticed the tall stranger who accompanied the man.

Hash spoke first, "Hello miss, my name is Hash Burton and my friend here would like to order some food. If you would be so kind as to see to him then I will excuse myself, I need to talk to my friend at the bar."

You could almost see the woman blush, either from being spoken to by this tall stranger or by the fact that he had called her miss. She said she would see to it at once. Hash looked at Spokes and said. "I'm going in the saloon to talk to the bartender. I won't be able to join you for dinner but I will be in the next room. If you need anything then come in there and find me." Spokes nodded and then turned his attention to the waitress.

Hash walked into the saloon and headed toward the bar. Burt walked the length of the bar and asked, "Where on earth did you dig up that dead body you came in with Burton?"

Hash turned back toward the dining area and saw Spokes talking to the waitress, undoubtedly telling her what he wanted to eat and drink. He turned back to Burt, "That dead body as you call him is the only witness who might be able to identify the man who hired them three gun hounds that tried to shoot me and did shoot Riley the other night."

Burt looked at the skinny stranger again. "You don't say. You think he'll live long enough to testify? I done heard what happened to that one that survived your six-shooter and my shotgun the other night. Someone said he got poisoned right here in our jail this very morning."

"You heard right Burt, and that's one of the reasons I came over here to talk to you. You remember the other night when you and I had that little talk right after they shot Riley?"

"Shore do Burton. I will never forget that night for as long as I live."

Hash lowered his voice. "Well when you told me the story about you killing, I believe you used the phrase 'double digits,' was that real or was it the whiskey talking?"

Burt smiled and then he frowned, "That is not a story I am proud of Burton. I would have never told it if I wasn't so upset about killing that man, but you know how whiskey has a lubricating effect on a man's tongue. The story is true and I would appreciate it if you would keep it to yourself."

Hash smiled, "You don't need to worry Burt. It's that story that got me to thinking that you could help me out."

"I reckon since me and you done been in a gun battle and survived then it kind of makes us brothers don't it? What is it you need?" Burt asked.

"Well Burt, we got to hide him away for a few days. I need someone to put him up and also that same someone needs to be handy with a gun if you know what I mean?"

Burt looked back at the stranger. "Is he tame or is he a troublemaker Burton?"

"He's tame Burt. He's from Cleveland Ohio and from what he has told me he's just down on his luck," Hash said.

"My guess is that his luck just got a little worse. Whoever killed that man in the jail will kill him once he finds out he's a witness. I really hate a murdering bastard. What can I do to help Burton?"

"Burt, you said you got a place over top of the saloon here where you stay. If you put him up here do you think you can keep it quiet?"

"Damn right Burton. I got two bunks up there and no one ever goes there but me. There is a couple of big windows that look out on the river, he can sit and watch that flood take over the town. I would ask one favor though, that you get him cleaned up a bit, I got standards." With that Burt busted out laughing.

"That sounds like it'll work. Two more questions though, do you keep a gun up there and can you sneak his food up to him so nobody suspects we got him hid here?"

"I don't keep a gun upstairs but I believe for the next few days I will take my Greener up there with me, might pay to use a little extra caution under the circumstances. And you don't have to worry about anyone trying to poison him either. The two women that cook here have been here for years and they are both good and honest. He'll be a lot safer here than in that jail, I can guarantee it."

Hash reached Burt twenty dollars. "That should cover the food for a few days. Where can he get cleaned up?"

"Take him around the corner. There's a barber shop there and they got a bathhouse attached. Tell you what, I know the man pretty well who cuts the hair, he drinks here each night before going home to that witch he's married to. You take that young feller over there and get him a haircut and shave." Burt took another look at the skinny trash heap and said, "Tell Bosco to put double suds in the tub, I don't think this is a time to be skimpy on the soap. Don't bring him back here when he's finished. I'll get someone to cover for me at the bar so I can go and collect him in an hour or so, might bring less attention that way."

Hash thought that was a good plan except for one thing. "You can't carry that Greener to the barber shop and back Burt. Here take this; you can give it back to me tomorrow." Hash made sure no one was looking and then reached into his vest pocket and pulled out the two shot derringer. Burt took it and slid it into his pocket without any lost motion. Hash could tell that Burt had been more in life than just a bartender who had ten kills notched on his gun. He would need to hear the entire story someday. "You ever shot a derringer before Burt?"

"Sure have, I carried one for years. You might say I earned two of my notches with a derringer, had to dispatch a couple of sour hombres one night after they jumped me and took my Colt."

Again Hash was impressed. "Burt, I'll see that you get paid for your trouble," Hash said.

Burt grinned and said, "I don't need any money Burton, tween you and me I'm set for life." Hash again was surprised. The bartender was a professional killer and had a substantial piggybank hidden somewhere.

Hash looked over and saw that Spokes was nearly finished. He said his so long to Burt and headed back to the dining room. When the waitress seen Hash she came back over and said, "He never ate very much, at least not as much as he should." Hash knew the man's stomach had undoubtedly shrunk.

"How much do we owe you miss?" Again the woman blushed.

"No more than he ate I'm ashamed to charge you anything at all but I guess a dollar and a quarter will cover it."

Hash reached into his pocket and pulled out two dollars and fifty cents. "Here you go, thanks for being so nice."

The waitress took the money and blushed her way back toward the kitchen.

"Spokes, how was supper?"

The young man picked up the cloth napkin and wiped his mouth. "That is more than I have had to eat at one time in over a month. Thank you Mr. Burton"

"Glad to help Spokes. How about you and me take a little walk, I need to fill you in on a few things." Both men headed out the door and went in the direction that Burt had mentioned. Just around the corner was another street with any number of small businesses. Down about halfway was a barber pole, the kind that was painted in a red and white swirl pattern. Hash and Spokes walked in; there were two barber chairs and only one customer. A stocky older man wearing a white apron was sweeping up. Another man, also wearing an apron, was working on the customer.

"Haircut today gentlemen?" The man with the broom asked.

Hash pointed at Spokes. "My friend here needs the works, shave and haircut and after that a trip to the tub. Burt over at the saloon said to ask for a man named Bosco. Would you be that man?"

The man smiled and said, "That would be me. I was just about to go over and see old Burt."

"Yea Burt said you're a regular," Hash said.

Bosco laughed, "Some days I need a little of that liquid courage he sells before I can go home to the wife. She can be a contrary bitch if you know what I mean?"

"That might have been something else that Burt mentioned but I am not one to judge. How much will it cost for my friend here, and one more thing, Burt said to use extra suds."

Spokes looked at himself in the mirror and said, "Extra suds is a pretty good idea."

"Let's see, that all comes to three dollars." Bosco looked at the rags Spokes was wearing. "You plan on getting them clothes cleaned mister? It'd be a shame to get all cleaned up and then put back on them dirty duds."

Spokes looked at Bosco and said, "Naw, I only got these and if they're getting cleaned then that would mean I would be naked."

That gave Hash an idea. If Spokes was clean and sporting a new haircut and shave he would be harder to recognize. If he also had different clothes it might just make him impossible to identify as the filthy young man he was earlier laying on the bench in front of the courthouse. Hash looked from Spokes to Bosco, "Is there anywhere close where he can get a pair of pants and shirt?"

"Two doors down they sell good solid work clothes at a reasonable price."

"Alright then, get started and I'll go and get him something to wear. Throw what he's wearing now in the trash. I'll be back in a minute," Hash said as he headed out the door. Just before he left he reached into his pocket and pulled out a five dollar bill. "Here's a five, keep the change."

Within a few minutes Hash was back carrying a clothing bundle. "Spokes, I got the tallest and thinnest pants they had, I told them what you looked like and they reached me these. In a few days we'll see about getting you a new pair of boots but for now them you got will have to do. Shirt, socks, and a new belt are also in the sack. Bosco, can you step out on the sidewalk for a second, I need to speak with you."

Bosco stepped out on the sidewalk and asked, "What's up mister?"

Hash stepped a little farther down from the door and said. "That man in there is important to the sheriff and the judge. I don't want anything to happen to him. Burt will come over in an hour or so and take him away. In the mean time I would like for you to lock your door. When that other customer is finished let him leave but don't let anyone else in, is that alright with you?"

"Well we'll be closing in a little while anyway. If it's for Sheriff Barnes then it's certainly alright with me."

"And one more thing, don't mention anything to anyone about what I just told you. A man's life could be at risk if you do," Hash said.

Bosco seemed to be pleased to help. It was apparent that his life must be a little boring and this would be excitement to him. "You can count on me. What did you say your name was mister?"

Hash reached the barber a couple more dollars and said, "This is for your trouble and the names Burton, Hash Burton. I got to go so keep a close eye on my friend in there until Burt gets here."

"Don't worry about a thing, everything will be as you asked," the barber said.

Hash turned and headed back toward the clinic.

Sheriff Barnes was also on his way to the clinic. He had worked out the details on where to stash the witness until he could figure out how to proceed. As Hash turned the corner and headed by the jail he stepped in and saw Jake. "Has the sheriff been in lately?" he asked.

"Haven't seen him since I brought that bunch over from the bank, them six been back there cussing this town to hell. I closed the door so they can cuss in private." Jake laughed at what he just said.

Just as Hash was about to speak Sheriff Barnes walked through the front door, "Burton, you are the man I been trying to find. They told me over at the clinic that you left with Spokes about an hour ago. Where you two been?"

"I took him over to the café for some food. He's at a barbershop run by a man named Bosco now. You know him?"

"Yea, I know Bosco, I get my hair cut there from time to time. You think it was a good idea to leave him there by himself Burton."

"I think so. No one knows who he is. I would doubt that the man he can identify could even figure out who our mystery witness is. I got him all squared away with Burt at the saloon. Burt is pretty damn tough if you ask me and I think he'll be safe there."

Sheriff Barnes walked over to the stove and picked up the coffee pot, it was empty. Jake seen this and said, "Sorry Sheriff, we been too busy to keep that coffee going today."

Barnes sat the pot back down and said, "Don't worry about it Jake. You get them six brought over and put away alright?"

"Sure did, have them all tucked away nice and quiet in the back. Got them all in one cell like you asked and it's pretty crowded."

"Why do you have the partition door closed?"

"I got tired of hearing them cuss. They done threatened to burn this town to the ground if I didn't let them out so I closed the door. They can still cuss and sling snot but I can't hear em," Jake said. "What do you plan to do with them now Sheriff, we got nothing to hold them for."

Barnes grinned. "Yes we do. They just threatened arson. Keep them in there until Monday morning. I'll have the county attorney draw up the charges and then we can march them in front of Judge Helton. I really didn't want to turn them bastards loose on a Friday night anyway."

The sheriff and Hash walked back to the Café and got a table as far away from everyone else as possible. Rebecca was now working her second job as a waitress. When she saw the two men she brought over a coffee pot and two cups. As she filled both, she told the sheriff that the three wounded men from the train were resting comfortable and should be alright in a few days. Riley would be there for quite a while. His chest wound did not want to heal properly but her father said not to worry, it would just take time.

Hash for fun asked, "What's the special tonight?"

Rebecca smiled and said, "Well Friday is a little different than the other week days, pulled pork barbeque along with baked potato and slaw."

The sheriff said, "That sounds fine with me Rebecca. Say how are those twin sisters of yours doing in the big city?"

"Just fine Sheriff, my dad says he can't wait until they graduate this spring. We can sure use the help over at the clinic. Will you be having the special also Mr. Burton?" Hash nodded that he would and she turned and went back to the kitchen.

After she left the sheriff told Hash that Reed and Mack wouldn't be able to join them for supper tonight, they just had too much to do.

The sheriff then told Hash about Rebecca's two sisters, both were in nursing school in Louisville and looking forward to graduation and then coming back to Prestonsburg to work in the clinic their father and Dr. Barnes ran. They had been gone for nearly two years, coming in about every two months to visit their father and sister. The town was growing and the twins would be the first nurses to work at the clinic.

"I got the judge to loan me the basement to the courthouse for a few days. He's going to have his bailiffs guard Spokes until he can figure out our next move. As soon as we get finished with supper I want to get Spokes and head him over there. The bailiffs are there now getting everything ready."

Hash thought it was a good plan but he already had his own plan with Burt. "Sheriff, I told Burt to put him upstairs over the saloon for a few days. That's where Burt stays and I feel comfortable with the arrangement. Burt can be his body guard. He keeps a twelve-gauge Greener shotgun under the bar, and this place is always busy. Kind of like hiding him right out in the open. No one would suspect he would be in a place like this."

Rebecca brought the food and when she left Barnes said, "I know very little about Burt but something tells me he's done some gun work in his younger days. You might be right about keeping him here Burton, but what do we do about the Judge's plan?"

Hash and the sheriff thought about this as they ate. Finally the sheriff said, "Tell you what. How about we keep him here like you said but we make the bailiffs believe they are actually guarding someone over at the courthouse. We put the bailiffs in the courtroom and tell them that the witness is going to be brought to the basement unseen. They guard the doors and I will have Jake and Scrappy bring the meals. They can sit down there and enjoy the food and then bring up the empty trays. No one will be the wiser and I'm sure the deputies will appreciate the free food."

Hash smiled and said, "You are a sneaky bastard Sheriff, I think that is an excellent plan."

"That would make both of us sneaky bastards Burton, you came up with the plan of using Burt's lodgings to hide him in." Both men laughed.

Burton paid the tab and said goodnight to Rebecca. He and the sheriff walked to the saloon and took a seat at the bar. Burt came over and asked what will it be?"

The sheriff declined, he never drank in public. Hash took a beer and ribbed the Sheriff about his tea totaling ways. "It's easy for you to say Burton but I got to get re-elected later this year."

"Tell you what Sheriff, you just sit right there and watch me enjoy my beer. I don't think that will cost you many votes."

Burt leaned over and said in a whisper, "Got Spokes squared away upstairs. I didn't recognize the scarecrow after he got cleaned up and put on them new duds." As he said this he slid the derringer across to Hash. "I got him all gathered up and brought over and didn't even get to try out this little toy of yours Burton."

"That toy can blow a hole in a man Burt. Glad everything went alright. You feel up to our little plan?"

"You damn right I am. Hell this is the most excitement I've had since I was down in................" Burt looked at the sheriff and then began wiping the bar with a cloth, "If you two need anything else just holler, you two ain't the only customers I got in here you know."

After the bartender moved away Sheriff Barnes said, "See what I mean. That man's got a story to tell and I'll bet it's a dandy."

Hash paid his tab and he and the sheriff went their separate ways. It was only a short distance to the Stanton

Hatfield house. By the time he got there it was completely dark outside. He wondered if Gray Bob was inside waiting on him. Before entering he walked around the big house, everything looked alright. He went inside the carriage house and then over to the ice cabinet. Hash opened the wooden door and sure enough Joe Tucker had it nice and full of ice and there on top was a six-pack of nice cold beer. He grabbed two and went to the front porch. After he found his key he unlocked the door and there sitting on the rug in the foyer was Gray Bob.

Hash re-locked the door and sat one of the beers on the floor in front of the dog. "Evening Gray Bob, I brought that beer in for you, find your own opener." Hash went up the stairs laughing. Within ten minutes he was sound asleep on the big bed. Hash thought he had played a pretty good joke on the old hound but he had made a serious mistake, he forgot to close and latch the bedroom door. The next morning before daylight Gray Bob got even by giving Hash another wet doggie-kiss across the face. Again Hash was awakened from a pleasant dream by a stinky dog's slobbery tongue.

"Gray Bob damn you," Hash shouted as he jumped from the bed and ran to the lavatory. As soon as he was out of sight Gray Bob climbed up in the big bed and immediately fell asleep. When Hash came back in to get dressed he saw the dog fast asleep in his bed. Hash put on the same clothes he had worn the previous day, he didn't know where the cleaners were and all his other stuff had been taken there by Joe Tucker the previous day. He told himself to check first thing this morning with the store keep.

As Hash descended the stairs he saw something that really surprised him. There on the sitting room rug was an empty beer bottle, beside it was the lid. Now how did Gray Bob manage to get that lid off? Hash looked back up the stairs and fully expected to see the hound standing at the top with a big, *'You really didn't think that lid could stop me did you?'* look on his face. Hash rolled the bottle to the side and as he went out the door he again said, "Damn dog."

It was just getting light and Hash wondered if the Depot Café was open yet, he doubted it. Maybe people would expect an early breakfast on a weekday but this was Saturday. As he walked by he looked inside, it was dark. He noticed the painting on the glass door and read the hours of operation, Saturday 9:00 till Midnight. He decided to head on over to the jail and see if the sheriff was out and about yet. He would come back for breakfast later and also check with Burt on whether anyone had tried to kill Spokes during the night.

There were several people on the street. Hash figured that a town like Prestonsburg was large enough to attract people at all hours of the day. Then he noticed a couple of wagons loaded with household belongings. As he walked he could tell that there was urgency in the way the early risers were acting. He stepped over to one of the wagons and asked what was going on. He was told that the river would probably break out of its banks late that evening or early night. He was told that people in the lower portions of town were trying to save what they could.

Sheriff Barnes had been out since four o'clock that morning knocking on doors and warning people that the river was still rising and that they should prepare. He and two of his deputies had notified everyone in the lower parts of town. Most people had already been taking precautions in the previous days, putting belongings in upstairs rooms. Those that didn't live in a two story house had been taking whatever would fit into lofts and attics. There was one portion of town that always flooded first and water was already creeping into the streets and yards of those homes. There were about fifteen houses there and they would all be flooded, no doubt about it. The families that lived there had been working for the last few days taking everything they could and storing it with neighbors, putting items in spare rooms of friends and even in the tops of barns.

Hash saw the sheriff and Scrappy coming up the street. He assumed they were headed for the jail and met them half way. "Morning Sheriff, looks like you got out early."

"Too early Burton, this damn flood is looking to be the worst one in fifty years, maybe even a hundred. How did our friend do last night?"

"Don't know yet. Everything is closed. I went there for breakfast and the door was locked and there wasn't any light inside. Sign on the door said nine-o'clock."

"Well I'm heading over to the jail, how about a cup of coffee at taxpayers' expense?"

"Sounds good to me Sheriff, I got a bad taste in my mouth and some coffee might just run it off."

Sheriff Barnes could tell that there was a story in that last statement. "Why Burton, what happened?"

"It's that hound dog of old man Hatfield's. This is the second morning in a row that that rascal has woke me up by licking me in the face. I'm starting to believe he knows magic, he even took the top off a beer bottle."

Barnes laughed, "Well, I see you've met Gray Bob, that hound is pretty smart. Hatfield said he could chew the lid off a beer bottle and I guess he wasn't exaggerating. You might want to sleep in one of the other rooms in that house; I believe Gray-Bob has dibs on the big one."

"I meant to lock the bedroom door last night but I guess I forgot, after the day I had it's a wonder I even found my way home. You know Sheriff, I did get a whiff of beer when that four legged bastard licked my face this morning."

"I really hated to evict that old man Burton. I still hate Reed a little for that," the sheriff said.

"Before I finish up my business in town I can promise you that old man Hatfield will be back in his house and he will possess a clear deed, no lean from the bank. I plan on doing a little horse trading and arm twisting with Reed. Hatfield will get his house back. Gray Bob probably wants the old man back there too."

Hash and Barnes entered the jail and headed straight for the coffee pot. Jake was in the back arguing with the six men who shared one of the jail cells. When he came out he slammed the big partition door and looked at the sheriff.

"Those six are getting pretty ornery Sheriff. Since you plan on keeping them until Monday you think I can use a couple more cells, you know two men to a cell?" Jake asked.

"Probably be a good idea Jake, but I want Scrappy here when you make the transfer. I don't want to take any chances. Have Scrappy hold a shotgun while you march them to the other cells. I'm not taking anything for granted with them strangers. As soon as Scrap shows up you can move em."

After Hash and the sheriff filled their cups Jake took the empty pot and refilled it with water. "How bad you think the town will flood Sheriff?" Jake asked.

"It looks pretty bad Jake. Everyone that can is moving their belongings now and some have even been moving for the last couple of days. You know though, I'm a little more worried about the troubles the town's got that aren't weather related."

"Know what you mean Sheriff, such as them six we got locked up in the back. Them is the most foul mouthed animals I have ever listened to. The sooner they are gone from here the better, "Jake said.

"Sheriff, as soon as the bank opens I would like to go over there and see if Mack has things under control. Did you ever get those lists from Reed and compare them?"

"Yea I did, he gave them to me after I left the café last night, I seen him on the street and he gave them to me. I glanced at all three lists and that is another thing that concerns me. I never realized that so many people had keys to that bank and the combination to the vault. Hell, it feels like the whole damn town is allowed a key. Those six cases of cash and gold, were they put in lock boxes in the vault Burton?"

Hash took a sip of his coffee. "All the lock boxes are rented. The money is still in the locked cases that arrived on the train and Reed and I are the only ones that have keys. Mack took the original set he had and had duplicates made at a locksmith here in town. After the bank employees counted the contents of the six cases they put the money back inside each case and then relocked all six. The keys were returned to Reed and he carries them on him at all times, same as I do. The cases are leather and reinforced. You can't just cut into them with a knife, it would take tools and that is just not going to happen during banking hours. Mack Ramsey will see to the security during the day and also make sure no employees enter at night. I am extremely confident that nothing will go wrong in the next few weeks. After that the problem solves itself. The proceeds in the six cases will have been spent."

Hash thought of another question. "Sheriff, is the locksmith in town an honest man?"

"I suppose so Burton; after all he is a locksmith, why do you ask?"

"Oh nothing I guess Sheriff, just thinking out loud."

"That is just an unheard of amount of money to be sitting in the middle of this town. I won't rest very well until it's spent. Let's me and you head over to the clinic and check on things Burton. After that we can look in on the bank and your six precious cases."

Both men sat down their cups and went out onto the street. The crowd had picked up a little. More people were either moving from the flood or were helping others with the move. It hadn't rained in at least three days and it looked like it was going to be another sunny day. All the water that had fallen in the previous weeks was now slowly moving down river and headed for the town of Prestonsburg. It was a little odd to be in bright sunshine while you watched the river grow and grow.

The clinic was busy this morning. One man had cut a deep gash in his shoulder when he fell from a barn loft while he was helping put away his neighbor's belongings. A young child had a high fever and a severe cough. Rebecca was tending to him while the two doctors cleaned and stitched the man's shoulder.

Hash and the sheriff didn't stay long, mostly because it is nerve-racking to see a child in distress and not know what to do. They both left knowing the little boy was in good hands. By the time the two got to the bank it was eight-thirty. Reed was there at the foot of the steps talking to Mack.

Burton asked, "How did everything go last night Mack?"

"No problems Mr. Burton. I stayed until a little past midnight and then went to the hotel. Two of the town's deputies took turns after that and when I got here they said no one approached the building the entire night."

Sheriff Barnes smiled and said, "A man wearing a badge and holding a Winchester rifle usually don't get asked many questions, especially after dark."

Reed went up the front steps and unlocked the door. By a quarter of nine most of the employees had already been let inside the building. Hash, along with the Sheriff and Reed went to the vault. After Reed entered the combination and opened the door all three men looked inside. Hash hadn't looked in the vault the previous day but had seen the plans and knew exactly what it would look like. The vault was large with three walls consumed by lock boxes, small ones at the top and the largest at the bottom. The vault door opened not in the center of the room but to the right. Hash had asked a vault company engineer why some vaults had the door offset. It was explained to him that when the door was open then anyone out in the bank could see inside. The people who rented lock boxes liked privacy when either putting items in or taking them out of their boxes.

This configuration left a large space to the left that wasn't in view of the rest of the bank. When a person was brought in then he used his key and the bank employee used the banks key to open the lockbox. It was then placed on a wooden table and the bank employee would exit. There was a door made of bars that would be closed during the day, never the vault door. When the customer was finished he would summon the bank employee to re-enter the vault and then the lock box would be secured back in the wall. The door with bars was always closed. When the three men stepped in they saw the six crates sitting against the wall, stacked three wide and two high. Everything was exactly the way it had been left from the previous day. Sheriff Barnes walked over and picked up one of the crates, it was heavy. He knew they had been in a locked bank vault the entire night but he just wanted to make sure they were still loaded with cash and gold.

Hash looked from inside the vault to the outside, to get in the vault you had to enter from behind the teller stations. This kept anyone from actually being able to look in the vault. His cases were completely hidden from view. You had to be in the vault to see anything to the left. It was a good set up.

As they left the vault Reed pulled the iron door made of bars shut. Hash stood and looked back through the bars. Still his cases and the table were hidden from view. No one could access his cases without a key. No one could haul away the cases without a lot of help and a wagon. Plus there were two men with guns in the lobby. Satisfied with the arrangement Hash and the sheriff left Reed to finish opening up his bank.

"You got time for a little breakfast Sheriff? It's nine-o'clock sharp and the café should be opening up."

"Are you buying Burton?"

"Why not, I hate to eat alone and you been out since four. I think a little breakfast will do the both of us some good. Plus we need to check on Burt and Spokes," Hash said.

When the two men got to the café it was already busy. Most of the people who were trying to get ahead of the flood must have hurried in to grab a bite of something. Burt was nowhere to be seen. The saloon would fill up later. The two picked a table against a wall and sat down. Hash thought it funny that men who carried guns always were a little shy about sitting in the middle of a room. Men who didn't carry guns sat anywhere they pleased and enjoyed their food without worry. He suspected that if you were prepared for trouble then you automatically expected it.

As the two sat eating breakfast and enjoying their coffee Burt came in. He walked over to the table and said good morning. The sheriff asked him to have a seat. "Why don't you join us for some breakfast Burt, I'm buying," Hash said.

Burt agreed and ordered the same thing, biscuits and scrambled eggs along with bacon and coffee. Although Hash and the sheriff never mentioned it to each other they could still see the tray of poisoned food in their thoughts and neither could stand the thought of gravy.

"Everything go alright last night Burt?" Hash asked.

"Just fine Burton; I took my Greener shotgun and a full box of shells upstairs last night after I closed the bar, kept it within arm's reach the entire night. That man Spokes never budged. I got up and checked on him a time or two; he was sleeping like a baby. This morning he asked me for something to read to help pass away the day. I got a couple of books up there, real old stuff; he looked at them and said they would do just fine. I plan on taking him some breakfast in a few minutes. I really don't think he can eat much though. It'll take him a few days to get used to having food again. He is the closest thing to a starved to death man that I ever did see."

"Where is the door that leads upstairs Burt, can you keep an eye on it and do your bartending at the same time?" The sheriff asked.

"Don't you worry any about that Sheriff. The door is back there in the kitchen. I had to tell Fern about Spokes staying here for a few days and she promised not to tell a soul except her husband, Henry. You know him Sheriff; he works in the mines during the week and runs the telegraph office over at the depot on the weekends. Fern said he talks telegraph talk in his sleep, you know dots and dashes, says he loves that job.

Anyway, the wires went down late yesterday due to the flood and he didn't have anything to do this weekend. When she told him this morning about Spokes being in danger and all, well he loaded up his twelve-gauge and she's got him sitting back there in front of that door doing guard duty. He was in the war you know, although he fought for the South. I asked Henry one time why he decided to fight for the South and he said it just happened to be closer. I guess that makes about as good a sense as any."

Hash liked to listen to Burt. It wasn't just what he said but it was also how he said it. "Burt, you think Henry and Fern can keep a secret about Spokes being here for a few days?"

"Yea I told them. Them are good people Burton, Spokes is hiding out here and that secret is safe," Burt said as he shoveled another spoon full of eggs into his mouth.

Sheriff Barnes finished his food and then drained the rest of his coffee. "I'd like to stay here and shoot the breeze with you boys but I ain't going to. Some of us have important jobs to do. And anyway the High Sheriff can't be seen with the likes of you two, might make me look less than respectable."

Burt looked at Hash and then at the sheriff, "You know I was thinking the same thing Barnes, people might start talking if they think I'm the type who would associate himself with a lowdown pistol packing tin badge carrying law dog like you. I got a reputation to uphold myself."

Barnes went out the door laughing. Burt looked at Hash and asked, "You think I might have hurt his feelings Burton?"

"I wouldn't think so Burt, I'm sure he's heard it all before." With that both men laughed.

As the day progressed Hash felt trapped. The roads in and out of Prestonsburg were now underwater. The sheriff had men checking all day and by three that evening the last road was covered by a foot of water and getting deeper with each passing hour. The fifteen low-lying houses had started to be surrounded by the brown muddy water early in the morning and by four o'clock water was entering through the doors of the lowest one. Jake and Scrappy were there to look things over and report back to the sheriff. A woman and four children were standing nearby and Jake saw the children start to cry, it was their house. He looked at Scrap, "Has Mrs. Handshoe got a place to stay until the water goes back down?" Scrap said he didn't know but was about to find out.

Scrappy went over and picked up the youngest child and wiped away her tears with his handkerchief. "Don't you worry none little lady. Me and some of the other men in town are going to clean your house up as good as new as soon as that mean old water leaves town, I promise you. Now you be brave and just remember that you got a whole town full of friends to take care of you." The little girl stopped crying and smiled at Scrappy. He sat her back down and asked her mother, "Where are you and the children staying?" He knew her husband was a hardworking man who worked the trains. He was probably stuck down around Ashland at that big freight yard and couldn't get home because of the flood.

Mrs. Handshoe smiled and said, "We're staying with my sister and her husband."

Scrap said, "I know who you're talking about. Why don't you and the kids head on over there, this is just too upsetting for the children."

"I know deputy, I was just waiting to see if by some miracle the flood water would stop rising and spare these houses. The miracle didn't show up though did it?" she asked.

For Lack of a Title

Jake took his eyes off the house and said, "No ma'am, it shore didn't."

As the woman and her children turned to leave Scrappy said, "Mrs. Handshoe, please stop by the sheriff's office later today. Some people have been leaving food and dry clothing there. If you need anything at all just see one of the deputies or the sheriff. This town always takes care of its own when there's a flood. I reckon that's the way it's been in every flood before this one and I hope everyone after." He looked at the little girl again. "Now you be brave little one, this ain't anything but a little bump in the road." The little girl smiled as she followed her mother and her three older brothers toward town.

Jake and Scrappy stayed a little longer. They assured the other families that anyone who got flooded could expect all the help they needed getting everything back to normal. The sheriff and Judge Helton had made that commitment the night before while they were discussing the matter of Spokes. The sheriff had informed all the deputies early that morning as to what he and the judge had agreed on. He told them to spread the word. The judge would see that any money that was needed would be found. In years past the town and its churches had come together with great results, this time would be no different.

When Hash left the café he really didn't know what to do with himself. His plans when he arrived a few days back had been completely changed, so much had happened in those few days. As he headed toward the center of town he decided to go back to the bank and check on Mack. He wanted to see if the sight of men in the lobby carrying long guns was causing any problems or concerns for the everyday customers that frequented the bank. As he walked he paid attention to the people on the street. Lots of folks were about; most were

283

making preparations concerning the flood. These people caused him no concern. It was the occasional man leaning against a building or standing just around a corner. It was obvious these men were not locals. Most had tied down guns and range clothes. Hash had seen the look before, lone wolf. He also saw the occasional group of three to four of the same type, all just standing around town taking everything in.

When he got to Reed's bank it was doing a brisk business. People came and went, all in a hurry. The pending flood seemed to have woken up the sleepy little mining town. Hash climbed the steps and entered the lobby. There were two or three people at each window. He saw Spurlock standing behind one of the tellers watching a transaction. When he noticed Hash he quickly looked away.

One of the town's deputies was standing at the back of the lobby holding a Greener twelve-gauge shotgun. Hash had seen him before but didn't know his name. He only knew Scrappy and Jake. At the top of the stairs was Mack holding one of the sheriff's new Winchester rifles. Hash climbed the stairs so he could talk to Mack.

"Howdy Burton, how was breakfast?"

"Good Mack thanks. Everything in here looks nice and secure. Anything unusual catch your eye?" Hash knew that Mack was well trained by the Baldwin-Felts Agency. Part of that training involved spotting anything out of the ordinary. It was almost eleven o'clock and he was sure that Mack had paid close attention to everyone entering and leaving the bank.

"Not really anything obvious Burton but I suspect something is in the works." As Mack spoke he never took his eyes off the lobby downstairs.

Hash looked down and only saw people.

"What do you mean?"

Mack answered, still not taking his eyes off the lobby. "Well, if you watch that double front door, the one on the right. Anyone on the outside could look through that door and see the teller lines, you follow me so far?"

Hash looked at the door and then at the teller windows, he saw what Mack was talking about. "Yes, I see what you mean, go on."

"Well wait just a minute and I'll show you what I'm talking about. There, watch that door."

Hash looked back at the door on the right. A man had stepped up and was peering through the glass. He looked over the lobby and then at the teller line. After a few seconds he was gone. "How often does that happen, Mack?"

"Pretty damn often Burton. Started about twenty minutes ago, there are at least three different men doing the looking. Something big is about to happen here Burton. I don't think they have seen me yet but they have surely spotted Zeke.

"Have you told anyone what you suspect?"

"Told Reed about five minutes before you walked in, he went downstairs and told Zeke what I saw and then he went in the vault just as you walked up here," Mack said.

Just then Reed came out of the vault and swung the big door closed and spun the wheel. "I think that was a pretty good thing to do under the circumstances Burton, what do you think?"

"I think I'm going out to have a little talk with the next man who looks through that door Mack. Regardless of what happens outside you and the deputy stay in here." With that said Hash turned and descended the stairs.

As Hash got near the bottom Reed took notice and walked around the teller line. He walked over as casual as could be and under his breath said, "Mack thinks we might have a problem Burton, I locked the vault just in case."

"Yea Mack has a good nose for trouble Reed." Hash walked over and noticed that the vault door couldn't be seen from the front door. If the men on the outside planned any trouble and wanted in the vault then they wouldn't know it until they were fully inside. "Closing that door might have protected the contents but it still won't prevent an attempt. They probably still think the vault is open."

Reed looked at the two doors. "You're right Burton; they might still burst in here with guns blazing. What do you think we ought to do?"

Hash knew he couldn't pull Mack or the deputy away from their positions and he couldn't go to the sheriff, time would not allow it. If he did nothing then innocent people might die. "I think I need to go and make a presence on the outside Reed." Hash headed for the door.

"Well I'm coming with you Burton."

Hash was impressed with the backbone Reed had shown in the last few days. "You still got that shoulder holster under your coat Reed?"

Reed patted his chest and said, "I do, and I also have a gun in it."

The two men walked through the big front door, Hash in front. Outside the streets were still busy, people going both ways on the sidewalks. Hash wasn't concerned with the ones moving, he was looking for the stragglers, anyone standing or sitting and looking at the bank. He counted seven but knew possibly more were around. "How long until you close the bank Reed?"

Reed took out his pocket watch and said, "Forty-eight more minutes, what do you think we should do?"

As Hash was running through the options available to him he realized that each one most likely ended with either himself or Reed dead, probably both. He felt events would make the choice for him. "We wait right here Reed. If they make a play on the bank then you try and make it back inside and lock those doors. Mack and Zeke will see to the safety of your customers and employees."

Reed looked at Hash, "And after I lock that door what will happen to you?"

"Someone needs to be out here returning fire to give you time to get everyone behind cover in there. I plan to shoot anyone that makes it to the base of the steps."

Reed looked across the street. A few of the men wearing guns were gathering. He counted five and it looked like there were several more on the way. "That's suicide Burton."

"I guess we'll see," Hash said.

Just then Sheriff Barnes, along with Jake and Scrappy, came down the sidewalk. Jake saw the gathering first and told the sheriff that it looked like trouble was brewing. The sheriff had seen Hash and Reed on the front porch of the bank. He headed across the street and straight for the group of men, Jake and Scrappy right beside him. The men saw him coming and began to scatter, walking as if they were minding their own business. By the time Barnes had crossed the street the men had thinned out considerably. There wasn't any reason for the sheriff to say or ask anything. If the group of strangers had something in mind it was over now or at least for the time being. Jake and Scrappy stayed on the sidewalk and watched the men leave as the sheriff walked back to the bank.

When Barnes got to the top of the steps he looked at Hash and asked, "What was that all about Burton?"

"Don't really know Sheriff, but your timing was impeccable."

Reed said, "If you think it's going to be alright now then I must open the vault back up. There are things that must be attended to before we can close for the weekend."

"I think the problem is solved for the moment thanks to the sheriff here and his two deputies. Finish up your work Reed. I plan on staying out here until you are fully closed for the day."

After Reed went back inside Hash looked at Barnes and said, "That was a close one Sheriff. What brought you to the bank; I thought you and your deputies were busy helping with flood relief?"

"We are but every Saturday at eleven thirty I come to the bank to cash the payroll check so I can pay the deputies. I usually come alone but I had Jake and Scrappy come with me so they could check out this end of town. Everyone in my department gets paid on Saturday. If I ever forgot to get here before they closed at noon then my deputies would probably put me in my own jail. You really think the bank was about to get hit Burton?"

"It was really looking like it. You take eight or ten hard cases with guns storming the bank right at closing on a Saturday, it just might have worked."

"Well, I think the trouble has passed. I better get inside so Reed can cash the payroll check. You staying out here Burton?"

"I believe so Sheriff, at least until noon."

When Reed locked the doors at twelve o'clock sharp Mack came down from his perch at the top of the stairs and walked up to Hash who had now come in from his guard duty on the front porch of the bank. "Mr. Burton, I need to talk to you a minute if you don't mind."

"Sure thing Mack, what's on your mind?"

"Well, I was just wondering if you have ever heard of a man by the name of James Arthur Pack?"

Hash thought about this for a minute, "I believe I have heard of him Mack. Isn't he one of the detectives with your agency?"

"He is. He was sent down here a few weeks ago to do some scouting around. He was to gather information and send it back up north if you know what I mean?"

Hash knew that Mack had to be careful with his words. Pack was an operative that was working in the shadows and there were still people in the bank. "I know exactly what you mean, why do you ask?"

"Well, he hasn't been heard from in a little over a week. It was one of my duties to find him and report back after I made the delivery to the bank. I asked around a little yesterday evening but no one has seen him in a few days. Jeremy Eisner said the last he saw of him was Monday, said he bought a ticket for one of the trains heading up past Martin."

Hash didn't find this out of the ordinary. "The flood up that way is bad from what I hear; my guess is that he's trapped up there. If he hasn't shown up by the time the flood recedes then I'll ask around. Right now it wouldn't be a good idea to ask too many questions though."

"You're probably right Mr. Burton, just thought I'd ask."

As the sheriff was leaving Reed came over to unlock the front door to let him out. "Are you planning on staying a little longer Burton?"

"No Reed, I think I'll leave with the sheriff."

"Well the bank will be completely shut down in about an hour. That little drama we had earlier has gotten us behind. Can't run a bank with the vault door closed you know."

Hash noticed the tellers were counting down their drawers and reaching them to Spurlock who was putting them in the vault. When both men were outside they heard Reed lock the door from the inside.

"Was Reed out here to back you up earlier Burton?"

"You know Sheriff, he really was. I have been in a situation or two in my life when I've had men on my side. I believe Reed would do as well as any of the others, maybe ever better."

When Hash and the sheriff made it back to the jail the large front room had been transformed into a relief center. There was baked food of every variety and several bundles of clothing, with more arriving every few minutes. Four women from one of the churches were separating and folding the clothing and sorting it into stacks. Hash wondered why this wasn't being done at the church itself but then realized that churches flood too. The couple of church buildings he had seen while in town looked like they were in the lower sections which were probably now taking on water.

Both men poured coffee. The deputy who had been taking care of the jail while Barnes, Jake, and Scrappy went to the bank was a new one Hash had never seen before. "Who's the new guy Sheriff?"

"Names Fred Miller, he's Jakes brother. I use him on the weekends so a few of the regular deputies can get a day off. The way things are looking around here though I believe he's going to be getting a few extra hours."

Hash thought about Fred and Jake, apparently his parents liked names that only had one syllable. He wondered if it was any indication regarding intelligence. Then he realized that he had been named Hash and let the thought drop.

As Hash watched the women sort and fold clothes he heard the front door open. "Why hello Judge, didn't expect to see you at the jail today," Fred said.

Hash turned to see a man who looked to be around fifty years old. He was bald and slightly overweight. He was smoking a cigar; it looked like the same kind Reed smoked.

"Hello Fred, I just came over to check on the town's preparations for the flood. How's it looking Sheriff?"

"Pretty bad Judge. The deputies and me been out since about four o'clock this morning. Water is already entering some of the lower houses, one of the churches too. Most everyone is ready though or at least as ready as they can be."

"Has everyone got a place to stay?" the judge asked.

"Most people are staying with family. A few are staying with some of their neighbors or friends whose houses shouldn't flood. Even got a couple staying in tents up on higher ground so they can keep an eye on their houses. I can't say I blame them. It must be a hard thing to watch that water invade a man's home."

The judge looked a Hash. He had never seen him but knew who he was; word had spread fast about the gunfight early in the week and the tall stranger who was involved. "You wouldn't happen to be Hash Burton would you?" the judge asked.

Hash stuck out his hand, "Yes sir, and from what I gather you would be Judge Helton."

Both men shook. The judge liked the fact that a stranger had heard of him, especially a stranger from New York.

"You've made quite a splash in our little town Mr. Burton."

Hash thought it ironic that the judge would use a term that referred to water, especially with all the water moving into town. "I assure you it was not my intention judge. I had hoped to enjoy the quiet and solitude of your peaceful little town but I guess it wasn't to be."

"Well you are surely filling up my docket. But you know no sooner does a man get a court date than he gets poisoned, very strange stuff Mr. Burton, very strange indeed. Prestonsburg has seen more mischief since you got here than at any other time that I can remember."

"Well Judge, I can't predict trouble, I can only deal with it when it shows up." Hash was still trying to figure out if he liked the judge. He could care less if the judge liked him.

"Yes Burton, I see your point. Anyway Sheriff Barnes, is there anything else the town can do to help its citizens?"

This was the opening the sheriff was hoping for. "Well Judge Helton, right now I think it would be important for our fine mayor to sober up and visit some of the residents. I haven't seen him in over a week and if he plans on getting re-elected then he better start doing his job." Barnes said this with as much deference as he could muster for the mayor. What he really wanted to do was to beat the shit out of the worthless son-of-a-bitch.

"Now Sheriff, Mayor Tillman has suffered a grievous loss and we need to give him time to work things out," the judge said.

Mayor Augustus Tillman had been mayor for four full terms and was nearing the end of his fifth. He was an excellent mayor as mayors go; he showed up for work each day and did what he could to run the town to everyone's satisfaction. He along with his wife lived in a large house that overlooked the town. After she died he kept the house and raised his five children alone, all the while holding down two jobs, one of which was mayor. He had three sons and two daughters. All three sons worked the mines near town and were starting families of their own. The two daughters had married and moved away a few years before.

Mayor Tillman was one of the most respected men in Floyd County, then tragedy struck. One morning the three brothers went under the mountain to pull a ten hour shift. None of the young men realized that they had just walked into their own graves.

Methane gas was always a danger in the mines. It lay dormant and harmless in the seams of coal for centuries. When a mine is driven into the side of a mountain this sometimes allows the gas to seep into the tunnels and accumulate. When a spark is produced from a hammer or a drill or any of a hundred other ways then the gas can explode with terrible force. That is what happened on the morning that the three Tillman brothers were killed, along with four other men. The explosion was of such force that the roof of the mine sat down on top of the men. It was decided after much heart wrenching deliberation that it was much too dangerous to attempt a rescue. The men were dead anyway, either from the explosion or the roof collapse. The force of the blast was so strong that debris was blown out of the mine and had hit the opposing mountain. It was like a shotgun blast, but with catastrophic force.

Augustus begged the mine's owners to at least make an attempt to rescue the men. He held out hope that the seven men were still alive, maybe trapped on the other side of the collapse. He wouldn't listen to reason. His sons were alive and might be at this very moment trying to dig their way out. You can't abandon men because you think they are dead, you have got to try he begged.

Throughout the day other miners had gathered at the entrance. These were men who knew the dangers of the business. A methane explosion, especially one strong enough to drop the roof of a mine, left no survivors. Any attempt to recover the bodies might lead to more deaths. All agreed that it was just too much to ask of any man.

The mine would be sealed, never to be entered again.

Sheriff Barnes wasn't a man without compassion. Quite the opposite, he was a man with a strong set of morals and he could empathize with those who were down on their luck or dealing with a personal tragedy. But he was also a realistic man. Everyone dealt with tragedy and his way of thinking was that life must go on. You allow the sorrow to carry you off to a dark place for a few days and then you step back into your own world again. You carry on. His mother many years before had told him a little poem that her mother had taught her when she was little. At times when others were hurting he always thought of the poem his mother had taught him.

If you speak it, make it soft and sincere,
If you sing it, make it pleasant to the ear,
If you do it, be just and show no fear,
If you lose it, hold the memory near.

The sheriff had always remembered that little poem. His mother told him that it contained the outline for a good life; he didn't understand this when he was young but now, many years later, he knew exactly what his mother meant. Mayor Tillman had lost something but now he was holding on too tight.

The mine explosion, and subsequent roof collapse, had happened a little over a year prior. The mayor had suffered terribly when no attempt was made to rescue his sons or the other four men. He stayed at the mine entrance for two days and nights hoping that his sons would walk out. He wanted to be there when they finally made it outside. After forty-eight hours it was decided by some of the men in town to forcefully bring him down off the mountain and take him home. He hadn't eaten a bite and as far as anyone could tell he had not had a drop of water to drink in all that time.

By the time the mayor was brought off the mountain he was too weak to resist. He was taken to his home and deposited in his own bed. Some of the men would check on him every few hours. He had no wife; she had passed away giving birth to the last of their five children, a boy.

Augustus was fortunate that the first two children, the girls, were ten and twelve years old when their mother passed away. They cared for the three younger boys which allowed their father to work and support the family. The men and women of the town admired Augustus. When he had ran for mayor the first time he was elected almost unanimously.

The loss of the three boys had devastated their father. When he finally ventured from his home after being deposited there by the town's men, nearly three weeks had passed. He now found solace in whiskey. He drank from sunup until sundown, sitting on his big front porch looking at the mountains that surrounded the town, the same mountains that had claimed the lives of his beloved sons. He had grown to hate the mountains. He was heard to curse them during the day.

It had been more than a year and Sheriff Barnes, who had once liked the mayor, now thought he had carried it too far. It was true that the sheriff had never suffered tragedy of that magnitude in his life, but it was time to move on. The town needed its mayor, especially with the flood of the century bearing down and now knocking on a few of the doors in town.

The sheriff looked at Judge Helton. He picked his hat up off of the desk and headed for the door. "I think I'll go up and have a little talk with our fine mayor."

Judge Helton looked at Hash and said, "Mr. Burton, if you have the time I would like for you to join the sheriff and myself." The judge knew it wasn't a good idea to allow Barnes to go to the mayor's house alone and he didn't want to go alone with the sheriff.

Hash didn't have anything better to do, for that matter he didn't have anything to do. He sat down his coffee cup and said, "I would love to Judge, might be better than staying down here and watching that flood consume the town."

"Oh, you will still get to see the flood. The mayor's front porch has the best view of all. He can sit up there and see almost anything happening in town," the judge said.

"That's when he's sober," Barnes added as he headed out the front door. "Fred, you make sure them six men in the back get some food soon." With that the three men headed for the mayor's house. As they proceeded down the street they could see the flood water at the lower end of town. Sheriff Barnes had always wondered why the river bank was higher than the land farther away. The flood wasn't spilling over the river's edge; it was backing up through the small streams and creeks that supplied it. As the water rose the back part of town was flooding first, not the homes and businesses that were nearest to the river itself. In all his years of living in Prestonsburg he had never heard of a single home or business near the river ever getting flooded. Mother Nature was a strange bitch he thought.

Two streets back was the road that led up the hill to the mayor's house. Along the way Barnes noticed more men wearing tied down guns. They were here and there either by themselves or in groups of two or three. They weren't here to help with the flood, for that matter it was as if they welcomed the flood and the isolation it would bring to the town. When the river rises it seemed the rats were the first to head for town.

As the three men approached the house up a fairly steep road it couldn't be seen at first, it was blocked from view by trees and shrubs. When they went around the last bend the house finally came into view. It was stately to say the least. On the way up the judge had explained to Hash that Mayor Tillman's father had done well in the timber business up until his death. His son, the mayor, was an only child and the house was left to him. It was overly large with a front porch that matched. The windows were also large giving the impression of a bright happy house. It was far from the truth. The house hadn't seen a smile since the day the mountain claimed the three sons.

A gravel path led from the driveway to the front porch, with the driveway continuing around back where there was a large carriage house. The elder Tillman and his wife were said to be nearly as wealthy as Stanton Hatfield, although Hatfield was now broke and living in a railroad shack. There were eight steps that led up to the front porch. At the base of the steps were two stone lions sitting on short pillars. Each lion held a steady gaze on whoever approached the steps, appropriate. The three men climbed the steps and the judge proceeded to knock on the front door.

There was a low moan down toward the end of the porch and all three looked in that direction. There in a swing lay a man sound asleep. The judge and the sheriff walked down in the direction of the swing, Hash stayed at the front door.

"Mayor, is that you?" Judge Helton asked.

There was no answer; the man in the swing snored away, oblivious to the men on his front porch. He was passed out cold. "Sheriff, you and Mr. Burton stay out here and try to wake him up. I'm going inside to make some strong coffee. When you get him up bring him inside, the sun out here will be a little harsh on the hangover he is going to experience." With that the judge went inside the house.

Judge Helton had been in the house many times. He played cards with the mayor and a few of their friends on several occasions. He hadn't been here though in almost a year. The place was still impressive even with a year's worth of dust. All the furniture was in the same place as it had been the last time he visited. He went to the kitchen and found the coffee pot which looked like it hadn't been used in months. There was still a small fire in the big white porcelain cook stove. He stoked the fire and filled the pot. The coffee in the bag was probably old but in the shape Tillman was in he didn't think it would matter. Before long the kitchen had the smell of strong coffee. Helton filled a cup, no sugar and no cream, just strong black coffee. He carried it into the front sitting room and sat it on a table beside Tillman's favorite chair. The men were still out on the front porch.

Judge Helton went out to see if Tillman had been brought back from the dead. Hash and the sheriff had managed to get him sitting up and he was holding on the side of the swing as if he might just fall out. "How is our man doing Sheriff?" The judge asked.

"He's dog drunk Judge, looks like he slept out here all night. I would say he hasn't drunk anything today but you can never really tell. You hold the door and me and Burton will try to get him inside." The two men grabbed Tillman under each arm and headed toward the front door. Judge Helton let the door go just in time to hit Tillman in the back of the head, there was a slight moan.

Sheriff Barnes looked at Helton, "You did that on purpose Judge."

"Well Sheriff, I don't think you can charge me with assault, I will just dismiss the charges. I thought a good bump on the head might wake him up long enough to drink that coffee I made."

The judge picked up the cup of steaming coffee as the sheriff and Hash held Tillman straight. The judge slapped Tillman on the face and said, "Augustus wake up, we need you to sober up and be a mayor for a while. Here take a drink of this, be careful its hot." He slowly held the cup to Tillman's lips and tipped it up. The coffee had cooled considerably but was still reasonably hot. As the coffee ran down Tillman's chin and onto his chest he started coughing.

He raised a hand and said, "What the hell are you trying to do, drown me?"

Sheriff Barnes said, "If you don't sober up soon then that's exactly what I'm going to do, drown you."

Tillman opened his eyes and said in a heavy voice, "Why hello Sheriff. I thought I heard Judge Helton a minute ago."

"You did hear me Tillman. The town is about to flood and we need you to sober up and do your job."

Tillman sat up under his own power and said. "Flood, what do you mean flood Judge, the sun is shining."

Judge Helton sat down the coffee cup and stepped in front of Tillman. He grabbed the mayor by both shoulders and shook him violently. "Gus, I need you to try to concentrate on what I am saying to you. The town is about to get one of the worst floods it has ever seen. We need you to pull yourself together and lend a hand, the town needs you."

Tillman put both hands on the arms of his chair and slowly stood. He reached for the coffee cup and raised it to his lips. He drank the entire cup and then reached it back to the judge. "I need more of that if you don't mind Isaiah."

Judge Helton went to refill the coffee cup. Barnes looked at Tillman and asked, "Did you understand what the judge just said Gus?"

"Yeah Sheriff, I heard him, why is everyone talking so loud anyway?"

"We aren't talking loud mayor; you're just suffering from a hangover. Are you going to straighten up and help or are we just wasting our time?" Barnes asked.

"Sheriff, go in the kitchen and put some vinegar and salt in a coffee cup. Half a cup of vinegar and one spoon of salt and then bring it out on the front porch."

Sheriff Barnes didn't know what he wanted that concoction for; it must be some sort of remedy for a hangover. He went and told the judge what Tillman had asked for. Judge Helton being a drinker from way back said, "Tabasco, he forgot Tabasco. Look in those cabinets over there and see what you can find." Within minutes the sheriff and Judge Helton were out on the front porch along with Hash and the mayor. They sat the remedy and the coffee on the railing and then stepped back, way back.

Augustus Tillman stood straight as he could and picked up the cup holding the stinky concoction. He took his free hand and held his nose as he turned up the cup and drank the contents in its entirety. When he finished he threw the cup in the yard and held on to the railing with both hands. He stood there holding on for dear life as he coughed and gagged. The sheriff looked at Hash and asked, "Now where have we seen that today?"

Before long the coughing stopped and Tillman picked up the coffee, he drank the entire cup, he then looked at the judge. "One more cup Isaiah, I think I'm starting to feel a little better." The judge winked at the sheriff and Hash as he hurried back to the kitchen.

Tillman looked at Barnes, "Now Ezra, tell me about this flood."

The sheriff filled in the mayor with as much as he thought a man in his condition could remember. It seemed to sober him up as he heard the troubles the town was having with the water. After he finished his third cup of coffee he reached the cup back to the judge and stood.

"You three head on back downtown. Give me time to clean up and get dressed. I'll come to your office first Sheriff and get all the up to date information. Does Scrappy and Jake still work for you?" Hash realized Sheriff Barnes hadn't exaggerated when he said the mayor had been drunk for a year.

"Yes they do Mayor, why do you ask?"

"Send both of them to all the businesses in town; I want to know what each intends to do to help the people of Prestonsburg. Have Jake do the writing, Scrap writes like a pig.

Oh I forgot, Scrap can't read or write, anyway I need that list fast Sheriff, so tell them to hurry. Judge Helton, can you go to the courthouse and see how much the county has in spare cash. And it better not be zero or I'll see that there's hell to pay." The mayor turned and headed inside the house, just at the entrance he turned and looked at the men. "Thanks Isaiah, thanks Ezra. And I want you to know that I'm sorry." With that he turned and went inside.

As the three men went down the hill the judge asked Barnes, "You still feel like kicking his ass Sheriff?"

"Not at the moment Judge. But if he slips back into his drunken ways after this flood I want you to authorize it."

The judge laughed and said, "You got yourself a deal Sheriff."

Back at the jail the preparations continued for the relief of the town's occupants. Sheriff Barnes sent Scrappy and Jake to get an inventory from the business's for the mayor. The six men in the back were being noisy again to the point that they could be heard out in the front room where the church women were working with the donations. Barnes had about had enough of their bitching and belly-aching. He grabbed five pairs of cuffs and told Fred to follow him.

The sheriff went into the cell area and once the six men seen him they all started yelping and yelling any number of obscenities. He unlocked one of the cells and reached in and pulled out the man he had hit the previous day. He knew now that that man was the leader of the bunch. Once he had him out in the big hallway the man drew back on the sheriff ready to strike him with his fist. Before he could Barnes hit him square on the jaw, the man got wobbly kneed and fell back on his ass. When he hit the floor he was out cold. It made twice in two days that the sheriff had knocked him out with only one blow. Sheriff Barnes was a tall powerfully built man and he also had a badge and a gun. The other five men immediately got quiet.

"Now you five have been screaming and cussing about being mistreated. Well you know what I think, you just got too much energy and I plan to fix that right now. This man beside me is Deputy Fred Miller. He has killed three men in the four months he's worked for me and I got a feeling that if any of you don't do exactly as he says then he might just make it four. Now I am going to put these five pairs of cuffs on you sorry son-of-a-bitches and you are going to go out and help people prepare for the flood. I don't think it's fair for you to be in here nice and safe eating for free while people are out there suffering. If any of you tries to run away then feel free. The town is cut off from the rest of the world and believe me you won't get far before old dead-shot Miller here has you on a slab in the undertakers office, got it?"

All five of the men looked at Fred and slowly shook their heads. "Now if you work hard and don't cause any trouble then I can promise you a good hot meal when Fred brings you back at dark. I won't order your food though until I see how many of you make it back alive. Remember Fred is looking for number four and anyone of you could be it."

After the sheriff cuffed the men's hands he winked at Fred and said just loud enough for the men to hear, "If you kill another man this month I'm going to take the burial expense out of your pay." The five looked at each other and then back at Fred. The sheriff made them drag their unconscious partner back into the cell. It dawned on the five that the sheriff had only brought five sets of wrist cuffs back with him. This sheriff was one mean bastard they must have thought.

Before they left Barnes told Fred to work the five men hard. He took away the young man's set of cuff keys, didn't want the prisoners to think they could overpower him and unlock their cuffs with his key. He made sure the prisoners saw what he had done. "Bring them back a little before dark, which will give you about three hours. Head down past Trimble, Jake and Scrap said some houses are already getting flooded down that way. They are cuffed but they can still lift and help some of the men move the heavier household belongings. If any of them so much as says one foul word then shoot him right between the eyes." Barnes hoped it wouldn't come to that but hey, no big loss.

After Fred led the five away one of the church women asked, "Sheriff, you don't think Fred would really shoot one of those men if he cursed do you?"

Barnes looked at her and said, "Yes ma'am if any of the men he just led out of here use the Lord's name in vain then he will shoot him."

Hash wondered how the four women would respond to what the sheriff had just said. They looked a little shocked at first but soon they were talking to one another again. Hash suspected the women wouldn't want anyone harmed but after the way those men had been screaming and using foul language then hell could have them and the sooner the better.

Soon the mayor entered the sheriff's office and you wouldn't believe the change. He was clean shaven, cleaned up and dressed in clothes that although nice were the type that would allow him to work in the mud alongside the town's residents if need be. "Sheriff, when do you think Scrap and Jake will be back?"

For Lack of a Title

"I don't know Mayor. I told them to get what they could finished before dark and then to report back here. It was a pretty late start, they can finish in the morning if need be. You really think the business in town are just going to give away stuff Mayor?"

"Yes Sheriff I do. This happened about fifteen years ago before you were in office. We had a pretty bad flood that year. I was new at my job and didn't really know what to do. I got to thinking that if the business could help out a little then the people in town might show their appreciation in the future by giving them their business. It worked. Each business owner I talked to later said it didn't cost that much and anyway, these were the people that were in and out of their stores on a regular basis. If the townsfolk could shop there in the good times then it didn't hurt to help out a little in the bad times."

Sheriff Barnes was impressed. He still wondered if this wasn't a little heavy handed. Some of the businesses that were barely making it would probably not be able to donate much if anything at all. He hoped the mayor would be fair with the people he was asking to donate. Still it didn't hurt to ask.

Before long Jake and Scrappy returned with the names of the businesses that had pledged to donate and what that pledge would be. The sheriff sent Jake down to help his brother Fred with the prisoner work detail. He let Scrappy stay and watch over the jail and help with any donations that might arrive. The four women had just left and said they would be back early in the morning. As the mayor sat at the sheriff's desk and looked over the list of donors Barnes walked over and told Hash, "I guess we've done about all we can do here today Burton. I think I'm about done in."

Judge Helton had been at the jail since their return from the mayor's house. He had spent the time helping the ladies sort the donations. He wasn't above working side by side with the people of the town. "Sheriff, you can't go home just yet, I don't care how tired you are, I wanted to have supper with someone other than just myself. How about you and Mr. Burton joining me for a bite up at the Depot Café? You know Saturday night is pork chop night."

Hash agreed that it had been a long day but he wasn't ready to give up just yet. "Judge, I think that is a great idea. You grab one end and I'll grab the other and we'll pack our tired old sheriff to the café."

Barnes held up both hands in defeat. "I give up, you two lead the way and I'll try to keep up."

The three walked out just as Jake and Fred came around the corner with the five prisoners. "Well Fred, how did it go with our new city employees?" the sheriff asked.

Fred shook his head. "I wanted to shoot every damn one of them Sheriff. These sorry bastards haven't said a word since we left and I tell you something else, they ain't done any work either."

The sheriff stopped and said, "You mean in two and a half hours they didn't do anything?"

"That's right Sheriff. They wouldn't pick up a damn thing to help them poor people. As men and women were hurrying to carry their belongings out these five just stood and laughed. I threatened to shoot them and that just made them laugh louder."

The sheriff walked over to the five and stood nose to nose with the biggest and the meanest looking one in the bunch. "Tell you what Fred, when you put these lazy bastards in their cells leave the handcuffs on, and then you take away the pillows and blankets that are on the cots." The sheriff stepped a little closer and said, "And they won't be needing any supper tonight, no work no food."

This was more than the man could stand. He tried to hit the sheriff with his cuffed hands but Barnes was expecting it. He side stepped and came up with a knee into the man's groin. The prisoner bent over and then fell sideways to the ground. The sheriff stepped to the next man in line and asked, "Anyone else like to express an opinion?"

Not a man spoke, not a man moved. Jake walked over and told the four to pick up their friend and get him into the jail. The four did as told and half carried, half dragged the man inside.

Hash looked at the sheriff and said, "Remind me to never cross you Sheriff."

Judge Helton couldn't help but laugh. "Sheriff, I really do like your style, I really do."

With the five prisoners of the work detail wishing they had worked instead of just watching the flood safely tucked away in the new jail the three men proceeded toward the Café. As they walked along a city employee was lighting the gas lamps that illuminated some of the streets in town.

Judge Helton was excited about pork chop night. He said he rarely missed it. The men entered through the saloon; it was doing a booming business with lots of strangers around, most of them armed.

The sheriff looked at Hash and asked, "You know any of these men in here Burton?"

Hash done a quick scan of the room and said, "Just Burt, looks like he's doing a booming business tonight."

"I just hope the booming isn't from a gun, this place looks like a powder keg," the judge said.

There were men playing cards while others were shooting pool at the county's only pool table. Some were smoking and talking loud, some were even arguing. Burt gave the sheriff a worried look. Barnes nodded back at the bartender as he and the other two men walked into the dining room where it was much quieter. Rebecca was working and came over when she saw the three men sit down at one of the tables. "Hello gentlemen, are you here for pork chops Judge Helton?" she asked.

"Yes Rebecca, and I brought two hobos along with me."

Rebecca looked at Hash and the sheriff and said, "I can tell Judge, you don't care who you're seen with do you?"

"Well, I thought I might see what kind of trouble these two might get into tonight. Come Monday morning I can testify against them in my own court." Judge Helton slapped his knee and began laughing. "I crack myself up sometimes, I really do," he said.

Sheriff Barnes and Hash just rolled their eyes. "Just bring pork chops and the fixings for the three of us Rebecca," the sheriff said. "Be careful and not trip on any of the judge's bad jokes though." The judge laughed even louder.

As the men sat and talked the sheriff kept a close eye on the saloon next door, it seemed to be getting louder. Hash also was on guard; after all he was the one who was shot at just a few nights before. Soon Rebecca brought out three big plates loaded with fried pork chops and three glasses of sweetened ice tea. Judge Helton was the first to dig in. He rarely missed chop night at the café. As he ate he was also aware of the loud crowd in the saloon.

"You know Sheriff, I don't ever remember it being this noisy, or this busy. I don't recognize half the people in here eating. And I don't think I could identify any of the saloon patrons. You got any idea about that?" the judge asked as he broke a piece of cornbread in half.

Barnes looked out again at the saloon and said, "With the roads outside of town cut off by the flood you would think the town would be dead. I had Jake check at the hotel and the two boarding houses a little while ago to see if any strangers were checked in. He came back and told me they were all full with town folks who were afraid the river would flood their houses."

The judge washed down a bite of cornbread with his glass of tea and then asked, "Well then, where are all these men staying? You know they aren't going to sleep in the saloon, even old Burt has got standards."

"That is a good question Judge. I think after I finish my supper I'll go over to the stables and see how many horses are in there. Willie might be able to shed some light on your question. You know he has at times rented out his loft to some of the men who keep their horses there."

Willie Tackett owned the stables at the edge of town. He was on the down river side of Prestonsburg and most people who lived in the city liked it that way. He had been given the stables when his father died a few years back. It had been in the Tackett family for years and Willie was third generation. He kept horses for a few of the people in town but mostly strangers, the ones that could afford room and board for their rides. He even rented out a buggy or two when it was called for. If any strangers were in town that couldn't, or wouldn't, put their mounts in the stables then they either kept their horses staked out in the bottoms around town or tied them to a hitching post. The town had a strict rule though; no horse was allowed to be tied to a hitching post overnight. The mayor felt it cruel to leave a poor animal without access to food or water all night long. The flood had covered all the low lying bottoms days ago so if anyone was in town with a horse the only place for it was most likely at the stables.

As the three men were finishing up their pork chops the judge looked at the sheriff and said, "Say Barnes, how about a drink before we head out, after all it is Saturday night and we are both off duty."

"Judge, I am never off duty. If a fight broke out in that saloon right now then I would need to respond," the sheriff said with a little bit of agitation in his voice.

The judge looked back at the saloon and said, "Well, there ain't any fight right now so as far as I'm concerned you're off duty, now how about that drink?"

Hash settled it when he asked Rebecca as she walked by, "Pardon me Rebecca, is it against the rules if we bring our drinks from the saloon into the dining room?"

She looked at Judge Helton and Sheriff Barnes and said, "These two men are the ones you should be asking, one makes the rules and the other enforces them. As far as I'm concerned none of you should be drinking anywhere." She patted the judge on the shoulder and smiled as she said this.

After she left Hash looked at the judge and asked, "How about I go and get a bottle and bring it back here along with three glasses Judge?"

Judge Helton grinned and said, "Make it a bottle of Old Fire Copper, it's the sheriff's favorite." Again the judge started laughing as Hash got up and went into the saloon to find Burt.

In the saloon most of the tables were filled with rough looking men who didn't spend much time indoors. The bar was nearly as full with men drinking mugs or bottles of beer. Burt was busy and you could tell he liked the amount of traffic he was getting. He slid two glasses of beer in front of two men and then noticed Hash standing down near the end. Hash walked over and sat down on an empty bar stool beside the two men who had just gotten their beer.

"Be with you in just a minute Burton." He looked at the two men and said that'll be two dollars. The man reached into his pocket and retrieved a nice wad of cash with his left hand, all new bills. He peeled off a twenty with his right hand and reached it to Burt.

Burt frowned and said, "I ain't got change for that, if you plan on drinking more then I'll just hold it for you and give you the change when you're ready to leave." The man who had given Burt the bill said that would be fine, he planned on drinking a lot.

"What will it be Burton?"

"The two men I came in with want a bottle of Old Fire Copper, you got any of that?" Hash didn't want to say Judge Helton or Sheriff Barnes; he didn't want to bring attention to himself or the two men at his table. Burt still held the new twenty dollar bill in his hand and that was when Hash noticed it.

Burt retrieved a brand new bottle of O.F.C. from the rack behind the bar and sat it down on the bar in front of Hash. "Give me three glasses Burt and how much do I owe you?"

Burt got the glasses and sat them down beside the bottle of whiskey. "I reckon six dollars will cover it Burton."

Hash reached into his pocket and pulled out a fifty. "Here you go Burt, if you got two twenties you can keep the other four dollars." Hash knew that Burt had put the new twenty dollar bill on top of his register and hoped he gave it right back to him; he wanted to have a better look at it without raising any suspicions from the two men sitting beside him.

Burt smiled and said, "I can do that Burton." He opened the cash register and raised the drawer. Hash thought Burt was going to put his fifty under the drawer and get two twenties from there too, he really wanted that new twenty that was in the drawer. Burt put the fifty underneath and then sat it back in its place. He then took two twenties out of the drawer and reached them to Hash. "Here you go Burton. I never saw so many twenty dollar bills in my life. I done run out of everything else and have to hold people's change until they either drink the entire twenty or I get some smaller bills."

Hash nodded and stuffed the two bills into his vest pocket as he turned to head back to his table. As he did he looked over the two men who were drinking their beer. Both had guns strapped to their waists, neither had the look of a coal miner. It was the lone wolf, gun for hire kind of look he had seen many times before. Neither of the two noticed Hash, they were content to yammer away with each other and drink their beer. They seemed excited about something, something that had recently happened or was about to happen.

Hash walked back and sat the bottle on the table and deposited the three glasses down beside it. He was deep in thought. "Sheriff, when you cashed that payroll check at the bank this morning what kind of bills did the teller give you, new or old?"

Sheriff Barnes took the top off the bottle and poured each glass a third of the way full, with just a little bit less in his than the other two. This was strong stuff and he didn't want to overdo it. He thought a minute and then said, "They were old and well circulated Burton, why do you ask?"

"Were there any twenties in the money she gave you?"

"Seven or eight I suppose, again why do you ask?"

For Lack of a Title

Hash pulled the two new twenties from his vest pocket and laid them in front of the sheriff. "Burt just got paid with a new twenty, said he had been getting them all night. Now what is the chance of that?"

The sheriff picked up one of the twenties and looked at it. "This bill looks like it ain't ever been used before tonight Burton." He grabbed the other one and inspected it closely; it was the same, brand new. He put the two new bills back in front of Hash and then reached into his own vest pocket. He pulled out a few bills and in it was a single twenty. Hash realized that the sheriff and his men didn't make much money.

"This is some of the money the teller gave me including this twenty dollar bill." He reached it over to Hash.

Hash looked it over closely, it was well worn and you could tell it had some miles on it, the series mark said 1889, that made it three years old. He picked up both new twenties and read the series mark on each, 1892. "Sheriff, these bills were produced this year and this is only April."

Sheriff Barnes picked up his glass and took a small sip. His throat burned and he wished he had some more tea in his glass to put out the fire. "That's only two bills Burton; maybe somebody came in here from out of town and got them at a bank someplace else."

Hash didn't reply, he just got up and went back to the bar. Burt came over and said, "Don't tell me that you and your two friends finished that bottle already? I see who you had dinner with and those two don't look like professional drinkers." He laughed when he said this, nothing like getting a shot in on the sheriff and a judge,

"No, nothing like that Burt, I need to get change for a hundred if you got it. I need it tomorrow and it's Sunday, the

313

bank will be closed." Hash reached Burt the hundred wondering what the response would be.

Burt grabbed it and went to the register. Again he picked up the drawer and put the bill underneath. He sat the drawer back down and counted out five twenties, five brand new twenties. When he counted it out into Hash's hand he said, "These been thick tonight Burton, I'm not complaining though, business is booming." Hash took it and thanked Burt.

He walked back to the table and spread the five bills in front of the sheriff. Barnes looked at each series mark, all 1892. "Well Burton, what do you think it means?"

Hash felt sick. "I think these bills came from one of the crates in the bank Sheriff. They all contained gold and uncirculated money picked up from the reserve in Philadelphia." Hash grabbed his glass and turned it up. He never stopped until it was empty. "I think we need to find Reed and go have us a look Sheriff."

The judge finished his drink and then put the lid back on the bottle. He had been watching and listening the whole time as he sipped his whiskey. "Sheriff, I think that is an excellent idea. And I think I'm going to tag along. You two sound like you might need my advice." The judge lived a pretty dull life. He, just like the mayor, had lost his wife years before and found his home life extremely dull. He didn't really have any close friends Hash had noticed. It seemed the judge had latched on to them this evening and wasn't letting go.

"Helton, are you still carrying that Smith and Wesson under your coat?" Sheriff Barnes asked.

The judge eased forward and whispered, "Yes I am, and until things get back to normal around town I don't intend to stop." Hash was starting to like the judge.

"What do you say Sheriff?" Hash asked.

Sheriff Barnes was in deep thought. He wasn't convinced that the new twenty dollar bills came from the crates that were stored in the bank's vault. Just because they were new was not a reason to hunt down the bank's president and drag him back to the bank at this late hour, it was almost eight o'clock. "I need more proof than that Burton. Seven new bills in the town of Prestonsburg is not a reason to assume the bank has been robbed, hell you got a man stationed down there carrying a Greener shotgun and at midnight two more men will relieve him. No I won't do it."

Just then there was a commotion in the saloon. Two men were going at it tooth and claw. The sheriff got up and headed that way followed by Hash. The judge looked at the bottle of Old Fire Copper and assumed it would be safe until he returned. He was going to follow his two dinner companions and see what all the commotion was about. In all his years on the bench he got to rule on crimes but rarely got to see one.

The two men were the same two who had given Burt the twenty and were determined to drink up that twenty and possibly another one. After a couple of beers they had changed over to whiskey. Both were shouting at each other and swinging their fists, as drunk as they were though neither was making much contact. Sheriff Barnes walked into the middle of the two and as he did he caught a wild left hook square on the jaw. He went down hard on the floor and then the two men decided he was a better target so they both jumped on the sheriff, kicking and swinging.

Hash reached down and pulled one of the men off the sheriff and threw him onto a table where four men were playing cards. The drunk landed on top, before he could struggle to his feet the table collapsed. Cards and money went everywhere. The four men jumped from their chairs and came after Hash who was busy pulling the second man off the sheriff.

Hash was grabbed from behind and pinned against the bar by two of the card players. He was dodging fists with his head but was still taking some good shots to his body. Judge Helton pulled his revolver and jammed it into the neck of one of the men holding Hash. As he pulled back the hammer he asked himself if he could really kill a man in good conscience. The answer was yes. If these men continued to beat on the sheriff and Hash he was prepared to take a man's life. Just then there was a tremendous thump on the bar. Everyone looked and saw Burt holding his shotgun waist high, he was pointing it at the two men who were beating Hash. The sheriff had made it to his feet and was ready to get back into things when he heard Burt shout, "Which one of you is first? After I kill that son-of-a-bitch then I'll ask which one is second."

Not a man moved, especially the one who had the judge's gun under his chin. The sheriff grabbed the one who had hit him with the wild punch and knocked him to the floor. Then he grabbed the man's partner and knocked him to the floor also. There was blood coming from the sheriff's nose and also from his mouth. He had taken a vicious shot and he was mad as hell.

The four card players had managed to rough up Hash pretty good. Hash finally jerked free from the two men who held him as the other two worked him over. He then hit both men that had been pummeling him. Now four men lay on the floor moaning. The sheriff walked over and pulled the bar polishing cloth off Burt's shoulder and held it to his mouth, it smelled of beer, the sheriff didn't care.

Judge Helton smiled as he lowered his gun from the man's chin. As he held the gun he walked from man to man and removed each of their guns. Before long there were six Colt Revolvers lying on the bar in front of Burt. One of the two men still standing protested, "You can't take our guns you bald headed bastard, you ain't no lawman."

Judge Helton was both excited and irritated at being witness to, and also part of, the barbarity of mankind. What he did next surprised everyone in the saloon. He put his Smith & Wesson .38 back in his shoulder holster and then he swung a wild overhand right and knocked that man to the floor. As he rubbed his knuckles he looked at the other man and asked in a calm voice, "Would you also like to say something about my receding hairline?" The man shook his head no.

Sheriff Barnes slapped the judge on the shoulder and said, "You really know how talk mean Judge."

It was more of an insult than a compliment but the judge didn't notice, "Why thank you Sheriff. It was a good thing for you two that I was here."

The sheriff and Hash managed to laugh. Barnes rubbed his chin, laughing hurt. Burt still held the Greener and was looking over the crowd. He noticed three more men he had been watching all night take off out the batwing doors and into the darkness. All three were big but one in particular was a monster of a man. "Sheriff, what are you going to do with these six men?" he asked.

"All six are going to jail," the judge said.

The sheriff picked up his hat and straightened it out. Before putting it on his head he looked at Burt. "You keep their guns under the counter and I'll send back either Jake or Scrappy to collect them. Can you get me an itemized list of the damages so the judge can levy it against these men Monday morning?"

"Not a problem Sheriff. I'm right proud of the fact that we got us a judge who gets into bar fights on Saturday night. Judge, if you ever need a second job come and talk to me, I think this place could use a good bouncer." The judge laughed as he rubbed his sore knuckles.

The sheriff went around and nudged the men on the floor and told them to get up, "You're all going to jail compliments of the judge over there. I don't want to hear a word out of any of you when we get outside either, some people in town are trying to sleep."

One of the men who had been knocked to the floor and was mostly drunk said, "But Sheriff, you can't put us in jail, we got us a job to do tonight. Me and some of these boys got to.........."

Before he could finish one of the card players who was not as drunk slammed him into the bar. When he hit there was a loud crunch and he went down in a heap. He didn't move after that. Hash grabbed the assailant, pulling him away from the bar. He held a gun on him while the sheriff checked on the injured man on the floor. After a few seconds he put his fingers on the man's neck. Slowly the sheriff got to his feet.

"This man is dead. I think you broke his back when you shoved him into that bar."

Everyone looked at the man Hash held the gun on. He was nervous and said, "Naw Sheriff, he ain't dead. Just give him some time he'll come to. I never hit him that hard anyway," the man said this without conviction.

"Come on, all five of you, and I don't want any more trouble out of a single one," Sheriff Barnes said. He had just had a man murdered who was under arrest. That made two prisoners in the last twelve hours he had lost.

For Lack of a Title

"Burt, don't let anyone touch or move the body until we get back. Send someone after the undertaker but just have him wait on me before he does anything."

The sheriff, Judge Helton and Hash marched the five men up the street to the jail. Not a word was said. Both Jake and Scrappy were there. The five men who had refused to help with the flood victims were locked away and not a bite of food had been served to them as per the sheriff's orders. Jake didn't know if it also meant the man Sheriff Barnes had knocked out but played it safe and refused to send for his supper too. He considered the six men as a team and that meant if one didn't eat then they all didn't eat.

When the additional five men were brought in Scrap said, "Looks like we got more business than the hotel tonight. I'm sure glad I don't have to make the beds." Judge Helton got a kick out of that. Hash had now figured out that the judge must never have any fun, he would laugh at just about anything.

The sheriff and Hash went back first, they wanted to see if any of the six men already in jail might show that they recognized any of the five being brought in now. Scrap and Jake had been told to put two men per cell and the fifth man, the one who would be charged with murder, in a cell by himself. When the partition door opened and the five were lead back it was apparent the two groups of men knew each other.

As the new group was being placed in their cells some of the first bunch were whispering to each other. Before being brought in the sheriff had instructed each man to empty his pockets on the big desk and for Jake to keep the contents separate and take the name of each man as he cleaned out his pockets, while that was going on Scrappy held one of the sheriff's new Greener shotguns at the ready, just in case. Each of the five did as he was told and they did it quick; safer to be in a jail cell than out here with a wild eyed deputy looking at them with a shotgun.

When the last cell door was slammed shut and locked the sheriff and Hash went back to the main room. On the desk were five small piles of personal belongings, the usual stuff like chewing tobacco and the makings for cigarettes. There were matches and four pocket knives. One of the men even carried a nice looking pocket watch. But the thing that caught both the sheriff and Hash by surprise was the number of twenty dollar bills, all brand new.

Jake was busy cataloging each pile and putting it under the name of the man who had left it there. Barnes walked over and started looking at each bill; all had a series mark of 1892. Hash walked over and compared one with the seven he had got from Burt at the saloon to one of the bills on the desk. The match was identical.

"You don't suspect these to be counterfeit do you Burton?" the sheriff asked.

"The judge too had now walked over to pick up one of the bills. "Looks real enough to me Barnes," he said.

Hash inspected the note very carefully. Unless he was bad wrong this was a legitimate Federal Reserve Note. "I have no reason to believe this, or any of these other twenty dollar bills, is not the real thing."

When they were all counted it came to eleven hundred and forty dollars. Each man had been carrying roughly two hundred and twenty bucks. "My guess is that these men were paid approximately three hundred dollars apiece for a job that was yet to be carried out," the sheriff said.

Judge Helton looked at the five piles and then at the Barnes and asked, "How do you figure that Sheriff?"

"Well, they had been buying whiskey and beer all evening. They were playing cards and don't forget, whatever money they had in front of them hit the floor when that card table collapsed. None of the players had time to pick it up and it's my guess that while me and Hash here were getting our asses handed to us some of the other patrons took the liberty of pocketing whatever was on the floor. It just makes sense. And the man who is over there dead was starting to say something about a job tonight just before he was killed. I would also suspect that when his pockets are checked there will be some additional twenty dollar bills, all new.

Sheriff Barnes went around and sat down at the desk. He opened the top drawer and pulled out a stack of wanted posters. As Jake finished up his tally and put away the men's belonging, Barnes scanned each poster carefully before placing it face down on the desk.

"What are you looking for Sheriff?' Judge Helton asked.

"I don't really know Judge, probably nothing but we got so many men in jail back there and none of them are from around here, I just got a hunch."

"Can you share your hunch with me, maybe I can help?" the judge asked.

The sheriff stopped at a poster, after a couple of minutes he reached it to the judge. "Why don't you and Hash look at that poster and see if you recognize that man."

Hash walked over and he and the Judge Helton studied the line drawing of a man wanted for the murder of a U.S. Marshal down in Georgia. The judge looked at Hash and asked if he recognized the face on the poster. Hash said he did as the judge reached it back to the Barnes. "Sheriff, I think that's the man who is lying over in the saloon," Helton said.

"What do you think Burton, is it the same man?" the sheriff asked.

"No doubt about it Sheriff, he looks a lot like the drawing and the description said he is missing part of the thumb on his left hand."

The sheriff read the description again. "How do you know the dead man in the saloon is missing part of a thumb?"

"I was standing on his left when I went over to buy that bottle of whiskey the judge said is your favorite."

Sheriff Barnes snorted and told Burton to go on.

"Well, when he pulled out that wad of cash it was in his left pocket. He held the money in his left hand and then pulled out the twenty he reached to Burt. His left thumb was on top of the stack and I couldn't help but notice part of it was missing."

At the bottom of the dodger it read,

$1000.00 Reward
Dead or Alive

The judge reached for the poster again and scanned it. "This dodger is recent Sheriff. How long have you had it?"

"It came in with the mail about a week ago. Why do you figure he ended up in Kentucky?"

The judge continued to look at the dodger. "My guess is that he knew he killed a lawman and figured it was a Georgia lawman at that. He thought that once he crossed state lines then he would be safe. What he didn't know was that the man he killed was a U.S. Marshal. That is a Federal offense and the state line won't protect him. I believe he was in Kentucky thinking that no wanted posters would be sent from the state of Georgia. While here he fell in with that bunch of no goods you got locked up back there. That's the way I see it Sheriff."

There were no other dodgers that matched any of the other men. The sheriff put the stack back in his desk and leaned back in his chair. "Burton, see if that pot on the stove has any coffee in it." Before Hash could check Fred said he had just filled it.

The judge walked over and filled three cups as the men considered their next move.

The sheriff asked for Hash and Judge Helton to come back to his office where they could talk in private. When they got there he closed the door. The judge had never been in the sheriff's new office, it was nice. There was a large desk and three chairs. There was another gun cabinet behind the sheriff's desk and it was filled with Winchester Rifles and Greener Shotguns.

The three men took a seat and Barnes said, "I wanted to come back here so we could talk without being heard. Judge, what does the charge of murder carry?"

"I assume you're talking about the man who killed the drunk at the saloon. If found guilty by a jury, which is a given, then I will sentence him to hang. Why do you ask?"

"We need information about what was going to happen in town tonight. Remember that just because we got five of the men locked up and another one dead doesn't mean that we've got everyone who's involved. Follow me now Judge. I say we bring that man in here and talk to him, just the three of us. You tell him that he is going to hang for the murder of that man in the saloon. You follow me so far?"

Judge Helton looked annoyed, "I got a brain Sheriff; tell us what it is you got in mind."

"Well, you make him think he's going to be hung and make it sound like it's going to happen quickly. Then when he thinks he's a dead man you cut him a deal for information."

"That sounds good but what kind of deal are you talking about?" the judge asked.

"I'd say you promise him a year in this jail, not the prison down state."

Judge Helton threw up both hands in frustration. "Have you lost your mind Barnes? That man committed a murder."

"Now hear me out Judge. That man killed a man who was wanted for killing a U.S. Marshal. The poster reads Dead or Alive. The way I see it he was only trying to collect the reward. He didn't murder anybody. He was upholding the law."

The expression on the judge's face changed completely. "Are you going to give him the thousand dollar reward too?"

"No Judge, I plan on you reducing his sentence to a year's probation if he will turn over the thousand dollars to the jail here. The jail can use the money, he will be free to go and I don't have to babysit and feed his sorry ass for the next year."

Hash liked it and hoped Helton would too.

The judge thought long and hard. "Tell you what Sheriff, if I do this then he gets set free quiet like and leaves on the first available train. The less people that knows about this the better. Now what if you talk to him and he refuses to give us the information?"

"Then we hang him. He swings for the murder of a man he didn't know was wanted dead or alive. But that won't happen, he'll talk and tell us everything he knows, believe me Judge."

Judge Helton stood. "I need a refill on my coffee. You bring him in here and we'll scare the living shit out of him Sheriff. Burton you better refill your cup too. I think we are in for a treat watching Sheriff Barnes interrogate his newest prisoner."

Barnes went in the cell area and unlocked the cell that contained the murderer. He threw in a set of handcuffs and told the prisoner to put them on. It wasn't really needed but it would make the man feel more at the mercy of the sheriff during the interrogation.

When the three men were back in the sheriff's office, along with the man wearing the cuffs, the sheriff had him to stand at the back of the office facing the desk while everyone else was seated. The prisoner was standing being stared at by three men he didn't know. Sheriff Barnes opened his desk and took out some paper. "What is your name mister?" he asked.

"Amos Spencer. Why have you got me in here Sheriff?"

"Well Amos, you killed a man a little while ago up at the saloon. This man seated to my right is Judge Isaiah Helton. He called this little meeting, just for you."

"What's gonna happen Sheriff?"

"Well Amos, we like to keep our court docket up to date. I am going to ask you a few more questions and then the judge here is going to find you guilty and then we are going to take you outside and hang you. That sound about right Judge?" Judge Helton looked at Amos and just nodded. He was enjoying this immensely.

"Hang me, you can't be serious Sheriff. I want a trial; I want to be able to say my part about this. I don't want to die."

The judge spoke up now, "We got us an ordinance in this town that if two elected officials witness a crime then there isn't any need for a trial," he lied.

The prisoner got weak kneed. The look of terror on his face was what the sheriff and Judge Helton were looking for.

The judge looked toward the man again. He was starting to feel like an actor on stage and he was enjoying it immensely. "Now Amos, can you tell us about what you and your friends were planning tonight. We know there was something going on or you wouldn't have killed your friend to keep him from talking."

"Those men are not my friends Judge, you gotta believe me. I just threw in with them yesterday. I was given some money and promised some more later after we done what we agreed to do."

Judge Helton could tell the man was nearly in a panic. He thought he was going to die and he would do anything to live. "Tell you what Amos, how would you like to avoid that noose we got hanging out back?"

"I don't want to die Judge. I never expected this time yesterday that I would soon be charged with murder and looking to hang for it. I just can't believe I got myself in such a mess."

"Well Amos, I'm willing to drop the murder charge if you answer a few questions for us. Might even be able to let you walk out of here in a week or two if you cooperate."

The look on the man's face went from gloom to excitement. "You serious Judge, I might not be hung tonight?"

"That's right. I would still need to keep you in jail for a few days, the town is blocked by the flood. If you cooperate and I set you free then some of the men in town might hang you themselves," Helton said.

The man looked down at his shoes, he was thinking. "You want me to tell you about what we were supposed to do tonight don't you Judge?"

"That's right Amos. You tell us everything you know and I will guarantee you walk out of here a free man in a few weeks."

"Those other men will kill me for sure."

"I'll kill you if you don't," Judge Helton said.

"Alright, you got yourself a deal," Amos said.

Sheriff Barnes got up and took off the handcuffs. He wanted the prisoner to get a little taste of freedom. He then pulled a chair from the corner and told him to have a seat. He opened the door to his office and told Fred to bring in a cup of coffee. When Fred brought it in the sheriff told him to give it to Amos and close the door on the way out. The prisoner looked like he was in shock. He had gone from a dead man a few minutes before to now sitting drinking coffee with the sheriff and Judge Helton.

The judge asked Amos to proceed and tell everything he knew about anything to do with the town of Prestonsburg.

He told them he was originally from West Virginia and had gotten into a little trouble there concerning a certain man's wife. After being run out of town he started riding the rails looking for work. Mining was hard dangerous work and it just wasn't for him. Shoed horses, worked in a saw mill, even herded cattle awhile but he just couldn't hang onto a job.

The judge just thought he was lazy, Hash and Barnes thought the same thing. The man stopped talking and took a sip of his coffee.

"Go on Amos, we need to know what you were planning in town tonight," the sheriff said.

He continued, "Oh it wasn't my plan Sheriff. Some of the boys you got locked up back there are working for a man here in town. Each of us were paid two hundred and fifty dollars at six o'clock this evening if we would agree to hit that big bank tonight at ten thirty. We were just killing time in the saloon until ten o'clock, and then we were heading to the bank."

"Who paid you the two hundred and fifty dollars Amos? Tell us so we can beat the truth out of him and find out who is in charge," the judge said.

"You can't talk to him judge; he's the one lying dead over at the saloon."

Hash, who hadn't spoken up until now said, "So the man who got killed in that little brawl is the only one who knows who is in charge. One thing I can't figure out though, why would you and the rest of that bunch agree to rob a bank for only two hundred and fifty dollars?"

"No sir, that two hundred and fifty dollars was just a taste. After we robbed the bank then we were to meet four miles out of town down river, you know, keeping to the high ground to avoid all that water. There is a big barn and lots of pasture down that way. Once we got to the barn we were to proceed up the mountain and wait for daylight. The man would be there thirty minutes after sunup to give us our share which was going to be a thousand dollars per man. Nine of us so nine thousand dollars."

Hash asked, "How were you going to rob the bank? We got an armed guard there until midnight and then two more men take his place."

Amos took another sip of his coffee. "The man who is running this show is supposed to know your guard. He was going to walk up to him real peaceful like and as they talked he was going to kill him with a knife. No gunshot to alert anyone. That was supposed to happen at ten o'clock. All of us were instructed to be there at ten thirty, not a minute before."

"Who is this man who Mack knows? Mack has only been in town for two days, he don't really know anybody," Hash asked.

"I don't know mister. If the guards name is Mack that you speak of then he knows him as just a respectable member of the town and would never suspect he's about to be killed. None of us has ever met the man in charge. The two men who got

For Lack of a Title

shot the other night knew him; they had been working for him for a while. That other feller that got poisoned, he knew him too. Those three and the dead man at the saloon are the ones who were following orders from whoever it is in town who's the mastermind."

The sheriff said, "There is just one little problem with your story Amos. You can't get in the bank without a key and you can't get in the vault without a combination. Hell even if you got in the vault everything is in lockboxes. You would need to use dynamite and that stuff makes a lot of noise."

"What we were taking wasn't in lockboxes Sheriff. We were told to get six shiny black crates and to forget the lockboxes."

The room went quiet. Finally Hash asked, "I know all you have to do is break the front door to the bank to get inside but how were you going to get into the vault."

"Oh no sir, we weren't breaking nothing, we got a key for the front door and a combination for the vault. We were told to be in and out in ten minutes so no one would know until the next guards got there and found Mack."

Judge Helton asked the next question, "Who has the key and the combination now Amos?"

"That same feller lying dead up at the saloon, you know the one who paid us."

Judge Helton was starting to believe what Amos had been saying. It was just too much information for him to make up on the spur of the moment. "If I find out you've withheld anything else we need to know then our little deal is over and you'll hang," the judge added.

"Judge, that's all I know, I promise. If there was anything else then I would tell you, you gotta believe me."

Sheriff Barnes looked at the judge and Hash. "You got any more questions?" Both men shook their heads no.

"Amos, I've got to put you back in your cell. I want you to act like we might just hang you in a few days. Tell them other prisoners that is why we brought you in here, to ask you questions about the murder. If you tell them you spilled your guts then not only will the judge here be mad but those other men will have a good reason to hunt you down and kill you if we do let you out of jail in a few weeks."

"You don't have to worry about me Sheriff. I won't let you down."

The sheriff got Fred to put Amos back in his cell. He then sent Scrappy and Jake to the bank with shotguns and told them to hurry. It was nine-thirty and he was afraid that if they waited then Mack might be killed.

Judge Helton said, "Let's go with them Sheriff. This is our chance to find out who is pulling the strings in that outfit.

The sheriff thought about this for a minute before saying, "I think you both know who is behind all this anyway."

Hash looked at the sheriff. "I know who you are thinking about Sheriff but I doubt he is the man who is going to attempt to kill Mack."

"And why not Burton, you said yourself everything points to him."

"I can give you three reasons why Greg Spurlock isn't the man who's going to the bank tonight to try to kill Mack.

"Number one, I don't think the sniveling little bastard has the guts to take on Mack.

"Number two, Mack has met Spurlock, that is true, but he is suspicious of him. He could never get close enough to Mack to use a knife and he knows it.

"And number three, if everything went according to their plans then Spurlock would be the first one suspected. I would bet he's been with friends this entire evening and will have a rock solid alibi when the bank is hit."

The Sheriff looked at Judge Helton. "I know of only one other man but I can't make myself believe it's him."

Judge Helton put together most of the story during the day and could see what Barnes was saying. "Reed, are you trying to say that Samuel J. Reed would commit a murder and then have his own bank robbed?"

Hash looked at the judge. "As hard as it is to believe, that is the only plausible explanation."

"You really think Reed is going to the rendezvous in the morning to pay the robbers and then keep all that money for himself Burton?" the sheriff asked.

"No Sheriff I don't. There was never going to be a rendezvous in the morning. Think about it, if you are one of the men who just risked your life to rob a bank would you really stop somewhere later to give away what you just stole for a thousand dollars. They would just take all the money and disappear."

"So you think Reed didn't think of this Burton. If you figured it out then you know he did too," the judge said.

Hash hung his head. He knew he had lost. "The money isn't in the six crates judge. Reed has already emptied them and put something back inside that is about the same weight. The money is already gone. When the robbers got far enough away then they would have sawed open those reinforced crates and found nothing of value. Then what were they going to do, ride back into town and say they had been robbed. The only man who knows who is the mastermind is dead up at the saloon."

"The money is gone and we don't even know who to blame. If we try to accuse Reed then he can just say it was Spurlock. You know yourself Spurlock counted the contents of the six crates while Reed was upstairs with us drinking bourbon. Reed will say that somehow Spurlock managed to empty the six crates and put something back inside to make them seem full. Reed has played us like a fine banjo," the sheriff said.

"But how would he be able to say Spurlock got the money out of the bank? The judge asked and then added. "He could claim that the money was taken out in the garbage."

"Judge, if you had this case without any eyewitnesses how would you rule with the information that we have on hand as of right now?" the sheriff asked.

Judge Helton thought for a minute. "Reed would be acquitted and so would Spurlock. No one can say with any amount of certainty what happened to the money."

"Well, enough got took to pay those men with brand new twenty dollar bills Judge. The money may not be in the six crates but it is still in Prestonsburg. All we got to do is find it," Hash said.

The sheriff got up from his chair and said, "First thing we gotta do is go back to the saloon and check that dead man's pockets. If the key is there to the bank and also the combination to the vault then we arrest Reed."

Just then Hash smiled. "Spokes, we do have a witness Sheriff, we got Spokes and nobody knows he exists. If he identifies Reed then the case is solved. Reed will cough up the money in a heartbeat once he is identified by Spokes."

The three men left the office and headed for the saloon. As they walked the sheriff looked at his pocket watch by the light of a gas lamp. "Ten thirty, I guess if Reed was going to waylay

Mack then he would be doing it about right now. I guess we missed our chance."

Judge Helton replied, "If we all were there as Reed walked up he would just say he was checking on the guard. I couldn't use the testimony of Amos Spencer at trial, hell he just killed a man himself. The testimony of a murderer doesn't carry any weight in my courtroom. Got to have proof gentlemen, got to have proof."

When the three men made it to the saloon the dead man was right where they had left him. Someone had been sent by the bartender to get the undertaker, his wagon was right outside. Shufflebarger was inside but was told by Burt not to touch the body. The sheriff walked over and began to empty the man's pockets. New twenty-dollar bills, pocket knife, tobacco, matches and one key. Also in the wad of twenties was a note with just numbers on it. The sheriff reached the note and key to the judge. The large key was evidently the key to the front door of the bank. Sheriff Barnes stood up and said, "I guess now Judge Helton I am going to request an arrest warrant for one Samuel J. Reed."

The judge just looked at the sheriff and shook his head yes.

"Herb, you can take the body now. You still got any room over at your place?"

"Got a little Sheriff, never seen so many dead men in one week." He thought a second and added, "I take that back, the mine explosion last year took seven but them men are still there." He then turned and went about his work.

Barnes and Helton thought about the mayor and both felt a bit sad. Outside the saloon Hash asked what was next. The judge said they should go straight to Reed's house to arrest him but wondered if he would be there; he probably had enough time to make it back home if he had seen the men in front of the bank and then backed out on killing Mack. He might have even heard about the fight at the saloon and knew his gang of thieves was locked up. Either way he could have aborted his portion of the plan and be home safe and sound right now.

It was only a few minute walk to Reed's house but still the three men hurried. The sheriff walked up on the front porch and knocked on the door. He waited a minute and then knocked again.

"We should go to the bank and see if he's there. I'll bet Mack and the two deputies have him," Judge Helton said.

Just as the three men were about to leave, the front door opened and Reed stuck his head out. He had his gun in his hand and when he saw who it was he quickly put it down. He looked at the three and said, "Judge, Sheriff, Hash; what on earth brings you out this evening?"

Sheriff Barnes stepped up and took the gun from the banker's hand. "Reed you're under arrest."

Reed didn't move he just stood there. Finally he said, "What do you mean I am under arrest Sheriff? I have never committed a crime in my life."

"Tell it to the judge; he's standing right behind me."

Reed looked at the faces of Helton and Hash. It was no joke. He was being arrested. "I can promise you gentlemen that whatever it is you think I have done can be explained."

"Come along Reed. You get to spend the night in jail," the sheriff said.

On the way there Reed never uttered another word. The three men thought his silence added to his guilt. He knew he was caught and his plan had failed.

At the jail Reed was placed in the last empty cell. None of the men already there acknowledged his presence. After locking the cell door and then going back to the front room Sheriff Barnes mentioned the fact that none of the other men in the jail said a word, about or to, Reed as he was being locked up. "That proves he is the unseen mastermind of this whole mess. Amos said the man in charge could only be identified by the four men who are now all conveniently dead. Burton, how about you and the judge joining me back in my office, we got some things to talk about. Fred you better keep that coffee pot brewing all night, I reckon there will be people in and out of here for the next few hours."

Once inside Barnes closed the door. "Judge, how do you feel about a conviction?"

Judge Helton sat down in one of the chairs and exhaled wearily. It was apparent the man wasn't used to so much exertion at such a late hour. He thought it over for a few minutes and said, "Well, as things stand right now he could be charged for several offences but in a courtroom in front of a jury he wouldn't be found guilty. No hard evidence, just circumstantial and no eyewitness."

"But we got an eyewitness Judge. We got Spokes all tucked away above the saloon in Burt's room," Barnes added.

"You do have an eyewitness, and I believe the number of people that know that little bit of information is limited to the men in this room and possibly Dr. Sables. He might have heard you talking when you found Spokes. As I understand it he was examining the last of the poison victims. Now mind you I wasn't there and am going just on what you have told me about how you happened upon this witness. If you can keep him safe then I plan to have a hearing Monday morning at ten o'clock."

"Why ten o'clock judge, hell have it at daylight. The sooner Spokes identifies Reed then the safer he'll be," Barnes again added.

"Well, two reasons Sheriff. First I plan on accompanying the two of you to the bank Monday morning when they open at nine o'clock. We will check the six bags and determine if the money has been taken. Then at ten o'clock we will convene our hearing in the main courtroom of the courthouse with your witness Spokes there to identify Reed."

Barnes thought about this for a minute and said, "Why don't we go to the bank now? We got the key to the front door and the combination to the safe. We can check everything out tonight." This was an idea that Hash liked, he wanted to know for sure if his money was there or had been taken.

Judge Helton liked the law; as a matter of fact he had liked the law even before he became a judge, when he was just a lowly lawyer. What he liked most was the slow methodical approach and argument, the debate, the give and take of the opposing sides. "No we won't go there until Monday morning when they open at their regular hour. Until then keep all visitors away from the men in the cells. We picked up Reed and I don't think anyone saw us bring him in. The workings of the town go on as normal until Monday morning at nine o'clock. If we go in there tonight then who is to say that we didn't take the money. We've got a key to the front door. We've got the combination to the vault. And gentlemen we've also got the key to the six black crates right there in Hash's vest pocket. It is a defense that Reed could use and at that point I would have to recuse myself because I would be implicated."

The judge thought a minute and then added, "I will be able to oversee the hearing Monday morning at ten o'clock but as soon as it's over I will need to recuse myself anyway. I have been involved in this since that fight broke out at supper in the saloon. I was involved when you interviewed Amos and I was there when you arrested Reed. As of now my only additional involvement will be to accompany you to the bank and oversee the initial hearing Monday morning. After that another judge will need to be appointed." There was a tone of sadness in Judge Helton's voice, he wanted to be on the bench at the trial but he knew now that he couldn't.

"Until Monday morning none of us should talk about what has happened tonight. I plan on going home and having me a large shot of O.F.C. and then I'm going to bed. Sheriff, could you meet me here tomorrow morning, say around eleven o'clock. I plan on going over to the County Attorney's house and see if he could come back here to write up the charges against Reed that will be needed for Monday's hearing. I plan on rushing this matter along in order to protect your witness. As soon as he identifies our man then he will be a lot safer."

The sheriff didn't mind being at the jail at eleven o'clock, he would probably be there anyway. What he did mind was going over to Preston Blair's house. Ever since he had first met Blair he didn't like him. He was a northerner who Barnes felt looked down his nose at the people of Floyd County. He had tangled with Blair more than once while testifying in court. Hell he thought he and the County Attorney were supposed to be on the same team. More than a few of the sheriff's arrests were not prosecuted by Blair and this bothered the sheriff to no end.

Blair had landed at the office of County Attorney about a year and a half earlier when the man who previously held that office died from some sort of influenza. Before a special election could be held to appoint a replacement word came down that the Governor had already appointed Blair. When he took office all the current cases were set aside for re-evaluation. A year's worth of the sheriff's work was dropped for insufficient evidence or poor investigative work on the part of Barnes and his deputies.

"Sure thing Judge, but isn't it something you could handle on your own?" Barnes wasn't sure why he needed to be there and suspected that Judge Helton wasn't on the best of terms with the County Attorney either.

"Well Sheriff, just between you and me, I am not one of Blair's favorite judges. You don't know this but in December of last year he filed paper work against me to have me removed from the bench. I was found to be competent of course but let me tell you something Barnes if I had been fifteen years younger I would have whipped his northern ass. Let him file that on me. So help me someday I will get even for that."

The sheriff hadn't heard about that little story. Now he understood why Helton wanted him to go along. "You be here at eleven in the morning and I'll go with you. Say Judge, what if he is at church tomorrow morning at eleven?"

"He won't be. I think he is an atheist anyway." Helton and Barnes both laughed at this although the subject wasn't a laughing matter.

After the meeting in the sheriff's office broke up Hash headed for the Hatfield place. He was deeply troubled about the loss of the money. It would devastate both his and the firm's plans for the coalfields of Eastern Kentucky. As he walked he noticed the streets were mostly deserted now. He saw very few people and liked it that way. The saloon was still doing a good business as he walked by. Just to ease the pain of most likely losing more than two million dollars of the firm's money he went in and sat at the bar. Burt came over and asked, "You alright Burton?"

For Lack of a Title

Hash looked up and smiled. "Couldn't be better, what do you suggest?"

Burt reached under the counter and pulled out a bottle. "Well, when someone asks me that question and they got a hangdog expression on their face like the one you were wearing when you walked in here, I suggest something strong." He put the bottle on the counter in front of Hash and got two glasses. He poured each three quarters full and slid one to Hash. "This one is on the house," he said.

Hash looked at the bottle, it was Old Copper Fire. "Ain't this the bottle we had at the judges table when that fight broke out earlier?"

Burt tipped up his glass and drained it, then said, "It is, that's why it's on the house."

Hash laughed. "Looks like you're still busy Burt, any reason why, it's almost one o'clock in the morning."

Burt looked around. "I always close at midnight on Saturday; I still need my beauty sleep you know. But tonight with all the cash floating around here I decided to stay open a little longer."

Hash slid his glass back to Burt, "I'll have another, on the house of course."

"Me too," Burt said.

Hash looked around and then asked in a low voice, "How is your guest?"

"He's fine Burton. I had to scrounge around for a few more books, he's a reading machine. Henry kept guard on the door all day and Fern took him up his food. They both went home at seven-thirty. I locked the door to the stairs and Rebecca locked the kitchen door before she left to go back to the clinic at nine-o'clock. She was the one who brought in this bottle that the judge left on the table."

Hash finished his second drink and then a third before saying so long to Burt. As he walked up the street to the Stanton Hatfield house he could feel the Old Fire Copper start to take hold. Suddenly he didn't feel as bad about getting two million dollars taken from him, not as bad but still bad. When he got to the house he couldn't find his key. He must have left it either at the sheriff's office or possibly it had fallen out of his pocket during the fight at the saloon. Now what was he going to do, he really didn't want to walk back to the jail and he for damn sure wasn't sleeping outside.

Suddenly he remembered the doggie door out back. He went around and up the stairs to the back porch. There it was installed in the back about six inches off the floor of the porch. He touched it with his foot and it swung in easily. He got down on all fours, lost his balance, and then fell backward off the porch and down the steps. It was one of those jump up real quick to see if anyone was watching kind of falls, and then he remembered it was the middle of the night. When he went back up the steps for the second time he realized he was drunk, damn the judge and his Old Fire Copper.

This time he was more careful when he got down. He looked the door over closely. He might be able to fit through but it would be a tight squeeze. He walked forward a step or two on all fours and realized he probably looked like a dog. Finally he worked up the nerve and stuck his head through the door. What he found on the other side was like a nightmare he and his friends told each other about when they were young.

He sensed a presence on the other side of the door, then he felt the hot breath of a wild animal and then he saw the teeth, big and white. Right when he thought he was a goner Gray Bob gave him a full face slobbery kiss. Hash rolled back out of the doggie door and continued backward until he was again rolling down the back steps. The Old Fire Copper took the sting out of landing flat on his back at the bottom of the stairs. And then he passed out.

At ten-o'clock the next morning Hash was sleeping soundly in the back yard when a foot nudged him on the shoulder. "Mister Burton, are you alright?"

Hash slowly opened his eyes to bright sunshine. He rose up on his elbows and saw that Joe Tucker from the General Store was standing over him holding a block of ice in one hand and a large clothing bundle in the other.

"Good morning Joe, what time is it?"

"It's a few minutes past ten-o'clock Mr. Burton. Why are you sleeping at the foot of the back steps?"

"That is a story that doesn't deserve telling." Hash struggled to his feet and realized that the sun was way too bright and Joe was talking way too loud.

"Well I brought you an ice delivery and also your clothes from the cleaners. You look like a man who needs some help."

"Well Joe, to tell you the truth I'm locked out and Gray Bob won't let me in." Hash realized he had just said something that probably sounded pretty stupid.

"Well Mr. Burton, there is a spare key hanging beside the door."

Hash looked at the back door and right there on the right hand side was a nail driven into the door jamb and a key hanging from it. Joe walked up and used the key to unlock the door and swung it open. Gray Bob walked out onto the porch and peeked over at Hash.

"Now why would that key be right out in the open like that Joe?" Hash asked.

"Old man Hatfield said that door locks are for sissies. He locked the front door to keep out visitors and left the back door unlocked, always. When he lost the house to the bank he wouldn't give them the keys, he just drove that nail and hung the key on it. I guess the people at the bank forgot to take it down. I saw it the other morning when I brought your first order of ice. I had heard the story and looked to see if he really did drive a nail in the facing. He did and there you have it."

Hash took both hands and dusted off his clothes, the same clothes he had worn for two days and one night, or was it two nights? Thinking about it was making his head hurt. He took the clothing bundle and thanked Joe. As he went in the back door he pulled the key from the lock and put it in his pocket. He wasn't a sissy but he still didn't leave doors unlocked. He didn't do it in New York and he wasn't going to do it here either.

Gray Bob was lying on the couch and looked like he could use a beer as Hash walked by but he was too tired to go back out and get it. He went upstairs and took off his clothes. He used the big tub and cleaned himself up. After that he went into the bedroom and fell asleep hoping to rid himself of a severe hangover.

A couple of hours of sleep did Hash some good. A couple more would have done him even better but Gray Bob wouldn't allow it. When the hound thought Hash had used his bedroom long enough he climbed up on the bed and flopped down in front of Hash's face, nose to nose. Hash slowly opened his eyes and then jumped to his feet. "Damn you Gray Bob," was all he could think of to say. Hash had spent four nights in Prestonsburg so far and he had woken up on three different mornings with Gray Bob. "I have got to remember to lock that bedroom door," he told himself as he went to the lavatory to shave and get dressed.

When he came out Gray Bob was sound asleep in his bed. "Damn dog."

Hash stepped out onto the front porch and pulled the door shut. There was his key sticking in the front lock; he must have failed to pull it out the previous day. He put the key in his pocket and laughed at himself. He had been locked out the previous night with a key stuck in the front door and another one hanging at the back door. What an idiot, he thought.

As he headed up the street he looked at his pocket watch, it was two o'clock. He had managed to waste half his Sunday. The café was open and doing a good business. He went in through the saloon and saw Burt sweeping up and cleaning.

"Well Burton, good to see you, thought you might have fell in the river last night after you left here. You was weaving all over the place when you headed up the street. I don't think you city boys can hold your liquor."

"Well Burt, I can hold my liquor, but I really don't think Old Fire Copper is liquor. I think that's the stuff they use to clean the locomotives down at the train yard."

"It is pretty powerful stuff, that's why I stopped at two. You though had three and the last one was a full glass. You poured it yourself."

"Well do me a favor and never let me drink it again. You open today?"

"Not today, it's Sunday. You know the day when all the drinking folks go to church."

Hash tipped his hat and went in the café. It was about half full. Sitting at the far end was the sheriff and Judge Helton. Hash walked over and pulled out a chair. He sat down and looked at the two but didn't speak.

"Hello Burton, you look like you've got a hangover?" Sheriff Barnes said.

"You know he does don't he Sheriff. I told you them city boys couldn't hold their liquor."

Hash just rolled his eyes. "Are you two eating or just waiting on someone to insult?" he asked.

"Oh we're eating. We just ordered, you look like you could use some food too, might help that hangover." The judge laughed at himself.

Just then a lady came from the kitchen and put two cups of coffee on the table. Hash reached over and picked up one of the cups and drained it. "Hey that's mine Burton, why didn't you take the sheriff's?"

Hash sat down the empty cup and said, "I think that's a good idea Judge." So he reached over and took the sheriff's and drained it too. He then sat that empty cup down on the table and looked at the waitress and said, "I'll have what they're having and I would like a cup of coffee with it also. "He looked at the two men and asked, "Aren't you two drinking anything?"

Helton and Barnes let it slide; they could tell when they were looking at a man with a nasty hangover. After the waitress left Hash asked how it went with the County Attorney.

"You know, I have never seen a man so happy to press charges against the president of the largest bank in town. He came straight back to the sheriff's office and drew up the paperwork. He agreed that after the hearing tomorrow I would have to recuse myself. I will most likely be called as a witness at the trial," the judge said.

"After he got all the facts does he think he has enough to make it stick?" Hash asked.

"You know Burton, he thinks he can get a guilty verdict from a jury of our fine citizens simply on the fact that most people don't like bankers. But I have my doubts about that. I like Reed, always have," Helton said.

Hash lowered his voice and asked, "What did he say about our surprise witness. I thought you said that was all we needed."

"I didn't tell him about our witness. The sheriff told me on the way over to Blair's house that Spokes was too valuable a witness to talk about to anybody. Hell, you know how people like to talk Burton. I guess the sheriff is right. I'll tell you something else, that damn County Attorney would find a way to make it his surprise witness and take all the credit for himself," Judge Helton said.

The food arrived and all three men ate. Hash reached over and swiped a piece of bacon off of each man's plate. He needed something greasy to settle his stomach. Helton liked to eat and he really liked his bacon. He reached under his vest and pulled out his Smith and Wesson and laid it beside his plate. The sheriff didn't like sharing either and did the same thing. Hash started to reach for more bacon and then he noticed the two guns that hadn't been there before.

"Please tell me you two wouldn't shoot a man over a piece of bacon?" Hash asked.

Both men nodded that they would and then smiled.

Hash kept his hands to himself for the rest of the meal. He realized that the drunk he had thrown the night before had made him act less like a gentleman and more like a hillbilly. He laughed when he thought he should be able to fit right in with his lunch guests.

"What do we do for the rest of the day Sheriff?" Hash asked.

Barnes said that he was going to help the mayor with the flood. Hash had forgotten all about the flood.

"How big is the water Sheriff?" He asked.

"It's big Burton, biggest I have ever seen. Before it's over I would say it will be in most of the houses on the back streets. I walked down toward the depot early this morning and started across the suspension bridge. About fifteen feet out I turned around and went back. The water is around the front edges of the piers and swirling fast. Out a ways on that bridge you could feel the movement, just too scary for me. I went around and checked the rest of the town."

"How was our men at the bank?" Hash asked.

"Fine, when Jake and Scrappy got there with their shotguns and told Mack what they knew he almost had a fit. He suspected it was Reed just like we had. It made sense; Reed was the only man he had met that could have come up to him late at night without raising his suspicions. He admitted that Reed could have lulled him into letting his guard down. He stayed there the entire night and Jake and Scrappy stayed there too. When the two men showed up at eleven to relieve Mack that made five men, all armed to the teeth. This morning they said that not a soul had approached the building the entire night."

"You know Sheriff; I would say that most of the men involved were locked up at the jail, along with one more at the undertaker's. There might have been two or three others but they weren't going to try anything, especially with the five men you had there," Judge Helton added.

The three men finished their meals and coffee. When the waitress came back by Hash asked her how much it was for all three. She said four fifty would cover it. He reached her seven dollars and said to keep the change. He looked at Barnes and Helton and said, "Would you two put those guns away, you ain't shooting anybody."

Both men thanked Hash for lunch. He told them it was the least he could do since they both shared their bacon with him.

The three walked down the street toward the bank. Mack was there along with the four other deputies. Hash sent him to the hotel and told him get some rest. He would be pulling another all night shift, starting that evening. The sheriff sent Jake and Scrappy home too. He wanted the two deputies to spend the night, along with Mack, guarding the bank.

After that the three went to the lower portions of town. The flood that had started to enter a few of the lower houses the day before was now halfway up the windows and still raising. They found the mayor along with some other men preparing the houses that hadn't flooded yet, trying to save everything they could. With each hour two or three more houses were starting to take on water. When Mayor Tillman saw Judge Helton and the sheriff he stopped what he was doing and walked over.

"That looks really bad Mayor. How much more of the town do you think will get flooded?" Helton asked.

The mayor thought for a second before saying, "My guess is that the river will raise another three to four feet. The good news is that the rate at which the water is raising has begun to slow and there are two reasons for that. One is that as the water gets higher it has more room to spread out. The second reason, and this one is more important than the first, is that the river has crested half way between here and Pikeville. I think it will crest here in the next ten to twelve hours. Some of the people that were moving their belongings in houses that I believe won't flood have stopped working on their homes and I have asked that they help with these homes you see before you now."

Hash looked at the mess before him. Houses in the lowest part of town had only the tops of their roofs sticking out of the water. He could even see the steeple of a church in the distance, just the steeple sticking out of the water. He assumed the rest of the church was under it. He guessed that the town had shrunk by at least half. "Where are all these people staying Mayor?" he asked.

The mayor looked around and then wiped the sweat from his forehead. "Mostly with friends or family in town, a few here and a few there, these are hardy people Mr. Burton. Most have lived through these floods before. Some of the older folks have been through this two or even three times but none say they've seen the water this high before. They are calling it a hundred year flood."

Sheriff Barnes slapped the mayor on the shoulder and said, "Glad to have you back Tillman. Do you think you're going to be alright after the flood goes away?"

Tillman looked in the direction of the mountain that contained the bodies of his three sons and said, "You know Sheriff, my sons grew up to be good hardworking men, outstanding men. I wouldn't want to be anything less than that myself. My day with the bottle ended when you and Judge Helton came up there after me. I have a life here taking care of this town, and I'm not going to let these people down. My sons will be better remembered if their dad is as good a man as they all were."

As the three men were about to leave the mayor stopped them. "Gentlemen, around six o'clock this evening there's going to be a big barbecue on the front grounds of the City Building.

For Lack of a Title

We've gathered food and I have Fern from the café and a bunch of her friends doing the cooking. Her husband Henry is over there now. He's roasting a pig in the ground and if you ain't ever had any barbecue that that man makes then you're in for a treat. I plan to have a big feast over there every day this coming week to help out the people who are dealing with this flood. It's going to be like a party and Judge Helton I want you to order everyone to have a good time. This damn flood has everybody in a bad mood and I think it's time the bad mood stopped."

Judge Helton walked over to the mayor and asked in a low voice, "You wouldn't mind if I brought a bottle of Old Fire Copper would you Mayor, I promise to keep it out of sight. The Sheriff and Burton over there have developed a taste for the stuff." Both Barnes and Hash heard this and then held up their hands, palms out.

The mayor said to bring anything the judge wanted but he himself was as of now a sober man. As the three men left the sheriff asked, "Why is it you think that turpentine you drink is something me and Burton like?"

"Because you do, you're both just too proud to admit that it's the best tasting stuff in the county, maybe even in the whole state."

Both Hash and the sheriff believed the judge needed more sweetened tea and less O.F.C.

Along the way Hash asked how Reed had done the previous night. "He did just fine Burton. He never complained one bit and he ate all his breakfast. I had him brought to my office so he could eat his meal without being in the same area as the other prisoners. In a way I felt sorry for the man, and at the same time I wanted to take him out back and hang him. Once he has had his trial, and if found guilty, how much time do you think he'll get Judge?"

"Well Sheriff, if he gives back all the money, that is the money that is left, he's looking at twenty years. Not easy years either. He won't be here in your neat little county jail, he'll be sent to the big prison down state."

Sheriff Barnes thought about this and added, "Reed is in his fifties Judge, a twenty year sentence is the same as a life sentence."

All three men walked in silence. Hash had grown to like Reed in the few days he had been in town. Now he found it hard to believe the man had stolen all his money and planned to kill Mack. He decided he would be there on the day of the sentencing.

Judge Helton then added, "The robbery is the least of his problems. Three men are dead because of him. One poisoned in the jail as a direct result of Reed and two more who died when they didn't know how to handle the arsenic. I don't know if that will be tried separately or added on to the robbery charge. My guess is that whoever the new judge is will try Reed for both crimes at once, and that crime gentleman, if he is found guilty, carries the death penalty. He will be hung right here in the city of Prestonsburg. That is quite the fall from grace if you ask me, from being president of the largest bank in the county to being locked up for robbery and murder."

Hash attended the barbecue later that evening. It was the largest gathering of people he had seen in one spot since he left Grand Central Station two weeks prior. Judge Helton was in his element. He laughed and carried on with everyone within earshot. Sheriff Barnes walked the crowd shaking hands and talking to as many people as he could. It seemed that everyone liked Judge Helton and the sheriff.

Hash hadn't seen Burt and walked over to ask the sheriff about it. "Burt wanted to come over Burton but he said he better stay at the saloon to make sure our witness is protected, and I agreed with him. I said I would send over a big plate of barbecue for him and he could share it with Spokes. I thought it might look suspicious to send over two."

Hash agreed that it was the best if Burt, and his shotgun, stayed at the saloon. He told the sheriff that he had already eaten and if someone could put together two plates then he would deliver it to the bartender. Anyone who saw him leave could be told he was just taking his and Burt's food to the saloon. After all Burt had saved Hash's life during the gun battle. The sheriff went over to Rebecca and told her what Hash intended to do for Burt. She fussed over the two plates and made sure everything was just right. She then covered them with a cloth and reached both to Hash.

"Here you go Mr. Burton. I hope you and Burt enjoy this," she said.

Hash took both plates and thanked her. As he turned to leave she added, "Too bad you can't stay, I think the mayor had convinced a couple of the men to play their guitars later. Might even be some dancing."

Now Hash really hated to leave. He could have spent the evening in the company of Rebecca and some of the other townsfolk but instead he would be seated across from Burt and Spokes in the locked up saloon. Hash apologized to Rebecca for leaving, she said she understood. He thought he noticed a look of sadness on her face as he turned to leave.

As Hash moved farther away up the street from the city building and made his way up town he noticed three men standing across from the saloon. The three men all wore guns and they were looking at him. Usually when men are just minding their own business they don't stare down a complete stranger. These men were not minding their own business; they were eyeing Hash and not being subtle about it at all. As he got closer he recognized them from the saloon the night before. They had been there but didn't get involved in the fight. He thought he had noticed the three leave just as the fight was over. He would bet a hundred dollars against a June Bug that these three men had brand new twenty-dollar bills in their pockets.

Hash was in a bad way. Both hands carried a covered plate and his Colt still had the leather strap across the hammer. When he was no more than fifty feet away the three turned to face him and spread apart. They were completely blocking the sidewalk. Hash stopped and stood. Just when he was ready to drop the two plates and reach for his gun the saloon door swung open and Burt stepped out, he was carrying his Greener shotgun at the ready. The three men were startled to be looking at the bartender and his shotgun; it was the same one they had seen the previous night just before they made their exit.

As the three were looking at the shotgun Hash quickly sat the two plates on a sidewalk bench and drew his Colt. Now the three were in a dilemma. They had two men with guns pointed at them and one of the guns was a Greener twelve gauge. The Greener alone could take out all three.

"Burton, those three have been standing over there for at least thirty minutes. I think they was planning something."

Hash assumed the something meant Spokes and this made him angry. He walked up and took the three men's guns from their holsters. After he had the men disarmed he took a few steps back and said. "You know Burt, I think at least one of these men is carrying a backup. I think they need to empty their pockets on the sidewalk. How do you feel about that?"

Burt walked across the street and stood in front of the three men who had yet to speak. "Burton, I think these three were going to cause me some trouble. They been over here staring at the saloon and pointing at me through the window."

None of the three denied what Burt had just said; they just looked at Hash and Burt with faces that could only mean trouble. Finally one of the men spoke.

"You and this puke bartender cost me and my friends here a lot of money when you locked up our friends last night." Why he said this Hash didn't know. He had just admitted to being part of the bank robbery that never took place. Hash figured the three men didn't know that one of the men that got locked up had spilled his guts and now the plan was out. They still thought it was a secret. Hash wondered if he could make a citizen's arrest. He didn't want the three roaming the streets, especially with Spokes hidden not more than fifty feet away.

"Empty your damn pockets right now and don't make me repeat myself," Hash said.

The three men did as they were told and emptied their pockets onto the sidewalk.

"Now each of you take a few steps back," Hash demanded.

Once this had been accomplished Hash looked at the contents they had dumped on the sidewalk as Burt kept his shotgun trained on the three. The contents of each of the men's pockets had several new twenty-dollar bills and the usual other stuff, matches, tobacco and pocket knives. And then there was the note. Hash stood up and then backed away; he still had the Colt in his right hand. He looked at Burt who was looking at the three men.

When he opened the note he was astonished, it read,

Five hundred per man if the job is done Sunday.
Nothing if done later than midnight. Tall stranger with mustache. Same one who had dinner in café with the Sheriff and Judge Helton last night.

"Burt, let me borrow that shotgun of yours if you don't mind," Hash said this as if he was still in a trance. He exchanged his Colt for the Greener and told Burt he would stay there until the bartender got the two plates of food and made it back inside and locked the saloon door.

"Where you think you're taking us city boy?" It was the first words any of the three had spoken.

Hash looked at the man who had asked the question and sized him up. He was big, real big with hands like a bear and feet as big as the end of a boat paddle. He had a beard and a scar down the right side of his face from his eyebrow to his chin, undoubtedly from a vicious fight.

"I figure you and your two sisters there need to go and have a little conversation with the sheriff."

"What fur?" the big man asked.

Either this man was simple or he was putting on a show. "He might want to hear the story behind that note you three were carrying." Hash didn't know which pocket the note had come out of.

"That note you speak of is worth fifteen hundred dollars when we kill you city boy."

Hash took a step away from the three. If the big one was either bold enough or stupid enough to talk to a man holding a shotgun in that manner then they were to be handled with extreme caution.

"Get moving, head down the street toward the sheriff's office. I figure you know which way it is."

None of the men moved. Now Hash had a problem. If they charged him and he pulled the trigger on the Greener then the blast would hit one, probably two of the men. Whoever got the center of the charge would be blown in half, the second one only injured and the third, not even a scratch. Before he could fire a second round they would be on him. He figured he could win in a fist fight with two, although any of the three were at least thirty pounds heavier than he was, the biggest a hundred. If it came to it he intended to let the biggest one take the full shot. Who were these rough looking men who weren't afraid of a twelve-gauge shotgun?

The three took a step toward Hash. No choice, he raised the Greener and fired a shot into the air. No sooner had the shot cleared the end of the barrel than he hit the biggest man in the mouth with the end of the shotgun and then took another step back. Either the shock of hearing the gun go off or seeing a chunk of the big man's lip hanging loose stopped the three. The biggest had both hands covering his face and blood poured from his injured mouth.

"Now I said get moving or the next shot won't be wasted in the air. I'll waste it on you."

The two grabbed the elbows of the big man and eased him down the street with Hash following behind, but not too close. They hadn't gone more than a hundred yards when the sheriff and Judge Helton came running up the street, both holding revolvers in their right hands. Hash told the three men to stop. They did.

"Now you're in trouble city boy. The sheriff is gonna arrest you for assaulting me," the big man said through busted lips. Hash couldn't figure the three out. Did they really think they were innocent?

Within a minute the sheriff was there breathing hard. Judge Helton was fifty feet behind him and looked like he might be packing a heart attack under his shirt. He finally made it to where Hash stood. The sheriff and Judge Helton stood and looked at the three, one man looked like a grizzly bear and he was bleeding from the mouth like he had been shot.

"Sheriff, I want to press charges against this city boy. He done shot at us and then hit me in the face with his gun."

Sheriff Barnes looked at Hash and grinned. "Well Burton, looks like you are on your way to making back that money that was stolen from you. I got posters on this big bastard. Probably on the other two as well. Get moving, all three of you. If you're real nice then I'll see if one of the doctors will have a look at that lip of yours. Did you say you tripped and fell Hoss?"

"Say Judge, you mind helping gather those three piles of belongings back there on the sidewalk?" Hash asked.

After the men's belongings had been picked up the judge and Hash joined the sheriff for the walk to the jail. On the way Judge Helton read the note that Hash had found.

"Well Burton, looks like whoever tried to have you killed at the beginning of the week also tried again at the end of the week. You got any idea who might be so dead set on you being dead?"

"At this point Judge I am afraid to guess. You think it's Reed."

"It would just about have to be wouldn't it? Hell, everyone else in town, including Reed, is locked up."

"Well if it is Reed then he is one murdering son-of-a-bitch. He has done killed three and un-telling how many more before I even got here. Sheriff, you think you got room at the jail for this bunch?"

Sheriff Barnes said he would make room. Probably need to put three men to a cell except Reed. He was afraid to put other prisoners in with him. He didn't want anything to happen to him before he got the chance to hang. Once inside the jailhouse Sheriff Barnes and Fred rearranged the prisoners. The big Hoss with the busted lip hadn't complained and the blood had stopped flowing so the Sheriff never bothered to send for one of the doctors. The scar on his mouth would match the one on the side of his face. By the time everyone was locked up nice and safe it was nearly ten-o'clock.

Sheriff Barnes, Judge Helton and Hash met back in the sheriff's office. The judge told them to meet him at the bank in the morning at nine-o'clock sharp. In the mean time it was up to Hash to stop by the saloon to check on Burt and Spokes. It was agreed that once the bank opened and the money was found to be either in the six crates, or not, then the two deputies and Mack were to go to the saloon and escort Spokes to the courthouse but were told to keep him out of sight as much as possible. It was also agreed that Burt would help with the escort. He was one of the few men in Floyd County that Hash trusted.

All three men said their goodbyes and Hash headed for the saloon. He wanted his Colt back and he knew that Burt probably liked the feel of the shotgun better than the revolver.

After the barbecue everyone must have went to their homes or wherever they were staying due to the flood. The streets were empty; after all it was late on a Sunday night. When he made it to the saloon he tapped on the door with the end of the shotgun. Burt walked to the door carrying the Colt but he already knew who it was, he had kept a steady vigil ever since the trouble earlier. He knew he had a very important witness stashed and he wasn't about to be caught off guard.

"Hello Burton, looks like you about lived to see another day after all. Say, how come it is that every other man in town is carrying a note with your description on it and a five hundred dollar reward for your scalp?"

Hash reached Burt the Greener and took his Colt. He checked the rounds and saw that it hadn't been fired. "You better replace that shotgun shell I fired in the street earlier. As to your question, I think you're the only man in town that ain't carrying a note." Hash looked suspiciously at Burt and asked, "You don't have a note do you Burt?"

"You can just shut the hell up Burton. I ain't no bushwhacker and if I was I would need more than five-hundred dollars to shoot your sorry ass." Burt thought a minute and then asked, "You think I could get more?"

"Burt, you need to get in line to try to kill me."

"That is the damn truth Burton, I never seen a man hit town and have so many enemies."

"You know what I think, I think I just got one enemy in town and he has just about got everyone else trying to kill me."

"Sounds about right Burton, and I think we know who that person is."

"Yea Burt, I think you're right. I am shocked that it was Reed though. He sure had me and a bunch of others fooled. He is a mighty fine actor, a mighty fine actor indeed."

"Say Burton, how about me and you finish off that bottle of Old Fire Copper. They might be two good drinks left in the whole bottle."

Hash smiled and looked at the bartender. After the week he had he said, "What the hell."

Burt pulled the bottle from under the counter and poured two glasses with equal amounts. He was right, it was a little better than a shot apiece. He slid one to Hash and said, "Bottoms up."

After his battle with a hangover that morning the whiskey went down smooth. The judge was right after all, he was developing a taste for the stuff.

"Burt, tell me, did you see them three in here last night?"

"Shore did, they lit out just after the fight. I figured they were going to get right in the middle of it with you and the sheriff but my Greener made them think twice. As soon as they seen that it was out of their hands they hit the door. I was watching the whole time just in case. They looked like back shooters."

"How come neither the sheriff nor Judge Helton remembers them being here?"

"They came in after the three of you sat down in the Café and they left just after the fight. I notice just about everything in here Burton."

"Well Burt, I'm on my way home, and by the way I want you to go along with Spokes when the deputies get here in the morning. I feel a lot better knowing you and that Greener are helping to keep the peace. You might have to open up a little late tomorrow. Judge Helton said that he wanted you to stay with the witness until he testifies."

Burt agreed and said he felt responsible for the boy after keeping him safe for the last two days. He said it would be an honor. Hash stepped outside and waited until he heard the door lock before continuing up the street. It had been some kind of a day, tomorrow would be worse.

Sunday night in the Stanton Hatfield house was uneventful. Gray Bob was locked out of Hash's bedroom and it had only taken four nights for Hash to remember to shut and latch the bedroom door. Early the next morning he was awakened by a scratching noise. When he got up and unlocked the bedroom door he found standing on the other side what he expected to find, Gray Bob.

Leaving the door open he hurried with a shave and cleanup, he wanted to look sharp for the first appearance of Samuel Reed before Judge Helton. As Hash left he made sure he took his key for the front door. The Café was open and he hurried in for a quick breakfast. Again he stayed away from the gravy, just coffee and scrambled eggs, along with bacon. There was no sign of Burt and he assumed the bartender was upstairs guarding the star witness, Spokes.

After breakfast Hash hurried to the sheriff's office. Helton and Barnes were already there. It was eight-thirty and the three were anxious to get to the bank to check on his six black crates.

"Morning Judge Helton, morning Sheriff," Hash said.

The two men stood and greeted Hash. "How did Reed survive his second night in jail Sheriff?"

"Just fine Burton. You know that is the quietest prisoner I have ever had the pleasure of locking up. He just sits and stares at either the floor or the ceiling. He eats his meals in my office and then he is taken back to his cell."

"Well gentlemen, I for one am anxious to get to the bank," Judge Helton said.

The three men left and headed off at a brisk pace. The sheriff sent Jake and Scrappy to the saloon to escort Spokes to the courthouse. The walk was pleasant enough; the sun was out again for the fourth day in a row. The river had reached its crest the previous night at three a.m. It hadn't yet started to recede; the Mayor said that would probably take at least twenty-four more hours. Hash could see that several more houses, and even a few businesses, had been flooded since the previous day, but only by a few feet.

The bank was quiet. Mack was there and looked tired. It was five minutes until nine and the employees were already inside. The three men waited outside and at nine-o'clock the door opened and they were let in. Hash looked around but didn't see Spurlock. He walked to the head teller's window and asked if he was at the bank or just hadn't shown up yet.

"Yes, Mr. Spurlock is upstairs in his office," she said.

"In his office, I wasn't aware he had an office upstairs," Barnes said.

"He does, he was appointed the new president of the bank and is in the office that was previously occupied by Mr. Reed who no longer works here," she informed the three men.

Judge Helton stepped to the window. "How could he have been appointed the new president over the weekend? Reed was the president as of close Saturday."

"Mr. Spurlock spoke to each of us this morning as we came in at eight-thirty. He has a letter from the board that states that Mr. Reed has been removed and will no longer have any dealings with the bank. The letter also stated that charges were about to be filed by the bank for the theft of a large sum of money as yet to be determined."

Judge Helton turned and headed up the stairs, followed by the sheriff and Hash. At the top he went to the big office in the corner. He didn't knock he just grabbed the door knob and twisted, it was locked. The sheriff walked up and beat on the door with his knuckles.

When it opened he was met by a man wearing a uniform, he was an armed guard. The sheriff pushed the door open and as he was stepping in the guard put a hand on the sheriff's chest and then pulled his gun. "You will stop and wait until Mr. Spurlock says it is alright for you to enter. The bank doesn't allow just anyone in these offices."

The sheriff smiled and then quicker than the guard could respond he grabbed his wrist and twisted it away. At the same time he knocked the gun barrel upward toward the ceiling before yanking it free from the guard's hand. As the three men stepped into the big office they noticed a second guard who was in the process of standing and drawing his own gun. The sheriff was still occupied with the first guard and was helpless to respond. Hash drew his Colt faster than the second guard and had it pointed at his face before the guard's gun had cleared leather. Hash reached over and forcefully removed the gun from his hand.

Hash and the sheriff were unaware that Spurlock was standing at his desk and had pulled a Colt himself from the top drawer. Judge Helton though was also holding his Smith & Wesson and it was pointed at Spurlock. "Unless you put the gun down on the desk I will be forced to fire." At this point both Hash and the sheriff also trained their weapons on Spurlock. He slowly put his gun down on top of the desk as instructed.

"What is the meaning of this? You can't barge into a bank and disarm my security guards. I will press charges if the three of you don't leave immediately," Spurlock said.

Judge Helton walked over and picked up the gun in front of Spurlock. "Press your charges Mr. Spurlock. My name is Judge Isaiah Helton."

Spurlock had met the judge only once and it was in the County Courthouse in the judge's own courtroom. He had been there to obtain an order to remove some families out of homes that the bank had foreclosed on. The judge hadn't wanted to grant the bank's request but the law was the law. The judge at the time had been seated and wore his robe. Now he was standing and dressed in a suit. Spurlock hadn't realized he had just threatened to press charges against that very same judge.

"Oh Judge Helton, I didn't recognize you, please accept my apologies," Spurlock stuttered.

Sheriff Barnes ordered the two guards to seat themselves and if either moved he would arrest them. Before either moved they looked nervously at their boss. Spurlock told the men to do as the sheriff had ordered. This made Barnes mad as hell. He walked over to the front of the big desk and pointed a finger at Spurlock. "I don't need you to tell anyone whether or not to do what I tell them to do. The people of Floyd County voted me in as Sheriff and that means you and your two guards can go to hell, is that understood?" Spurlock slowly shook his head.

"Sheriff, before you do anything that might get you in trouble with the law yourself let me explain something to you. This bank has a charter from the State of Kentucky to operate in Floyd County. It is authorized to maintain a level of security that insures the safekeeping of the bank's deposits. You have just barged in here and disarmed two of the bank's guards and threatened them along with myself with arrest. I will be sending off a telegram shortly describing what you have just done and I will request federal authorities intervene as soon as possible. You may have already gone too far and be subject to arrest yourself along with these other two men," Spurlock said in a haughty tone.

"Return the weapons to the guards so they may escort each of you from the bank," Spurlock added.

This was more than Hash could stand. He walked over and around the big desk and grabbed Spurlock by his jacket. "I don't know what kind of stunt you pulled to get yourself appointed president of this bank before Reed's chair even had time to cool but you can be damn sure I intend to find out. In the mean time you will escort the three of us to the vault so we can check on the six crates I have had there since Friday."

"I will do no such thing. You can leave now. Neither you nor your two friends are allowed in the vault. You pose a threat and it is my intention to see that the three of you are arrested as soon as I can obtain a Federal Warrant," Spurlock said.

Hash drew back and hit the haughty bastard square on the chin. Spurlock was knocked completely across the top of the desk and landed at the feet of Sheriff Barnes and Judge Helton. Helton looked from the unconscious Spurlock to Hash. "I couldn't have said it better myself."

Barnes had the two guards pick Spurlock up from the floor and place him in a chair. He was coming to. Once he was aware of the fact that his words could get him clobbered again he chose his words with more caution. "What is it you intend to do now Mr. Burton?" Spurlock asked as he rubbed his jaw.

"I intend to do what I have already told you. We are going to go down and inspect those six crates and we are going to do it right now."

Spurlock stood and wobbled a bit before walking to the door and heading down the stairs. Once at the vault he opened the iron bar door and stepped inside. Hash looked at Barnes and Helton. He walked over and picked up one of the crates. It was heavy. The sheriff also picked up a crate and checked the weight. "It feels about right Burton, feels no different than when we took them off the train Friday," the sheriff said.

Hash sat the one he had in his hand on top of the table and then took the key from his vest pocket. He unlocked the padlock that held the straps secure and then opened the crate. Judge Helton and Sheriff Barnes looked inside along with Hash.

Hash slowly reached in and pulled out a brick. Barnes and Helton did the same. The crate contained at least a dozen bricks, no money, no gold, no government securities. All three looked at Spurlock who walked over and looked in the crate himself. "It was in there Friday, let's check the other five," he said.

All six crates contained thirteen bricks. They looked like the same type that adorned the veneer of the bank.

"You can now see gentlemen why I was appointed president and Reed is in jail. Only he had the means to remove the contents of these crates from the bank. He had a key to these six crates and it is my understanding that Mr. Burton here has the only other. When I heard Sunday morning that Reed had been arrested then I contacted some of the members of the bank's board here in town and they unanimously appointed me as the new president. As soon as the telegraph lines are restored I intend to have the three of you answer to the authorities for what you have done to me this morning."

Judge Helton wasn't the least bit worried about what Spurlock might or might not do. "Well gentlemen, we should hurry along to the courthouse." Before exiting the building

Helton turned back to Spurlock and said, "You know where to find me." With that the three men left.

Hash, Barnes, and Helton made it to the courthouse at twenty minutes before ten. To everyone's surprise the place was packed. Upon entering the courtroom the scene was nearly one of bedlam. All the seats were filled and even the jury box was totally occupied although these seemed to be attorneys here to watch the show. More people stood around the back wall unable to find a seat.

Sheriff Barnes led the way and Judge Helton and Hash followed. Once through the crowd they proceeded to the door at the back of the courtroom which led to the back offices which included Judge Helton's. The senior bailiff, Ben Anderson, was standing at the judge's office door and asked what needed to be done. Judge Helton asked how many bailiffs were in the building and was told that they all were, seven total. The judge told Andersen to get them all in the courtroom and have everyone seated that could find a seat and to have everyone else to stand quietly at the back. He would make a decision on whether or not to have the courtroom emptied once he was on the bench.

"Where is the witness Sheriff?" the judge asked.

"He's in the basement with two of my deputies and Burt from the saloon Judge. I had him brought over this morning before first light. I felt it would be safer that way. Anyone looking to bushwhack Spokes would expect him to be brought over just before this morning's hearing."

"That's good thinking Sheriff. When will Reed get here?"

"Any minute, I told Fred to have him here at five minutes before ten."

Judge Helton looked at Hash. "I want you to go down and bring up the witness. I will have Anderson to clear out two spaces for you and Spokes on the front seats. Please have the two deputies and Burt stand at the back of the courtroom and keep an eye on the crowd. I really don't think anyone knows who the witness is or for that matter what he even looks like. If there is any trouble in the courtroom then they can help my bailiffs take care of it."

Hash left the judge's chambers and headed to the basement. He found Spokes and his body guards sitting at a table drinking coffee. "Morning boys, how was the trip over?"

Jake said there was no problems and wanted to know when and what to do. Hash filled them in on the plan and said to give himself and Spokes enough time to enter the courtroom before they came in, he didn't want anyone to think the three armed men were with Spokes, best to be low key.

Hash and Spokes entered the big courtroom and went to the very first row of benches. Bailiff Andersen was there and had two seats waiting. "Sit right there Spokes and let's wait and see when you're needed," Hash whispered.

The two deputies and Burt entered and took up positions at the back of the courtroom. All three men carried shotguns and this fact wasn't lost on the crowd. Soon Judge Helton came through the back doors wearing his black robe and a bailiff said "All rise," which everyone did.

Judge Helton took his seat and told everyone to be seated, which left at least fifty other people standing around the back wall. He then looked at the charges that were in front of him. After he scanned the document he looked up and saw Preston Blair sitting at his table. He motioned for him to approach the bench.

"These charges against Samuel Reed may need to be amended at some point in the near future. There may be additional charges," the judge told the County Attorney.

"That won't be a problem Judge. I haven't talked to any one that is representing Mr. Reed, do you know if he has council?" asked Blair.

"He was arrested very late Saturday evening. I would doubt if he has even talked to anyone other than the sheriff. If he doesn't then I will enter a not guilty plea on his behalf." Judge Helton looked at the jury box. It contained twelve chairs and each was occupied by an attorney. "You think any of these gentlemen are here hoping to pick up Reed as a client?"

Blair had already seen the men and knew exactly why they were there. They all suspected that the banker would pay dearly to have his name cleared. An acquittal or a not guilty verdict would also draw in more business in the future.

"After Mr. Reed posts bail he can hire one of those vultures sitting in the jury box if he likes," Blair said.

"Oh there won't be any bail. He's going to remain in the county jail until trial," Helton said.

Blair looked at the judge. "Why wouldn't you grant bail. His most serious charge is theft?"

"His most serious charge is about to be upgraded to murder and I never grant bail in those instances," the judge said.

Blair looked at Judge Helton and said in surprise, "Murder."

"That's correct. Take your seat and let's get started."

After a couple of minutes Fred came through a side door of the courtroom along with Reed who was in handcuffs. They walked over and stood in front of the judge. Preston Blair picked up some papers and walked over in front of the bench.

Hash looked at Spokes and asked, "Do you see the man who put that tray of poisoned food in front of the jail?"

"I sure do Mr. Burton that is a face I will never forget. I almost ate that food myself and if that had happened then I wouldn't be sitting here right now."

Judge Helton asked Reed if he had an attorney and was told he did not. He then asked how he wanted to plead and was told not guilty. As the judge and Reed were talking Spokes looked at Hash.

"What's that feller being charged with Mr. Burton?"

"He will be charged with murder and theft," Hash said.

"You mean both of them men are being charged with murder?"

Hash looked at Spokes and whispered, "What are you talking about?"

"That heavyset fellow that the judge is talking to, is he being charged with murder too?"

Hash looked back at the front of the courtroom. "The heavyset fellow is Samuel Reed, he's the one you just identified as the man who placed that tray of poisoned food in front of the jail."

"No sir, when you asked me if I see the man who put that tray in front of the jail I said yes, but it ain't that Reed feller, it's the man with the suit standing to the left."

Hash was astounded, the man Spokes had just identified as the murderer was the county attorney, Preston Blair. Sheriff Barnes was standing at the back of the courtroom with Scrappy and Jake. Hash turned and got his attention. The sheriff eased up front and leaned over. Hash whispered as low as he could so that no one in the crowded courtroom could hear, "we got the wrong man. It's Blair."

The sheriff stood and looked at Blair and then at Judge Helton. Helton had seen the Sheriff move to where Hash and Spokes sat and by the look on the sheriff's face he knew something was wrong.

"Sheriff Barnes, do you have something to add to our discussion?" the judge asked.

"Yes your honor. May I approach the bench?"

"You may," the judge said.

Sheriff Barnes went through the gate in the bar that separated the spectators from the business section of the courtroom and walked quickly to the bench. Blair also approached the judge but was stopped when Helton motioned for him to return to where he was standing.

"Judge, I believe we might have arrested the wrong man."

Helton had seen the sheriff speaking to Hash , "What have you found out Sheriff.

"Spokes told Hash that Reed isn't our man, it's Blair."

Judge Helton looked straight at Blair and instantly wished he hadn't. Blair had been watching and when the judge looked at him he turned pale. Andersen was summoned by the judge and told to clear the courtroom. The judge motioned for Hash and Spokes to approach the bench.

It took several minutes for the crowd to make their way out. When they were gone the sheriff had Burt and Scrappy stand guard so no one could enter or leave.

Judge Helton observed Blair as this was going on and noticed the man was nervous, very nervous.

"Alright then, we will proceed. You sir, what is your name?" the judge asked as he looked at Spokes.

"My name is Monroe Spokane sir, but people just call me Spokes."

For Lack of a Title

"Well Mr. Spokane, can you identify the man who placed the tray of food in front of the jail on Friday morning of last week?"

"I certainly can your honor. It is that man standing right there." Spokes was pointing at Preston Blair.

Blair finally found some backbone and said, "What in the world is this man talking about Judge? I have never seen him before in my life." Blair was now feisty and arrogant.

The judge looked at Spokes and said. "Can you describe what happened that morning Mr. Spokane?"

"Yes sir. I was lying on a bench in front of the courthouse here when a man, that man, came by carrying a tray of food covered with a cloth. It smelled so good and I hadn't eaten in so long that it made me take notice. Well, he walked right by me not more than ten feet away and then crossed the street and placed the tray in front of the jail. After he put it down he looked around as if to see if anyone might be watching. He never gave me a second look, either he didn't see me lying on that bench or he thought I was drunk. After he looked around he darted down the alley beside the jail."

Blair was shuffling from foot to foot when he looked at the judge. "That is the craziest thing I have ever heard. It sounds like this man was drunk and imagined I was carrying a tray. Hell for all he knows I wasn't even there."

"Were you there?" Judge Helton asked.

"Well your honor, I usually go by the jail in the mornings but that don't mean this skinny drunk saw me there."

"Mister, it was you and as for the drunk accusation, I don't drink," Spokes said. "I don't like the stuff and for that matter I can't afford it either."

Sheriff Barnes walked over to Blair and said, "Blair, you're under arrest. Jake escort him to the jail and put him in the same cell that Reed was just brought from. After you get Blair situated come back for Reed."

Jake came up and cuffed Blair who was now silent, once cuffed they headed for the rear door. After they were gone Reed asked, "You mean to tell me that you thought I poisoned those men Judge?"

"At this point I don't know what to think, but there is still the matter of the missing money from the six crates and all indications point to you," Judge Helton said.

"When I was arrested Saturday night you said that I had robbed my own bank. So I assume the six crates are empty, is that what you're telling me?" Reed asked.

Hash looked at Reed and said, "The crates only contain bricks Reed, the money is gone and you are the only one who could have removed it from the bank."

Reed thought about this for a moment and said. "I see what you mean. The only person at the bank capable of having the money removed from the building would be me. I could have had it taken out in any number of ways. Anyone else though could be a suspect, not a strong suspect, but a suspect just the same. You're saying I'm the only man who could have removed the money, but I didn't."

"Then explain why the money isn't in your bank Reed if you didn't take it?" Hash asked angrily.

Reed smiled and said, "That Mr. Burton is easy, the money must still be in the bank."

Hash looked at the judge and then at the sheriff. "What are you talking about Reed?"

"Gentlemen, I request that we proceed to the bank and figure out what has happened. The money is not in the six crates and you think I took it. I say that I didn't take it and it is still in the building. It is a possibility that with me gone it may not be there much longer. We should hurry," Reed said.

Suddenly Hash had a hope that the money could be recovered if Reed was telling the truth. He knew the money wasn't in the bank but he wanted to hurry over there anyway. He prayed the banker could explain but out held very little hope.

Judge Helton adjourned the proceedings and said he was going along too. Burt and Scrappy were told to take Spokes back to the saloon and keep a close eye on him. He might still be in danger. Before leaving the courthouse Sheriff Barnes removed the handcuffs from the wrists of the banker. He had never considered him a risk and didn't want to parade him through town in chains.

Judge Helton, Sheriff Barnes, Hash and Reed headed for the bank at a brisk pace. No one spoke along the way but each man was trying to figure out what had happened to the money. If Reed had in fact taken the money then he would answer for his crime and if he didn't take it then who did.

The four entered the bank with Reed in front. Once inside Reed looked over the lobby and the teller line. He looked at the sheriff and asked if he could see the six crates. The four men entered the vault and Reed opened each of the six cases and peered inside. Brick, they all contained bricks as he had been told.

"Gentlemen, this adds another side to the story. The bricks had to have been stored in the bank for some time. They couldn't have been brought in at the time the money was removed from the crates. Someone would have noticed. Where is Spurlock?" Reed asked.

"Well Reed, when we came here at nine-o'clock this morning he was upstairs in his new office," Hash said.

Reed wheeled around and ran from the vault. He bolted up the stairs with the three men following. This was going to be good. Reed didn't knock but grabbed the knob and entered the office. He was met by two security guards and told to stop. When the two guards saw who was following the banker they stepped aside.

"Where is Greg Spurlock?" Reed demanded.

Neither of the two guards offered a response.

Judge Helton told them it might be best if both cooperated before he authorized the sheriff to arrest them.

"He has gone to the telegraph office at the depot to see if the lines have been repaired. He prepared a message requesting help after the three of you barged in here and assaulted the three of us this morning. He is requesting arrest warrants," the taller of the two guards said.

"What the hell is he doing in my office," Reed demanded.

"It isn't your office anymore. You have been removed as president and are looking at years in jail for theft," the other guard said.

Reed looked at the judge and said. "I have no authority here if that is true but if you will authorize something I would like to do then I might just have an idea."

Judge Helton looked at Hash, he had the most to lose if the money wasn't found. Hash told him to hear Reed out.

"Gentlemen, I have racked my brain on the way over here trying to figure out where the money could be. I still believe it is in the building for the reasons I have stated earlier. Judge, I need to look at the register for all the banks safety deposit boxes. If you will authorize it then I might be able to shed some light on the disappearance," Reed said.

"Mr. Reed, for the moment you have my authorization but it better not be some sort of trick."

Reed headed down the stairs followed by the three men. The two guards stayed at the top of the stairs not wanting to tangle with the sheriff or Hash again. The register was kept in an office behind the teller line and Reed went straight to it and spread it on the desk. He scanned all the entries made in the last two months until something caught his eye.

"Look here gentlemen. Eight of the bottom boxes have been rented in the last five weeks. That is about the time you wired me Burton that a substantial sum would be arriving within two months. Those bottom boxes are some of the largest that we have," Reed said

He continued to look at the names of the men who had rented the boxes. He didn't recognize any but he did recognize the bank employee who had filled out the paperwork for the boxes and signed for the bank, Greg Spurlock. He stepped aside so Judge Helton and Sheriff Barnes could have a look. "Do you recognize any of the names other than Spurlock's?" Reed asked.

Both Helton and Barnes said they did not, but both did know Spurlock. Judge Helton also observed that the addresses beside the names were out of county. Not a single one was a local address.

"How do we get into those boxes?" Judge Helton asked.

Reed thought a moment before answering. "Each box has two locks. The bank has a key to one of the locks and the customer who rented the box has the other. Without the customers key I'm afraid the only way is to use a heavy hammer and chisel on the lock we don't possess a key for."

Judge Helton asked a question that he was pretty sure he already knew the answer to. "Do you have a hammer and chisel handy Mr. Reed?"

Reed smiled, he hoped the judge would ask that question. "Yes judge. The bank has a hammer and chisel." He reached into the desk where the ledger was kept and retrieved the two tools. "We from time to time need to access a box that a customer has lost his or her key to. It destroys the lock of course but they always agree to reimburse the bank."

The four men went into the vault and Reed used the bank's key to unlock the top lock. He turned and reached the hammer and chisel to Burton. "I feel the honor should fall to you Mr. Burton, if you please."

Hash took the two tools from Reed and said, "It would truly be my pleasure."

He got down on one knee and put the chisel against the bottom lock. He drew back with the hammer and with a powerful blow against the face of the chisel the lock snapped inward. He stood and looked at Barnes. "I believe this is now a matter for the High Sheriff."

Sheriff Barnes bent down and grabbed the door and pulled it open. He then grabbed the box that sat in the drawer. He pulled with one hand but it only moved a few inches, it was heavy. He used both hands and pulled the drawer completely out on the floor. It took both Sheriff Barnes and Hash to lift the large metal box onto the table.

Judge Helton walked over and raised the thin metal lid that covered the contents, the box was filled nearly to the top with cash. At the back were some canvas bags of gold coins. Reed said, "Well gentlemen, I believe we have found what we were looking for."

The sheriff looked at Reed and said, "How do we know you didn't put the bricks in the crates and put the cash in the safety deposit boxes?"

Reed smiled and said. "I don't do the boxes Sheriff. That is a task I let the Assistant Vice President do. Any of the bank's employees will verify that I was never in the vault after the money was delivered Friday except when I was in the company of you. And to add to my innocence is the fact that Spurlock was the man who rented the boxes that contain the money. I would bet that after you run down the names of the people that rented the boxes you will find that they either don't exist or if they do then they are unaware they have rented a safety deposit box here at the bank."

As they stood and pondered whether to sledge hammer open the rest of the locks Spurlock made a dramatic entrance. "Well gentlemen, you are just the men I was going to go find. You will be glad to know that the telegraph lines have been repaired. I sent off a message to the state capitol explaining the serious crimes the three of you committed this morning against the bank and I have been notified that the authorities will be sending a U.S. Marshal down to investigate. I can only imagine the look on your faces when he slaps the wrist irons on the three of you."

As Spurlock finished talking Reed stepped from the vault. "What is he doing here. He is supposed to be in jail?" Spurlock said.

Judge Helton stepped aside and motioned for Spurlock to have a look inside the vault. Spurlock stomped over and looked at the table holding the box filled with cash. For the moment he was speechless. Hash brought the ledger from the adjoining office and laid it on the table. Spurlock didn't need to look, he knew.

"Sheriff, I would like for you to put Mr. Spurlock under arrest. Please have him placed in the same cell as Preston Blair. I'm sure they have a lot to talk about," Helton said.

"It would be my pleasure Judge." The sheriff used the same cuffs he had taken off Reed not more than an hour earlier.

After the sheriff and Spurlock left Reed again headed up the stairs. Hash and Helton hurried along after him not knowing what he had in mind. Reed stormed into his office and notified the two guards that they were fired and had sixty seconds to vacate the building. The two men scampered down the stairs and out the door without a word. "Either of you ever see those two in town before today?" Reed asked. Neither one had.

Reed looked over his office and threw up his hands. "How the hell did that bastard get the board to replace me so quickly? My father started this bank and I am the leading shareholder." He went to the cabinet and found his bottle of Bourbon. "At least I wasn't gone long enough for him to throw this away."

He poured three generous glasses and gave one each to Hash and Judge Helton. Reed sat down at his desk and looked at Hash but didn't speak. Hash felt he owed the banker an apology but it was Reed who had allowed the swindler into the bank's business to start with. "What happens now?" Reed asked.

Judge Helton took a taste of the bourbon. It was good but it wasn't O.F.C. "Well Mr. Reed, you are still under arrest until the charges are dropped and that can't happen in your office, it will need to be done in the courtroom. But don't let that bother you, it is just a formality and I can assure you that you can do as you please. How about we head over there, along with Mr. Burton here, as soon as we finish our drinks, I never waste good whiskey."

"What do you want done with the money Burton?" Reed asked.

"I prefer it be left in the safety deposit boxes, assuming you can repair the broken lock and find a key for the other boxes."

"That won't be a problem. I will have someone sent over to inform the locksmith here in town and I will make sure there is an official accounting of the funds in all your new security boxes. After all the rent has been paid in full for an entire year."

Reed thought a minute and then added, "I suspect that Spurlock somehow made an impression of the keys to the six crates when they were brought in Friday. He is the only employee that spends much time in the vault alone. That must be how he put the money in the lock boxes. He already had the bricks there, brought in a few at a time in a bank bag. He is the only employee that had the opportunity and the means to carry out the plan."

Hash agreed and so did Judge Helton. The three men sat in silence for a few minutes and pondered the events of the last week.

"There are a couple of things I want done before I leave town Reed," Hash said.

"Leave town, you've only been here a week, you can't possibly leave now."

"I will be leaving on the seven-o'clock train tomorrow morning. I heard this morning that the broken down engine has been repaired and trains are back on schedule since the water has started to recede. Down river isn't as bad as it is here. It is my intention to go back to New York and find out who in the organization has sold me out. It's no coincidence that as soon as I got here all hell broke loose. I suspect someone has been sending information to some of our competition for several months, if not years. Blair and Spurlock didn't just happen to land here in the last year or so and somehow put this plan together on their own. They are just minor functionaries of a much larger organization."

"Sounds like you are correct in your assumptions, I wish you luck. What are the things you need from me here Burton before you leave?" Reed asked.

"First I want the deed to the Stanton Hatfield place delivered to the old gentlemen living in that railroad shack first thing in the morning, and it is a gift from the bank. Let's call it a goodwill gesture from a man who narrowly escaped the hangman's noose."

Reed thought for only a second before agreeing.

"Secondly, I think the position of Vice President or Assistant Vice President or whatever in the hell you call it just became vacant. I have a man I promised a job and I want you to hire him. His name is Monroe Spokane and he knows nothing about banking, but he was a chemical engineer in Cleveland and I would assume you would be willing to personally train him," Burton said.

Reed looked at Hash. "I don't know this man you speak of and doubt I would be willing to hire him."

"Oh the two of you have met. As a matter of fact it was your good luck that this man happened to be in Prestonsburg last Friday morning."

Reed smiled. He knew now who the man was. "You mean that skeleton that identified Preston Blair this morning?"

Hash nodded, "That's the man."

"Well Burton, it will be my sincere pleasure to take the boy on. Where is he staying?"

"I want you to advance him two hundred dollars on his first month's pay so he can look presentable at his new position. Also the place he will be staying will cost the bank another hundred and fifty dollars a month in rent," Hash said.

"Reed felt generous, after all two hours ago he was in jail with no hope of getting out. "Fine Burton, where will he be staying?"

"I want you to put him up at the Stanton Hatfield place. The old man is way up in years and should have someone there to help look after things. Spokes is a good honest man. He can use one of the rooms in the big house and also help Mr. Hatfield around the place. I think the old man could use the company and Spokes needs someone as a father figure. The hundred and fifty will guarantee that the old man has a little money coming his way each month."

"Well Burton, I will gladly agree to your request and we have Judge Helton here as a witness. When will you be back?"

Hash drained the last of the Bourbon in his glass and sat it on the desk. "Before the trial, the judge here can keep you posted and you can let me know. I want to see those two sitting on the witness stand. You might even learn some more facts about the happenings around here." The three agreed and shook hands.

The next morning Hash met Reed at the depot at a quarter till seven. Reed possessed the deed and Hash looked it over. He reached into his pocket and pulled out a hundred dollars. "Here, give this to Mr. Hatfield if you don't mind Reed. Tell him it is rent paid by a stranger who stayed at his place for the last week. Also, Jeremy Eisner and Josh Osborne have agreed to help the old man move today. You know both of them; they work here at the depot."

"Well Burton I must say that it has truly been an adventure." Reed stuck out a hand.

Both men shook and then Hash boarded the train. He walked down the passenger car and picked a seat by an open window. The engineer tooted the whistle and the train jerked. As it started to move Hash looked toward the old railroad shack. There was a little smoke coming from the pipe that protruded through the roof. Sitting on the porch looking at Hash was Gray Bob.

The End

Made in the USA
Las Vegas, NV
13 March 2023

68964213R00213